Tough Blood

The Skylark, P.I. Series
Volume 1

Susan Tuttle

WRITER
WITHIN

Tough Blood

The Skylark, P.I. Series
Volume 1

DEDICATION

This book is dedicated to the brave men and women who work tirelessly to keep us all safe and secure: all law enforcement personnel from Patrol Officers to Detectives to FBI Agents to Sheriff's Deputies and US Marshals; Park Rangers; Firefighters; First Responders; Paramedics; Private Detectives; our Armed Forces—and all those who support them behind the scenes—the front-line heroes of our lives. You are invaluable, irreplaceable, and appreciated more than words could ever express.
So just let me shake your hand and say, "Thank you."

CONTENTS

ACKNOWLEDGMENTS

Though writing is a solitary occupation, no novel is ever written in a vacuum. It truly takes a village to produce a book.

Thank you to my invaluable critique group, The Friday Night Writers Group: Debra Davis Hinkle, B. Carter Pittman, Shirley Radcliff Bruton, and Christine Taylor. Every time I thought I had it "perfect", you showed me the error of my ways. And helped me get that much closer to my dreams.

Thank you, too, to my beta readers: Patricia Akey, the world's best proofreader (I'm still embarrassed about all those typos!); writer Priscilla Gruenewald (thank you for all the great feedback!), Yvonne Avila, and Midge LeNoue, who gave it one last "tweak".

A special thanks to Mark Arnold, my Starbucks, writing, and brainstorming partner. I couldn't have done it so well without you.

Thanks to all those who've been such good sports about being in my book—even if it means you got "killed off" (most didn't, though I wasn't necessarily "nice" to the rest of them): Heidi Coffey, Javier Soto-Osorio, Yvonne Avila, Heather Hurley, Maureen Overton, and Clancy D'Angelo. A nod also to my cousin, Garrett Gallivan, and my grade and high school friend, Nancy Roessler, whose names I also "borrowed".

A huge thanks goes out to the brave men and women I met at the PSWA Writers Conference in Las Vegas—first responders, police officers, detectives, crime scene investigators, government agents—all great writers themselves. They selflessly shared their law enforcement experiences, and let me pick their brains. I thank you, Skylark thanks you, and Dunwitty thanks you! And if I screwed anything up, it's all on me.

Thanks, also, to Collin Wiseman from First Defense Firearms, for letting me "sample" all the wonderful revolvers and pistols, and for talking me through my firearm needs. You're the best!

And of course I can't forget my cover designer, Aaron Kondziela. I don't know how you do it, book after book, but I definitely have the best covers ever! I'm so glad you drank so much orange juice when growing up.

And thanks always to you, my readers. I'd be nowhere without you. I hope you love Skylark and company as much as I do.

 *CHAPTER ONE*

I don't particularly like insurance fraud cases, but with my bottom line I wasn't in a position to turn down fairly easy, lucrative work just because it didn't suit my sensibilities. And this guy, Mitchell Argus, was a real slime ball. The case was one of those no-witness, slip-and-fall injuries that didn't result in any pictorial evidence—i.e., x-ray proof—the kind of case that drained insurance company coffers and raised rates for everyone.

I'd almost caught him on film yesterday, but a van drove between us before I could snap his non-crutch-assisted steps. That was why I was on Argus again today, sitting outside Trader Joe's grocery store with camera in hand, waiting for him to exit. Maybe, since he'd have to juggle loaded bags as well as crutches, fate would smile on me and I could digitally immortalize his fakery. Then I'd find that bathroom that had been beckoning to me for the last few minutes, after which I'd head home, ditch my stupid bra, write up my report, then celebrate with a shot or three of Glenlivet.

And fate, that lovely lady, did smile. TJ's door swung open and out strode Argus, sure-footed, with three heavy bags in his hands and one set of crutches perched atop a shoulder. I grinned as I raised the camera, tweaked the focus and moved my finger toward the button.

Then fate—the bitch—quit smiling.

My Jeep door was flung open; a pair of meaty hands grabbed me and yanked me out of the car. The camera tumbled onto the ground.

"Gotcha, sweetheart." The deep growl gouged into me. A huge ape towered over my five-feet-eleven-and-three-quarter inches and outweighed me by about seventy pounds. "You're under arrest. And you ain't getting out, not ever."

He spun me around. Cold metal clamped tight around my wrists.

"Hey!" I yelped. "What the hell? That hurts!"

"So what? Getting a little of your own back is a good thing, I'd say."

"Who the hell are you? Why are you doing this?" I twisted and bucked in his hard grasp. "Let me go, you cretin!"

"Shut the fuck up," the suit snarled, and shook me like I was a wet dishrag. We stood surrounded by his goon squad, all with guns pointed at little old, trussed-up me like I was still some kind of threat. "I don't wanna hear one more squawk outta you. I'll duck tape your mouth if you say another word. You got that?"

Duck tape? I thought as he wrestled me over to the huddle of squad cars blocking traffic in the parking lot. *Is this guy for real?* He yanked me around and I bit back a cry of pain, hoping my shoulder didn't dislocate—

again. Then he pulled open the back door of a county-supplied plain-clothes vehicle that fooled nobody and shoved me in, accidentally-on-purpose forgetting to push my head down. He muttered something at me, some kind of chant I couldn't decipher through the pain. I spent most of the ride to the cop shop with blood trickling down my face and my brain on fire, as I tried to blink stars out of my vision and prayed I'd throw up on his fake leather seat.

I decided compliance was the better part of valor at this point—at least until I unleashed my lawyer on him —and kept my mouth shut as ordered.

He brought me all the way back to the Sheriff's substation in Los Osos from where he'd snatched me in San Luis Obispo; just my luck he was county affiliated and not part of SLO's local police force. That made for a torturous twenty-minute drive up to the coast instead of the four or five minute in-town journey it might have been.

I couldn't stifle a few grunts of pain as he hauled me out of the back seat once we arrived, though I managed—barely—not to call his parentage, ancestry, or intelligence into question. Not out loud, anyway. Then he muscled me through the front door and into the bowels of the station, his hands not any gentler than they'd been so far. He shoved me into the interrogation room, secured the cuffs to a chair bolted to the floor, and walked out, slamming the door behind him.

All without saying one word to me. No enlightenment as to why I'd been invited to this little shindig. No explanation about the cuffs. Or the mauling. Or the "under arrest" crap. Just abuse and silence as an intimidation tactic.

As if. It takes more than silent battering from a Neanderthal throwback to intimidate me. I rolled my aching shoulders to try to ease the stress—not that it helped much—and pretended I was anywhere but in that room.

The handcuffs had been cinched tight enough to cut through skin and scrape against bone as I'd been hauled into and out of the squad car. I was pretty sure the moisture I felt on my fingers wasn't sweat. My shoulders burned from the way my arms were pulled behind my back. All I could do was wait for Ape-Man-the-Cop to return so I could demand answers. And unleash the "L" word. Not that lawyers are any better than cops, but through experience I'd discovered that mentioning my particular "L" word made law enforcement types shudder in their boots.

I sat there alone as the seconds ticked away, my eyes closed. I practiced visualization and did deep breathing exercises for what was probably about thirty minutes—though it felt more like two hours—pretty sure Ape-man and his cronies stood watching behind the one-way glass, hoping for a melt down. What they would get was a lawsuit once I threw Maureen into the mix, especially given the way legal rules had been ignored or broken. I knew I hadn't done anything—not for a while, anyway—so I was more pissed than scared. I just wanted to get this mistaken identity thing over with so I could go home to where that bottle of Glenlivet was waiting for me. I spent part of the time composing a report in my head that explained why I hadn't yet finished the surveillance on Argus, though I had to get a bit creative with the wording since I hadn't any idea what had caused this particular delay. And I spent the other part of it wishing my bladder wasn't still demanding attention. I doubted Ape-man would uncuff me for a restroom visit no matter how politely I asked. I could just hear his response...

As soon as you confess, sweetheart, I'll have you taken to the bathroom.

Said, I was sure, with all the sadistic glee his pebble-size heart could manufacture.

Rats. Another deep breath and more visualization exercises, ones that didn't include water of any kind.

The pain in my head, shoulders and wrists was starting to impinge on my Zen state when the door finally swung open. In walked Ape-man, accompanied by a shorter, slimmer, younger, black-haired detective with an olive complexion. He moved with catlike grace, reminding me of a leopard. Ape-man sat opposite me and slapped a folder on the stained Formica tabletop. Leopard situated himself against the wall, arms crossed, eyes lapping up every nuance of my body language. Ape-man opened the folder.

Let the games begin, I thought.

"Skylark," he said in his deep grating rasp. "Skylark. Huh. What kind of weirdo name is that?"

The one Social Services saddled me with, I thought as I stared into his narrowed, calculating eyes. Since he'd so politely requested I remain mute, I didn't grace him with an audible reply.

"And no last name either, just plain old Skylark. Guess you think that makes you special. Better than the rest of us. No, I know," he snapped his fingers then pointed a thick index finger at me, "you think you're another Cher, or Madonna. A real 'freaky' one." He air quoted freaky. "Hey, we got us a celebrity here, José."

He grinned his sarcasm at Leopard—who grinned his own back—looked at the paper again, then up at me, face now flooded with scorn.

"Haven't had no last name, not since, let's see," again he looked down and appeared to read for a few moments, not that I for a second believed he needed to, "you turned eighteen and went and had it erased. Before that it was... let's see... *Friday*. Skylark *Friday*. You believe that one, José?" He turned eyes filled with incredulity on his partner, who shook his head.

"Not in this lifetime," Leopard purred.

Ape-man turned back to me.

"Skylark *Friday*," he repeated, again emphasizing my last name. "Sounds made up, you ask me."

I didn't ask, I thought, but again didn't respond aloud to his ridicule. Since he'd somehow gotten hold of sealed records, he already knew I'd been named by the State of California which, in its infinite non-wisdom, took my last name from the day I'd been discovered abandoned on the steps of the Los Angeles Social Services building—without once considering what it would do to me, coupled as it was with my odd first name. I was closing in on thirty and still not over the teasing I'd endured all through school.

"Sky-lark Fri-day, Sky-lark Fri-day." Ape-man crooned the syllables like they were the latest romance ballad. "Sky-lark Fri-day... Oooh, that would make you a *girl friday*, wouldn't it? You work alone, or are you some guy's *girl friday*, huh? Do whatever he wants, like a good little *girl friday*? Do all the dirty work for him? Or are you just dirty all on your own?"

I locked my stare on him, glared my venom directly into his eyes. My jaw ached from grinding my teeth together. Ape-man was damned lucky my arms were still fastened behind my back, or he'd not have a face left. How the hell had he opened sealed records? What was going on here? Just what the hell had I been arrested for? I almost asked, almost opened my mouth, but when I shifted my gaze and saw the look of anticipation on Leopard's face I decided not to give either one of them any satisfaction.

Ape-man turned a page and again pretended to read. I squirmed in pain and seized the moment.

"You gonna take these cuffs off any time soon?"

"Depends." He looked up at me and grinned. "You gonna sit there nice and quiet like a good little girl?"

That did it. It was past time to show this Neanderthal ape just who he was dealing with.

"No." I let scorn tinge my stare, ignored the way my hands itched to teach him a lesson in civility, and let my snark ooze out in a quiet, measured tone. "I'm going to sit here quietly like the adult woman I am and watch you preen, and pose, and act like the adolescent asshole you are." Leopard snorted a laugh and Ape-man's face turned a lovely beet red. As did his ears. "*And* wait for my *lawyer* to show up," I added just as he started to speak.

The magic "L" word seemed to stop him cold. He stared at me a moment, blinked his beady eyes, then, to my surprise, burst into derisive laughter.

"Ohhh, I'm so scared. José, she said the "L" word!"

"I want my phone call," I said.

I tried to put all the scorn and anger I felt behind the words, but the pain bouncing around in my body weakened my voice and it came out sounding a bit shaky. With an underlying pleading whine I so could have done without.

Ape-man turned another page, then slapped a huge palm on the paper.

"Tell you what, you tell me why you killed this guy and I'll let you use the phone."

This is about a murder? I shook my head.

"What are you talking about? What guy? What murder? I haven't killed anyone."

I knew it was a mistake when I saw the way his eyes lit up. I should have stuck with the "L" word and not engaged him at all, but somehow my mouth got ahead of my mind. Pain does that to me, sometimes.

Ape-man's eyes grew big. His brows rose. His mouth opened into a disbelieving "O"—a fairly well-feigned proximation of incredulity given his know-it-all personality. Behind him, Leopard sucked in his cheeks to hold back a grin.

"Haven't killed *anyone*? Not *ever*? What about that Kaiser fella, what was his name?" Ape-man glanced at, then tapped, the file. "Pietr. That's it. Man, you carved him up good, sweetheart. Not much left of him once you was done, was there?"

"That was self-defense," I said, my teeth clenched with rage. "He attacked me first, and I have the scars to prove it."

"Ohhh, I'd *love* to see *those*."

His beady eyes inspected my body like his mind was busy undressing me. I turned my head away and closed my eyes in a not-entirely-successful attempt to rein in my anger, before turning back and meeting his stare again. After another moment of tying to unnerve me—it didn't work, he wasn't that good at lascivious leering—he went on, naming a few more turds I'd had run-ins with over the last seven years.

I hate the more violent aspects of being a P. I., which is why, now that I was finally on my own, I specialized mostly in corporate cases with their nice, clean, non-violent computer searches. Not that it stopped the area's underbelly from stepping on me every once in a while; my being a woman in what's traditionally been a man's occupation just brings out the best in some people. So there'd been times I'd been forced to use my fists. Or my Glock. Each encounter left me riddled with either guilt or ghosts.

Then Ape-man went one too far.

"And let's not forget little Billy Cranston."

A wave of heat washed over me. How *dare* he bring up Billy? I could feel Vesuvius begin to rumble deep within. I drew in a breath through clenched teeth and looked daggers at him.

"I never hurt Billy." I forced the words through lips gone numb. "He killed himself."

"Yeah, probably because you hounded him to death."

"You son of a—"

I snapped my mouth shut and glared at this cretin of a man who sat blank-faced, staring at me with a glint of expectation and triumph in his hazel eyes. The pain of failing Billy all those years ago roared through me like a tsunami. If the chair hadn't been bolted to the floor, the way my body shuddered from rage would have walked it across the room.

"Oh, my, my. That hit a nerve. Didn't it, *Skylark Friday*?" Ape-man purred. It took all my strength to unlock my jaw enough to force out words.

"Where's. My. Lawyer?"

Ape-man made a big show of looking around the room, then ducking to check under the table. He turned to look at Leopard.

"You know where her lawyer is, José?"

"Nope." Leopard shrugged his own feigned ignorance. "Not a clue."

"You hear her ask *for* her lawyer, José?"

"Nope. Just where hers was."

Ape-man turned back to me and shook his head.

"I'm astounded. *Your* lawyer, not *a* lawyer? You actually got one on call? Just like a real celebrity criminal, huh? Wow. How the hell do you afford your very own shyster mouthpiece? You dealing drugs outta that office of yours?"

I closed my eyes; it took a count of seven before I could open them again and speak without telling Ape-man and Leopard where they could go, and what they could do to themselves once they got there.

"I want my lawyer, now," I said, enunciating each word with clipped precision. "I want to confer with my lawyer, Maureen Overton, before we go any further. I am asking for my lawyer. Call Maureen Overton, *now*. I will not speak to you until I have conferred with Ms. Overton. Is that *clear enough* for you, *Detective*?"

Ape-man stared at me for a long moment, emotions flitting across his face so fast I couldn't decipher them, ending with disgust that stayed and twisted his thick features. Then he closed the file.

"The Overton is your lawyer?" He pursed his lips and shook his head. "I should have known."

Then he rose and the two detectives left the room, slamming the door behind them, leaving me alone, in increasing pain, and still tethered to the chair.

CHAPTER TWO

"Where the *hell* is my *client*?"

Maureen Overton's strident voice echoed through the closed door, and if my pain—and increasing need for a bathroom—had been any less, I'd have smiled. Five-foot-two and a cross between a steamroller and a jack hammer, The Overton hadn't yet met a cop she couldn't flatten in ten seconds or less.

I couldn't make out Ape-man's response, though from his tone I could tell he was trying for conciliatory. So not the way to go with The Overton.

"I don't want to *hear* any of your *crap*, Dunwitty." Maureen's screech only emphasized her trademark accented-speech patterns. "I have it on *good authority* that she's been held here, *after asking for me*, for well *over an hour*. While *you* stood around, twiddling your thumbs, and I only got called *twenty minutes ago*. So *don't*," she added, steamrolling over his anemic response, "get in my way, or I'll have you up on charges faster than you can blink your *beady little eyes*. You *got* that? *Where. Is. She?*"

Five seconds of silence punctuated by the click of Maureen's signature four-inch stilettos, echoed by the clop of cop shoes, and the interrogation room door swung open. Maureen—Reenie to the very few of us she considered close enough to use the moniker—designer-clothed from head to foot, halted in the doorway. Her mouth dropped open when I raised my head; for her, the equivalent of a volcanic eruption. That's how I knew I looked a real mess; it takes a disaster of epic proportions to rattle The Overton.

We stared at each other a long moment, then her blue-gray eyes turned to steel and she ground out words from between scarlet-painted lips.

"Get those cuffs *off her. Now.* Then get *out* of my *sight*," she added as Leopard sidled past her, keys in hand—no way would Ape-man's bulk fit between her and the door frame—"before I *do something* you'll regret for the *rest of your lives!*"

I groaned when Leopard removed the cuffs and my arms swung free, my teeth clenched in an effort to hold back the tears that threatened. Leopard walked back to Maureen and stopped in front of her, his back to me. Something passed between them, something I wished I had seen, because she moved aside and let him exit the room without handing him his head. It was such a rare occurrence that I knew it was important, momentous even, something I could use to blackmail the Leopard—or at least manipulate him—if I ever needed to. I wondered if I could weasel it out of Maureen—not that anyone had ever weaseled anything out of her, ever.

Maureen stepped into the room, then spun and took the edge of the open door in her hand.

"Go. *Now.* If I find out *anyone* is in this corridor, in the observation room, or *anywhere* in ear- or eye-shot while I'm in here with my client, *heads will roll.* Is that *perfectly clear*, Dunwitty?"

Ape-man squared his shoulders and glared at her, but he turned and marched away like an obedient little lemming, towing Leopard in his wake. Maureen watched their progress a moment, then slammed the door and teetered her way to my side as fast as she could on those stilettos without breaking an ankle.

"I'm gonna bury that man so deep, he'll never climb out." She inspected my bloody wrists, then pushed my hair away from my throbbing temple and winced. "This might need stitches. I'll file charges as soon as we get this straightened out. Dunwitty might think he's above the rules, but he's gone way too far this time."

I took a breath and licked my cracked lips.

"Bathroom? Please," I whispered. It had been an increasing struggle, but I'd managed not to simply let my bladder loose where I sat. Satisfying as it would have been to stink up the room and maybe ruin the chair and a few floor tiles, I'd have been the one sitting in cold, acidic urine, not the Ape-man.

"You got it, Skylark. But in silence, right?"

I nodded my understanding, wincing as the motion ramped up the throbbing in my head. She had to help me stand, and she held on tight as, guarded by guys with guns, we shuffled down the corridor and into the ladies' room. I wasn't sure I'd make it once I started moving, what with the pressure on my bladder, the nausea digging at my stomach, and the way the walls kept shimmering in and out of focus. It was touch and go the whole while, but in the end my fears were groundless. It wasn't until I went to wash my hands—fingers only, and Maureen insisted on doing the honors—that I realized how deep the gouges were in my wrists, how much they'd bled. I checked my reflection and suppressed a moan: face drawn, skin pale, eyes sunken, temple gashed, the left side of my face bloody and bruised. Maureen stopped me when I bent over the sink to splash cold water on the aching bruise.

"No." She turned off the water. "Leave it be. I want to document all this before we do a full clean-up. That idiot is going to pay for this, I promise you."

"I don't care, Reenie, I just want to go home. Get me the hell out of here."

"As soon as I can, Skylark. Let's go sit you down where it's safe to talk, before you fall down and compound your injuries. Then you can tell me what's happened so far."

In a few minutes I found myself back on the chair in the interrogation room, this time sans handcuffs. But reaction had set in and I couldn't stop the shudders that made speech impossible. Maureen demanded hot coffee for both of us. She snapped pictures of my injuries with her iPhone—and even shot a video when I groaned and rested my aching head in my trembling hands—and then waited for the coffee's soothing heat to permeate my body. When I regained a modicum of coherence, she listened in silence as I described how I'd come to be tethered to an interrogation chair in the sheriff's substation for over two hours, waiting for two still-un-introduced detectives to get to the point.

"What do they have on you?"

"I don't know. The big one spent most of the time belittling me about my name. No specifics. He did ask why I killed some guy, but didn't say who. Or how." I took in a deep breath and blew it out. "He unsealed my records, Reenie. He knows about my name and what I can do. Everything. This is just the start. He's got it in for me, now."

I'd always kept my special abilities a deep, dark secret—hell, they even made me uncomfortable—because when most people learned about them, they thought I was a freaking nutter. Or was pulling some kind of scam on them on. Or they just pitied me. My business would never survive a public outing; a P. I. who glimpsed images from the past and could see connections between people as glowing lines of light wouldn't attract anyone but other kooks and crazies. I'd already suffered enough derision and censure while growing up because of something I had no control over. I sure as hell didn't need the local cops to mount the "Skylark's A Freak" bandwagon. Now that he knew, it was a sure bet the Ape-man would be at my door, hauling me in for every infraction that crossed his desk. Maureen was one of the two people in my life who accepted me the way I was; no judgments, no mockery, no censure. My surrogate brother, Garrett Gallivan, was the other.

"Don't you worry, I will deal with Dunwitty," Maureen said, her voice hard as flint.

She stared at me and I watched her eyes spark. The Ape-man was now on her shit list. If it had been anyone else, I might have felt sorry for him. She grinned at me and I managed an anemic smile in return. She stood up.

"Dunwitty thinks and acts like the rules don't apply to him. Well, this time he's got one *hell* of another think coming. It won't take me long to grind him into the ground."

She walked over, opened the door, and proceeded to bellow for Ape-man and Leopard. They shuffled into the room and sat opposite us, looking like chastised schoolboys though Ape-man-nee-Dunwitty blustered in an attempt to regain his macho standing. The Overton shut him down with one raised, scarlet-nailed finger. I planted my elbows on the table, propped my head on my hands, and watched the show through my fingers.

"All right, *here's* how it's going to go, *gentlemen.*" Maureen fixed the two detectives with an icy glare that moved into subzero temperatures as she continued to speak. "*We* don't say a word. Not one. *You* do. *First,* you explain my client's *injuries. Second,* you explain why I was not called *immediately. Third,* you explain why she was *handcuffed to that chair* until I got here. *Fourth,* you tell us what you *think* she has done, and *to whom.* And *fifth,*" again she stepped on Dunwitty's attempt to speak, "you show me *everything* you have against Skylark, *all* your *so-called evidence.*" She sat back and crossed her arms. "*Mi capisce?*"

Take that, Ape-man, I thought as the two detectives sat motionless, attempting, I was sure—with the fuzzy lint that passed for brains—to figure a way out of the mess they'd made. I'd have enjoyed Dunwitty's discomfiture more had my headache not ramped up into the stratosphere since I'd returned from the restroom. That stroll up and down the corridor had so not been a good idea, necessary as it was. Or maybe Dunwitty'd put something in the coffee; I wouldn't put it past the big ape.

Colored lights flashed intermittently in my peripheral vision, and some invisible someone had taken to drilling a hole through my left temple. All I wanted was to go home, climb in bed, and sleep until maybe the next millennium began. Hopefully in that order, though right then I'd have settled for just number three. But there was no going anywhere until The Overton handed these jerks their heads and earned me my freedom.

Dunwitty wasted a good thirty seconds trying to stare Maureen down, then he sighed, tapped his fingers on the table—a slight sound that echoed like thunder through my brain and made me wince—and shook his head.

"Okay, we'll do it your way, Overton—"

"Excuse *me*, Detective?"

I suppressed a grin at the way Maureen's body tensed and her eyes spit sparks at the discourtesy. Maybe this wouldn't be such a bad end to my day, after all.

"Sorry," Dunwitty growled, not sounding the least bit sincere. "*Miss* Overton." He once more tapped his thick fingers on the table; white hot light shot through my head at the sound and I hunched my shoulders. "We'll take it in order. First, your client was fighting like a banshee. Not my fault she hit her head when I put her in the car. Wouldn't a happened if she'd cooperated."

I drew in a breath at the lie, but Maureen's hand on my arm kept me silent. And from leaping across the table to strangle the cretin.

"Second," Dunwitty gave me a smug look, "she didn't ever ask for her lawyer—"

"I did too," I snarled. Dunwitty smirked at me.

"Not right away."

I drew in a breath to blast him into the next county, then Maureen's hand tightened on my arm and I skidded back into sanity. *Silence*, I thought. *Right. Don't give him any more fuel.* Dunwitty looked at Maureen.

"And it took us a while to figure out who her lawyer was," he added, neglecting to admit I'd given him her name. "Third, as for the handcuffs, she's a dangerous felon, a killer who was out of control. She needed to be restrained."

Maureen turned to me.

"Any truth to all this?"

"Not in the least," I murmured.

"Didn't think so," she said. She turned back to the detectives and crossed her arms. I counted to ten before she broke the thickening silence.

"Well, while your revisionist history is *amusing*, Dunwitty, let's try looking at actual *facts* for a change. Skylark was working, minding her own business, when you yanked her out of her car, cuffed her *with no explanation*, then threw her into your ride, severely injuring her in the process."

"I arrested her, was the explanation. Told her that." Dunwitty's beady eyes glinted as he attempted to regain some footing. Wouldn't happen on Maureen's watch.

"She did *not*," Maureen again held up a scarlet-nailed finger, silencing the burly detective, "struggle banshee-style, or *any other style*. She kept quiet—*as ordered*—and went with you without complaint. You brought her in here and secured her to a chair, *without* telling her *why* she'd been arrested. Then you walked out, giving her *no chance* to ask for me. When you came back in, you sat there and mocked her, belittled her, and berated her about things that have *nothing* to do with *why* she is here, but that have *everything* to do with why *you* are an *ignorant, uncivilized boor* indulging in some kind of *personal vendetta*. When she *finally* was able to ask for her legal representative, you *walked out again*, left her in pain and distress *for an hour*, denied her both needed medical attention *and* legal representation, and *never even read her her rights.*"

"Oh, we read them, all right. Not my fault she didn't pay no attention."

Maureen looked at me, and I carefully moved my head from side to side. I had no memory of hearing any such rights being read to me.

"Not unless they did it after they shoved me in the car," I said. "I wasn't in any shape to hear or understand anything at that point."

Maureen turned back to the detectives and placed her hands flat on the table.

"*Not legal*, then. And so, *gentlemen*, we'll be *leaving*."

Before I could psych myself to stand—and at this point I wasn't really sure my legs would hold me upright —Dunwitty shook his head and once more tapped his finger on the table.

"Uh-uh, there's still that little matter of a murder to settle before she goes anywhere." He grinned at me. "We got your gun, sweetheart, we're just waiting on the ballistics. Once the match comes in, you're gonna be our guest for a long, long time."

"My gun?" I blinked at him, my heart thudding at the thought of my sweet Glock being mauled by slimy cop hands, then looked at Maureen. "How did they get it? I didn't have it on me. It was in the glove box, in the Jeep."

"Yeah," Dunwitty nodded, "and they're tearing that Jeep apart as we speak, Miss One Name Wonder. There's proof in there and we'll find it—hairs, fibers, little drops of his blood. It's all in the forensics these days, yes, indeed." Another tap on the table.

"My car? You can't—" Again Maureen's hand on my arm stopped my words.

"Warrant," she demanded.

Dunwitty took his time producing it. Maureen snatched it from his hand and scanned the closely-typed lines while I tried not to visualize the forensics guys dismembering my beautiful Jeep. Would they even bother putting it back together again? Maureen nudged my arm and I read the disastrous news in her eyes when I looked at her.

"It's legal," she said. "Nothing I can do about it, sorry."

"But why?" I whispered, trying to wrap my mind around the enormity of what was happening. This was way beyond a simple mistaken identity.

"Because of this." Dunwitty slapped a couple of crime scene photos on the table, two stark, vicious depictions of a mutilated, faceless body drenched in blood. I gagged. "Takes a real sicko to do something like this. A sicko freak like you."

"What?" I looked up at Dunwitty, stared into his hating, condemning eyes, my head reeling. "I-I can't... Wh-who is it?"

"Like you don't know. Your good buddy. Garrett Redmond Gallivan."

 *CHAPTER THREE*

And just like that, with three words—*Garrett Redmond Gallivan*—my world fell apart.

Garrett, *dead*? *My* Garrett?

"No," I moaned. "It's not true, it can't be."

"There's the proof of your handiwork, right there." Dunwitty gestured at the photos, his voice filled with disgust and condemnation. "A bit of overkill, don't you think, obliterating his face after you shot him? What the fuck did the poor guy do to deserve that?"

"Stop!" I shoved the photos across the table, as far away from me as I could get them. I turned to Maureen, feeling like a huge hole had been gouged out of my core. My whole body had gone numb; I could barely draw enough breath to speak. "It's not him, it's not possible. I just saw him, we had dinner—"

"And when was that?" Dunwitty's eyes lasered in on me.

"Not another word, Skylark." Maureen glared at me, but I couldn't stop the flow of words to save my life. All I could see, all I could think about, was Garrett.

Dead.

Murdered.

Mutilated.

"Two... no, three days ago. We met for dinner at that new place, Garcia's."

"Skylark, *stop.*"

Maureen put her hand on my arm but I shook my head.

"No, Reenie, it's *Garrett*. It doesn't matter what they learn about me. If it'll help find whoever did this, I'll give them my whole life story, warts and all."

"Oh, we already know who did this, sweetheart." Dunwitty's sneer echoed around us as he picked up the photos and set them out in front of me again. "We just want you to tell us why."

I drew in a deep breath and looked directly into the detective's hard eyes. I had to force myself not to look down at those vile pictures. I could feel my left eyelid twitch in tempo with the throbbing in my head.

"I'm only going to say this once." I tried to spit it out, but with the way I hurt it came out more like a shaky plea. "So you'd better listen. *I did not kill Garrett.* There is no *way* I would kill him, not for *any* reason. He's like my brother. He was fine when I left him. He was *fine!*"

I cradled my head in my hands and told him about meeting Garrett at the town's new restaurant instead of at my favorite haunt. Valley Liquor's mini deli might have—in my humble opinion—the best burgers in the area but, according to Garrett, my usual table-by-the-window in a liquor store's corner eating area, complete with Sports TV, lacked "ambiance". I had balked at first —I'm not the least bit adventurous on a culinary level— but in the end I had to admit Garcia's burgers came in a somewhat-close second. Meaning they were edible— and that, from me, was high praise. Over a burger and fries for me, enchiladas and frijoles for Garrett, and Mexican beers for both of us, we discussed my plans for moving into Garrett's rental house. I gave him a check for the first month's rent, since the jerk refused to sell the house to me—mostly because I couldn't afford it and my credit rating stank to high heaven. We'd parted with plans to meet at my current place on Saturday so he could help me schlep boxes.

And now he was dead. Gone. I sat in silence as icy shivers slammed into me, and my heart felt like it was about to explode.

"All right." Dunwitty exhaled a forceful burst through his nose. "Now tell us about the fight, why you threatened him."

I blinked up at him.

"Threatened him? What fight?"

"The one the owners and the waitress told us about. Got pretty heated, from what we heard. You said, and I quote," he opened the file, turned a page, and read, "'You horse is ass, Garrett. You so fucking stubborn. I shoot you and buy house from you estate.' And this: 'You better must sleep with the one eye open. With my Glock, I shoot you on sight.' And, 'Fuck you. I do it, and no one ever not able to prove it. I that good.'" He grinned at me. "Beg to differ on that last statement, sweetheart."

"Oh, for God's sake." I sighed and pressed a hand to my head. "I don't talk like that. *No one* talks like that. Who the hell told you this? Whoever overheard our conversation, had no idea what was going on. I wanted to buy Garrett's house and he wouldn't sell it, so I got on his case. We've been teasing each other about it for months. It's a running joke between us, we're always kidding—"

Maureen pulled me around to face her.

"Not another word, *you hear me*?"

I blinked at her as the door opened and a uniformed officer strode in. She handed Dunwitty a paper and left. The door closed with a sharp snap that echoed in the silence. We watched Dunwitty read the report, his eyes shining with anticipation, watched his face sag, his shoulders slump, the light in his eyes go out. Maureen pursed her lips—to hold back a grin, I'm sure—and took a breath.

"Bad news, Detective?"

The sweetness in her tone would have killed a diabetic. Dunwitty passed the sheet to Leopard, who'd so far sat beside him in silence, watching the interplay between us with an avid expression in his eyes.

"Ballistics don't match." Dunwitty's hard tone grated into me. "Guess we'll need to look for another weapon. Care to let us know where it might be located?"

"I only have the Glock," I said before Maureen's tightening hand warned me to obey her order for silence.

"So, let me get this straight," she said. "You brought Skylark in here, *mistreated* her like this, on the strength of an *ear-witness account* from busy workers in a restaurant filled with chatting, laughing diners and energetic background music. Workers for whom, I might add, English is *a second language*. Under those circumstances, *anyone* could easily mishear or mis-understand what anyone else says." She narrowed her eyes at Dunwitty. "You don't have *anything* other than that, do you? *No* ballistics, *no* fingerprints, *no other* forensics, just the fact that two good friends had dinner together and teased each other like siblings. This was just a *fishing expedition*, fueled by your *personal dislike* of my client. Do I have that *right*?"

Dunwitty had the grace to look chastened, though he wasn't gracious about it by any means. If looks could kill, I'd definitely be six feet under. Maureen urged me to my feet and kept a strong arm around my swaying body. I had to grit my teeth against the throbbing pain in my head.

"You have no probable cause to hold Skylark. I've *been* to Garcia's, gentlemen. They hire young people who have never worked before, most just arrived here from Mexico. *Few* of them have any proficiency in English. I am taking my client to the *emergency room*, and then home to *discuss charges*. Should you wish to *speak* to her in the future, you will do so *only* through me. *Is. That. Clear*?"

Dunwitty nodded as he and Leopard rose and followed us out of the interrogation room.

"This isn't over, Miss One Name Wonder," he growled. "We'll be watching you."

"If you harass my client—"

The dizziness defeated me. Maureen's words cut off as I lurched out of her hands and stumbled across the hall. I leaned against the corridor wall, Maureen's comforting presence nearby, and closed my eyes, hoping to ease the throbbing pain a bit before attempting to move again.

"Are you all right?" she asked.

"Yes," I murmured. "Just a little dizzy."

"We should get an ambulance."

"No!" My heart stuttered in my chest. EMTs might solidify Maureen's plans to press charges, but I'd never weather the indignity of being hauled off like a namby-pamby weakling. "Please, no. Just give me a minute, I'll be okay."

"Are you sure?"

I made a sound of assent deep in my throat, then opened my eyes, looked at her, and gave her as much of a smile as I could muster.

"Yeah, I just need a minute... or three..." I sighed as the walls again danced around me. "Or a maybe bit more..."

My words trailed off as my gaze slid away from her and I looked into the room we'd just left. Time shifted and my psychic curse took advantage of really disastrous timing to kick in. I froze, staring, as the past ghosted over the present. Four see-though figures appeared, one a distraught, handcuffed, tattooed young man in the chair I'd just been sitting in. A uniformed woman was seated at the head of the table bent over a pad of paper before her, pen in one hand, handkerchief pressed to her eyes with the other. A suited detective, long-limbed and burly, leaned across the table to pat the young offender on the arm, the gesture one of obvious comfort. Beside the cuffed miscreant stood a young, much-thinner version of Dunwitty in uniform, arms crossed, a truculent glower on his face. The older man turned to look up at him and I gasped at his uncanny resemblance to the hefty Dunwitty of today.

"Skylark?"

Maureen's soft voice broke into the vision as I watched the older figure—none other than Dunwitty's father, I assumed—gesture at his son. His mouth moved, silent words of rebuke to judge by the angry look on his face. Dunwitty-past merely shook his head and clenched his jaw, obviously refusing to understand whatever the detective was trying to impart. Not for the first time did I wish these visions came with surround-sound.

"What is it?" Maureen again. Words only; she knew from experience not to touch me. The vision began to waver and fade. "What do you see?"

Dunwitty elder shook his head, his face a study in disappointment. Then he moved around the table, shoved Dunwitty junior aside and patted the prisoner on the shoulder, his face now filled with compassion. I closed my eyes and shook my head. When I opened my lids again, the room was empty. The past had returned to where it belonged.

I looked in confused wonderment at Dunwitty, who stood staring at me, arms crossed, legs spread, face twisted with the same leering dislike he'd given that tattooed young man. He snorted.

"What kind of game you playing now, sweetheart? Trying for an insanity defense?"

I shouldn't have spoken, wouldn't have if the pain in my head hadn't distracted me. It only made things that much worse between us.

"That man I saw in there was your father, wasn't he? He was better looking than you," I said. "And a much better cop. I could tell he really cared about people, like that poor young guy with the lion tattoo. You should have listened to him when he tried to teach you about compassion."

The sneer on Dunwitty's face morphed into shock, then horror as my words penetrated his thick skull. I so wanted to enjoy the sight, but the throbbing in my head chose that moment to rise to a crescendo. My brain imploded, and I slid down the wall in a dead faint.

CHAPTER FOUR

"There." God-the-doctor applied one last Steri-strip to the gash on my temple; seemed I didn't need stitches after all. "Good as new, almost. It should heal with minimal scarring."

He walked over to the sink in the corner of the room and began scrubbing his hands like he'd just touched Typhoid Mary. I took a deep breath and eased my way off the bed I'd been sitting on, moving slow, making sure my legs wouldn't collapse beneath me before trusting all my weight to them. Maureen, standing at the foot of the bed, crossed her arms and glared at me.

"We'll need to keep you a couple of days for observation," the doctor said, pitching his don't-dare-disagree-with-me voice over the noise of the running water, "so I'll send someone—"

"Not happening," I said, my words not quite as loud or forceful as I wanted them to be. Still, he must have heard for he turned from his ablutions, water dripping from his hands, his face frozen in disbelief that I'd dare contradict him. "I'm going home."

"I don't advise that. You have a concussion—"

"I. Don't. Do. Hospitals."

He sighed, turned away, pulled a couple of paper towels from the dispenser, dried his hands, then looked back at me, his expression stern and uncompromising.

"Leaving isn't an option, Skylark." He kept his words slow and precise, like he was speaking to a recalcitrant two-year-old. I shook my head—carefully, so I didn't wake any sleeping dragons—but he didn't give me room to voice any further objections. "You have a head injury and you lost consciousness. This isn't something you can just shrug off. Even though the tests didn't show an obvious problem, you shouldn't be alone until we're sure there's nothing else going on inside your head. Something hidden. And to know that, we need to observe you. In a room. Here." He spread his hands and nodded like it was a done deal. "Just for the weekend."

"I can't," I said. His crossed arms and glare mimicked Maureen's. I looked over at her. "I can't lie here in a bed like some helpless little twit while—"

The words jammed in my throat and I gagged. I pressed a shaking hand to my lips and closed my eyes. The image of my surrogate brother's mutilated, faceless body superimposed itself over the memory of Garrett laughing and joking with me at the restaurant, the image so clear behind my closed lids that it took all my strength to hold back the flood of tears that threatened. But I did not cry, I never cried, not even when I was alone, not since I'd turned fourteen, not even when Billy died. And I certainly would not cry now, not in front of an unsympathetic ER doctor with a god complex and a hot-shot attorney with legal machinations up her sleeve. It took a few moments and every ounce of willpower I owned, but my eyes were clear and dry when I opened my lids and stared at the bandages on my wrists.

"I won't stay here. I *can't*. I need to go home, need to be in my own place." *Need to find the creep who killed Garrett*, I clarified to myself.

"*I'll* make sure she isn't alone for the next few days, doctor." Maureen's soft voice held a note of steel even I knew better than to argue with. "*And* I'll bring her back immediately if I even *suspect* something isn't right."

The doctor's long-suffering sigh rattled around the room.

"All right, under those conditions I'll allow it. *But*." He glared at me. "You will have to sign a release that you left AMA." He narrowed his eyes and gave me a snapped explanation I didn't need. "Against. Medical. Advice."

"Fine." I looked up at Dr. Cover My Ass and glared back. "Whatever makes you happy."

I endured his macho, don't-mess-with-me stare for a long moment, until he realized I wasn't about to be cowed, or change my mind. He shook his head, stalked to the door, then turned and pointed a long, slender, well-sanitized index finger at me.

"Stay here," he growled, then swept out of the room.

I sighed, made my shaky way over to a chair, and lowered myself into it to wait for whatever I needed to sign. And for the pain med he'd given me to kick in. I felt completely disconnected from everything: my body, my mind, the room, the situation. *If I sit here and don't move, don't think, don't even breathe*—it was more a prayer than a mere thought—*it won't have happened. The world will right itself again.*

Maureen wiggle-hipped over and sat on the edge of the bed.

"You should stay here, and not just because of your health," she said. "It would pad out our lawsuit nicely to include a few days in the hospital."

"I don't care about any lawsuit. Besides, aren't you good enough to win on what we already have without throwing in a hospital stay?"

"Damn straight I am." She studied me a moment, then nodded. "Okay, we'll go with what we have already and skip the hospital bit. But you do realize that if you leave AMA, your insurance won't pay for any of this, don't you? Just how big *is* your bank account these days?"

"Not that big, and getting smaller fast thanks to Dunwitty." I gave her a wry smile. "Why not add the bill for this to the suit? Let Dunwitty pay for it, I'm sure it'd put quite a dent in his salary. That'd teach him not to toss the rule book out the window."

"I like the way you think, Skylark." Reenie grinned at me. "Now, like I told the doc, you'll come home with me for a few days so I can keep an eye on you," she said, but I held up my hand.

"No, Reenie. I'm going home."

"Skylark, *someone* has to watch you for a couple of days, just in case this is more serious than it appears. There's no room for me at your place. You don't even have a bedroom, all you have is a pull-out couch. A *single bed size* pull-out couch? Trust me, if I *ever* sleep with someone in a single bed, it *won't* be a *woman*."

I looked at Maureen and, beneath the brittle humor, saw—on her face, in her eyes—the same need I felt grinding away at me. The need to do something, anything, to bring life back into some kind of focus. And I remembered that Garrett was her friend, too.

Maybe not the same kind of friend that he was to me, not as close or as vital, but a good friend, a Reenie-level friend, nonetheless. Watching out for me would help ease her hurt. The least I could do was give her one night. I was still too shaky to venture out on my own, anyway. But tomorrow morning, all bets were off. She'd just have to deal with that.

I summoned another smile from somewhere and nodded. She grinned back.

"Good. We'll stop by your place and pick up what you'll need for the weekend, and maybe order in a pizza. Or would you rather Chinese? Oh, and a couple movies —"

The door snicked open and Dr. Personality strode in, stepping on her overly-enthusiastic Girls Only plans. Good thing, since they were pointless; I was only giving her one night, after all, and the way I felt, I'd be spending most of it asleep.

The doc took his time re-examining my injuries with less-than-gentle hands—to punish me for ignoring his advice, I'm sure—then he gave me a stern lecture on activities I could and could not do. He had me sign an AMA release form and thrust a prescription for pain medication at me. Maureen took it, snapped a photo of it with her phone and sent it to her personal assistant to fill, so it would be waiting for us when we arrived at her house. Then doctor-god left without a backward glance or a consoling word. Such compassionate treatment. And he'd left us to find our own way out of the ER warren, too. It wasn't until we'd gotten in the car, and I had buckled my seatbelt and reached for my non-existent purse to fish out my house keys, that I realized how truly bereft I was.

I had nothing. No keys, no cell phone, no wallet, no ID, and—most importantly—no Glock. It had all been in the Jeep when they'd hauled me out of it. And then the cops had hauled off the Jeep and all it contained, which left me without more than just transportation. Pretty much everything that defined me was being pulled apart and scrutinized by Dunwitty's nosey forensics teams. Violated didn't begin to describe how I felt. I needed to get home, needed to be in an uncontaminated space where I could lick my wounds in peace and gather the shreds of my identity back together. *And* locate another weapon. I clenched my shaking hands around the shoulder strap of the seat belt.

"My keys," I said as Maureen drove down Foothill Boulevard and turned onto Los Osos Valley Road. "The cops have my house keys."

"We'll figure something out. Giuseppe should be home, he can let us in."

Despite my benumbed state, I had to chuckle at the image that name brought up: my soon-to-be-ex-landlord, Enzio Napoli, a short, rotund, bald, gleaming-eyed Italian immigrant with an accent so thick his English was almost incomprehensible even after twelve years in this country. Maureen often said all he needed was a long-nosed puppet to make the picture complete.

"You shouldn't call him that," I said.

"I don't. Not to his face, anyway." She grinned at me, then went back to scrutinizing the ink-dark road; rural San Luis Obispo county was famous for its dearth of streetlights. "Besides, I won't have to worry about that anymore, since you're moving..."

Her words trailed off and I sat stupefied, wondering for the first time what I would do now, where I would go. My current place was already rented out, I'd given notice two months ago; new tenants were arriving in ten days, and I had only five left before I had to vacate the premises so Signore Napoli could get the place cleaned and painted in time. Garrett owned the house I was supposed to move into, but Garrett was gone. Dead. And dead landlords didn't rent out houses or collect rent checks. Their properties got sold out from under the people who lived—or were supposed to live— in them.

Somewhere to lay my head... One more thing to add to a "to do" list dominated by "Find Garrett's Killer," the only item I considered worth accomplishing.

Darkness surrounded us as we passed night-shrouded farmland. Stars studded the firmament overhead. A half moon shed a soft glow through the BMW's side window. We passed the local cemetery, descended a steep declivity, then rose up the other side into Los Osos proper, passing Palomino on the right, the street that now I wouldn't live on.

"I'll gather up what you'll need," Maureen said, the long silence having grown more than uncomfortable, "the doctor said you're not supposed to be moving around too much. No bending, no lifting, no straining. You just sit and tell me what you want me to pack, okay?"

"Yeah, whatever works," I murmured, my mind busy sorting through ways to lay my hands on another gun. Preferably a nice big one. Deadly. And untraceable.

Something in my tone must have tipped off Maureen. Her hands tightened on the steering wheel and she huffed out a breath.

"Skylark—"

"I'm going to find the asshole who did this, Reenie. Don't try to stop me." I looked over at her, my eyes burning as we sailed through the green light at South Bay Boulevard. "It's *Garrett*. I *owe* him this."

"It's not smart to interfere with the police investigation, Skylark. You'll just get arrested again."

"*What* investigation?" I snorted my derision and watched Ralph's Grocery flit past the window. "That jerk, Dunwitty, hasn't a *clue* how to be a real cop. He couldn't investigate his way out of a paper bag. He's already decided I killed Garrett. He won't even bother looking for the asshole who really did do it. So there's nothing to interfere with."

"And you think *you* can find him?" Maureen yanked the wheel to the right and we jolted onto 9th Street, just slipping beneath the yellow light. "*Without* getting in worse trouble? Or getting yourself *killed*?"

"Damn straight I can. I *will*."

"Not on *my watch* you won't."

Which was one more reason I'd only give her one night. Damned bossy-bitch. Maureen sighed again and we drove a few more blocks in silence. Not until she turned onto El Morro, toward the Bay, did I speak again.

"I'm going to kill him Reenie. For Garrett. Track him down and kill him like the rabid dog he is."

"Damn! Don't tell me things like that, Skylark. I'm an *officer of the court*, I have to *report it* if someone tells me they intend to commit a crime." She looked over at me; her eyes gleamed in the lights from an oncoming car. "I'm going to pretend I didn't hear that. And pray like hell I never have to defend you for a deliberate murder you actually *do* commit. It's bad enough trying to get you off on one you *didn't.*"

We turned onto 5th, now just two blocks away from my tiny little one-room apartment behind a house situated one block from the Bay. I started to shake again. The empty numbness that had insulated me from reality had shredded, giving way to rolling waves of emotion that almost doubled me over. My best friend, the man who'd stood as my surrogate brother from the time I turned nineteen and met him our first day at the police academy, was gone. Horribly, brutally murdered. Mutilated. Faceless. Tears again threatened. I leaned my head back, shut my burning eyes, and swallowed hard.

"What am I going to do without him, Reenie? He's my anchor. How do I go on without him?"

She reached over and clasped my icy hand with her warm fingers.

"One step at a time, Skylark," she whispered. "One step at a... Huh." Her voice rose, grew hard. "What the hell is going on up there?"

My eyes jerked open as I sat up. Midway down the block squad cars half-clogged the street. Unmarkeds filled Signore Napoli's driveway; others canted up onto his pristine lawn. All the lights were on. I spotted my landlord's rotund, back-lit silhouette hovering at the living room window. Shadowy figures moved up and down the driveway at the side of the house that led to the minuscule one-car-garage-turned-in-law-apartment in the back yard where I'd lived for the last three years. Uniformed cops formed a perimeter around the front, holding back curious neighbors.

"Dunwitty!" My heart beat with fury in my chest. "That son of a bitch!"

I had the door open even before Maureen steered the car onto the dirt berm at the side of the road, my feet outside as soon as she came to a stop.

"Skylark! Wait for me," she yelled as she yanked the shifter into park and killed the engine.

But I was in no mood to listen, much less obey. All I could see was the violation of the one safe place left to me. And the Neanderthal ape who'd instigated it. He had no right. He knew I had nothing to do with Garrett's death, had no evidence of any kind except spurious hearsay testimony from those restaurant people. No forensics, nothing, because there wasn't any. *Couldn't* be any. And still he came after me instead of looking for the real killer. Wasted time and resources on a wild goose chase because his little bitty ego had been bruised. By a woman.

I wasn't in any shape for physical confrontation despite the pain med I'd been given, but fury and adrenaline lent me strength and kept my feet beneath me. I shoved my way past the nearest uniform, Maureen screeching in my wake, and stumbled down the walkway like an Indy-500 race car with engine trouble. CSU techs jumped out of my way. It seemed to take forever, those fifteen seconds, until I rounded the back of the house, crossed the yard, and stomped up the three steps to my door, which stood open to the night.

All my lights were on. A warm glow streamed out the open door, spreading a few feet into the unlit back yard. Inside the apartment, four detectives carelessly dumped out the contents of the boxes I'd so carefully filled for the move. A fifth cop busied himself emptying the kitchen cupboards of the food I hadn't yet packed, opening and spilling onto the counter boxes of rice, oats, pasta and pudding, spices, tea and coffee. Dunwitty stood just inside the door, my laptop cradled in his meaty hands.

"You son of a bitch!" I screamed as I launched myself at him. The uniform guarding the door grabbed me, pulled me down the steps and held me, kicking and squirming, outside my now-ruined safe haven. "What the *hell* do you think you're doing? You have no right! Leave my things alone, you asshole!"

Dunwitty smirked at me, then raised his eyes to look past where I stood fighting with the uniformed cop.

"I suggest you control your client, Miss Overton." He pulled handcuffs from the back of his belt. "Or I will arrest her for interfering with a police investigation."

"*Investigation*? This isn't an investigation, it's a *witch hunt*! You fucking—"

Maureen jerked me away from the uniform, spun me around and slapped her hand over my mouth. Her nails dug into my arm and she held me in place until I calmed enough to be somewhat rational.

"*Shut up* and *stand still*, you *hear* me?" she hissed into my ear. "*I* will deal with this. *Don't you move* from this spot until I say you can. *You got that*?"

I stared into her blazing eyes and took two shuddering breaths before I was able to force myself to nod agreement. She let go slowly, not moving toward Dunwitty until she was sure I wouldn't launch myself at him again. The uniform stood close by, alert. I watched Reenie mount the stairs, walk up to the detective and hold out her hand. He slapped the warrant in it and it took all my strength not to run up, snatch it away from her and tear it up in Dunwitty's face. She took her time reading it, then she crossed her arms and glared up at the hulking detective.

"Pretty thin grounds, don't you think?" She gave him her shark smile and damn if he didn't quail just a bit. Too bad I wasn't in the mood to enjoy his discomfiture. "Who'd you have to pay off to shove this one through?"

"Don't be such a poor sport, Miss Overton." Dunwitty rocked back on his heels. "It doesn't look good on you."

They stood side by side a moment, watching the cops tear apart my life. The uniform turned away from me now that I appeared calm—basically, it was all I could do not to crumple to the ground, not that I let him know that—his attention claimed by three teens who had decided to scale the back fence in order to get closer to the action. I edged up the steps on weak, shaky legs until I stood just behind Maureen and Dunwitty.

"My laptop, Reenie." Dunwitty turned at the sound of my voice, and tightened his clutch on the device. "It's got all my client information on it. *Privileged* information," I added, glaring at the Neanderthal. It didn't phase him, he merely smirked at me again.

"Should have thought of that before you offed Gallivan," he said.

I tensed and Maureen grabbed my arm.

"It's listed in the warrant, Skylark, he can take it. But he *can't*," she turned her glare on the detective and he backed off a step, "take note of *anything* that does not pertain *directly* to Garrett Redmond Gallivan. *Meaning*," she added as Dunwitty tried to speak, "if Garrett's *name*, *address or any other pertinent information* is *not* found in a file, he cannot note down or use *anything* that's in it. Isn't that right, Detective? And she *will* get the laptop back in a timely manner, and in working condition, *correct*?"

She lifted her chin and continued to fire off more questions before he could formulate any answers to those first ones.

"They're being a bit sloppier than usual, aren't they? Following *your orders*, maybe? You *are* going to have this *cleaned up* before you leave, aren't you?"

Dunwitty blinked at us, then tried on his smirk for the third time that night.

"Sorry, not our job description."

"Reenie," I said, but a deep voice from behind me cut through the cold night air.

"Skylark? What the hell is going on? Why are the cops tearing your place apart?"

Heart thudding, unable to breathe, I slowly turned around and found myself staring into the mystified face of Garrett Redmond Gallivan's ghost.

 *CHAPTER FIVE*

Don't get me wrong; I do have paranormal "gifts"—at least that's what the so-called experts dub them, though I'm reserving judgment since they've always seemed more like a curse to me—but seeing ghosts, especially the ghosts of dead surrogate brothers, had never been one of them. Not, at least, until then.

I stood transfixed, unable to utter a word. I mean, how could I explain talking to blank air space to the cops who were systematically destroying my life? To say nothing of my attorney, who I knew would slap me in some psych ward quicker than she could pick up a new pair of Jimmy Choo's on sale if I embarrassed her by conducting a public conversation with a dead man. My mouth opened and closed, goldfish-style, but no way in hell would I let anything audible come out.

"You're not talking to me?" Garrett's shade spread his hands and gave me his signature WTF look. "Come on, woman. Not fair. What did I do?"

Both Reenie and the jerk-off, Dunwitty, turned to look out into the dark yard, probably prompted by my fascinating deer-caught-in-headlights act. Then Reenie gasped in a scared-sounding breath, which scared more than the hell out of me.

"Hey, Maureen, maybe you can tell me what's going on, since Skylark's giving me the silent treatment for some reason."

"Who the hell are you?" Dunwitty's growl echoed around my head and stepped on whatever reply Reenie might have made. My heart froze in my chest. "And how the hell did you get in here? Aranda! Get this gawker out of here!"

I turned and gaped at Maureen and Dunwitty.

"You can see him?"

I didn't mean to say it out loud since I didn't relish a sojourn in a rubber room, but my stunned brain seemed to hold no power over my mouth. Dunwitty took a step back, eyeing me as though I had suddenly sprouted another head. I could read the derision on his face and knew some blistering snark was about to roll my way, but Maureen's soft, awe-struck voice filled up the tiny inch of silence that had fallen.

"*Garrett?* My God, it's really you! You're not... dead?"

"Are you nuts?" Garrett reared back, his eyes as round as ping-pong balls. "Why the *hell* would I be *dead*?"

He stood there, his eyes shifting back and forth as he looked at me, then Maureen, then Dunwitty, and back at me. The detective—and I use the term loosely—started forward, blustering about Garrett getting the hell out of his crime scene, and the total idiocy of the huge ape burst on me like a bomb exploding. I whirled and shoved Dunwitty with both hands. He staggered back and smacked into the door frame. My head started to pound again.

"You fucking *idiot!*" I screamed. "Didn't you even bother to verify the *identity of the victim* before you came after me for killing my best friend—*who isn't even dead*?"

The cops sifting through my belongings stopped. They stood transfixed, staring at our little soirée in the doorway. Maureen grabbed onto my arm to keep me from further attacking Dunwitty. Said Ape-man held up a meaty hand to halt the outdoor uniforms who'd come in response to his bellow. He glared at Garrett, who looked like he was sorry he'd bothered seeking me out.

"Hold on." Dunwitty's raspy growl echoed in the still air. "You claim to be Garrett Gallivan?"

"Only for the last thirty-one years." Garrett's grin faded when no one else seemed amused at his little joke. "Hey, I can prove it."

He reached toward his rear pocket; the three uniforms surrounding him drew their weapons and shouted for him to halt. Garrett froze, echoing my proverbial deer-in-headlights stance. Dunwitty's grate rasped on.

"Where the hell you been since Monday night?"

"Uh, I lost my wallet? Spent Tuesday in San Luis, getting my driver's license and Social Security Card replaced, then I drove down to Santa Barbara and spent the night with a friend. I had client meetings there all day Wednesday. Stayed overnight again, came back today and spent the afternoon at my banks, straightening out credit cards and stuff. I stopped for something to eat, then came over here. Why?"

Dunwitty waggled his fingers. Garrett, his movements slow and precise, pulled out his wallet and handed over a newly-re-issued license. I watched the detective frown as he scrutinized the photo, then lifted his head to study Garrett. *Good thing licenses carry photos*, I thought; I doubted Dunwitty could correctly decipher actual words. After a long, tense moment, with his men still standing motionless, watching—one with his hands in my stash of exotic coffee beans, three with guns still drawn—Dunwitty nodded and handed Garrett back his license. Tension eased; weapons got reholstered.

"This is an interesting little puzzle we have here," the detective muttered, his confused gaze staring over Garrett's head into the darkness. The stupidity of his statement rolled over me like a blistering wave from a blast furnace.

Interesting? Skyrockets shot off in my head. *Little puzzle?* Red rage misted over my vision and I gasped in a breath.

"You stupid *shithead!*" I pulled out of Maureen's grasp, reached for my laptop and yanked it out of Dunwitty's hands before he could react. Then, ignoring the elephants that again began stomping on my brain, I shoved him away from the door with all my strength— which wasn't much, given the events of the day; he only moved back two steps. "You have *no right* to be messing with my things! *Get out of here!*"

Garrett scaled the steps in two strides and pulled me into his arms, which saved both Dunwitty and me; Dunwitty from being pounded into the ground by *moi*, and me from being tossed into jail on a charge based on actual fact and not Dunwitty's fantasy.

Maureen turned and glared at me.

"Let *me* handle this, Skylark. It's what you're *paying* me for, *right?*"

Oh, she just had to bring up the money issue, didn't she? Especially since Dunwitty had made sure I wouldn't get paid any time soon by my latest client. Maureen turned her patented glower on the huge detective, morphing into The Overton in the blink of an eye.

"Get your men *out* of here, Dunwitty, before I add *trespass and vandalism* to the brutality charges. Your *warrants*," she added, again inspecting the one she still held, her tone of steel overriding Dunwitty's attempted bluster, "are for evidence in the murder of Garrett Redmond Gallivan, who is *standing right there*," she pointed at where Garrett stood with his arms wrapped around me from behind, "very much *alive*. So, your warrants have *no basis in fact*, are *invalid*, and you have *no business* interfering with my client. *Or her possessions*." She crossed her arms and lifted her chin. "*Leave. All* of you. *Now*."

Dunwitty pursed his thick lips and lifted his gaze to the ceiling. Then he nodded.

"That's it, guys," he called to his men. "We're outta here."

The cops dropped whatever they held, left it lying where it fell, and moved toward the door. I squirmed in Garrett's grasp and held out an arm to try to block their exit.

"Hey, wait, you can't leave it like this. You've got to clean it all up."

Dunwitty gave me one last smirk.

"Sorry. Like I said, not our job."

I lunged for him, only missing because Garrett shuffled us back, out of the way of the exiting cops.

"You imbecilic moron, I'm gonna break every bone in yo—"

Garrett's hand clamped on my mouth before I could finish telling Dunwitty what I was going to do to him, and then what he could do to himself once I was through.

"Let's not get you arrested for threatening a police officer," Garrett breathed into my ear.

I shrugged off Garrett's hand and watched Dunwitty's broad back vanish into the darkness of the yard.

"He has *no right* to the title, *or* the job," I spat, pitching my voice loud enough for the so-called detective to hear, wishing every word were a poisoned dart that could pierce Dunwitty's rhino-thick hide. "He's a *jerk* and an *asshole* who has no idea *how to be a cop,* much less a *detective!* Anything I could do to him would be considered *justifiable imbecilicide!*"

I caught my breath on a sob and turned around in Garrett's arms, laid my pounding head on his warm, broad chest so I could hear his heart beat. And his bubbling laughter as he repeated "imbecilicide" to himself. Not that I needed the reassurance, but still...

"They said you were dead, Garrett," I whispered, no longer able to maintain any appreciable volume. "And that I killed you. They showed me pictures, horrible pictures."

"It's okay, Skylark. I'm fine and I'm right here."

The adrenaline that had flooded my body ebbed away. I began to shake and whatever strength I'd held onto fled into the next county. The increasing drumbeat in my head was getting harder to ignore, pain med or no pain med. Garrett half-carried me to the one kitchen chair still upright and sat me down as Maureen moved further into the mess that used to be my private oasis.

Garrett righted the second chair and sat facing me. He picked up my hands and inspected the bandages on my wrists, then gently pushed the hair away from the butterflied wound on my temple and the surrounding bruise slowly growing in size.

"What happened to you?" he asked, and I trembled even more at the dangerous undercurrent that rode in his soft, caring tone.

I told him everything, starting with being pulled out of the Jeep, through the interrogation at the cop shop, and ending with the humiliating arrival at the emergency room via ambulance—everything except the vision from Dunwitty's past. Like Dunwitty—hell, like most people—Garrett had no real belief in paranormal abilities, and no patience for what he called "imaginary nonsense." If he had to, he'd listen without much protest —he accepted the parts of me that made him uncomfortable because that's what surrogate brothers did—but I knew he hated hearing about something he didn't believe in, couldn't understand, and had no control over. So I rarely told him when, or how, the paranormal stepped on my life.

Garrett smiled at me when I'd finished my recitation.

"I'm only gone two days and look what you do to yourself. Cuts, bruises, bandages and a concussion. You're hopeless."

"Damn straight she is." Maureen walked toward us, settling items into a couple of cloth shopping bags she'd unearthed from somewhere in the mess surrounding us.

"I think I've got what she'll need, for a few days, anyway. Let's get out of here."

"No." I shook my head, then winced; bad idea, moving. "I'm staying here. I need to start cleaning this up."

"No, you're coming home with me, like we planned. You've already broken just about every rule the doctor gave you. This will all wait a couple of days, until that concussion settles down. Can you help her out to my car, Garrett?"

I started to protest, but Garrett pulled me up onto legs that felt more like overcooked spaghetti than useful limbs. I staggered against him, which bounced up the pain in my head a few more notches, and I couldn't bite back a groan or two. Maureen sighed.

"Maybe you'd better carry her, Garrett."

He grinned and swung me up into his arms. Garrett's six-foot-seven frame might be lean, but hours in the gym had built him some formidable muscle strength, enough so that he handled my hundred-fifty pounds as though I were a dainty, petite damsel in distress and not the almost-six-foot giant I was. I gave a few seconds of thought to insisting I could maneuver on my own, but I knew there was no way I could have taken even one step. Not without falling. My head whirled, so I just gave in and let myself relax in his embrace, and smiled when I felt him kiss the top of my head. The last thing I remember before waking up the next morning in Maureen's guest sleigh bed was Garrett carrying me down the three steps into the back yard.

 *CHAPTER SIX*

I had my fingers clamped on the front doorknob, with freedom only a few steps away, when Reenie's voice rang out across the room.

"Excuse *me*. Just *where* do you think you're *going*?"

I took a breath, turned, and gave her the innocent look I'd stayed up half of Saturday night practicing in the mirror. I didn't let go of the doorknob.

"Jail break?"

"I see. And *how* do you plan to get anywhere? The cops still have your purse, your ID, your house keys, *and* your car."

"I'll manage, somehow." I shrugged and tried on the innocent look again, while behind my back I twisted the knob. Reenie's eyes narrowed; she must have heard the click. Or maybe my innocent look didn't work; so much for forgoing all that sleep.

"Oh, no, you don't." She wagged a manicured finger back and forth, then pointed into the living room. "Get your ass back in here."

"And if I don't?"

"Then I'll make you."

She propped her fists on her hips and lifted an eloquent, plucked brow; she obviously expected The

Overton act to have a cowing effect on me. As if. I lifted a brow of my own. Granted, not half as dramatic—or plucked—as hers, but still.

"You think so, shrimp?" I looked her up and down, scanning all hundred-five pounds of her. "*You're* gonna stop *me*?"

Reenie crossed her arms and scowled.

"Don't force the issue, Skylark."

"Hah. Take one step closer and I'll pick you up and toss you across the room. Then I'll raid your rainy-day stash for funds and call a cab."

"No, you won't."

"Oh, won't I?"

"You better believe it."

"You willing to test that theory, Counselor?"

"Don't need to. You won't do any of that because if you do, I'll sue you for everything you own. *And*," she added when I opened my mouth, "I'll throw in a few things you don't, just for fun." She grinned at me. "Sometimes it pays to be The Overton."

I heaved as dramatic a sigh as I could manage—not that it affected Reenie in any way—then let go of the knob, trudged over to the sofa, and dropped down onto the pearl gray, shot-silk upholstery on which she'd spent more than I grossed in good month. A really good month.

"I hate when you do that," I muttered.

"What? Out-maneuver you?" Reenie gave me a pleased smirk. "Don't know why. *I* find it eminently enjoyable."

I shook my head and closed my eyes so I didn't have to see her triumphant glow. Friendship hell might be tolerable in short bursts, but for the last endless three nights and two days she'd been stuck to my side like Superglue. I'd endured more than any rational human should have to of nail polish, face cream masks, intimate disclosures, and heartsick sighs over cinematic dreamboats. Reenie's idea of "Girl Time" consisted of an endless round of pajama party popcorn, greasy pizza, hot fudge sundaes, outdated college yearbooks, and saccharine chick flicks. She had *The Divine Secrets of the Ya-Ya Sisterhood* scheduled for this afternoon. I knew that if I saw so much as the opening credits my brain would dissolve and run out my ears. My headache was gone, thanks to the pain pill I'd taken an hour before. My watery bones had almost re-solidified, if I didn't move too much or too fast. And the asswipe who had sentenced me to this torment was still out there, running around free. As was Dunwitty.

"I can't just sit here anymore," I whispered. "I feel so useless."

I felt the cushions bobble as Reenie sat down near me. I opened my eyes to look at her. She gave me a sad smile.

"I understand, sweetie. You're a woman of action," she reached out and brushed my hair away from the cut on my temple, "and this enforced stillness is driving you crazy. But hurting yourself because you can't sit still until you're fully healed won't help anyone. And getting arrested for interfering with a police investigation is counterproductive. You can't accomplish *anything* from a *jail cell*."

"Dunwitty isn't capable of conducting an effective investigation, and you know it." My breathing sped up as anger again stirred inside me. "He wasn't even smart enough to confirm the identity of the dead guy! He'll *never* find out who did it, because his pea brain is convinced *I'm* the killer. That means it's up to me." I glared at her. "And *don't* call me *sweetie*."

Reenie chuckled and I sighed out a breath through clenched teeth.

"You are *so* predictable. Listen," she added before I could take another breath, much less blast her to kingdom come for being so condescending, "Dunwitty might be a dinosaur and full of himself, but he really *is* a good detective. It might take him longer than it would take—what was it he called you? Oh, yes—Miss One Name Wonder, but he'll eventually get there. Even *without* your help."

"I wouldn't help him if he were the last detective on the face of the earth," I growled. "And how many other innocent people's lives will he tear apart before he solves this crime? *If* he ever does."

I looked at Reenie and knew by the sympathy on her face I hadn't been successful at hiding the pain I still felt over hearing of Garrett's so-called death and being accused of causing it. I couldn't stand the thought that someone else might go through what I had at the hands of that idiot cop.

I shoved myself up and began pacing around the room, from the couch to the mahogany-mantled fireplace, to the French doors that opened onto a rear-yard patio with its stunning view of Morro Bay and its famous Rock, and back to the couch where she sat watching me. And around again. And again, my fury rising with every word, each ever-more-wobbly step.

"You've got an in with the Coroner's office, right? I need to know how he was killed, and with what. What injuries he sustained. Were there defensive wounds?

How many, and where? And I need to find out who the guy was, his name, where he worked, who his friends and coworkers were. And his family. Maybe there are some clues in all that I could follow to find out who did it."

The drum in my head started up again, echoing my pounding heart as I waved my hands around, searching for a viable plan.

"I need to figure out where he lived, check out his house and go through his stuff. And his work place. I also need to know what was left at the scene, what kind of evidence they found. Would Dunwitty even *know* evidence if he saw it? You're chummy with the DA, maybe—uh!"

An arrow of white light shot across my vision. I stumbled and grabbed onto the fireplace mantle with both hands. The room seesawed around me for a few moments and pain stabbed through my head. I pressed a hand on my left cheekbone. Mr. Invisible had once again picked up his handy-dandy temple drill, despite the pain meds.

"Okay, that's enough moving around for now." Maureen rose and came over to me. "Let's get some lunch and then you can go take a little rest."

I protested as she led me into the dining room—well, wrestled my protesting body is more accurate, I wasn't capable of more speech right then and the damn midget is a hell of a lot stronger than she looks—then pushed me down in a chair. She stood staring at me, hands fisted on her hips.

"You won't get far if you don't eat, Skylark, and *don't* tell me *one* piece of toast four hours ago is enough. One piece you *didn't even finish*, I might add. Now *shut up* and *sit still*, and let me get some *real* nourishment into you."

I nodded agreement, knowing I would simply attempt another escape when we'd finished our meal. She had to use the bathroom sometime, right? The room executed a graceful swoop around me, and my stomach lurched. I set my elbows on the table, propped my head on my hands, and waited for stability to return as I listened to the rattling sounds Maureen made in the kitchen, wondering what she was whipping up this time. *Please, no more popcorn. Or pizza,* I thought, though Reenie was actually a good cook when she bothered with it. Unlike me, who specialized in freezer-to-microwave-to-table. Or fast-food take-out. Or my ultimate favorite, reservations—when someone else was paying.

"Here," she said, carrying in a tray laden with steaming bowls, "this should fix you right up."

She set a Limoges porcelain bowl in front of me, along with a matching plate bearing two warm, homemade-looking biscuits and another holding a few pats of real butter—no imitation anything for The Overton. She added silverware—sterling, of course—set her own place, then sat down facing me. I looked up from the delicious-smelling broth.

"Chicken soup? Really?"

Maureen shrugged and grinned.

"It's good for what ails you."

I took a sip and almost sighed aloud at the luscious flavor. This was definitely homemade, not the canned variety I invariably attempted to force into myself whenever I got sick. I could feel the soup's warmth threading down through the fibers of my body, feel the burst of energy it imparted. It tasted like heaven, not that I'd ever admit as much to Reenie. I looked over at her, sitting all smug and virtuous, her bright-eyed gaze fastened on me.

"If I'm predictable," I said around another mouthful of the broth, this one laden with luscious bits of carrots, peas, and diced potatoes, "then you, my dear Ms. Overton, are an anachronism."

"*Thank* you." Maureen beamed at me. "Now, let's discuss your *lawsuit.*"

"I've been thinking about that. I don't want to sue anyone, much less Dunwitty," I said, dunking a piece of biscuit in the broth. "It'll only cause me more trouble than I'm already in."

"He *needs* to pay for what he did to you." Reenie narrowed her eyes at the wound on my temple. "Think of that *emergency room bill.*"

I had to admit, she had a point; the hospital tab hadn't done my dwindling funds any favors. Still, what I wanted more than anything was off Dunwitty's radar, and shifting his net worth into my depleted bank account was so not the way to accomplish that. I shook my head.

"No, Reenie. I can't—" My words choked off when I saw thunderclouds amass in her expression, and I rethought turning her down flat. "I just can't deal with it right now. It's not something we have to do, like, tomorrow, is it? I'm still having trouble with everything that's happened. Can you give me a few days to process it all?"

"Of *course*, sweetie. I'm sorry, I didn't mean to push you," she added, though I knew damned well that she's the one who invented pushing. "We have some leeway before we have to file against him; not a lot, but *some*. We'll see how long it takes him to return your property, and what shape it's in. If there's any damage, we can add that to our bottom line."

I gave her as non-committal a nod as I could manage and we ate on in silence. I watched Reenie's eyes glow and I knew that, despite my not wanting to further complicate my life, she was busy planning Dunwitty's monetary downfall. I alternated between spoonfuls of soup, bites of flaky buttermilk biscuit soaked in the broth, and scheming out my next bid for freedom. I had almost finished the bowl when the spoon suddenly became too heavy to lift. Alarm bells rang in my head.

I sat staring at the bowl, barely able to move, while Maureen cleared her plates from the table. By the time she returned to the dining room for mine, I could hardly lift my head. I tried my best to glare at her from eyes that stood at half mast.

"Wha shid ooo—"

My tongue fumbled among the syllables and in trying to find my way through them I lost track of what I wanted to say. Maureen helped me out of the chair and guided my weaving body down the hall to the guest bedroom. Once there she pulled off my T-shirt and jeans, slid a nightgown over my head and pulled back the bed covers. A gentle shove and somehow I was on my back, head nestled on the pillow as she settled the covers over me. My eyes started to close of their own volition.

"You... *drugged*... me."

"I didn't *drug* you, I just put a sleeping pill in your soup." Maureen smiled at me. "The doctor said you need to rest, which you haven't been doing. Now you can."

I groaned and forced my eyes open.

"Thass assault, or kinnapping, or somesing. I'm gonna sue you. Know any good lawyers?"

"I'll write out a list for you while you sleep. But none of them are anywhere *near* as good as I am, so you'll just waste their time. And *your* money. Sleep well."

She turned and left the room, leaving soft laughter and lilac perfume in her wake as she closed the door behind her. I couldn't even lift my arms to shove off the bedcovers, much less get up, get dressed and get out. As I felt the drug pull me under, I realized I'd have to give up Maureen. And Garrett, too. It was all too painful, this thing called friendship. There was too much closeness, too much sharing, and way too much pain if I ever lost one; I'd over-learned that at Dunwitty's hands. And now I was drowning in the anguish of betrayal. Having friends made me way too vulnerable, and that was something I'd sworn I'd never be again.

No, friendship might be okay in the short term, if kept on the surface and at arm's length, but in the long run it just wasn't worth it. Not at all.

 *CHAPTER SEVEN*

Seven a.m., Monday morning; the start of another workweek. Another house. More treasures to be discovered. It should be exciting.

It wasn't.

Magellan Carstairs stood before the far shelves in the dim warehouse in San Luis Obispo and tried to think it out, step by step, tried to construct a plan for this new week. This new job. Just as he'd always done. It should have been easy, but memories of last week's fiasco kept intruding. They bombarded him; the carefully thought-out scenario, his every action, what had gone right, what had gone wrong.

Yes, wrong.

For the first time.

It should have scared him.

It exhilarated him.

Not that he wanted to repeat it, at least not in the chaotic way it had happened. He could still remember the terror he'd felt as it unfolded; mind-numbing, paralyzing, suffocating fear. The memories alone made him shudder. He'd stood there in the dark, listening to sounds he'd never before encountered, sounds he'd never thought he'd hear. He'd always planned so thoroughly, knew exactly what to expect from moment to moment. But all his care went down the drain when the unforeseen—the unthinkable—finally caught up to him. All he could think was, *this isn't happening, it* can't *be happening!*

But it had happened. And somehow, in the blink of an eye, as the blood roared in his ears and his body broke out in a cold sweat, as dread had made breathing almost impossible, he'd known what needed to be done. Knew exactly how to extricate himself from the situation. And he'd done it; without a thought, with no hesitation. Step-by-step, as though he'd done it many times before. He'd sprung out, heart pounding, adrenaline surging through his body, and faced the crisis head on. He'd solved the problem, righted the wrong. Saved the day.

He'd had the time of his life.

And now he didn't want to go back to living as usual. Not that he particularly wanted to go forward, either, not quite in *that* way, but he had to admit there was something strangely hypnotic about it all, something addictive. It called to him, as though he'd inadvertently uncovered his true path to happiness. Discovered just exactly who, and what, he was. What his purpose in life was. What he was capable of. What made him different. The one thing above all others that filled him with sublime exhilaration.

Despite the mistakes.

Or... maybe because of them.

Mistakes. Yes, despite all his care, all his training, all his experience, he'd made mistakes, two of them. *But did I really?* He frowned as he thought it over. Perhaps he'd had nothing to do with either occurrence. Perhaps it was only the intervention of Fate itself, steering him in the right direction. Yes, he liked that thought. The Intervention of Fate.

The First Intervention—as he now thought of it— the homeowner coming home unexpectedly, had pointed Carstairs toward his true path, a path he knew he'd more than enjoy exploring in various ways. Blinking, he lifted down a gallon of paint and squinted at the label on the can he held until he could make out the name: *Sheer Ivory*, the color needed for the current job. He nodded and set the can in the case at his feet, with the result of fate's Second Intervention now in the forefront of his mind.

The loss of his reading glasses.

He'd not thought to leave them home. And why would he? He was almost blind without them, he needed them on the job, and so he'd kept them tucked into his shirt pocket. And now, thanks to Intervention Number One, they were gone.

He'd first noticed them missing late Wednesday afternoon. He'd taken the day off to recuperate and so hadn't missed them until the evening paper had arrived. He'd spent the rest of the week, and even the weekend, looking for them, starting with the work truck, both in the cab and in the bed. He'd checked the warehouse, all the places he'd gone into and even some he hadn't. Then he searched his pickup, under and between the seats, in the glove box, even in the bed. He'd gone through every room in the farmhouse, every drawer in every room, outside along the walkway, the garage, and even in the musty old barn, though he'd never gone in there before. He'd delved into each shirt, pants, and jacket pocket, even those he hadn't worn in weeks. He'd even risked going back to The House and searching there, too.

Nothing. They were gone. Lost.

A trickle of fear again shuddered down his spine at the thought, but he stepped on it. Ground it into oblivion. Fear served no purpose, his father had taught him that. It made a person careless and caused stupid, halfwitted mistakes. Not the kind that led to bigger and better things, not the kind that were really the Intervention of Fate, but the kind of mistakes that came from being a moron. A cretin. The kind that were completely his fault. Those kind could ruin everything. He had no room in his life for idiotic mistakes. Or the fear that caused them.

Carstairs set a second gallon in the box at his feet and reached for another can. He didn't want to admit it, but deep inside he knew his glasses were in the one place they shouldn't be. The one place that could spell disaster for him.

But would it really? The thought caught him up. He frowned and let the implications filter into his head. *No, probably not*, he decided. It wasn't like anyone could trace him from the glasses, they weren't prescription. He'd bought them off a display at a drugstore. It was unlikely that someone would realize they shouldn't be where they were, that they didn't belong to the dead guy. It was equally unlikely someone would recognize their true significance even if they did figure that out. And if they did, so what? The revelation would just lead them to a dead end—pun intended.

Unless...

If he'd left behind some trace, and if they found that trace...

"Carstairs! Feinstein's waiting on you. What's taking so long? Ain't you packed those cases yet? You blind or something? Or just sleeping on the job?"

Carstairs turned and looked at his hated boss, Vince Eddington. The shift supervisor stood in the open doorway of the warehouse, backlit by the glare of the early morning sun. Sneering at him as usual. Putting him down. *Pain in the ass lazy shithead*, Carstairs thought. His hands tightened on the paint can handle. *I'd like to bash his frigging head in.*

"No, sir." He forced a note of servile enthusiasm into his voice. "I got it right here." Carstairs gave the man an inane grin and lifted the can.

"Well, quit mooning over the damned stuff and get a move on. You guys ain't got all day."

Eddington shook his head then walked away, muttering to himself about the lack of intelligence and initiative he had to deal with on a daily basis, a mutter loud enough for Carstairs to hear. One more thing for Carstairs to hold against the shithead.

His lip curling, Carstairs added two more gallons to the two already in the box, packed another case on top of that one, then hefted them both and lugged them out of the building, grateful he'd remembered where the color for the job on 4th street had been stored. If he hadn't been tapped to off-load the shipment last week when it had arrived—not in his job description, but his boss didn't care about that—he'd have been sunk. Between the lost reading glasses and the dim lighting in the warehouse, he'd never have been able to tell the difference between *Sheer Ivory* and *White Blush*.

"I'd like to *Sheer Ivory* that asshole," he muttered, glaring at his boss's retreating back as he staggered toward the truck, muscles bulging. He pictured pelting Eddington with the heavy cans until nothing remained but a bloody pile of pulp and bones. It would be so satisfying. But no; he had a bigger problem to solve, first.

Those reading glasses.

"Get a move on, Carstairs," Larry Feinstein growled. "Fuck, we're late now 'cause it took you so long."

Carstairs grunted at his painting partner—another shithead—who stood beside the truck with his own expression of disdain on his beak-nosed face. Arms crossed, foot tapping on the asphalt. Not about to lend a hand with packing up the paint. Or carrying the heavy load. They didn't get along, couldn't stand each other, actually, and the supervisor knew it. Yet he kept pairing them up on jobs, probably just to ruin Carstairs' life. Yet another reason to hate the fucker. Both the fuckers.

Carstairs shoved the cans of paint into the truck bed, closed the tailgate, then hoisted himself up onto the cab's passenger seat. They headed out, Larry behind the wheel as usual; he never trusted anyone else to drive. They stopped at a Starbucks and coffeed up before aiming for the house in Los Osos, another Larry ritual Carstairs could have done without. But it wasn't worth yet another argument about it.

Once they left the coffee shop, Carstairs watched the storefronts lining Broad, then Higuera, then Los Osos Valley Road whip by them as Larry pushed the accelerator down, well past the posted speed. He'd get stopped for it sooner rather than later, and have to face Eddington, the office, and traffic court. Maybe even lose his job. Not that Carstairs cared. As long as he wasn't behind the wheel and the cops disregarded him like they usually did, he was happy to let Larry do the driving. And take the heat.

He sipped his coffee, glad of the silence in the truck's cab. He and Larry-the-jerk didn't go in for small talk. They had nothing in common. They split each job by room so they didn't even have to see each other much during the day, which suited Carstairs just fine. It gave him time to reconnoiter, to think, to plan, without the aggravation of being social with the dickwad. And he really needed time alone today; he had problems to solve. If he had lost the glasses where he thought he had, who would have found them? What would have happened to them? Where might they be now? And how could he get them back without anyone being the wiser?

"All right, we're finally here," Larry said, steering the truck into the driveway of the house on 4th Street and pulling Carstairs from his ruminations. "I'll take the living and dining rooms. You do the bedrooms. 'K?

Carstairs merely grunted his agreement to Larry's curt tone—he knew 'K?' was merely lip service added to what were orders and not a real question—and slid down from the passenger seat. In the distance, Morro Rock rose like a beached whale from an ocean that glittered in the strengthening sun. Nearby, birds chirped in the live oaks surrounding the large, one-story, rambling stucco house. It sat atop a low hill that overlooked Morro Bay and the dunes beyond, a location that raised the price tag on the property into the stratosphere. The scent of salt and seaweed rode the gentle breeze that wafted across the bay. They got out of the truck and began gathering the painting supplies. Then Larry broke their tacit no-talk rule.

"Gregg, you know Gregg?" he asked as he hefted the tote with their brushes and rollers—he always took only the light stuff—and they walked toward the house, Carstairs behind him lugging one heavy case of paint. "Saw him at a bar last night, and man was he complaining. Boss got him slated to start on what Gregg calls the Body Building tomorrow, and he's scared shitless. Thinks the dead are gonna rise and walk while he's there."

Larry brayed the hyena laugh that always made Carstairs shudder, then he unlocked the door and shouldered through, letting it swing shut behind him. Carstairs grunted as he shifted his hold on the unwieldy case of paint cans, yanked the door open, and walked into the foyer, his heart thudding.

"Man, he was shaking in his boots, though I don't really blame him." Larry set his paraphernalia just inside the living room archway and stood, arms crossed, back to Carstairs, eyeing the living room walls. "Man, just the thought of that place gives me the shivers. You couldn't pay me enough to so much as step inside that place. Eesh!" He looked over his shoulder. "Go get the rest of the paint. And the ladders. 'K?"

Carstairs nodded, set down the case of paint in the hallway, then headed back to the truck, for once not resenting the way Larry ordered him around. His whole body started to tingle; he'd thought he'd have five anxious days on this job, eggshell-walking around Larry and trying to figure out a solution, but it had happened again. Fate had intervened, had given him a clear sign: Intervention Number Three.

Carstairs grinned.

"She damn well *does* have something to do with this!"

Detective Carrick Dunwitty's deep rasp rang out across the squad room, underscored by the whack of the file he slammed onto the desktop. Detectives and Uniforms alike turned to look at him. Javier Soto-Osorio, his partner for the last six years, lifted his gaze to the ceiling to commune with the Almighty in His heaven. He'd done a lot of communing since being assigned to Dunwitty.

"No, she doesn't," Soto said. "We have no evidence, Dunwitty, and you know it. Nothing. *Nada.*" He dropped into his chair and peered up at his partner. "I mean, the guy she's supposed to have killed is still walking around, as alive as you or me."

"The one who's dead sure as hell isn't, José," Dunwitty snarled. "We gotta be missing something, some connection between our victim and Miss One Name Wonder. I just know it. I feel it."

"Listen, partner, I don't mind you calling me José during interrogations, but the rest of the time could you at least *try* to remember that my name is Javier? *Por favor?*" Soto knew it was a lost cause; he'd been trying to get Dunwitty to call him by his given name for six years now, with no success.

"José, Javier, what's the diff?" Dunwitty gave a dismissive wave of his hand. "All those Hispanic names sound the same."

He threw his bulk into his chair, which groaned a pained protest, then he slapped open the file and began scanning pages for what Soto figured was probably the hundredth time.

"You are such a prejudiced jerk, Dunwitty. And we haven't missed anything. We need to re-think this, start looking elsewhere. Skylark didn't do it."

Dunwitty ignored him. He continued turning pages as Soto again turned his eyes up. Asking for patience. Asking for the right words to turn his partner from this obsession. After about ten minutes of silence punctuated by the crackling of paper, Soto narrowed his eyes at Dunwitty.

"What's got you so damned fired up about her, anyway? All that stuff she was spouting off about your father?"

"Don't." Dunwitty glared at him and stabbed a thick finger his way. "Shut up about that."

"You mean she was right about him? And about that kid with the lion tattoo? I thought so." Soto blinked at his partner, surprised Dunwitty would admit to it, that his father had been the better cop. "Man, did you see her face, that blank stare, when she had that vision? That was really spooky."

"No, it was *shit*." Dunwitty shoved away the file and leaned back in his chair, his hands clenched on the armrests. "She's a *con artist*, Soto, don't let her fool you."

"Then how did she know all that stuff about you, about your family? She didn't even know your *name* until her lawyer showed up."

Dunwitty made a dismissive gesture, his face screwed up as though he were in pain.

"She researched it ahead of time, and went into that act just to throw us off. She's probably got something on every one of us, just in case she needs it."

"I don't know, Dunwitty. It looked pretty real to me." Soto shivered as he remembered Skylark's face, the way her whole body had reacted, when she'd that eerie vision. He frowned, thinking she could be a seeress; she'd looked just like the local village *adivina* his *abuela* had taken him to see when he was a small boy.

"Real?" Dunwitty snorted. "You notice she didn't home in on you, did she? 'Cause she didn't know *your* name. And she had to wait until her lawyer, that Overton bitch, mentioned mine. She had a couple hours to pull her shit on us, Soto; *hours*. But she couldn't do it earlier, 'cause she had to wait until she found out who at least one of us was, so she could pull out the correct info she's got stored away." He tapped a finger on his temple, then picked up a pen and began drumming it on his desk. "She's a damned good little actress, that one. Damned good."

"I think you're wrong, Dunwitty." Soto shook his head, trying to rid himself of the premonitory shivers that still ran down his spine. "I think maybe she's got The Gift. People do, you know, they can see and hear things others can't. Back in Mexico—"

"Ah, don't give me any of that Hispanic culture crap of yours. You were born here, José, you know better than to believe those old wives' tales. There ain't no such thing as 'psychic visions.'" Dunwitty air quoted his sarcasm. "Or spirits rapping on tables. Or messages from the dead. Or people reading other people's minds.

Or any of that other so-called psychic crap. It ain't real. *Trust* me on this. If you can't see it, hear it or touch it for yourself, *it ain't real*. All this psychic stuff is just *woo-woo shit*. Con artists use it to manipulate and hoodwink gullible idiots." He threw down the pen, stood and glared at his partner. "You're supposed to be a cop, Soto. A detective. Try acting like one."

He picked up his mug and headed for the door. Just before he reached it, he turned and pointed at Soto.

"I'm getting coffee. That'll give you time to get your head on straight. When I get back, we're going over those reports, letter by letter, until we find what we missed and we can haul that murdering con artist back in here for good. You got that?"

Soto watched Dunwitty turn and vanish through the doorway. He knew his partner had a point. Most of what was touted as genuine psychic phenomena was mere chimera, used to bilk money out of desperate, lonely or grieving people. But he didn't think this Skylark woman had been yanking their chains. There was no way she could know something private about every officer in SLO county, to say nothing of each of the cities that had their own forces. Just in case she *might* run into one of them *someday*? That was hundreds of officers; she'd have to have a memory the size of an elephant's.

No, he'd watched her face when she'd stared back into the interrogation room, seen her eyes shift as though following someone's movements. He'd seen her body stiffen, the color drain from her complexion. He'd seen the confusion and hesitation on her face, heard the plaintive, wondering tone in her voice when she'd told Dunwitty what she'd seen. And he'd seen Dunwitty's face when she'd told him about his father, and mentioned that boy with the lion tattoo. There was no mistaking the shock and horror that had rolled over Dunwitty as her words had spilled out.

Something uncanny was going on with that woman. Something other-worldly. Soto shivered again.

His heritage not withstanding, Soto was convinced that not everything that was real could be seen, heard or touched. God, he knew, was real, but He wasn't ever seen, heard or touched. Not in a physical sense, anyway. In Soto's estimation, the human mind was capable of far more than most people could comprehend, things that could bring a strong man like Dunwitty to his knees. There truly were, to paraphrase the Shakespearean quote, more things in heaven and earth than were dreamt of in Dunwitty's narrow-minded philosophy.

Soto smiled to himself as he watched Dunwitty return to the squad room, steaming mug in hand. It certainly was going to be interesting to see how things played out between his intolerant, closed-minded partner and Miss No Name Wonder with her so-called woo-woo shit.

 *CHAPTER EIGHT*

I gave Reenie the silent treatment on Monday morning, not that it fazed her in the least. She went about her business, as curt and snarky as usual, insisting I "supervise" her morning ablutions. Help her with zippers and stuff. Give her the benefit of my fashion sense—as if I had any. It was just a ruse, I knew, her way of keeping an eye on me so I couldn't complete the aborted jail break of the day before, the details of which I'd dreamed about all night long.

I really hate it when people know me that well.

Watching Reenie get ready for the day wasn't all bad, though. It gave me a glimpse into how the other half lives. We might be friends, but Reenie and I are cut from diametrically opposed cloth when it comes to fashion of any kind. She started with a La Perla Floral Vibes underwire bra ($301, and I hated her for actually needing an underwire) with matching Lacey Story Brazillian briefs ($241), topped with a Dolce & Gabbana lace-trim camisole (a mere $695—all this just for underwear, mind you). From a closet filled with designer apparel, she selected a BOSS blue and yellow power suit (a snippet under $1,000 for the three pieces) to which she added yellow sapphire stud earrings from Tiffany's, a matching yellow sapphire pendant—set in platinum, of course—and a thin, delicate solid platinum bracelet. The jewelry alone set her back close to five grand. She wrapped her petite feet in Louboutin Empiraltissima lace and suede Victorian teardrop platform shoes with five-and-a-half-inch heels that "only" cost $1,195. Her makeup and perfume came courtesy of Hollywood designer Tom Ford; the lipstick alone (a sassy burgundy-to-die-for called Saboteur) topped out at $60. Foundation, blush, mascara and shadow clocked in at over $500, and she'd spent $990 for half an ounce of Black Orchid Perfume. Yes, only half an ounce. Oh, and $265 for the chic hairstyle, color, and mani-pedi.

She had three adversarial meetings that day, she told me, and she needed to level the playing field. You ask me, it was more than leveled; it was mown down and plowed under. Even if she never opened her mouth, everyone else in the room would be intimidated up to their eyeballs just by what she layered on her body. She spent an hour and a half getting ready, and left the house worth more than I made in half a year.

I, on the other hand, spent a whole ten minutes getting ready to face my day of cleaning up the mess the cops had made of my home. I donned my usual white Jockey cotton briefs ($17 for 3 pair on sale but, hey, at least they were French cut) and a blue New Balance T-shirt Bra ($4.99 online, my favorite kind of shopping), then slipped into Walmart jeans ($21.95 on sale) and an "I need my Space" NASA logo T-shirt ($8 at the Salvation Army store). I pulled my long hair back into a ponytail (scrunchie, a whole buck at the Dollar Tree). No makeup. No luscious, understated, discreet scent, though I did add a pair of simple gold-colored hoop earrings ($4.99 on sale at K-mart)—I never go anywhere un-earringed. All told, I tallied up to less than a C-note; bag lady, *par excellence*, that was me.

Maybe I should have become a lawyer instead of a penurious private investigator.

I felt like a new woman that morning, though. Broke, but new. I had to admit—only to myself, never to Reenie—the full twelve hours of sleep forced on me via that sleeping pill had done me a world of good. My head no longer pounded and my bones were solid once again. I didn't need any more of those pain pills, and I had a sneaking suspicion that my invisible driller had put away his hardware for good.

But I wasn't about to let Reenie off the hook quite yet. Some admissions to her made things better; others merely led to overbearing arrogance. I knew which way this one would go, and I wasn't about to give Reenie any more room for gloating. She got way too much amusement out of it, mostly at my expense. I kept my head down and my mouth shut all through breakfast, really stretching out that silent treatment. When we'd finished and I'd gotten up to help clear the table, still mute, she shook her head and sighed.

Gotcha, I thought, suppressing a grin. I set the dishes in the sink.

"Listen." She cleared her throat. "I know you're pissed off about the sleeping pill, but you weren't following the doctor's orders. You had to get some rest or you wouldn't have gotten any better. You hadn't settled down at all, you were up most of every night except the first one, you spent hours on your laptop, working, you wouldn't sit still... I could see how much pain you were in..." Another sigh. "I did it for your own good, Skylark."

I stood with my back to her, not answering, until I heard her swear under her breath, heard the tears trapped in her quiet tone and knew I'd made my point. I turned around, crossed my arms, and gave her my most annoyed look.

"It was a dirty trick to pull, Reenie. You're not my mother, my doctor, or my babysitter."

"I might as well be," she said. "You need at least one of those, if not all three, since you refuse to take care of yourself."

"I take care of myself just fine."

"Only when it comes to snooping, fighting, or shooting your damned gun. But when it comes to your safety or your health..."

She spread her hands and gave me a mock-indignant look. I ground my teeth together. Maybe I'd let her off the hook too soon.

"Don't you have to go into the *office* today?" I snapped. "Like, *now*?"

"Yes, you're right." She stood up from the table, balancing on those sky-high platform heels like a model on the runway. "Come on, let's get going."

"*Us*? What us?" I took a step back on my own, heel-less Nikes ($58 at a discount shoe store). "I'm not going anywhere *near* your office."

"Of course not. Don't be silly." She picked up her Kate Spade New York Healy Lane Lilith Crossbody purse ("only" $298, I should be so lucky) and the keys to her BMW i8 (don't even ask) and blinked at me. "I'm dropping you off at your place, so you can finish packing. Since you have no money, and I moved my rainy day stash to somewhere you'll never find it, you have no other way to get there."

"I could so easily hate you," I muttered as I picked up the jacket she'd packed for me Thursday evening ($12 at the local thrift shop), and followed her out of her multi-million dollar house.

It took only about seven minutes to navigate down from her monied aerie high in the hills overlooking the Bay to my humble one-room converted garage. I wondered what I'd find when we finally arrived, how badly my belongings had been treated by Dunwitty's monkey-gang. How much was broken, torn, or trampled? I also wondered where Garrett was, why I hadn't heard from him since he'd shown up at my place on Thursday night and carried me off to Reenie's house. I wondered what shape my precious Jeep was in, and if it would—or could—be put back together. And what about my Glock? Would I ever see it again, or would the cops confiscate it on a permanent basis? Or at least until Dunwitty was convinced I'd had nothing to do with the crime. If he ever was.

But I didn't talk about any of that with Reenie. I was still a bit pissed about the sleeping pill—though she'd had good intentions, I will admit that—and a whole lot freaked out about the pressures of friendship. I was still struggling with whether to simply dump both Reenie and Garrett and retreat all the way back into the shell that had helped me survive the worst of my life so far, and wondering if I could outlive the pain and isolation if I did. At this point, I wasn't sure I could.

Having friends really sucked.

I looked at Reenie in surprise when she pulled into Signore Napoli's driveway and shut off the motor. I'd expected she'd just drop me off curbside and jet on down to her exclusive, pricey firm in SLO.

"You're coming in?"

"I've got a few minutes."

I shrugged but didn't question her, my mind too consumed with worry over what I'd find to care about her intentions. I got out and trudged the rest of the way into the back yard, trailed by Reenie, my steps slowing the closer we got to my garage-cum-apartment. I didn't look at where I was going, just kept my gaze on the uneven ground. I might make my living by cleaning up other people's messes, but when it comes to my own I'd rather stick my head in the sand. It's so much easier to simply ignore it all and hope it'll go away on its own.

I think I was probably an ostrich in a former life.

"La mia provera bambina!"

Before I could look up, I was wrapped in a tight hug. Well, about two-thirds of me was, since the top of Signore Napoli's head only made it as high as my collar bone. I patted his shoulder and gently extricated myself from the embrace, though he kept a grip on my arms.

"You all-a right?" Damn if he didn't have tears in his eyes. "I worry so about-a you when I see Signore Garrett-a carry you off-a." He stared at the cut on my head, and the purpling bruise that now snaked halfway across my forehead and down onto my cheekbone. "Just-a look at you, your head, *il proveri testa.*"

"I'm fine Signore Napoli. It's not as bad as it looks, really."

"I watch-a your house for you." He pulled himself up to his full five-foot-three, over-bursting with pride and self-importance, and let go of me to use his hands to punctuate his words. "Not let in-a anyone who not-a belong. No-a one. *Nessuno*."

I mustered up a smile from somewhere and gave his shoulder another pat.

"Thank you. I wish I could take you with me when I move. I'm going to miss you, Signore Napoli."

"You will always-a be *mia cara ragazza*. Those *polizia, come stupido*. Everyone who know-a you, know-a you no do wrong. *Più*!" He took out a dark gray handkerchief and blew his nose with a loud honk that scattered the birds from a nearby tree. "Now I go start *il mio cacciatore* for *questa notte*. I bring-a you some later. If you need-a help, you knock-a the door, *va bene*?"

Reenie and I watched the rotund *Italiano* lumber off to his house and vanish through the back door. I shook my head. Talking with that sweet old man was always an adventure. I was never sure I correctly deciphered the Italian he peppered into his English. Made for some interesting misunderstandings over the years. I'd miss that, too, when I moved.

"You *really* need to get him a marionette as a going away gift," Reenie murmured.

That broke my dispirited mood and made me laugh, and the laughter carried me the rest of the way across the yard. Only then did I notice that my apartment door stood open, and I realized that Reenie must have called my landlord to open it for us, since the cops still had my keys. That was why he'd been there to meet us. How had I not heard her do that? As Desi would say, she had some 'splaining to do. I started up the steps.

"Reenie, when did you—"

I broke off at the sight before me when I reached the top step. Not the mess the cops had left, my clothes, linens, books, papers and food strewn all over floor and countertops, furniture upended, cushions scattered everywhere. Instead I saw neat, orderly piles of possessions awaiting the boxes that had been stacked to the right of the doorway. A wave of heat washed over me.

"What? Who did this? It sure as hell wasn't the cops. Was it?"

I turned to Reenie, who stood at the bottom of the steps grinning up at me.

"Not the cops. I'm sure Dunwitty would have fired anyone who came back to help you out. Or at least made their lives miserable. No, it was Garrett. And a few others."

"Others?" I turned again to the interior of the place and took a few steps in. "What others?"

Everything had been picked up, straightened out, and cleaned off. Clothing folded. The furniture set upright, cushions replaced on the sofa and chairs. The floor swept, countertops and table wiped down. It even looked as though the windows had been washed. The hours of disheartening work I'd envisioned lying ahead of me had instantly morphed into maybe one. Or two.

I stopped beside the sofa and shook my head.

"Shirley Matthews helped," Reenie said, leaning against the doorframe. "And so did Felipe Silveras and Joe Gorman. And Mattie Davis. Garrett told me that Hank Landry even stopped by for a while."

"But why?" I looked at her, totally perplexed. "Why would they do that?"

"Because *you* helped *them*. You found Shirley's grandson, brought him home safe and sound. You figured out who was embezzling funds from the bank and saved Hank's job. You discovered who was stealing the animals from the pet store and saved Mattie's business. You helped all of them in one way or another, so when they heard about this," she gestured around the room, "they wanted to help you in return."

"But... I don't understand." Garrett I could see, we were like brother and sister, it made sense he'd want to help me. Plus, he knew what I'd do to him if he didn't. But those others, they weren't friends, they were clients. People who hired me to do a service for them. For money. Why would they waste their time helping me, of all people? Surely they all had better things to do. "That's... my business, they paid me to do those things. They're just... clients. Why would they... ?"

I looked around again, so stunned I could barely breathe. My eyes filled. Shivers ran down my spine. I sank onto the couch. Reenie walked over, sat beside me and took my shaking hands in hers.

"It's about time you understand more people care about you than you realize, Skylark. Yes, they're clients and yes, they paid you to do a service for them. It's not *what* you did, but *how* you did it. You're willing to go the extra mile, to even put your *life* on the line, for other people, to help make their lives easier. To solve their problems. To bring them peace. You *care*." She smiled at me and squeezed my hands. A traitorous tear broke free and tracked down my cheek but I ignored it, hoping Reenie wouldn't notice. "You're a very special person, Skylark. It's time you started to see your true value, the way the rest of us do."

She stood up, smoothed her skirt, nodded at me and, that quickly, switched into The Overton mode, complete with condescending look and sardonic inflection.

"Now get started on the repacking. Garrett's bringing the truck after work, around 6:30, to help transport your stuff to the new place. He'll be pissed if all you do is sit there and cry like an overemotional little girl, instead of reacting like an adult and getting all this..." she shuddered, "crap ready to go."

She turned then and wiggle-hipped out the door, which was a good thing because, as I watched her go down the steps and cross the yard, I did break down. I cried for the first time in years, my heart so full I feared it would break. I cried for myself because I hadn't known, could hardly believe, that anyone other than Garrett and Reenie cared about me, or even liked me enough to care. Then I cried for those poor, deluded people who'd done all this for me, because they had no idea who I really was, how unworthy I was of the caring they offered. And in the end I cried for the lonely little girl whose own mother hadn't wanted her, who'd been given a mockery of a name by Social Services and then was shuffled off to be used and abused by heartless foster parents because she was unnatural. No good. A freak.

If Reenie had stayed and witnessed that— hiccuping breaths, red swollen eyes, runny nose and all —I'd have had to shoot her.

 *CHAPTER NINE*

Carstairs stopped just inside the door of the fourth bar he'd visited that night and closed his eyes for a moment before he ventured any further in. He was damned sick of this search. He'd been attacked by noise in the other three places, waves of pulse-pounding music, along with shouts and laughter from the buzzed twenty- and thirty-somethings as they released the tensions of the workday and ignored family obligations waiting at home. And no sign of who he'd been looking for. Now it was after nine o'clock, and he feared it was too late. What he'd thought was Intervention Number Three had turned into a frigging nightmare.

Had he somehow misinterpreted the sign? He thought back to the morning's revelation. No, the sign had been clear, the Fate-incidence—that sounded more accurate to him than coincidence—well timed. Much as he wanted to chuck it all and go home, he knew he needed to be patient. To keep looking. To follow where Fate was leading him.

This place, Kelley's Bar & Grill, had little to recommend it. Off the beaten main path where the other bars congregated in downtown SLO, it was grope-around dark, slightly worn and a bit dingy. Pool balls clacked discordant notes as they smacked into each other in the far corner. Only a dozen or so people peppered the tables scattered on the floor or manned the booths along the side wall. There was, thankfully, no music of any kind playing, and only a very low hum of voices involved in private conversations. This was his kind of place, the kind that catered to locals and not students or tourists, the kind where he could sit in anonymity for hours.

He waited until he sidled up to the bar before looking for his target. To the side of the mirror that backed shelves on which perched various dusty bottles of booze, stood a poster listing a dozen or so local micro brews. He read down the list, in between each line shooting a glance at the room reflected in the mirror. When the bartender ambled his way, Carstairs shook his head, rejected the anemic Millennial quaffs and ordered his usual: a double Jack Daniels, neat, his fourth of the night.

He'd already spotted Gregg in the mirror. The small, overly-muscled man sat hunched over a tall stein in a booth along the far wall. When the bartender set the drink in front of him, Carstairs picked up the glass, slid some bills onto the counter, then turned around as he took his first sip, resting an elbow on the polished mahogany. He gave what he hoped was a casual look around the place, doing a well-feigned double-take when he saw Gregg, just in case anyone had noticed. He nodded, plastered a grin on his face, and walked across the room.

"Gregg? That you?" he said, putting as much surprise as he could in his voice.

The small, timid-looking man looked up, blinked, then smiled at him.

"Carstairs. What you doing here?"

"Drowning my sorrows, what else?" Carstairs lifted his glass, gave Gregg a self-deprecating smile, and gestured at the bench on the opposite side of the table. Gregg nodded.

"Take a load off and join the club. What's going on?"

"Same old shit." Carstairs slid onto the bench and grimaced as he took another sip of his whiskey. "Eddington hates me, I swear. He's the supervisor from hell. Partnered me with that shithead Feinstein, again. I spent my whole day being ordered around by that dickwad." He shook his head. "Nice week-long job up in Los Osos, pretty house overlooking the bay, seven whole rooms, could be a dream and I gotta spend the time with Feinstein. Guy hates my guts and really lets me know it, like, every minute of the day. Life's a bitch, sometimes, you know?"

"Hell, I can top that." Gregg took a long draught of his beer and wiped his thick lips with the back of his hand. "I'm thinking of quitting."

"No." Carstairs blinked well-feigned disbelief and let his mouth drop open. "What the fuck?"

"Yep. Not sure I can handle what they got me assigned to now."

From the corner of his eye, Carstairs noticed a pretty, slender young woman approach their table. About five-feet, five-inches tall, she had sparkling eyes, a lean body, a sweet smile, and dark hair that waved down past her shoulders, the kind of hair a man could get lost in. To say nothing of a rack that made his manhood stand up and take notice. His mouth began to water.

"The kitchen's closing in about fifteen minutes, gentlemen. Can I interest either of you in something to eat? We've got a great cook back there and some of San Luis Obispo's best food."

She gave them an encouraging grin and held out two sheets of coated paper. Carstairs made sure his fingers lingered on hers just a moment when he accepted one of them, then glanced quickly at the abbreviated offerings. He looked up and smiled into her lovely brown eyes.

"I'll take your word for it. How about an order of those sliders, with a side of nachos, Miss...?"

"Coffey." She blushed, the red stain on her creamy white skin visible even in the dimness of the room. "Heidi Coffey. My uncle owns this place, I'm not really the waitress, Janie got sick so I'm just helping him out tonight." She pulled an order pad and pen from her pocket and busied herself writing down Carstairs's order.

"Well, he's a lucky man to have you to call on, Miss Heidi Coffey. And so are we, to have you as our waitress. Add another double Jack Daniels, neat, to that order, please."

He gave her another grin, the one he kept especially for women, the one women didn't seem able to resist. Invisible he might be most of the time, but when he wanted to be noticed—by specific women—he knew exactly what to do. His father had taught him well.

And he wanted to be noticed by this woman. Girl, really, she couldn't be more than nineteen or twenty.

Too young to even drink what she served, but with a body that deserved to be served in the way only Carstairs could serve it. Maybe this wouldn't turn out such a bad night, after all.

Gregg ordered a personal pizza with extra onions and another beer and Heidi gave Carstairs one last shy, almost apprehensive, smile before she turned and walked over to the next occupied table, halfway across the room. Carstairs watched her hips sway and for a moment fantasized about what he could do with those long legs, that sweet piece of ass, then turned his attention back to the matter at hand.

"What you saying, man? Quitting? No way."

"Yep. Not sure I can do this one." Gregg shook his almost-bald head. "It's got me so scared I can't even go home. Gotta be around people, or my 'magination's gonna do me in."

"Come on, it can't be worse than a week of Feinstein. Nothing can be worse than that."

"It's way worse. Tomorrow... I start on..." Gregg looked around the room, shuddered, then leaned across the table and whispered. "The Body Building."

"Huh?" Carstairs blinked and did a double-take. "The what?"

"The Body Building. You know." Gregg drained his glass and smacked it down on the table. "The morgue. Where all those dead corpses are. Iggghhhh." He gave a theatrical shudder and scrinched his beady eyes shut.

"No shit? The morgue? That's... well, icky, yeah, but also kinda cool, don't you think?"

"Cool? Are you nuts? It's creepy, that's what it is. All those bodies being cut up, organs lined up in jars of that formalide stuff, guys running around in gory aprons with bloody knives in their hands... sheesh!" Another theatrical shudder. "Gives me the heebie-jeebies just thinking about it."

"You been watching too many horror movies, man." Carstairs allowed himself a small chuckle; Gregg might be an attention-loving nutcase, but Carstairs doubted he'd appreciate the full belly laugh that wanted to break free. "Reality ain't like that. It's all bright lights, everything clean, and the bodies all hidden away. You'd never see anything that'd disturb your dreams. Just walls and fresh paint. You want horror?" He took another sip of his Jack and shook his head. "Try spending a day with someone who hates you and is out to get you. That'd give you *real* nightmares."

"That's nothing. This is the *morgue*, man. I'm telling you, there's no way I can walk through that door. I had horrible dreams all last night just at the thought of it. I can't imagine what it'll be like if I ever see the inside of that place. I'd take your Feinstein over the Body Building, any day."

Heidi brought their food and Carstairs enjoyed the sight of her supple body as she leaned down to place the plates on the table. He again earned a blush when he gave her his patented 'I want you' smile, and he made a mental note to get her contact information before he left. He scooped up a nacho and sighed.

"You know, life's just shit-not-fair. Here we are, two nice guys trying to make ends meet, working as best we can, and now I gotta spend the week with my nightmare and you gotta spend the week with yours. I mean, all we're doing is painting, for fuck's sake. Shouldn't be so damned hard. Too bad they don't let us pick our own jobs."

They ate in silence a moment, Carstairs waiting with tightly leashed impatience for Gregg to tumble. He began to count in rhythm to his chewing, wondering if he'd have to prod even more. Just how thick was Gregg, anyway? He'd sure as hell dropped enough clues. *Twenty... twenty-one... twenty-two...*

"Hey." Gregg set his beer mug on the table and again swiped the back of his hand over his lips. "I got a great idea."

Carstairs looked over at the little bald elf, at the small dark eyes lit now with a modicum of intelligence, at the half-eaten slice of greasy pizza in one thick-fingered hand. *About time*, Carstairs thought.

"Yeah?"

"Yeah. How about... we trade jobs?"

"Trade jobs?" Carstairs frowned and shook his head. "We can't do that, can we? Now without permission. I mean, I already started on my job. I'll get in trouble if I walk away from it, I'm sure."

"Nah, I got it figured out. We'll do it tomorrow morning, last minute, just show up at each other's jobs. I'll tell your nightmare that you're sick and I'm filling in for you, and you tell my nightmare I'm sick and you're filling in for me. They'll be happy as shit, no scrambling for replacements at the last minute, no losing any time at either job, so who's gonna care? And you and I both get an easier week. Whatta ya think?"

"I don't know... If Eddington finds out..."

"How would he? And so what if he does? As long as his job gets done on time, why would it matter to him who does it? He might grouse a bit, but he's not gonna fire you. And I won't be, neither. Not for being, what do they call it? Consencious or something about the jobs—

you know, getting them done right and on time. Hell, we might even get a medal or a raise, or something. Come on, Carstairs, it'll work, you know it will."

Carstairs let Gregg sweat it out a few minutes longer.

"Me, do the Body Building?" he asked. "I don't know."

He shuddered a bit, just for effect, loving the despair that began flooding Gregg's expression. Then he screwed up his face and gave a masterfully-reluctant nod.

"All right," he said. "Let's do it."

Gregg's face cleared and almost split in two, his grin grew so big. They exchanged locations and supervisory information, clinked glasses in celebration and drained their drinks. Then Gregg wadded up his napkin, threw it on his empty plate, gave Carstairs the money for his meal, and set off for home, crowing about how he'd now get a good night's sleep. Carstairs moseyed over to the bar, where little Heidi Coffey stood talking to the bartender. He handed her Gregg's check and money, along with his.

"Gotta tell you," he said, smiling into her eyes, "you were right. The food here is good. But the service is even better."

When he left for home, he wasn't alone.

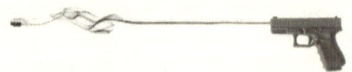

"Yes, Reenie, I know you're right. You're always right. It's just... I'm still not sure."

I rolled my eyes and drew in a breath at the lie. I was as sure as I could get, but Reenie wasn't the kind to take no for an answer. Not when she'd decided she knew better than I did, which was most of the time. Besides, I never could get away with handing her a line.

"How can you *not* be sure?" Her imperious tone shivered down the line, through the handset and into my ear. "It's not like it'll hurt anyone. That's what insurance is for, after all, especially the county's. They're insured up the wazoo, just for things like this. Besides, you know it's the right thing to do. Dunwitty needs to be taught a lesson, and this is the perfect way to do it."

"Maybe, but—"

"There's no frigging maybe about it, Skylark! Or any buts."

I pursed my lips at her unexpected shriek—very un-Overton—and listened to the silence that thrummed through the wire. At times like this I really missed my cell phone; it was hard to feign a call breaking up while using an old-fashioned wired house phone that didn't lose reception. I really hoped the cops would release my cell soon. Being tethered to outdated technology made me both antsy and nervous as hell.

"Listen," Reenie said, her tone now a few decibels down into human-hearing range and much more manipulative, "don't do this for yourself. Do it for all the other poor souls out there who have been on the receiving end of Dunwitty's little games. People who didn't have access to someone like me. Most of all, do it for all the others who will be in his crosshairs *in the future* if we *don't* do this. Can you really *live* with yourself if you could have done something to stop him, and you *didn't*?"

Damn, she had to bring up responsibility. And guilt. I could feel all my failures lining up, just waiting for another crack at me. I glanced at the pile of boxes yet to be unpacked, wishing I weren't such a coward, then sighed as I felt my resolve crumble. Reenie heard it, too.

"It's not the money, Skylark, it's the *principle* of the thing. A message to the powers that be. And Dunwitty."

My resistance vanished in a puff of Reenie's self-righteous smoke.

"All right, Reenie. You win. We'll sue. But," I raised my voice so she'd hear me over her celebratory hoot, "only for reimbursement of my hospital and doctor bills, and what I'll lose on the Argus job. Nothing more."

"What do you mean, what you'll lose on the Argus job?"

Damn, did she have to sound so happy about it?

"National Insurance fired me first thing this morning. Well, not *technically* fired, they merely canceled the remainder of the contract, gave it to Mike Fairmont up in Paso, since the cops still have my car and my camera. Can't really follow anyone around without transportation, can I? Or take pictures without a camera." I sighed. "They said they can't wait any longer. They'll pay me for the time I've already put in, there's no worry there." To be honest, I'd probably have to give back part of the retainer, and of course I'd never see the huge bonus covered in the canceled portion of the contract. "But what I'd have earned by finishing the job is history."

"All right, how much will you lose? A couple thousand? More?"

"Nowhere near that high, maybe five hundred at the most. I was almost finished with the job." That amount would cover anything I'd have to return, and no way was I telling Miss Eager Beaver about the five grand bonus I'd kissed goodbye.

"Okay, I'll add that on, too. And of course there's always pain and suffering, we can tack on a few hundred thou—"

"*No*. I mean it, Reenie. This is not a get-rich-quick deal," I clarified over her grousing moan. "And we're only naming the county, the Sheriff's department as a whole. I don't want to single out Dunwitty personally, you got that? He already hates me enough. I'm not about to give him even more ammunition."

"But he *owes* you, Skylark," Reenie said. I could tell from her tone that she was upset about my not agreeing to a high six-figure payout. "And you *deserve* it."

My doorbell rang. For the second time that morning. And—I glanced at the clock—it was only nine-fifteen.

"No. We do it my way, Reenie, or we don't do it at all." The bell rang again. "Listen, I gotta go, there's someone at my door. I'll talk to you later."

I hung up over her protest, looked down at my ratty jeans and stained T-shirt—the no-company-allowed, house-settling outfit was nowhere near social attire—sighed, and opened the front door.

A wrinkled elderly couple stood there, both not much taller than five-foot-five, their button eyes bright with anticipation. She was stick-thin with dentures two sizes too big; he had no chin and wore Coke-bottle-bottom glasses that enlarged his eyes to tennis ball size. She had a helmet of blue-white hair; his head smooth and shiny as a flesh-colored bowling ball. Backlit by the rising sun, she held a large glass bowl filled with what looked suspiciously like tuna salad. She grinned and held it out to me.

"Hi, we're the Mobleys, Renee and Aaron." Her high-pitched voice grated down my spine. "We live a couple doors down. Welcome to the neighborhood. Are you really a private detective? Can we come in?"

 *CHAPTER TEN*

I should have been fully settled in my new place in just a few hours, considering I had only a shoe-box-size amount of possessions to fit into the refrigerator-box-size abode. Unpack a box or two, then shift a few things from one place to another, just because I could—a luxury I hadn't had in my old apartment—then repeat. An easy, fun Tuesday, topped off with a "Skylark Burger"—a half pound of beef with lettuce, tomato, provolone cheese, avocado, bacon, mushrooms, and a mayo/catsup mix—accompanied by fries and a brew from Valley Liquor. Then, on Wednesday, I'd be back to business as usual.

But I hadn't figured on being interrupted every couple of hours by the street's nosy-nellies, who dropped by with homemade offerings in the guise of being "neighborly" and didn't leave for an hour or more. The two curving, extra-long-blocks of Palomino had a rural feel. The street might boast only fifteen houses half-hidden on sprawling lots before the road dwindled down into a narrow trail that led to a secluded farm, but the people living in those homes appeared to be endless in number.

The one-story, faded blue house, which Garrett said I could treat it as if it were mine even if he wouldn't sell it to me, was small even by Los Osos standards, though it sat on a good half-acre of land. Real estate agents often describe this kind of miniature abode as "cozy," which doesn't fool anyone but them. Little is little no matter how many euphemisms one might employ.

The slightly-rundown place, one of the few non-stuccos on the street, sat back a good thirty feet from the road. An abbreviated porch led to a front door with peeling paint that opened directly onto an 18' x 25' all-purpose room, which felt palatial to me after my sojourn in that converted one-car garage. A long narrow addition had been tacked onto the driveway side of the structure. Three-quarters of the way down the addition, just beyond the carport, a side door opened onto a four-foot-wide no-man's-land of a pathway that led into the main room. The kitchen, just barely over efficiency size, stood to the left of the pass-through; to the right was an eating area that could fit a table just big enough to seat six really skinny people. At the back, behind the living area, were the two tiny bedrooms with a minuscule bath sandwiched between them. I measured and figured I could just fit the king size bed of my dreams in the larger one, though I'd have to forego a dresser if I wanted to walk around all three sides of the bed. The smaller bedroom, no bigger than 8' x 12', would work as an office, and maybe even hold a dresser if I traded down to a pint-size desk. Small the place definitely was, but I couldn't imagine ever needing more space.

Finding places for possessions that would fit into a closet with room left over for clothing should have been no problem. But the doorbell kept ringing—starting at seven-thirty that Tuesday morning—and answering it meant I had to keep stopping every hour or so to play hostess to a steady trickle of people I didn't want to meet and had nothing in common with. But Garrett, the big rat, had "let slip"—as the Mobleys termed it—that I was a private detective. I found myself deluged not only with containers of homemade desserts, soups, stews, and every variation of tuna salad known to man, but also with questions about the life of a P.I., and queries about how realistic TV detective shows were. Turned out no one was interested in any of my work details after I told them I specialized in computer searches instead of shoot-outs and car chases, though they did ask how many times I'd had to use my Glock. And went away disappointed that I couldn't show it to them, since the cops still had it in their possession.

By the time I was ready to leave to meet a new client on Thursday—one I desperately needed since nothing else that promised actual income loomed on my horizon—I was ready to wring Garrett's neck, since I still didn't have a gun with which to shoot him. Instead, I called and insisted he housesit until my new-to-me, thrift shop-purchased couch arrived. I'd stashed my old pull-out one in the back room until I could earn enough to buy a real bed—of any size. When he arrived, he stood in the middle of the living room and cast a jaundiced eye at the barely opened boxes.

"You haven't finished unpacking yet?"

"I've been too busy playing hostess to the natives." I glared at him while trying to stop steam from shooting out my ears; he was damned lucky the cops still held onto my Glock. I gestured toward the kitchen table. "Can't you tell?"

He walked over to the archway and eyed the home-baked goodies that covered the tabletop.

"Nice," was all he said, and my blood pressure went up another few notches.

"No, *not* nice. My freezer is full of stuff I suspect is poisonous, or at best inedible, and the fridge compartment is jammed with all sorts of tuna salad." I huffed out a breath. "I *hate* tuna salad."

"Poor baby," Garrett murmured, but the sparkly glint in his eyes belied the professed sympathy.

"Why the *hell* did you tell them what I do for a living, Garrett? It's bad enough you didn't tell me this was a fish-bowl neighborhood. Now, because of your big mouth, there's someone here every couple of hours, putting me through cross-examinations and expecting insider information. And tea or coffee. And homemade munchies. Homemade—from *me*. *You're* the reason I'm not yet settled. It's all your fault."

I gave him garbage bags for the tuna salads and a goodly portion of the freezer crap, orders to do something about the mess of desserts littering the kitchen table—except for the ones containing chocolate—and instructions about where to situate the amazing, oversized, overstuffed 1970's avocado green and harvest gold paisley print sofa I'd found at the Salvation Army last-chance shop for only forty-five dollars. Then I left for Starbucks, which had doubled as my meet-and-greet office for the last year and a half, since there was no way on God's green earth—or under it, for that matter—I could afford to rent legitimate office space. I was relieved that Garrett had gotten both my purse and car back the day before, though the cops still hadn't released the camera or my Glock. And I was more than grateful that he and not I would have to field the afternoon drop-ins.

I arrived about ten minutes before my prospective client, enough time to secure a large mocha java with a shot of vanilla and snag a table by the window, since my usual back-corner table was already occupied. She arrived right on time. I recognized her the minute she entered—she looked exactly as she'd described herself—then stood and gave her a discreet wave. A small, compact dynamo of a woman who strode with an attitude, she seemed dressed more for an LA boardroom than a Los Osos coffee shop. She wore a light gray silk pantsuit with a soft green blouse, and three-inch pale green heels on her feet. Opals gleamed on her lobes and at her throat. She sported an imperious look on her high-cheekboned face.

"Araceli Aguayo? It's nice to meet you," I said, offering my hand. She merely looked at it, kept her own hands clasped on her purse, then raised her eyes back up to mine. "Thank you for contacting Skylark Investigations. Would you like something? Just let the barista know you're with me and she'll put it on my tab. I'm Skylark, by the way."

"I don't need anything." She sank onto the chair opposite where I stood and her cold brown stare lingered on my bruised face as I reseated myself. "Skylark Investigations," though, was all she murmured, her voice as dark and smoky as her eyes and hair. She gave me a disapproving glower. "I thought Skylark had to do with your business, not your actual name."

Yet another blast about my stupid name. I probably should have changed it, but I didn't want to give Social Services the satisfaction of knowing they'd completely defeated me; dropping my last name had felt like failure enough. I plastered as pleasant a smile as I could on my face and folded my hands around my Starbucks cardboard cup, searching for warmth that wasn't there any longer.

"Actually, it's both, my name and my business." I took a sip of the lukewarm dregs to marshal my thoughts, then looked again into her disdainful brown eyes. "From what you told me on the phone, I take it Peter Dufferin recommended me?"

She turned her head to the window and gazed out at the traffic flowing past on Los Osos Valley Road. Her lips twisted, then she nodded and faced me again.

"I assume you're Native American, then?"

I could tell from her pinched tone that wasn't a pleasant thought for her. I so wanted to knock her down a few pegs, but I needed the work more than I needed to put her stupid prejudice in its place. I also wondered how anyone could equate my almost-six-foot height, exotic Romani looks, and dark gray-green eyes with any known—or unknown—Native American tribe.

"No, I'm not, I was just named by someone with a very quirky sense of humor." I tried out my smile again, but received none in answer. *Off to a roaring start*, I thought. "So, what is it I can help you with?"

She blinked at me, and I watched the minute changes in her face as she decided to drop her displeasure with my name and shift into the business at hand. She told me she owned an internet-based firm, LOAC (Los Osos Apparel Crafts), that brokered unique, one-of-a-kind clothing items handcrafted by local artisans for women with a dramatic flair. I took another look at her conservative outfit and decided she didn't patronize her own shop. She said she'd been turning a good profit until six months ago. The puzzling part was that sales hadn't fallen off, they'd actually increased. But profits kept going down; at this point, they were almost non-existent. If the trend continued, she'd have only another six months or so before she'd be out of business.

She told me all the things she'd done to try to solve the problem herself, which included upping her internet security and changing bank accounts. That told me someone very sophisticated, or with insider information, had latched onto her cash flow. When I mentioned my fee—$150 a day plus expenses—she stiffened and drew in a breath. I feared I was about to lose her business. Her dismissive expression softened, though, when I offered her a courtesy discount since Peter Dufferin, with whom I'd trained and who sent local work my way instead of paying one of his agents to drive up from Santa Barbara, had recommended me. We settled on $100 a day plus expenses—not that I expected there'd be many—with a $500 retainer, and she groped in her purse for her checkbook.

"I'll need a complete list of all your crafts people and suppliers, passwords for your websites, your banking information, and contact information for anyone else you do business with." She nodded. "Also the names of your bookkeepers and/or accountants."

"It's not them, I can assure you of that." She slapped the checkbook on the table and glared at me. "We've been friends forever. They would never do anything to harm me or my business. Never."

"I'm sure you're right," I said, though I knew that in too many instances the criminals were those you least suspected. "But I need to be as thorough as possible, make sure I cover every base. That's what you're paying me for. I'll be discreet, I promise. If they've done nothing wrong, they'll never know I looked into them."

"Well, perhaps," she murmured, looking more distressed at the thought of my checking out her friends than she had about the prospect of losing her business. And that raised a red flag for me. I wondered if maybe, on a subconscious level, she suspected one of those "friends" was at fault.

"Don't worry," I said, trying to both soothe her and get her to write that retainer check. "This is what I do, and I'm damned good at it. Let's see what I can find out over the next few days. Chances are I can find the culprit by this time next week."

"Really? That soon?"

"It's possible, as long as I get *all* the information I need from you."

She looked up and smiled her hope at me. Then her gaze slid to the side and up, and the smile faded. She frowned as a deep rasp showered down on me.

"Well, well, Miss One Name Wonder. I been looking all over for you."

I turned to find Dunwitty's ugly hulk beside me. He gave Araceli Aguayo his shark smile and pushed aside his jacket to show off the badge clipped to his belt. Then he grabbed my arm and lifted me out of the chair.

"You been ducking me, Skylark? Now, why would you want to do that?"

"Your own mother would duck you, Dunwitty. What do you want? I'm in the middle of a meeting, here."

"Got a dead, faceless body I need to identify. Thought you could come take a look at it, see if your handiwork jogs any memory cells."

"I had nothing to do with that, and you know it." I tugged at my arm, but he tightened his grip. "Let go of me."

Opposite us, Araceli Aguayo shoved her checkbook and pen in her purse and stood up.

"I-I think I'd better go," she stammered. "This sounds pretty official."

"No, please, I—" I said, but Dunwitty spoke over me.

"That's a good idea, Miss. This *is* official, a *murder* investigation. You don't want to find yourself in the middle of that, do you?"

Araceli shook her head and took a step back.

"Ms. Aguayo, please, wait—"

"No, I'd better leave." She continued to back up. "I'll call you. Yes," she added over her shoulder as she turned and scurried out of the coffee shop, "I'll call you."

We watched her leave, Dunwitty's hand still squeezing my biceps. I took a deep breath, then turned my head and glared at him.

"You couldn't have waited another five or ten minutes to come in here and grab me? Are you trying to run me out of business? You just lost me a client—one I really needed. Because of *you*, I might add."

"What?" He raised his brows and gave me a mock innocent look. "She said she'd call you."

"Yeah," I muttered as he began to move toward the door, towing me with him. I barely had time to snag my purse from the chair back. I tried to ignore all the eyes marking our progress, the excited buzz we left in our wake. "We both know that's not going to happen. Thanks to you."

Kirsten, the barista, lifted the phone and frowned at me; I shook my head and mouthed 'It's okay' to try to reassure her. Dunwitty pulled me through the doors and we stopped just outside them so he could slide on his sunglasses with his free hand.

"What do you want with me?" I asked again.

"Like I said, I need you to come look at the body, see if you can identify him."

"Why the hell would you think I'd have any idea who he is?" Again I tried to yank my arm free, and again he tightened his fingers until I winced. "I have nothing to do with this, and you know it."

He turned his head. I could feel his glare even through the dark lenses.

"Are you resisting me?"

"Are you arresting me?"

We stood staring at each other a long moment, me wishing my eyes were also hidden behind dark lenses, while Starbucks patrons veered around us with curious looks. Finally, I huffed out a breath and rolled my eyes.

"Fine. Give me the address and I'll meet you there."

"And have you take off in the opposite direction?" He pulled me across the parking lot toward his car. "I don't think so."

"This isn't necessary." I dug in my heels and twisted my arm, but nothing I did slowed down that behemoth of a man.

"My car is right over there, I can follow you—"

Dunwitty swung me around and shoved my back up against his passenger door. He put his hands on top of the car, one on each side of me, leaned down close to my face, and growled out his words.

"No, you *can't* follow me. What you *can* do is sit your ass in my car, keep your trap shut and not give me any of that woo-woo shit you spouted at the station. And you can tell me everything you know about my victim or I'll make your life a living hell."

"More than you already have?"

I clenched my fists so tight, my nails dug into my palms. We stared at each other while traffic threaded through the parking lot and a pair of gulls flew overhead. I couldn't tell, from Dunwitty's closed face, what he was thinking, but I know I was grateful he'd been wise enough to have not yet returned my Glock. I don't think I could have resisted using it on him. After an hours-long minute or so, he moved me to the side, opened the passenger door, and gestured at the seat.

"Get in the car, Skylark. *Please*."

I stayed motionless and let him squirm another minute, then I took a deep breath and straightened out my fingers.

"Fine. We'll do it your way."

I bent to get in. He put a hand on my head and pushed down with enough force to throw me off balance. I fell onto the seat in an awkward sprawl.

"Be careful, now," he said, his shark grin firmly in place. "Wouldn't want your poor head to get hurt. Again."

I barely had enough time to pull my legs in before he slammed the door. I straightened myself out as he marched around to the driver's side, yanked open that door, dropped onto the seat, and slammed the door shut. I wondered, as I fastened my seatbelt, how often the department had to replace his poor, abused county rides.

We didn't speak, or even look at each other, as Dunwitty backed out of the space and turned left onto Los Osos Valley Road, toward San Luis Obispo. We drove out of town in silence. The road dipped down and then up. We passed St. Benedict's Episcopal Church on the right and the town cemetery on the left, then the surrounding area gave itself over to farmland: horses, goats, and cows; rich, dark soil; newly planted crops. He glanced at me a couple of times before we got to Turri Road, but didn't speak until we passed it and rounded the curve to where our one lane widened out to accommodate a passing lane.

"That looks pretty sore."

His subdued tone surprised me. If I didn't know better, I might be fooled into believing he was capable of remorse.

"It'll heal." I raised a hand to my left cheek and temple, trying not to wince as I touched the still-tender yellow-green bruise and the mending cut. "Eventually."

Another mile passed in silence. The divided road ended. Then Dunwitty spoke again.

"I really am sorry that happened, Skylark. Sometimes... I just get too... focused, you know? And so damn pissed off at all the shit people do to each other."

"So you thought you'd add your own shit to it? That makes a lot of sense."

Dunwitty growled deep in his throat. His hands tightened on the wheel until his fingers turned white.

The speedometer edged up from the posted fifty-five to a bit over sixty.

"Damn it, I'm trying to apologize here, Skylark. Give me a break, will you?"

I let another mile go by in silence. Then I looked at him and shook my head.

"Sorry, but being nice to me now isn't going to stop the lawsuit, Dunwitty. Or get Maureen Overton off your back."

Another low growl. The muscles in Dunwitty's jaw worked as he gritted his teeth. We accelerated to over seventy and quickly caught up to the other cars in the single lane, all driving close to the speed limit. Dunwitty mashed the brakes and we hung about two inches behind the car in front of us. I faced forward, biting the inside of my cheek to keep from grinning. I still wasn't happy about the lawsuit, but Reenie had been right. It was the principle of the thing, a way to rein in Dunwitty, to let him—and his superiors—know he couldn't keep getting away with his rogue cop antics.

But since Dunwitty had no idea I wasn't going after him personally—and I wasn't about to enlighten him—I had the pleasure of seeing him squirm. And watching him take out his anger on the road. Besides, given that his little stunt today had cost me yet another paying client, I just might have to re-think dipping into his assets.

At least a little. I doubted his coffers were anywhere near full; he was a county employee, after all. Still, Dunwitty's discomfiture, the little flare of panic in his eyes, and the lovely, if fanciful, daydream of a multi-million-dollar payout occupied me the rest of the way to the coroner's office on Sendero Court.

 CHAPTER ELEVEN

The cold and the smell—rotting flesh buried beneath an acrid overlayment of antiseptic cleaning solution—hit me like a fist the moment we walked into the huge room. I froze, my skittish gaze taking in the stainless steel that seemed to be everywhere: walls, cabinets, doors, autopsy tables—two of which had naked bodies on them being washed by assistants, in preparation for the coroner's ministrations. Dunwitty took a few steps without me before he realized I wasn't beside him. He turned and skewered me with a glare.

"I don't believe it." He shook his head. "The big, bad female P. I. is afraid of a few corpses?" He walked back to me and leaned close. "Or is your woo-woo shit acting up again? No, don't tell me, I got this." He nodded, opened his eyes wide, and used his ham-hands to air quote his mocking words. "You see dead people."

I took a deep breath. This was the last place on earth I wanted to be; dead bodies didn't necessarily scare me, but they did give me nightmares. Like they would any normal, rational human being—which left

Dunwitty out. I gave him a look searing enough to burn off his skin and lifted my lip in a snarl.

"Now I understand why cops are called pigs."

That earned me another deep-throat growl; Dunwitty seemed to have an endless supply of them. He grabbed my arm, adding even more bruises to those he'd gifted me with at the coffee shop, and pulled me over to the far wall. A tall, bald, eagle-beaked, gowned-and-gloved man, who looked to be in his mid-fifties, stood beside a rolling stainless steel cart that held a sheet-draped figure.

"Hey, Doc. This here's the One Name Wonder I told you about. She's gonna tell us who our unknown guest is."

"Good. Welcome, my dear. We definitely need help with this one," the man said in a quiet, gentle voice. It seemed he, at least, did not automatically assume I was the cause of the victim's demise. "I'm sure there must be someone somewhere missing this man. I'm Marshal White, MD, your county coroner; you could say I'm the resident 'internal' investigator." He winked, his understated joke twinkling in his bright hazel eyes, then he held up his gloved hands and gave me a warm smile. "And I'm truly sorry I can't shake hands with you right now. It is lovely to meet you, though." He raised his bushy brows. "You really have only one name? Or is the detective pulling my leg again?"

"No leg pull," I said, returning his smile with one of my own. Had Dunwitty not still had his meaty hand clenched on my arm, I might have enjoyed meeting Dr. White, despite our surroundings. "My name is Skylark. No last name, just Skylark."

"Oh, no, my dear." Dr. White shook his head and his eyes gleamed. "If you are named for that amazing bird, you could never be 'just' Skylark. Birds are one of my passions, I read extensively about them. 'Higher still and higher, From the earth thou springest, Like a cloud of fire...' I believe Shelley's *To a Skylark* best captures the essence of a bird that lives in two worlds, both earth and sky. Did you know it sings longer than any other bird, up to four minutes, as it hovers high above the land, a mere speck in the firmament? What a joy to be named for such a unique creature."

"I guess," I said, feeling my face flush beneath Dr. White's flattering words. I gave him a tiny shrug. It had never occurred to me that my name might have any significance other than to make my life miserable.

"Oh, yes, indeed." Dr. White's delighted smile lit up his long, narrow face. "You see, the skylark has been associated with the majestic hush of dawn, the prospect of warmth and ease returning after the cold bleakness of winter, and with both humility and ascendency. That's quite a legacy to live up to. Though," he added, looking me up and down, all five-feet-eleven-and-and-three-quarter inches of me, "you appear to be up to the task. Even Wordsworth wrote of this bird, 'Type of the wise, who soar, but never roam, True to the kindred points of Heaven and Home.'"

"Thank you, that's beyond flattering," I murmured as a wave of heat washed through me. "And here I thought it was just my name."

We smiled at each other and for a moment I wondered what it would have been like to have a man such as this—gracious, caring and encouraging—for a father. Or even a foster father. How different my life could have been.

"All right, that's enough of this mutual admiration society crap." Dunwitty's harsh tones yanked us back to the grisly business at hand. "Quote poetry on your own time, Doc, we got a dead guy to inspect."

Dr. White's smile died. He nodded and moved to the other side of the cart, his expression now sober. Dunwitty let go of my biceps, then wrapped his arm around my shoulders, hugging me close to his side, as though he feared I would bolt for the door the first chance I got. Which probably wasn't too far off the mark. The last thing I wanted to do was to see what was under that sheet.

Dr. White's hand reached out. He looked up at me.

"Are you ready for this?"

"Sure, she's ready," Dunwitty said, tightening his grip until I winced. "She's a big, bad private investigator. A little violence ain't gonna bother her, not the way she dishes it out."

I turned my head and gave the detective a glare that could have ignited a bonfire. When I turned back, my heart—and my stomach—leapt into my throat.

Dr. White had uncovered the body to the middle of the hirsute chest. He'd been a long, lean man, with a slender neck, broad shoulders, and narrow muscles, though his body seemed diminished now, the skin gray and criss-crossed with welts, bruises, and jagged cuts. The face was completely gone; no skin, no nose, no eyes, just a pile of raw meat clumped at the top of the neck with glints of ashen bone showing through the rents.

I'd already seen the vicious destruction in that photograph Dunwitty had slapped in front of me five days ago, but this wasn't anywhere near the same. At least the photograph had given me a bit of distance from the reality of the violence. A small distance, to be sure, but still a space in which I could fool myself into believing—even if only for a moment—that it was trick photography and not a real person.

But there was no space here. No way to distance myself from this horror. The reality of what this man had suffered, the savage depravity visited on him by his assailant, hit me like a sledge hammer. My stomach rebelled. The room seesawed. My nails again dug into my palms as I searched for stability. I turned my head toward Dunwitty and grated words out from between clenched teeth.

"If you don't let go of me, in about three seconds you'll be wearing my breakfast."

Alarm widened his eyes. He dropped his arm and jerked back a step. I stumbled over to the counter against the wall and stood with my back to the body, eyes closed, hands pressed to my mouth as I tried to keep the contents of my stomach where they belonged— in my stomach. *Breathe*, I told myself. *Just breathe.* Over and over, like a mantra.

"Skylark? My dear, are you all right?"

As Dr. White's words penetrated my mantra, I realized from his close-to-panicked tone that I hadn't answered the first few times he'd asked. I took a final deep breath, nodded, and reached for my voice.

"I'm fine," I said, turning around just as Dunwitty added his two cents.

"Given your track record, I'm really surprised this kind of thing bothers you at all."

"You don't know anything about me, Dunwitty." I spared him one disgusted glance, then fixed my gaze on the body. "You just think you do."

I walked closer to the cart, shoving my emotions as far away as I could as I searched for something, anything, that seemed familiar. Both Dunwitty and the coroner watched my every movement, though from their expressions I could tell it was for widely different reasons.

"Can you uncover more of him?" I glanced at Dr. White, who nodded, his face, his whole demeanor, one of compassion and concern. "I'd like to see his hands. And then his legs."

He pulled the sheet down to just below the body's navel—I ignored the neatly stitched "Y" incision that defaced his battered torso and the jagged hole the bullet had made in his chest—and folded the man's arms across his abdomen, giving me a clear view of the hands. They were narrow, like the rest of his body, and soft, with long fingers and well-maintained nails. No sign of love handles around the waist. A flat abdomen, though the laxity of death had eliminated almost all sign of the cultivated six-pack I expected to find.

His legs, when the doctor pulled up that end of the sheet, were even more hairy than his chest. They seemed equally well-maintained, the muscles tight to the bone without a hint of flab, the feet sleek and un-callused with close-trimmed nails. I shifted my gaze to the thick, dark hair on his head, which lay in obedient waves despite its disheveled state—trying my best not to again take in the ruined face that shouted 'look at me, look at me!'—and shook my head.

"I don't recognize him, nothing looks familiar. But I can tell he took care of himself, spent money on things many men might consider frivolous. Even un-manly. Probably because of whatever his job was."

I nodded my thanks to Dr. White and turned away from the cart as he moved to recover the body. Dunwitty stomped closer to stand over me, his eyes narrowed in anger. Or suspicion: it was hard to tell, they both looked the same on him.

"You're lying about not recognizing him. How can you possibly know so much about him if you don't know him?"

"It's called *deduction*, Detective." I crossed my arms and returned his glare. "It's obvious that he's taken good care of his body, gotten regular exercise, kept himself in shape. There are no calluses on either his hands or feet, so he didn't do a lot of physical labor. He's had a recent manicure and pedicure, his hair has been expertly styled, not just cut, and I can still see the shine of hair gel even after..." I shuddered, "all the blood that covered it, and having his hair and body rinsed down here. Most men aren't that fastidious about their appearance, so it's logical all that attention to grooming had something to do with either what he did or where he worked."

Dunwitty grunted, glanced at the coroner who was handing off the cart to an assistant, then stared at me a long moment. His expression held a mix of surprise and calculation and I wondered what was now going through what passed for his mind, what further deviousness he was planning. Then he again wrapped his hand around my arm—but gently, this time, which surprised the heck out of me—and led me across the room to another counter on which was spread a variety of miscellaneous objects, most spattered with dried blood.

"All right, we found this at the scene. Take a good look. See anything you recognize?"

Although I knew it was stupid—and just asking for trouble—I simply couldn't help myself. Dunwitty had, after all, left himself open for it.

"Yes. A ring, a pair of glasses, a handkerchief, a couple of quarters, ow—"

His hand clamping down on my forearm cut off my words. He kept squeezing and I wondered if he'd break the bone.

"Nobody likes a smart ass, Skylark. So, cut the crap."

"Maureen Overton," I whispered. He dropped my arm as though he'd just touched scalding water.

"You can be a real bitch, you know that?"

"You'd better believe it," I said, rubbing my aching arm.

"Stay here." He pointed a meaty finger at the floor, like I was a dog. "Don't move. And don't touch anything. That's evidence, I don't want you fucking it up. Hey, Doc!"

He turned and walked away from me, but I didn't pay much attention. I stared at the bloodstained items. It wasn't all of the evidence that was found, I was sure, since Garrett's missing wallet was absent. It was only that which Dunwitty the dimwit thought had any relevance, so none of it probably did. Not for the first time did I wish my special abilities included psychometry. It would be way more useful to be able to touch an object and learn useful information than to see the silent past superimposed over the present, or a bunch of lighted lines that connected people together but really didn't tell me anything specific.

I glanced over at Dunwitty, who stood in deep conversation with Dr. White, his back to me. Maybe it was the frustration eating away at me because of having stupid, useless abilities, or maybe it was the fact the big, bad detective had ordered me stay. And not to touch. I couldn't help myself. I reached out a hand and used a forefinger to poke at the items on the counter.

I figured the stuff had already been processed to death—no pun intended—or they'd not have been spread out like a smorgasbord for any Tom, Dick or Harriet to play with. So I didn't really feel any guilt at touching them or turning them over, and I didn't fear messing up any evidence. Another shudder rippled through me as my finger touched the dried blood stains on the ring and the handkerchief and my stupid brain pictured how they'd gotten there, but my poking and prodding gained me nothing.

Until I touched the glasses.

A shock corkscrewed up my arm. I stifled a gasp and yanked my hand away, then looked back at where the two men still stood in conversation, joined now by one of the assistants. My heart beat so hard and fast I feared it might break through my chest wall. I was stunned no one else could hear it. I looked back at the glasses.

What the hell was that? I'd never before ever had any kind of physical reaction to something I touched, other than a slight tingling deep inside when I laid my hand on somebody and let the light lines come to the fore. I peered closer at the glasses. The black frames were bent, the small, oblong lenses shattered as though stepped on. I saw 2.25 stamped on the inside of one bow and realized they were standard reading glasses, the kind you could purchase at any drug store. I touched them again and got another shock, milder this time, and I knew. Those glasses held a clue of some kind, something important. I just had no idea what. And, of course, with Dunwitty about to arrive back at my side at any moment, no time to figure it out right then.

I didn't stop to think. I snatched them up—ignoring yet another even milder shock—and tucked them into my pants pocket just as Dunwitty shook hands with Dr. White, who went over to one of the stainless steel tables where a new body awaited him. I walked over to Dunwitty, hoping he'd not bother going back to scan the evidence. He frowned over at the counter, then at me, but he didn't move. I blinked up at him, grateful I wore a loose top that was long enough to hide the telltale bulge in my pocket.

"There's nothing I recognize over there. Do you think you could manage getting me home now?" I could only hope my snark would keep his attention off that evidence pile. "My entire life doesn't revolve around you and your cases, you know."

The snicker from an assistant across the room narrowed Dunwitty's beady eyes. He snarled, grabbed my arm and towed me out into the hall, which smelled a hell of a lot better than the autopsy suite since it was being refurbished. I inhaled the scent of wet latex primer as though it were fresh air, and in my periphery noted a man on a ladder at one end of the long hallway, busily plying his brush to the juncture of wall and ceiling. We'd not taken a half dozen steps before a deep voice behind us called out.

"Detective Dunwitty! There's a call for you, they said it's urgent. You can take it in Dr. White's office."

We turned to see a uniformed cop standing a few yards away.

"Why don't you give me your keys?" I gave Dunwitty a smirk and held out my hand. "I'll go wait for you in the car."

Dunwitty glared at me, then again pointed at my feet.

"Not even if hell froze over. You stay right here. Don't move an inch from this spot. You got that, Skylark? Not an inch. You stay."

I crossed my arms and rolled my eyes, praying he wouldn't order the uniform to stand watch over me. He didn't. He stormed down the hall and vanished through a doorway without once looking back. I stood still a moment before walking a few feet further away from the autopsy suite, toward the exit door, and leaned against the unpainted part of the wall. I glanced at the man on the ladder, who worked on, ignoring me as though nothing interesting had happened, then pulled the glasses from my pocket, being careful not to cut my fingers on the broken lenses. I turned them over in my hands, hoping for revelation but receiving none, not even a shock this time. Suppressing a sigh, I stowed them in the bottom of my purse. I barely had time to slow my heartbeat and erase my puzzled expression before Dunwitty emerged out into the hallway, his face a dark thunder cloud. He looked at where he'd told me to stand, then at where I leaned against the wall. He stomped down the hall to loom over me, glaring.

"I told you to stay put, Skylark," he practically shouted. "Don't you ever do what you're told?"

"Sorry." I shrugged. "I don't do orders. I'm a person, a human being, not a dog."

"Cute. Well, get a move on." He grabbed my arm, giving my bruises bruises, and began towing me down the hall. "We gotta get back to Los Osos."

"What's going on? What was the call about?" I asked as we hustled past the painter. Dunwitty merely growled at me again.

"None of your business, Skylark."

None of my prodding did any good. Dunwitty shoved me in the car, and maintained a terse silence all the way back to the Starbucks parking lot. He wasn't smart enough to look inside my purse.

Carstairs positioned his ladder against the wall just inside the door to the parking lot, set the primer can and brush on the shelf, and climbed to the top. As he worked, he tried to figure out what to do next. He'd started on Tuesday, relegated to the office complex, then on Wednesday he'd switched with the pansy-ass who didn't want to paint the corridor outside the autopsy suite and evidence labs. Now he was where he needed to be, but all the rooms here had keypad locks; you needed codes to get inside them. The place was crawling with cops, who patrolled at regular intervals. And, unlike Eddington, this shithead supervisor kept a close eye on his painting crew. There was no time to wander around, looking. Unless he got assigned to paint the one room he needed to be in—and who knew which one it was?—

this whole job, his supposed Intervention Number Three, would be a waste of time.

"Shit, fuck 'n damn," he whispered just as a door halfway down the corridor opened. A huge bear of a man, towing an exotic-looking woman, began walking his way, then someone further up the hall called out to him. Shit, he was a cop. A detective. Carstairs's hands began to shake. *Cool it*, he told himself. *This ain't about you, it can't be about you.*

He kept his face turned to where the wall and ceiling met, and dug his brush into the cracks. He heard the cop order the woman to stay where she was, then he walked away. Carstairs risked a glance. It was hard to tell from his position, but she looked tall, way too tall for a woman, and skinnier than he liked them. She had dark hair that tumbled halfway down her back, creamy olive skin, and dark-looking eyes that tipped up at the outer corners. She reminded him of the gypsy woman who told fortunes at the summer fair when he was a boy. Man, did that gypsy bitch freak him out.

He kept painting, his attention split between the wall and the woman, and almost dropped his brush when he saw her pull a pair of glasses from her pocket. She gave a surreptitious look around the hallway, then bent to study the specs. His specs! He could see that even from this far away; his distance vision was twenty-twenty. Black frames twisted, lenses broken in the struggle; yeah, they were his. It was all he could do not to descend the ladder and snatch them away from her. She shook her head and shoved them down into her purse. What was she doing with his glasses? Who the hell was she?

The cop came back, looking pissed as hell.

"I told you to stay put, Skylark," the asshole yelled at her. "Don't you ever do what you're told?"

Skylark, her name's Skylark, Carstairs thought. Weird, but easy to remember. His stomach churned at the insolent tone in her voice, the uppity look on her face, as she answered the cop. No woman should treat a man with such disrespect.

The detective grabbed her arm as Carstairs watched from the corner of his eye—*I hope that hurts*, he thought—and hauled her down the corridor and out the door, his words ringing in Carstairs's ears: ... *get back to Los Osos.*

A too-tall woman with exotic looks and a weird name, who lives in a small town. Shouldn't be too hard to find, he thought, as he dipped his brush into the primer. He grinned. Unless he was mistaken, and he knew he wasn't, Fate had just handed him Intervention Number Four.

 *CHAPTER TWELVE*

"You did *what*?" Garrett stared at me as though I'd just crawled out from under a rock.

"I can't be here," Reenie said, raising her hands and taking a step away from the table.

"Oh, come on." I glared at both of them and cocked my fists on my hips.

We'd just finished dinner, a christening celebration for my new home which caused me no end of angst since I did the cooking. Well, reheated stuff from the deli in the supermarket, which in itself was no mean feat, for me at least. When I cleared the dishes I'd set the offending item—the broken reading glasses, all innocent and pathetic looking—on the table, and said, "I need your help. I took these from the morgue."

I couldn't figure out why Garrett and Reenie were getting so bent out of shape. Sure, I probably shouldn't have lifted the specs, but what good were they doing hidden away in an evidence locker? The fact that Dunwitty had allowed me to see them meant the cops, despite all their forensic technology, had no idea of their significance. Neither did I—yet—but that was beside the point.

"I can't believe you stole evidence in an active case," Garrett muttered. "You know better than that."

"It's a *felony*." Reenie glared at me. "I'm an officer of the court. I have to report this, you know that."

"No, I don't. You've bent the law before, don't try to deny it."

"I might have bent it, but I've never *broken* it."

"Oh, don't go getting all righteous on me. I didn't take something crucial, it's not like those glasses are important or anything. If they were, they'd never have let me within ten feet of them. I doubt those idiots will even realize they're missing."

"If they're not important, why did you swipe them?"

I closed my eyes and winced. Trust Garrett to zero in on the heart of the matter.

"You got a *hit* off them, didn't you?" Reenie pointed at me. "And instead of telling the cops, you decided to take them and look into it yourself." She shook her head, pierced me with her glare, and itemized on her long, slender fingers. "Stealing evidence. Withholding information. Interfering in an ongoing murder investigation. Have I *missed anything*?"

"Damn. I thought you guys would be on my side."

"We are, Skylark." Garrett reached out and tried to pat the shoulder I twitched out of his reach. I so did not need comforting.

"*I'm* not." Reenie pursed her lips and crossed her arms. "Not unless you're completely honest with me."

"All right, yes!" I rolled my eyes. "I got a hit off them. Are you happy now?"

I blew out my frustration in an audible breath, stomped over to my new-to-me couch, and flopped down. Not even its overstuffed softness eased my irritation. Things had finally started going my way. I hadn't seen hide nor hair of my nemesis—or heard from him—for three whole days. I had my cell phone, Jeep and camera back, though Dunwitty still hadn't released my Glock. Garrett had gifted all the salads and most of the frozen junk to the local homeless shelter in my name so I had a righteous tax write-off, and no neighbors had rung my doorbell since Wednesday night. Granted, Araceli Aguayo hadn't returned my call of abject apology, but I was still hopeful she'd reconsider.

And now, just when there was light at the end of the tunnel, my friends—my only friends—turned on me.

I sighed again and looked at them both, Garrett sitting on the other end of the couch looking wary and thoughtful, Reenie leaning up against the kitchen archway, arms still crossed, face glowering. I shook my head.

"What was I supposed to do? Tell Detective If-you-can't-see-it-touch-it-or-hear-it-it-don't-exist that I felt something, that I got a 'hit' off those glasses? That they mean something, but I have no idea what, or how it relates to the crime?" I snorted. "Like he'd believe that. No, he'd figure it proved I was involved. He'd have hauled me in and arrested me again faster than you could blink an eye."

"Maybe, but—"

"There's no maybe and no but, Reenie. It was a miracle I got to see as much as I did. You think they'd ever let me get that close to the evidence again? Uh-uh."

I shook my head. "Not even in your dreams. I did what I had to do."

"She has a point, Reenie." Garrett, ever the mediator, jumped in to head off the argument that was brewing, like he always did. "It might have been ill advised, but at least I can understand why Skylark did it." He sent a placating look Reenie's way, then turned back to me. "Tell us, what have you learned from the glasses?"

I winced again and drew up my shoulders. I so did not want to admit defeat.

"Not a thing," I whispered.

Reenie groaned and rolled her eyes, then turned and headed for the bathroom. We listened to her heels click on the hardwood floor until the door shut—with more force than absolutely necessary. I sighed yet again. She really was pissed about this.

"What do you mean, not a thing?"

"I mean," I said, looking not at Garrett but at the side wall where my almost-empty four-shelf bookcase stood, "nothing. Nada. Zip, zero, zilch. I was just poking around the stuff—from his pockets, I guess, there was a ring, a handkerchief, a couple of receipts, some coins, all blood-spotted—then I got to the glasses. The first time I touched them I got a shock, a real zinger, then lesser ones the next couple of times, and now... nothing." I shrugged. "For all I can tell at this point, they're just a broken pair of drugstore reading glasses."

Garrett stared at me a moment, then he rose, went into the kitchen, brought back the glasses and handed them to me.

"Do your thing," he said, then sat down again, his gaze glued to me.

I knew it wouldn't do any good, but I saw Reenie return from the bathroom, still disapproving, and the expectant look on Garrett's face, so I nodded and closed my eyes. *Maybe a miracle will happen*, I thought. Yeah, and maybe I'd win a hundred million in the lottery without even buying a ticket.

I sat in silence as the seconds ticked into one minute, two minutes, feeling nothing—no shocks, no deep inner tingle that heralded the presence of my psychic ability. Then I opened my eyes. All I saw was what was supposed to be there: my living room, Garrett, and Reenie. No mystical light lines shooting off to who knows where. No past super-imposed over the present. Not one shred of paranormal anything.

I shook my head and set the frames on the cushion between us.

"Nothing. It only works with people, you know that. I don't know why I got that shock, but I did. I know it means something, I just can't tell what."

"Did you at least touch the body?"

"No." I looked at Garrett. "I'm sure Dunwitty would have stopped me. Besides, there was no point, unless either Dunwitty or the coroner did him in, which I highly doubt. I'd only have gotten lines of light that went nowhere helpful. Maybe, if they figure out who he is and there's a funeral, I could try it then."

But I hoped not. The thought of touching a body in its coffin gave me the willies.

"This just keeps getting worse," Reenie muttered. She held up a hand to stop my protest. "I don't mean to be judgmental, but I don't like what's happening, the way you're getting obsessed. It's not like this is your case. No one's hired you to look into it. It was just bad timing,

Garrett losing his wallet and then you two being overheard arguing, which was what got you pulled in. But you're cleared now. You need to drop it. Walk away."

"I don't know that I can."

We stared at each other and I became aware that something was going on that I didn't understand. Something inside Reenie. Or maybe me. She finally nodded.

"I figured you'd say that. All right, I'll forget I was here, but this is the *last time*. I can't do it any more. I can't look away, can't pretend I don't see these things." She gave me a tiny shrug and a little moue with her lips. "It's not fair to me, Skylark. I'm a *lawyer*, in case you forgot. I took an *oath*."

"I'm sorry," I said, and I was—sorry at least that what I'd done had caused her a problem, not that I had taken the glasses. "I didn't think—"

"That's just it, you *don't* think. You get a notion in your head and you go off half cocked. You never consider how what you do might impact the people around you." She sighed. "Do you think I want to be forced to turn in a good friend, my *best* friend, to the cops? You mean too much to me, Skylark. So, I've got no choice. I'm bowing out. Call me when it's over. Or if you decide to smarten up and drop it."

"Reenie—

"No," She held up her hand. "My mind's made up. I'm leaving."

We watched in silence as she walked out of the house. I wondered how long it would be before she'd be back in my life. Or, if I kept investigating, if she'd even speak to me again. Yet another friendship test I'd failed.

"Shit," I whispered.

"She has a point, Skylark."

"She *what*?" I stared at Garrett in disbelief. "I thought you said *I* had a point. We can't *both* have points."

"Yes, you can." He grinned at me. "They're not mutually exclusive, you know."

"They sure feel like it to me."

We sat together for a few minutes while I sat fighting tears I refused to let fall, even though my heart was breaking and I could have used Garrett's arms around me, comforting me. But no way would I allow myself to be that weak. Then Garrett sighed.

"Don't sweat it, Skylark. It's true you might not give your friends enough thought. Or credit. But, bottom line," he added, placing a finger on my lips to stop my protest, "Reenie loves you. She won't stay away forever. She'll get over it, eventually. Just give her some time. Meanwhile..." He picked up the glasses and nodded at me. "Let me take these. I have an idea about what to do with them."

"What?" He didn't say anything. I gave him a jaundiced look and my best sarcastic tone. "Oh, you gonna pull a Reenie and turn me in to the cops?"

"You'll find out soon enough." He bent down and kissed the top of my head, then mussed up my hair. "I'll get back to you."

He gave me a mocking salute with the broken specs, then turned and walked out. The door slammed behind him. The day darkened around me as I sat on alone, deserted, betrayed yet again, and hurting. There was no point in turning on a light, it wouldn't illuminate anything worth looking at.

That was my life—business as usual.

"Hi, honey, I'm home!" Carstairs sang out as he entered his cabin.

He grinned. He'd always wanted to say that, and now he had a reason. He tried to picture her in the dark inner room. He'd boarded up the windows so no daylight leaked in. And he'd turned out the lights after their first session. Would she still be defiant, or would there be tears in her eyes now? Maybe fear coated her body with sweat. He pictured her crouched in the corner where he'd left her, far away from the comfort of bed and blankets, cowering at the sound of his voice. The way a woman should.

He'd really only planned to talk to her, to get to know her better after that first evening. Maybe even go on a few more real dates. But she'd been so scared when he'd shown up outside her apartment without warning that he couldn't deny the adrenaline that surged in his body. Couldn't keep his hands from grabbing her, hitting her into submission. Couldn't deny the anger he felt, or the thrill that lit him up from the inside.

The special something that had lain dormant all these years had insisted that now was the time. Time to see just what he enjoyed. Time to see how long he could make it last. Time to practice, to get ready for that uppity one he'd seen at the morgue, the one with the weird name. The one with that insolent mouth, who needed a man to tame her. To break her. The one who had meddled in his business.

Skylark.

He set the bags on the kitchen table and began unpacking them while he sang the song that had been running through his mind all day at work, putting in his own version of the words to the classic tune.

"Every tear of yours will satisfy, I will hurt you until you comply, just remember baby, 'til you die, you belong to me. I hold all the power, darling. In my hand I hold your breath... or death..."

It tickled him no end to think she heard—and was terrified by—every luscious sentiment. He held up the remote wireless camera and grinned at it. The man at the store told him that, once hooked to an internet transceiver, it could send a signal over quite a distance. And he could switch from regular to infrared with the push of a button. He'd be able to check on her while he was at work, watch how her day went, see what she was up to while he was gone, if she tried to escape or if she obeyed him. And plan her rewards and punishments accordingly.

Oh, yes, he thought to himself as he paired the camera with the remote receiver he hooked to his television, and connected it through the internet, *this is going to be instructive. And fun.* He shivered in delight at the thought of it, a video record of her alone, waiting, imagining, anticipating, then the film-at-eleven-worthy taping of the two of them engaged in all the wonderful activities he had in mind. He hoped she had good staying power, he'd hate for this kind of fun to end prematurely. Just in case, he decided to upload the files, make a little home movie out of it all, something to help him remember the good times once it was over.

He unlocked the door to the back room, flicked on the light, and smiled at his little honey, who cowered into the corner as though trying to melt into the rough wood-plank wall.

"Please, please let me go." The abject fear in her voice, not quite buried beneath the tears that erupted at his entrance, thrilled through him. "I won't tell anyone, I swear. Please, I just want to go home."

Over and over she repeated the words, babbling her pleading, as he went about considering angles, looking for the best placement, the fullest coverage, completely ignoring her. Once he had the camera firmly mounted, he pressed the record button, then turned and looked at her. She shrank back, the chains on her legs and arms rattling with both her movements and the trembling of her bruised, naked body. Or maybe it was the cold, since he hadn't bothered to turn on any heat. Was it fear or the chilly air that peaked her nipples so tight? Maybe it was the combination. Something else to explore more fully. Just the thought made him stiffen.

"Did you miss me, honey? Look, what I got for you." He gestured at the camera, at the red light blinking its readiness. "I'll immortalize you. You'll be the star of our little show."

He grinned at her and pulled off his belt.

"Smile pretty, now. Let's start with act one."

He swung the belt. The heavy silver buckle glinted in the overhead light as it descended, and Heidi Coffey screamed.

 *CHAPTER THIRTEEN*

I didn't hear from Garrett the entire weekend, and wondering what he was doing with those glasses just about killed me. I ached to call Reenie, see if we could work things out, but I couldn't stomach the thought of her hanging up on me. So I kicked around doing pretty much nothing until I couldn't stand it anymore, then took off for Bishop's Peak on Sunday afternoon. I spent four hours out there between toiling up and down the steep, winding trail and sitting in isolation on the crest, hoping the exercise and panoramic view would exorcise my ghosts.

Vain hope. All I got out of it were sore muscles and an over-abundance of sun. Since I'd been too focused on my fucked-up life to remember sunscreen, I was definitely hurting by the time I arrived home, the setting sun blinding me the whole way. My silent cellphone mocked me as I ran a hot bubble bath that I couldn't even sit in, I was so burned. I ended up draining the tub, filling it with cool water, and drinking half a bottle of Glenlivet while I soaked away the physical pain.

There wasn't much help for my emotional pain.

The booze didn't ease the poor-me's I wallowed in, but at least it helped me sleep a few hours Sunday night. Monday loomed dark and dreary. The Central Coast's fabled June Gloom fog, which had descended a month early, socked in the land, and the aftereffects of too much Scotch Whisky socked in my head. Not that a clear head mattered, since I didn't have any clients, or any work to do. Took me 'til late afternoon to pull myself together enough to make the phone call I'd been putting off.

Dunwitty wasn't around—so they claimed—and when I asked about my Glock I was transferred to his partner, Leopard—a.k.a. Detective Soto-Osorio—who, surprise of the century, said he'd been wanting to talk to me. My heart began to thud. Had they discovered the glasses were missing? Or had Reenie—or Garrett—actually turned me in? No; I quickly dismissed those fears. Had either happened, Dunwitty would have pounded down my door, cuffs in hand, and not waited until I called the station hoping to shake loose my pistol.

"Why don't you come over to the station and we can talk?" Detective Soto-Osorio asked. "I'll be here another hour or so. Your weapon should have been released before now, I'm not sure what the problem was."

Maybe he couldn't figure it out—or maybe he just didn't want to out his jerk of a partner—but I had no such problem. I knew Dunwitty-the-Dimwit was behind the delay, and I was sure he'd be livid that Soto-Osorio had gone behind his back and released it to me. Not willing to risk my nemesis showing up and putting an end to my weapon retrieval, I shot out of the house and arrived at the sheriff's substation on 10th Street in about three minutes flat, since the traffic lights—all two of them—were with me for once. Like I said, Los Osos isn't a very big town.

"Please, come this way." Soto—by this time I'd dropped the hyphen, his double surname took up too much space in my head—led the way through the locked door, into the bowels of the station. "We'll see if we can locate your weapon, and I've got a few questions for you."

I'll just bet you do, I thought as I followed him down the corridor, expecting to be shoved back into that interrogation room. To my surprise, we by-passed it and ended up in the tiny office Dunwitty and Soto shared. It held three mis-matched chairs with an ancient four-drawer file cabinet in the far corner. Two wobbly-looking, battered gray metal desks were home to oversize black telephones and ancient plastic cups that held a few ballpoints—freebies from the local bank, I recognized the orange and white color scheme. And there, centered on one not-so-gleaming desktop, sat my Glock.

Locate my weapon, indeed, I thought as Soto gestured me to the hard wood chair facing his desk. All I wanted was to grab the gun and get out of there before Dunwitty showed up, but the novelty of not being relegated to an interrogation room lent me a smidgen of politeness. I sat and stared at Soto a moment, waiting to see what kind of crap he was going to dish out. And how long it would be before he handed me the Glock. Finally, the silence—and nerves about Apeman—got to me.

"Where's Dunwitty?"

"Dentist. He broke a tooth on an olive pit at lunch."

Couldn't happen to a nicer guy, I thought as I eyed the nameplate on the desk.

"Your first name's Javier?" Soto nodded. "I thought Dunwitty called you José."

"Yeah, he has trouble remembering what he calls 'Mexican names'. Six years, and I still can't get him to call me Javier."

We smiled at each other—that was so Dunwitty—then Soto bent his head and looked up at me through long, thick lashes most women would kill for.

"Look, I'm not quite sure how to say this, so I'm just going to let it roll, if that's okay with you?"

I blinked at him and shrugged; I doubted anything I could say inside the cop shop—or outside it, for that matter—would make a hill of beans of difference to what he was about to unleash on me. Better to get it over with quickly.

"Can you tell me more about what happened the last time you were here?"

"What... happened?" I frowned at him, not sure where he was going with this, and hoping it wasn't where I feared; could he really lock me up just for being a freak? "What do you mean?"

He leaned forward, his arms crossed on the desktop.

"Unlike my partner, I do believe in the paranormal. My *abuela*—my grandmother—took me once to see an *adivina*, oh, I guess you'd call her a soothsayer, or prophetess. Or even a fortune teller, though that's not really accurate. I was about seven and we were visiting her village in Mexico." He gave it the Spanish pronunciation, making the 'x' into an 'h'. "Doña Mago said the *adivina* had the Sight; she knew things just by looking at you. Or by holding your hand or an object of some kind. She'd see things no one else could see. Something like that happened to you here that day, didn't it? I could tell by the way your eyes shifted that you were seeing something that wasn't there for the rest of us."

I sat there staring at this strange aberration of a cop, not sure what to say, how much to admit. Had Dunwitty put him up to this? Was that why he was "absent"—in other words, lurking in the back room, waiting for Soto to entice me to spill the beans? I looked around the room, sent my gaze over the filing cabinet and desks, but found no sign of a recording device. Of course, they'd never have set it out in plain sight, it was probably tucked snug in a drawer or some such place.

What difference does it make? I thought. They had already opened my sealed file. They already knew of the psychic abilities that had reared their ugly heads when puberty hit. It wasn't like I could tell them a lot more than they already knew.

I took a deep breath and let it out slowly.

"Something like that," I finally admitted. "But completely different, really. Nothing happens when I touch objects," so blithely I dismissed the hit I'd gotten from the glasses, "and I have no control over what I see. Or when. It's just that sometimes I see the past superimposed over the present." *Yeah, at the worst times,* I thought, refraining from rolling my eyes. "It's just pictures, like a silent movie I can see through. I rarely understand what it means, it's just there one minute and gone the next." I shrugged. "It's a bit disconcerting, to say the least."

"I can imagine." Soto stared at me, his dark eyes blazing. He looked so enthralled and intent that I wanted to 'fess up, come clean, admit I'd lied; often what I saw held the key to the puzzles I was trying to solve. I didn't think I could be arrested for that. An instant later, I remembered who he was and where I was. Then I wanted to knock the guy off his chair, grab the Glock, and sprint for the door. That *would* get me arrested.

"No, I don't think you *can* imagine it." I crossed my arms and lifted my chin as I continued to match his stare. "I don't mean to be rude, Detective, or dismissive, but unless you've gone through something like this, you haven't the foggiest idea what it really means. People think you're a freak. They act like you're crazy. Or a scam artist fishing for money. Or just a jerk out for attention. I don't usually let anyone know when it happens, not anymore, not if I can help it. If I hadn't been in so much pain, I'd never have blurted out what I saw."

"Especially to my partner." Soto gave me a grin I wanted to share—but didn't—then he sobered. "You were right, you know. Everything you said. It happened almost twenty years ago. That boy with the tattoo? He was Dunwitty's cousin. They were really close, more like brothers, palled around together all the time. Dunwitty thought he knew Harry, trusted him implicitly. They'd just brought Harry in, he was part of a local auto theft ring, one of the organizers of it, actually, and Dunwitty had had no idea. He was so angry, felt so damned betrayed, he could barely see straight. And no," he added when I looked my question at him, "he didn't admit anything. I looked it up. And asked around. On the sly."

He grinned again and I relaxed just a bit.

"There was also a woman there," I said, crossing my mental fingers that Soto would continue to share the truth of what I'd seen—I almost never got confirmation on the random pieces of the past that I saw, unlike the self-explanatory non-random ones that were attached to my cases. "She was mid-to-late twenties, maybe, wore a uniform, looked like she was doing steno work of some kind, but she was also crying."

"Yeah, Harry's sister, Eleanor. I can't imagine how hard that had to be for her, she was an auxiliary cop, the station's stenographer. Her uncle and cousin were cops, too, and there's her brother, a felon." Soto shook his head, his face a study in pity. "Hard times for that family."

"Well, I thank you for the confirmation, anyway. I just wish I hadn't said anything out loud. Dunwitty…" I sighed.

"He has a hard time accepting things he can't see for himself. Doesn't trust anyone or anything, not since Harry. It's what makes him a good cop, but, well," Soto shrugged, "it also makes him too hard-nosed at times. Plus, he's still trying to live down his father's expectations. Nice guy, the dad, but he wanted his son to be a carbon-copy of himself: the dogged detective with a heart of gold. Mr. Empathy. He never did accept his son for who he is."

Yeah, the obnoxious detective without a heart of any kind, I thought. Soto leaned forward again, arms resting on the desktop, hands touching my Glock. I so wanted to snatch it to safety.

"The whole department expected the same thing, up until the new Sheriff took office a couple years ago.

He didn't ever know Dunwitty senior, so he had no preconceived notion about who and what Dunwitty junior was supposed to be. Too little, too late, though. Dunwitty's spent so much time being the square peg in a round hole, that it's ingrained into who he is now. He's like a bull in a china shop, plowing everything down that's in his way. He's constantly on the Sheriff's bad side because of it."

We sat in silence a moment, while I tried to digest information I didn't want to know. I could feel a sense of connection with Dunwitty materialize deep inside—one misfit to another—and I tried to shove it away. The last thing I wanted was to see Dunwitty as a human being.

"Um, I shouldn't have said all this." Soto's face reddened. "It's just, you were up front with me, so… You won't repeat it, will you?"

"Not in this lifetime." We shared an amused smile, both knowing it was Dunwitty at issue and not our information exchange, me thinking how young Soto was —even though he was probably a few years older than me—how much he still had to learn. I almost wished he wouldn't learn it, wouldn't turn into the Dunwitty clone he was sure to become in a few years, considering who his Jedi master was. I rose and held out my hand.

"Thank you, Detective, this little tête-à-tête has been a lot of fun. If I could have the Glock, I'll get out of your hair."

Soto shook his head.

"There's just one other thing," he said.

I froze, my heart thudding, the thought of those glasses in the forefront of my mind. I sank back onto the chair.

"And that would be…?"

"This other ability of yours. How does that one work?"

Oh, crap. I'd have rather dealt with them finding out I'd stolen the reading glasses than talk about the light lines. A tremor moved through my body. I looked at Soto, shook my head, and remained silent.

"All the file said is that you see connections between people when you touch them." Soto plucked up a pen and played with it, almost as though he wanted to take notes. So wasn't gonna happen if I could help it. "But there were no details. I'd like to see how it works. Can you give me a demonstration?"

"I... I don't think so, Detective. It isn't a sideshow act, something I do on demand. In fact, I'd rather not do it at all. Ever."

He studied me a moment, gave me a calculating smile, and laid his hand on my gun.

"You want your Glock back?"

It felt like a slap in the face. I took in a deep breath and lifted my chin.

"Really? You're going to *blackmail* me, in the *police station*?"

"Don't think of it as blackmail." His smile widened, became more amused. "Think of it as an exchange. One little sideshow"—he used a sideways nod to air quote the word—"for one honkin' big gun."

I crossed my arms and looked at the far corner of the room while I thought it over, what it might mean having a cop—a detective, Dunwitty's partner, no less—privy to the details of my light lines ability. Reading about it was one thing, seeing it in action a whole other ball game. Not that I had much choice, it seemed, not if I wanted to take my baby home with me.

"If Dunwitty hears about this..." I said as I looked back into his eager face.

"He won't. I swear." He held up his hands in pledge. "This is just between you and me."

I gave it a few seconds more thought, then nodded and rose.

"Fine. Come with me, then. And bring my Glock. I'm not coming back in here when we're done."

I led him down the corridor and stopped outside the squad room. Four uniforms sat at desks, pecking away at keyboards. Through an interior window, we could see the reception counter behind which a male intake officer sat, along with a petite, red-haired female dispatcher. Across the hall stood the Sheriff's closed door. I turned to Soto.

"Don't talk, and don't ask me anything. Just watch and listen. You got that?"

He nodded. I laid my hand on his shoulder, closed my eyes, and stilled my mind. It took only two seconds before it began, the tingle deep inside that heralded the onset. It spread rapidly through my body until my insides shifted, and I felt myself semi-detach— metaphorically speaking—from the world around me. When I opened my eyes, glowing lines of light snaked out from Soto, who stood staring at me, his face a study in both wonder and fear.

"I see four, no, five light lines. Two fairly faint ones —they look like thin rope—connect to two of the officers at the desks, the one in the far corner, and the one with the mustache. You don't have a close connection with them, at least not for the past few months. It was probably something work-related, a case you all worked on together. There's a stronger line, a thicker rope, attaching to the Sheriff's door, which makes sense, since he's your boss and you probably have to report to him pretty much daily."

Soto's body began to tremble. He licked his lips, but I held up a hand to stop whatever he was about to say.

"There's a really wide, bright line, looks like a thick cable, that goes out the front door, probably to wherever Dunwitty is. Its width and brightness means you've got a really strong connection to him. Doesn't look like you keep much from him." I shot him an acid look to remind him of his promise not to let Dunwitty in on this little show. "May I have my Glock now?"

"You said five lines," he all but whispered. "What's the last one?"

Crap. Why the hell had I told him how many lines I'd seen? I looked along the last one, the line I knew was trouble. It resembled a glowing golden chain although, like the others, it now had begun to fade. The links sparked a rosy hue where they joined together. I'd only seen that a few other times, and I knew what it meant, especially since the glowing chain attached to the dispatcher. She sat in profile to us—long lashes, tipped up nose, red bow of a mouth, a curvaceous figure. She looked to be maybe twenty, a bit young for Soto. She spoke into her microphone, oblivious to us.

"It connects to the dispatcher," I said. "It's the shape of a chain, and from the looks of it, you're a couple, been dating—well, at least sleeping together—hot and heavy for a while now, I'd say last night was—"

Soto grabbed my arm, yanked me down the corridor away from the squad room, and shoved me up against the wall, pinning me with an arm against my shoulders.

"Keep your voice down," he growled at me. "How the hell do you know that?"

I blinked at the panic and anger in his voice, the strength of his grip.

"Hey, you're the one who wanted me to do this. Shouldn't ask if you can't take the truth."

"Truth? Those first four could have been lucky guesses, though I don't see how you could know which of those guys I'd worked a case with. But there's no way you could know about Betsy." He let go of me, stepped back and shook his head. "She usually works the night shift, she's just filling in today for Karey, who's sick. No one knows about us, not even Dunwitty."

I could see there were reasons, serious reasons, maybe even career ending reasons—department regulations, probably—why they were keeping their relationship a secret. I didn't really care, and I so didn't want to know any more details than I already did. Still, I couldn't quite help myself. I smiled my usual snark at Soto and gave him back some of his own.

"Yes, but now *I* know about Betsy, and my spilling the beans could make your life rather *difficult*, maybe get someone *fired*, or *reassigned*, so..." I shrugged. "You know the drill, Detective. Don't think of it as blackmail, think of it as an *exchange*. The Glock for my silence."

He glared at me, his jaw working as he processed the sentiment, and I watched whatever goodwill I'd earned go down the drain. After a century-long twenty seconds of infuriated silence, he handed me the gun. I put it through its paces, making sure it hadn't been wounded or unalterably scarred by its sojourn in the land of the enemy. The clip was, of course, empty; I didn't bother to ask if I'd get back any ammunition remaining after they'd done their test shots. I knew what the answer would be. I just chalked up the loss to the cost of doing business. Once I was satisfied my baby hadn't been damaged, I nodded and dropped the gun in my purse.

"Thank you, Detective Soto, this has been a very *interesting* meeting. Enlightening *and* informative."

I gave him a perky smile as his hands clenched into fists, then spun on my heel and walked out of the station. I expected he'd come after me, trump up some charge to keep me in custody, but he didn't. No one followed me when I drove off. Still, I didn't breathe fully until I reached home and had the door shut and locked behind me.

Damn, I thought. *First Dunwitty, now Soto.* Seemed that no matter what I did, I just kept getting in deeper and deeper.

 *CHAPTER FOURTEEN*

Tuesday started with a bang—on my front door. The noise yanked me from sweet visions of tropical beaches, heady drinks embellished with umbrellas, and a dream of a dreamboat doing his sexy thing on a steel drum, all the while winking lascivious promises at me.

I moaned as the wanton night-time mirage vanished, cracked open one eye, and squinted at the clock: 5:12 am. Barely four hours since I'd gone to bed. *Shit*, I thought, and pulled the covers back over my head, searching in vain for the hot bod behind that steel drum.

The banging didn't let up. Not even my blanket-burrow could block it out. Then over the pounding came a deep, grating roar.

"Open the door, Skylark, or I'll break it in! Open up! Now!"

Dunwitty, in full-blown, obnoxious form. Over and over, bellowing nonstop, like a moose in rut.

By this time, I was sure the entire neighborhood was up and staring out their windows, if not actually lining the street. I groaned, slid out of bed, threw a robe over my sleep attire—an old, washed-out camisole and threadbare boy shorts—and stomped to the front door, eyes only half open. I held the robe closed with my hands, since I'd lost the sash somewhere in the distant past, but when I reached out to open the door—it was recalcitrant enough to need both hands—the two halves of the robe parted like the Red Sea. I should have covered up again, but I was too pissed at the ongoing racket to stop and rectify the matter. Dunwitty was so on my shit list. I caught him with his fist raised, ready to put another dent in the wood. I glared at him.

"What the *hell* do you think you're doing?"

"I got questions for you, Miss One Name Wonder."

His growl still rang on the cool early-morning air as his gaze wandered south to my breasts, peaked nipples clearly visible through the thin, semi-sheer fabric. Then he pushed his way into the living room, his big semi of a body forcing me to step back before he ran me over. I slammed the door shut and stomped over to where he stood beside the couch, staring around the room. I propped my fists on my hips and glared at him.

"I don't remember inviting you in," I snarled.

He was tall enough that I had to look up at him, not something I was used to doing with most men, and the fact that I stood half naked while his eyes did their male-intimidation thing on my body made me even angrier. I pulled the two halves of the robe across my chest and held them there with crossed arms. Who the hell was he to think he could just push into my house any time he wanted? And then stand there, silent, like he was lord of the castle or something. I huffed out a breath.

"It's practically the middle of the night and I've had barely four hours of sleep, Dimwitty. What's so all fired important it couldn't at least wait until the sun came up?"

"What did you call me?"

He narrowed his eyes at me; the rage in his tone sent a shiver down my back. What *had* I said? I tried to recall my words, but the hatred in his eyes froze my mind.

"The name is *Dunwitty*, Miss One Name Wonder. *Dun. Witty.*" He spelled it, spitting out each letter like a curse. He stepped close to me; the couch stopped my backward retreat. "You got that?"

"Tit for tat, Detective." I gave him my patented cocky grin, still not sure what had his panties in a twist, but not about to let his looming size or animosity—or the fact I was pinned against the couch—cow me. "You remember *my* name, and I'll do my best to remember yours. In case you forgot, mine is *Skylark*. S-K-Y-L—"

He grabbed my arm and yanked me close, cutting off my defiance.

"Don't get cute with me, Missy. I ain't in the mood."

"Fine." I yanked my arm from his hand and stepped to the side. "You and your pissy mood can take a hike. *Now.*"

I hitched a thumb at the front door and glared at him, not that he noticed. He crossed his muscle-bound arms and shook his head.

"Sorry," he said, his eyes telegraphing how not sorry he was. "I need answers."

"*Sorry,*" I parroted back, letting my snark have free rein. "I ain't *got* any this time of night." I rolled my eyes.

"I'll meet you at the station at a decent hour *after* the sun comes up. Say, eleven?"

"No. Now."

"All right, what—"

"Not here. At the station."

I could tell by the way his face tightened and his jaw worked that I wasn't going to win this battle. I closed my eyes, took in a deep breath, and let it huff out into the early morning stillness.

"Whatever you say, *Detective*."

I turned and started for my bedroom. Dunwitty grabbed my arm. I pulled away from him and the robe fell open again.

"What do you think you're doing?" he growled.

I should have been more circumspect—or, better yet, humbly asked permission—but once more anger trumped my ability to think before I put my fury into words. Though I did frame said words in an almost-polite, if thoroughly sarcastic, tone.

"I am getting dressed so I can accompany an irrational, pigheaded, idiotic detective to the sheriff's station, at an unreasonable hour of the night, in order to answer a bunch of stupid questions that could easily wait until after the sun comes up and normal, rational people start their day."

I turned away again, and again he grabbed me.

"You're dressed enough. Come on."

"Are you nuts?" I twisted, but this time couldn't break his hold. "I'm not going anywhere like this."

Dunwitty grinned.

"You're resisting. Good."

He pulled out his cuffs. Before I could blink my arms were secured behind my back, and Dunwitty was dragging me out the front door into the cold darkness.

"You son of a bitch!" I shouted as my shoulders burned and the cuffs dug into my not-quite-healed wrists. The gravel and sticks littering the front walk gouged into my bare feet. "Ouch! Damn it, that hurts! Let me go!"

He wrestled me to his car, my gaping robe leaving my thin, semi-see-through sleepwear in full view of the half dozen neighbors who stood at the edge of the property, eyes goggling at the sight. And damn if I didn't spy a cell phone or two aimed my way. Dunwitty threw me in the back seat—overly careful once again to make sure I didn't smack my head—slammed the door, then dropped into the driver's seat and took off, spraying gravel on the onlookers. When I looked back through the rear window, I caught two definite camera flashes. A half-dressed, slightly porno version of yours truly would probably go viral in the next few minutes.

Fuck social media.

"You are going to be *so sorry* you did this, Dunwitty," I muttered, trying to find a semi-comfortable position on the hard, unyielding back seat. In answer, he slid open the front windows. A cold wind surged into the back of the car and wound down into my core, raising goose bumps on my arms and legs. I started shivering and couldn't stop.

"Threatening a police officer, are you?" He grinned at me in the rear-view mirror. "I'll add that to the charges."

"It's not a threat." I met his amused glance in the mirror, and let him see the full venom I felt. "It's a *promise*."

I spent the rest of the five-minute trip in silence, reciting Reenie's phone number over and over in my head. She might be mad at me, but she'd never abandon me to the mercy of the cops. Especially not Dunwitty.

I hoped.

We parked behind the station. I stumbled twice when he pulled me out of the car—the gravel in the station's lot was a lot sharper than the gravel on my walkway—and by the time we got indoors I was sure my soles were cut to ribbons. Then I had to endure the amused grins and lustful eyes of the other cops when he marched me through the station, robe agape. I bore it all with my head held high, not saying a word, but when he shoved me down on the chair in the interrogation room, I glared up at him.

"What bogus charges are you considering this time, Dunwitty? No," I said when he opened his mouth, "don't say a word. You'll only waste your time. Go call Maureen Overton. *Now*. I'm not answering *any* questions until she arrives." He straightened up and glared at me. "And you'd better take these cuffs off before you leave this room, or Reenie will hand you your head. It's bad enough you'll be waking her up at this hour."

He stared at me a long moment while I tried to control my shivering, and schooled my face not to show the pain from my shoulders, wrists, and feet. Then he bent down and removed the cuffs.

"This is an interview, not an arrest, Miss One Name Wonder. You don't need no lawyer." He pocketed the cuffs and turned toward the door. "I'll be right back."

"Call The Overton!" I shouted as the door shut behind him. "You dimwit," I added under my breath. Then I almost laughed when I realized that's what I must have unknowingly called him earlier. Out loud. *Dim*witty, not *Dun*witty. No wonder he got so pissy.

He left me alone about an hour, which gave me plenty of time to inspect myself for damage. I found a few bleeding spots on my wrists where the healing scabs had torn loose, but only a little blood on my soles—not the gushing river I'd expected, which surprised me. Sharp pains poked into my feet when I flexed my toes, though, so I knew that, despite the dearth of blood, the sticks and gravel had done some damage. I feared walking might be difficult for a day or two. As would typing, if the ache in my hands was any indication.

I sat in silence, shivering, since there didn't seem to be any heat in the room. The thin, summer-weight robe was no help at all. Being on Dunwitty's radar was getting old really fast. Maybe Reenie was right. I needed to drop this 'obsession,' as she called it, and get on with my life. Once Dunwitty turned me loose, I'd see about getting Garrett to anonymously spirit those reading glasses back to where they belonged. It wasn't like they were going to impart any crucial clues—not to me, anyway, since they'd inexplicably gone silent. Let the cops figure out who the guy was, and who killed him. *It's no skin off my nose*, I thought. *Though with Dunwitty at the helm—*

The door opened.

Well, see? It works: Think of the devil and up he pops. In waltzed my nemesis, carrying a file under one arm and two steaming cardboard cups in his hands. A uniform controlled the door for him; he closed us in again without too much ogling, since I'd overlapped the robe halves around my body in my vain search for heat. Dunwitty placed a cup on the table within my reach. He sat opposite me, set the file off to one side, and took a sip from his cup. All without taking his cold, calculating gaze off me.

"Wasn't sure how you like it," he said, nodding at my untouched cup. "But I figured, a tough girl like you, you probably drink it straight. Right?"

He grinned at me, so sure he'd pegged me.

"Wrong," I said as I picked up the hot cup and drew in a breath of nature's indispensable mind and body jump-starter. "For a tough *woman* like me, cream and two sugars. Though in a pinch, I can *force* down black."

I took a sip of the hot liquid, which was slightly burnt and bitter tasting. It wasn't all that bad, though; I'd definitely had worse. Still I forced myself to wince a bit as though it were truly awful. Let him think what he would; no way would I admit to him that he was right. I'd never adulterate coffee with either cream or sugar. I closed my eyes as the soothing heat slid down my esophagus, warming my still-shaking body. The shudders began to ease. I took another couple of sips before opening my eyes and setting the cup on the table.

"Did you call The Overton?" He shook his head. "What the hell is this, then? You can't possibly think one cup of lousy coffee will loosen my tongue."

"I need to know." He stared at me, then opened the file and slapped a photo down in front of me. "Where is she?"

Despite my resolve not to be drawn in, I studied the picture a moment, a bust shot of a cute, dark haired girl with an impish grin and sparkling eyes. She looked maybe nineteen or twenty. I'd never seen her before. I frowned up at Dunwitty.

"I don't know. Who is she?"

"We're not playing twenty questions here, Skylark. I want to know where she is. She's been missing for five days now. *Five.* Her family," his face, his voice, softened, "they need to know what's happened to her, where she is."

So they can bury her. His unspoken words rang in the air between us and my heart clenched. I looked at the photo again and shook my head.

"Why do you think I'd know anything about her? I've never seen her before."

"Don't give me that crap. You've been to the bar her uncle owns, so you do know her."

"No, I *don't* know her," I said, my mind busy sorting through the images his words conjured up. I didn't often go to bars to drink—that was so not my scene, I do most of my drinking alone at home—though I did meet Garrett or Reenie once in a while at Gaylord's here in town if we had something special to celebrate. But that was a serve-yourself, pay-as-you-go bar; you went up to the bartender for your drinks, and picked up any pre-paid finger food orders from the side counter. Gaylord's didn't employ cocktail waitresses.

"Damn it, Skylark, you were in Kelley's just three weeks ago." Dunwitty's voice rose. He slammed his hand on the table; I reached out and grabbed my cup before it could tip over. "They recognized your picture. So don't tell me you don't know her!"

"*My* picture? You're showing *my* picture around? Why?" I asked even as my mind sorted through where I'd been before all this shit had hit the fan. Then it came to me, what I'd been doing during the time in question. "You mean Kelley's in San Luis? Yeah, I was there, for all of about fifteen minutes. I was doing a skip-trace and someone told me my mark spent his evenings there. I talked to a few patrons, asked the bartender a couple questions, got a possible address, and left." I looked down at the photo again, then back up at Dunwitty. "If she was there that night, I don't remember seeing her."

"Fifteen minutes, huh?" He narrowed his eyes at me. "You made quite an impression on the clientele for only being there a mere fifteen minutes."

"So I'm a memorable person." I sat back, crossed my arms, and shrugged. "Sue me."

Dunwitty leaned forward and shook a thick finger in my face.

"You listen to me, Miss One Name—"

The door opened and Leopard, a.k.a. Soto, stuck in his head. He didn't so much as look at me.

"We got a tip on the Coffey case, Carrick. Let's go."

Dunwitty sent his glare to Soto, then back to me, as though he suspected we'd cooked up the interruption just to spoil his fun. Then his face cleared and Mr. Cop-on-a-Mission reappeared. He stuck the photograph back in the file, stood, and tucked the folder under his arm. Then he picked up his empty cup and looked at me.

"You can go home. But don't try leaving town. I still got more questions. A lot of them."

"Wait a minute," I said as he moved toward the door, where Soto now stood eying my outfit, obviously enjoying my state of deshabille. "You dragged me out of my house like this. I don't have any way to get home, and you know it." I stood up on my aching feet and braced myself with my hands on the table top. "I don't even have shoes! Take me with you and drop me off on your way to wherever."

"Ain't gonna happen. Call one of your freaky friends. I don't have time to play chauffeur, I got a missing girl to find."

He walked out, leaving the door ajar. I sank onto the chair and listened to their footsteps recede down the corridor, the distant voices of the other cops going about their business, the faint sound of a ringing phone. I had no car, no money, no shoes—no house keys—and would probably be arrested if I pranced down the street in my scanty nightclothes. Not only did I have to suffer the humiliation of another walk—or, rather, hobble, given the state of my feet—past the day shift, to say nothing of begging to use their phone, but I'd also have to swallow the ridicule of either Garrett or Reenie, whichever one I could talk into coming to get me.

Shivering again, now that the warmth of the coffee had worn off, I put my elbows on the table, rested my head in my hands, and wondered if I would survive until I got home. And it was just after 7:00 a.m.; I still had the whole day ahead of me.

CHAPTER FIFTEEN

It was ten-thirty before I got home, bleary-eyed and mushy-brained from lack of sleep. Reenie hadn't answered her phone when I'd called around seven-thirty —God forbid she lose any of her beauty sleep, or maybe I was still *persona non grata* for her. Damn caller ID. Garrett, once he stopped laughing, said to hang tight for a while. He had to stop in the office and finish a stack of important paperwork before he could come get me.

Hang tight. The office. Paperwork.

He'd suffer for that.

In the meantime, I was the one who suffered, since the cops—considerate assholes, every one of them— wouldn't let me wait secured out of sight in an office or the interrogation room Dunwitty'd left me in. Instead, they stashed me in the outer lobby in full view of everyone, humorous fodder for the day shift that moseyed in around seven-forty-five, and for every Tom, Dick and Perv they hauled through the front door.

Skylark's role for the morning—comic relief.

By the time I tottered though my own front door on my still-sore feet, I knew who was truly at fault—not that I'd let Garrett off the hook, by any means. Reenie was so right, Dunwitty-the-dimwit more than owed me. I had finally had enough. No more pussy-footing around, no more worrying about his radar. He deserved everything I could do to him—legally speaking. Once I got hold of my "L" word, I'd have her add everything he owned to the lawsuit and—borrowing a leaf from Reenie's book—even a few things he didn't. That'd make him think twice before not letting me at least get dressed before dragging me out of my home in the middle of the night.

But it wouldn't happen, not until I'd gotten some sleep—and gotten Reenie to answer my phone call. Barely able to keep my eyes open, I shed my robe on the way to the bedroom and collapsed on top of the disheveled covers, dead to the world. Two hours later, something urged me back into daylight well before I was ready to admit I was still alive, much less willing to face the next huge crisis in my life.

I lay there, eyes burning and blurred, lids at half mast, mind in a befuddled fog, and listened. Nothing: no scraping or bell-like noises, no flashes of light, no movement of the bed or the house around me. Which meant no one breaking in, no ringing phone, no storm raging, no earthquake tremors. So what had awakened me?

I waited a while for either enlightenment to burst in my brain or sleep to pull me under again, but neither happened. Eventually I got up, eyes barely open and brain still mushy, and shuffled on my still tender feet from the bathroom into the kitchen for coffee. Life's blood. Can't start the day without at least two cups of the high octane stuff. This, though, felt more like a three- or four-cup day.

The coffee had barely finished brewing my current indulgence, Peet's heady Uzuri African blend, before I filled my favorite mug—*I don't have nose trouble, I'm a P.I.*—to the brim. Inhaling the sweet, pungent aroma, I stepped into the living room, looked up, and jerked to a stop with a gasp. The mug dropped from my hand; hot coffee splashed up my legs. It took all my control not to dance around from the pain, movement not being a good idea with all the knife-sharp shards of mug littering the floor around my bare feet.

"Shit!" I yelped. "Damn you, that was my favorite mug!"

Quiet laughter filled the space between us. I glared at the man sitting in the maroon leather armchair that floated a foot off the floor beside my couch, a small mahogany occasional table hovering at his side: Bass Ehrler, my oh-so-irritating mentor, who'd first shown up when I was eleven. His thin, aristocratic lips curved up in an annoyingly handsome face; hazel eyes glittered with amusement. Dark hair, without even a hint of silver after all this time, flowed in sculptured waves down to his shoulders. He wore his usual leather slippers, black dress slacks and maroon smoking jacket, with an ascot folded beneath his clean-shaven, square chin; I'd never seen him in anything else. One long-fingered hand clasped a glass of dark red wine. The ring on his finger glinted in an unseen ray of sunshine that I knew didn't originate anywhere on my foggy Central Coast.

The fact that I could see my front door through him still disconcerted me even after all this time.

"I'm glad you find this so amusing." I rolled my eyes.

"Love the outfit." His deep velvet voice stroked down my spine like it always did.

"That's what you get for showing up unannounced. Call ahead next time and I'll make sure to dress for the occasion." I blew out a breath and shook my head. "How the hell did you find me?"

"Surely you understand by now that we are psychically linked. I will always be able to find you."

"Yeah," I said as I took a giant step over the mess on the floor, trying to avoid impaling my instep on the breakage, "I just hoped I'd have a few months of peace in my new place before you barged in on me again. Clean that up while I get dressed, will you? And you owe me a mug."

I gave him a rude, middle-finger wave over my shoulder as I headed into the bedroom, glad that he'd at least never totally invaded my privacy. He'd only shown up in the more public rooms of my abodes, and waited until my bed was folded back into a couch in my last place, since the one room was both public and private.

I sat on the edge of the bed a moment, wishing I was anywhere but where I was. The last person—no, second last, Dunwitty held the ultimate last place of honor—I wanted to deal with was Bass Ehrler. Every time he showed up my life went to hell. And I was far enough in hell already without his brand of help. There was little I could do to banish him, though; it's not like I could grab his astral-projected blob of ectoplasm and chuck it out the door. I was stuck with him until he decided to vanish back to his Minneapolis suburb, if that's where his physical form still resided. After about five minutes I got up, pulled on jeans and a T-shirt, stuck my feet into flip-flops—they still hurt too much for my usual sneakers or boots—and went back out to where my psychic nemesis awaited me.

Ehrler saluted me with his wineglass as I walked past him to the kitchen, though—smart man—he remained silent while I cleaned up the mess, totally ignoring him. I thanked the powers that be that my new place had hardwood floors and not wall-to-wall carpeting. Not until I'd poured myself another mug of coffee and semi-reclined on the couch did Ehrler open his ectoplasmic mouth.

"We need to talk about what's happening, my dear."

I held up my hand to stop him.

"Don't you have any other clothes, Ehrler? These have to be getting pretty ripe by now, don't you think? It's been what, sixteen years since I first saw you. In that same outfit." I shuddered. "You've got to be crawling with bugs by now."

Ehrler sipped his wine, set the glass on the side table and folded his hands, his expression on the annoyed side of patient. I pierced him with a glare, if one can actually affect ectoplasm.

"And despite the 'yardarm' adage, it's a bit early in the day for wine, isn't it?" I took a huge gulp of my coffee, and closed my eyes with pleasure as warmth flooded my body and caffeine burst in my brain. "What are you, a certified alkie?"

"Must we do this every time, Skylark? You are well aware that this is merely a psychic projection, an ectoplasmic image of our first encounter. I shouldn't need to explain it yet again. This," he spread his arms, "is not what you get in person. It's unchangeable, like a photograph. Now." He uncrossed his legs and set his hands on the chair arms. His eyes hardened. "Can we dispense with the childish nonsense and get down to business, please?"

"We have business? You want to hire me?" I gave him a smirk. "I'm not sure you can afford my rates."

Ehrler closed his eyes and shook his head. I sipped my coffee and let the silence lengthen.

"You've always been a challenge, right from day one," he murmured.

"Maybe because I don't want what you're offering. Never have and never will. So, you can take back your 'psychic gifts,'" I air quoted the words with my free hand, "and leave me alone."

"I didn't give you your abilities, you know that. They're part of who you are. I am merely here to help you learn how to fully use them."

"Yeah, yeah, so you say." I waved his words off. "What is it this time? And don't tell me some new freak-ability is being dumped on me. I've got problems enough with the ones I already have."

"No, no new abilities for you, not at this point. But there will be a new person arriving in your life, one you need to listen to. Her words will hold the key. Pay attention to this, Skylark. She will be the beginning of the next phase of your life."

I popped up from the couch and set one fist on my hip. I clutched the poor coffee mug so tight it's a wonder it didn't break apart in my hand.

"Oh, my God, will you give it a rest, Ehrler? No new phases. Absolutely *not*. I'm not buying what you're selling. I did that once, when I was young and stupid. I'm not either now, not anymore."

"You cannot fight what you are, Skylark. And you cannot ignore your destiny. The hit you got off the glasses was just an indication—"

"Thanks for the heads-up, Ehrler." I curled my free hand into a fist, my heart thudding. How the hell did he know about the glasses? Then again, how did he ever know about anything concerning me? "But you're too late. I'm dropping the thing with the glasses. It's got nothing to do with me. Not anymore. I'm having Garrett take them back to where they belong and I'm going on with my life. *Without* any new phases. *End* of story."

"I don't think so, Skylark." He began to fade. "This is just the beginning. She's waiting for you, waiting to usher you into your future. Pay attention..."

"I'll usher myself into my own future!" I yelled at him as his image wavered into points of light. Damn, how I wished I could slug him. "And you owe me a mug!"

The lights vanished, leaving behind echoes of his laughter. And leaving me trembling, worried about the meaning of his pronouncement. Ehrler's arrival always meant more psychic crap messing up my life, and his messages were always cryptic, like there was some messed-up kind of psychic law against clarity. Just who would I be meeting, what the hell kind of "key" did this person hold, and what "new phase" was in store for me? With the cops dogging my heels and stolen evidence in my hands, the very last thing I needed in my life was more of what Dunwitty called "woo-woo-shit."

Damn, look at her, she's not much bigger than a minute, Dunwitty thought when the apartment door swung open to reveal the slender, elfin-like creature who dwelled within. Though he knew his size dwarfed most people, especially women, this woman—girl, really, he figured she was barely out of her teens—couldn't possibly be an inch over five feet tall.

"Miss Hurley? Heather Hurley?"

"It's Mrs. Hurley, I got married a couple of months ago," she murmured, looking both anguished and terrified. Her deep blue eyes were puffy and blood shot. Her full lips trembled. Straight auburn hair arrowed down to kiss the tops of her shoulders; deep bangs cut across her forehead just above her eyebrows. Her nail-bitten fingers tightened on the door's edge.

"I'm Detective Dunwitty. This is my partner, Detective Soto."

Dunwitty held out his Sheriff's Department ID, as did Soto. Hurley's eyes filled with tears. Blinking, she opened the door wider and stepped back to allow Dunwitty and Soto entrance to the apartment. Without a word, she shut the door behind them, then led them into a minuscule living room and gestured at the couch.

"I don't have a lot of time, I have classes today, starting at eight-thirty. But I have coffee on." Her voice was as quiet and tiny as her body. "Can I get you some?"

Dunwitty declined, but Soto smiled and nodded.

"Just black would be great, thanks," he said.

They watched her hesitate, then turn and vanish down a hallway, presumably into the kitchen. Dunwitty turned his gaze to the room, assessing both the contents and the owner who'd arranged them. Neat, almost obsessively so, not a thing out of place in the sparsely furnished room. A couch and one armchair, both upholstered in dark beige faux suede, between them a round coffee table made from a slab of wood rimmed with bark. Built-in shelves covered one wall, holding books that looked to be arranged according to size rather than subject or author. A small, flat-screen TV—not much over 20", Dunwitty estimated—was mounted on the back wall, and a small basket loaded with various balls of yarn perched on a tiny stand in one corner. A pair of knitting needles stuck up from the yarn like antennae. There were blinds on the front—the only—window; no curtains softened their angular silhouette. One knitted afghan in blue and cream centered itself on the back of the couch, which didn't look as though it had been sat on in ages.

Nothing else. No dirt, no dust, no newspapers, no discarded books or food wrappers, only one picture on the walls of the happy couple in wedding garb. No paintings or other photographs anywhere except one on the bookshelf. It felt very OCD to Dunwitty, nothing like most young people's exuberant, messy living spaces.

Dunwitty walked over to the built-in unit. There, at his chest level—Heather Hurley's eye level, he realized—sat a framed photo of two young women at some kind of party, holding glasses of something frothy he could tell they were not old enough to be drinking. Wide semi-drunken grins on their faces. An arm around each other. Heather Hurley and Heidi Coffey.

He heard Heather Hurley returning before she appeared in the archway.

"Are you sure you won't—"

She broke off when she saw that neither detective had yet seated himself. She stood holding a steaming mug, her head swiveling from Soto to Dunwitty, alarm on her face. Soto stepped forward and took the mug from her.

"Thank you," he said, his tone soft and soothing. "That smells divine."

He gave her his most charming grin, then took her arm and led her to the armchair before seating himself on the couch. Dunwitty grabbed the photograph and brought it back with him.

"Does anyone else live here with you, other than your husband?" he asked, studying the slant of her shoulders, the tip of her head; someone a bit uneasy around law enforcement, or perhaps just the situation, but not exhibiting any noticeable sense of guilt.

"No. My parents died when I was four. A plane crash. My grandmother raised me. I lost her last year. We'd moved from Santa Maria to SLO when I started high school. I met my husband in chemistry class last year. At Cal Poly."

Dunwitty dropped onto the couch beside Soto and set the picture frame on the coffee table.

"You two were good friends." It wasn't a question, but she nodded as though in answer. "Mrs. Hurley—"

"Heather, please call me Heather. Mrs. Hurley just... I don't know." She shrugged. "It still sounds weird."

She tried to smile and failed; her voice still shook. She sat rigid, dwarfed by the chair, her hands clasped so tight her fingers looked white. Dunwitty smiled at her.

"All right, Heather, thank you. You said you had some information for us when you called?"

"I-I probably shouldn't have bothered you, Dennis said not to, it's nothing, really. I just..." Tears again threatened and she swallowed hard, then drew in a few deep breaths. "I can't believe she's gone, just gone. Why would someone take her? Where can she be?"

"That's what we're working to find out," Soto said, again using his quiet, soothing voice. "We don't know why she's missing, and we want to make sure she gets home again, safe and sound. I'm glad you called. Anything you can tell us, no matter how small or insignificant it may seem to you, could be the one thing we need to find her."

"You knew her well?" Dunwitty asked, then clenched his teeth when she winced at the past tense. Damn, he wished he had Soto's finesse in these situations. "I mean, you're close friends, you two?"

"Yes." Heather nodded. "Best friends, since high school. We're like sisters. We tell each other everything. Share everything. Just... everything."

Heather closed her eyes, obviously fighting her emotion. Silence fell. Soto sipped his coffee. Dunwitty studied the photograph. Finally, Heather sighed.

"What did she tell you?" Soto asked.

Heather blinked at Soto, looking startled.

"How did you know...?"

She lifted the back of her hand to her lips for a moment, then sighed out another breath. Hands once again clasped, she pulled up her shoulders.

"She said she'd met someone, at the bar. Her uncle's bar, Kelley's?"

The detectives nodded. Heidi took in a deep breath and let her shoulders drop on the exhale.

"Three days before she disappeared she filled in for the regular waitress who was sick, spring flu or something. She said he seemed so nice at first. Walked her to her car, for safety, he said, 'cause it was so late. The next night he asked her to dinner. Heidi expected a restaurant, but he took her on a picnic at the beach, in Morro Bay, right around sunset. There wasn't anyone else around, and she felt a bit uncomfortable, being alone with some guy she didn't really know. He said he liked being on the beach because of his work, something with marine biology."

Heather paused and looked at both detectives.

"Heidi said he asked all kinds of questions about her; how many friends she had, how big a family, how often she worked at the bar. She said anytime she asked about the ocean, his answers sounded like he didn't really know much about it. She started feeling spooked. When they were done eating, Heidi told him she was tired and had a paper due and needed to go home."

"Did he argue with her or seem upset about her cutting the evening short?" Dunwitty asked.

"No," Heather shook her head. "Heidi said he just nodded then packed things right up, kind of fast, like he wanted to be rid of her or something, though he was still nice to her, and polite. That spooked her, too. But what really made her feel weird was when he dropped her off. He put his hand on the back of her head like he wanted to kiss her, but all he did was stare into her eyes. Then he told her next time he'd like to have dinner at his cabin. He said..."

Heather closed her eyes and the two detectives looked at each other.

"'You'd really like my cabin, baby. It's just made for you.'" She opened her eyes and looked at them. "That's what she told me he said. That's kind of weird, isn't it?"

"I'd say so." Dunwitty nodded. A cabin made for someone the guy'd just met? That definitely landed on the weird end of the scale.

"She said he had a funny look in his eyes, kind of empty and blank, like no one was home, you know? Then he smiled and the look vanished and she wasn't sure she'd really seen it or not, it was kind of dark in the car. Then he kissed her cheek and said he'd call her. She told me she got out of the car as fast as she could and didn't look back until she was inside with the door locked and bolted. When she looked out the window, he'd already driven away. I told her to forget about him and she said she'd already decided never to see him again."

Heather looked at the picture on the coffee table. She shivered and wrapped her arms around her torso.

"Do you think *he's* the one who kidnapped her?"

"We don't know she's been kidnapped, but this guy is definitely worth looking into," Soto said, setting his mug on the coffee table. "Did she tell you his name?"

"Uh, Jerry, I think. She only said it once..." She frowned. Her eyes moved back and forth as she searched her memory. "Yes, Jerry, I'm sure of it. She didn't mention a last name. I should have asked her more questions."

She looked up at them, her unspoken *I'm sorry for not knowing more* seeming to echo in the room around them.

"Sounds like she told you everything she could. Is there anything else?" Dunwitty asked.

Heather shook her head. Slow tears began to dribble down her face. Dunwitty rose and pulled a card from his pocket.

"You can reach me at this number anytime, if you think of anything else, no matter how small. This has been a real help, Heather. You've given us a lot to look into."

"Don't get up," Soto said as he rose. "We'll let ourselves out. You take care, Heather. We'll find her for you, I promise."

They left the girl sitting in her puddle of misery and walked out to Dunwitty's car. Not until they belted themselves in and Dunwitty fired the engine did he speak.

"You shouldn't promise things you can't deliver on."

"Yeah, I know." Soto sighed and ran a hand through his dark hair. "I just couldn't stand seeing her so unhappy. And I only promised to find Heidi, not to find her alive. Hopefully, we can at least do that much. Find her."

They drove back toward the station in silence, Dunwitty fearing there was no way they'd find Heidi Coffey alive. Not after all this time. It had already been a week since she'd vanished. When they'd parked in the station lot, he turned to look at his partner.

"Well, if this Jerry is our guy, if he's responsible for Heidi's disappearance... Probably took her to that cabin he mentioned. Somewhere out of the way, isolated, where no one would hear any screams. That increases our search area exponentially. She might not even be in San Luis County."

"Well, it's more than we had yesterday." Soto shrugged. "A direction, at least. Let's go see how many Jerrys we can find who own cabins somewhere in the wilds along the Central Coast."

Yeah, all 350 miles of it, Dunwitty thought as he followed his partner into the station.

CHAPTER SIXTEEN

"I think I found the bitch," Carstairs called through the open door to the back room as he sorted through the items that lined his bookshelf. "Almost didn't bother with the phone book, since I don't know her last name. But I thought, what the heck? Why not try? And I found a business called 'Skylark Investigations'. Only gave a phone number, though, no address. I figured that was probably her, given the name, but there was no way to know for sure, since I didn't want to risk calling."

His little angel had been a very bad girl today, trying to dig through the wall to release the bolts that held her chains. He couldn't imagine where she'd gotten the screw she'd been using. He'd police the room better from now on—after he dealt with his angel. She needed a very strong object lesson, more than the few hard smacks he'd already administered. He listened to her whimper as his hand passed over the stun gun, the lighter, the cigarettes, the knife, the nails. He rejected each item.

"And I couldn't ask around about her, in case anyone remembered me, you know? That would never do. I spent some time driving around the town, just looking, hoping to spot her, but no joy." He laughed as he continued his search among the shelves. "I just love that expression, don't you? It really says it all."

He walked to the kitchen area, picked up a bottle, and took a deep swig of beer, a local brew the shift supervisor on the morgue job had raved about. The stuff wasn't as good as the man had claimed, but it wasn't bad. Had a nice aftertaste Carstairs liked, and half a bottle had already given him a warm buzz. He stood a minute, watching the beagle puppy he'd acquired a few days ago cower in her cage in the corner. The way a dog should.

"Then I got lucky when I stopped at the coffee shop. A casual remark to the idiot behind the counter and wham! Got what I needed. She uses the place as an office. I'm sure it's her, now I just gotta wait til she shows up again, then follow her home." Anger began to boil inside him, and he kicked the cage. The dog yelped. "I can't believe the bitch is a P.I. It's not right." He kicked the bars a second time. "Another woman horning in on a man's work, forcing him into unemployment. Ruining good work with her so-called feminine wiles, all that women's intuition crap."

He finished the beer and slammed the bottle onto the counter. The rage had built to towering proportions; it felt like a volcano getting ready to blow. He could barely breathe. Damned women, always ruining things for men with their smart mouths and their frigging need for 'independence.' Thinking they can do everything better than men. And the way they kept their legs shut tight unless a guy greased them open with money. Or dropped to his knees and begged for what was his by right. It was so fucking wrong.

But not this guy, he thought, *not any more. No stupid woman is gonna get the better of me ever again.* It was his game, now, and he held all the cards. Just the thought calmed him down enough to be able to breathe again.

He stalked back to the bookshelf and found what he needed. He felt the volcano rumble again, but it didn't matter. He was in control this time. He grinned.

"You and me, babe, we got a problem to discuss." He picked up a knit ski mask and pulled it down over his face. "You got a lesson to learn. And we're gonna film it, so other women can learn it, too."

He picked up a ten-inch length of pipe and walked into the room where a bruised and bloody Heidi writhed on the floor, begging him not to hurt her. He looked at the camera and winked; it tickled him no end that he'd decided to post these sessions to the internet. No reason he should be the only one to benefit from Heidi's training, which is why he'd purchased the mask. And gotten the fucking dog. *How To Train A Bitch,* he'd call his show. He'd alternate between the beagle and the woman, just for variety. And because he loved the double entendre: Canine bitch—human bitch. He hoped both Heidi and the mutt would be very naughty little girls, and need a lot of training.

"Come on, Babe, it's lesson time," he said. "Smile pretty for the camera."

He released the chains from the wall and dragged Heidi across the room. He hauled her onto the bed and affixed the chains to the bedframe. Then he climbed on top of her, shoved her legs apart, and positioned the pipe just so. He looked at the camera.

"This, bitches, is what happens when you don't obey your man," he crooned.

Giving his invisible audience one more wink, he turned back to Heidi and began thrusting the pipe. Heidi's shriek split the air.

No matter how many times I called Reenie's cell, day or night, she wouldn't pick up. I cursed Caller ID to the deepest depths of hell and finally, around 4:00 pm on Wednesday, bit the bullet and phoned her office. The dragon who guarded the gate—Reenie's personal assistant—had hated me since the day we'd met, so I wasn't sure how far I'd get with her. Still, I did my best to suck up: kept my snark to a minimum, used my indoor voice, and even said please. Granted, it was jammed behind clenched teeth, but at least I'd said it.

"I'm sorry, no," Danielle chirped even before I'd had time to finish my request, not sounding the least bit sincere. On the contrary, she sounded tickled pink. "Ms. Overton has left strict orders for me *not* to put you through to her, not for any reason. *Or* to listen to your begging."

Begging? No way in hell. I closed my eyes and huffed out a breath at her snide intonation. I was sure she'd stuck her pointy nose high in the air, too. I took a deep breath and quickly spoke before she cut the connection.

"Just give her two words, Danielle, that's all. Two words: Dunwitty, and lawsuit." Silence answered me, but I could hear her breathing so I knew she hadn't hung up —yet. "You can manage that much, can't you? It is only two words. Let me repeat them for you: Dunwitty; Lawsuit."

A sharp click echoed in my ear and I wondered to what desperate lengths I'd now have to go to get Reenie to talk to me. Pull my Glock on her, maybe, or nuke her house or something. But the phone rang not ten minutes later—Danielle, not Reenie—and I received curt orders to meet the woman who was supposed to be my best friend, but who wouldn't talk to me, at Starbucks late the next afternoon.

Okay, I thought as I put the appointment on my calendar app, *I'll take what I can get. She just better not bring the dragon with her.*

It didn't start out a fun meeting, though Thursday began on a positive note. The phone skewered me back to the land of the living just after ten-thirty that morning. I was usually up by seven, but not having any work had really thrown off my circadian rhythms—or maybe it was all the Glenlivet I'd imbibed the night before—and I groped for the offending item from beneath my blanket cocoon.

"Skylark Investigations."

It came out a bit rumbly-grumbly, and was met by a deep chuckle.

"You still in bed at this hour, Miss Lark? Business that bad, or did you drink your dinner again last night?"

I sat up and swung my feet over the side of the bed. All thought of hermiting vanished in a flash, though the headache lingered, tsk-tsking at me for having the gall to move.

"Duff, you old coot. How are you?"

I'd trained with Peter Dufferin—who'd sent Araceli Aguayo my way—down in Santa Barbara, cut my investigator teeth under his tutelage. He had fifteen years on me, I stood four inches taller than he did, and snark sparks had flown between us since day one. I'd never called him anything but Duff, and he'd always separated my one name into two. He was like the quirky uncle I'd never had. He'd whined when I rejected his offer of permanent employment, said he'd never forgive my betrayal, but had belied that sentiment by referring whatever work he could to help me get established. I wondered now if Araceli Aguayo had called and given him an earful after Dunwitty's interruption of our initial meeting.

"Couldn't be better, Miss Lark. Full plate down here. How's your calendar?"

So, it wasn't a complaint. Good.

"Got a few holes in it," I said, not about to let him know the huge gaping nothing that was my life at the moment. "I can fit you in if I juggle things a bit. What d'you need?"

"Client with a skip-trace, but the mark is up in your neighborhood. Figured I could save the guy some bread by not sending any of my operatives after him. You got time to take it on?"

"Sure." My tone was a bit tentative, since skip-traces were mostly done online these days. I wasn't sure why Duff had chosen to sub this one out to me. I picked up the pen I kept on my nightstand and took down the details as he dictated them. "So what's the timeline on this?"

"Whatever you and Rosen agree on, Sky, it's your case now."

"Mine? Uh... thanks, Duff." He'd handed the entire case over, not just hired me to do his legwork; that really made me wonder. "Who you been talking to?"

"Lord a'mighty, woman, can't you just take a gift in the spirit it's offered? Teach me to do nice things for people," he added in his best curmudgeonly tone.

"I *said thanks*, Duff. You getting so old you can't hear anymore?"

"Don't be a smart-ass, Sky. It's just..." He paused and I wondered if maybe Garrett had been telling tales out of school. "I worry about you, Miss Lark, all alone up in the wilds of SLO County."

"Yeah." I snorted. "It's a real drag being so far from civilization. But don't worry, Duff, I hear tell we'll be getting electricity and running water any year now."

We insulted back and forth for a few more minutes —our standard way of showing affection—then said good-bye. I headed in for a shower, then forced myself to sop up any lingering booze by fixing a bowl of oatmeal for breakfast instead of relying on my usual: just coffee. It's hard to jiggle computer keys into readable words with shaking hands. I'd just finished the bowl when the phone rang again, this time the manager of a local branch of a national insurance company who needed deep background checks on three prospective employees.

Things were definitely looking up: two new jobs and Reenie agreeing to speak with me. I felt like throwing a party but couldn't think of anyone to invite

—who might actually come—then thought maybe I'd call Garrett and tell him to ditch those glasses. Before I could, the phone rang once more and that devil thing worked again.

"I'll pick you up tomorrow at eleven-thirty." Garrett's deep voice rolled into me, sans hello, how are you, or any kind of personal identification.

"And what if it hadn't been me who answered the phone?"

"Who else would pick up your cell phone? It's not like it ever leaves your side."

He had me there, so I went with the obvious.

"That's true. Uh, who is this?"

"Don't be a smart-ass, Skylark. Just be ready tomorrow. Eleven-thirty."

"Okay. Where are we going, Garrett? Is this about the gla—"

He cut the connection, leaving me with an uncomfortable mix of curiosity and annoyance. And I had to meet Reenie in less than an hour, which was really winding up my nerves. I tried deep breathing exercises, then a few Aikido moves—the physicality involved usually soothed my inner beast—but nothing worked. I left for my appointment with Reenie with my nerves still strung painfully taut. I just hoped I could keep myself in check and not alienate her more than I already had.

 *CHAPTER SEVENTEEN*

Reenie was about ten minutes late, but then I'd been more than twenty minutes early, so to me the wait felt like forever. The place was, surprisingly for the hour, half empty; I was able to camp out at what I considered "my" table, a two-fer set in isolation in the back corner, away from the other, larger tables. It sometimes surprised me that the staff, knowing I met clients here, didn't post a *Reserved* sign on the thing.

More than one patron sent amused looks my way; heads tilted close, and fingers pointed. Even the guy in the lounge chair near the front door got in on the act. Mr. Non-descript—and trust me, there was nothing at all remarkable about him—kept looking up from his newspaper and sending secretive little smirks my way. My half-nude infamy had obviously preceeded me. I was staring into my second cup of high octane, positive Reenie'd stood me up and just about to flee the fishbowl, when the reason for this little jaunt out into the big, cruel world appeared beside the chair opposite me, coffee cup in hand.

"Hi," was all she said.

I looked up and gave her as much of a smile as I could muster, which wasn't more than a slight stretch of my lips. My heart gave a painful thud, then both it and my nerves eased up. Damn, it was good to see her. Yes, I know it had only been four days since she'd walked out, but it had felt to me like a year or more. She smiled back at me, her smile wider and more easy-looking than mine felt, then sank onto the chair.

"Reenie, I—"

She held up a hand, stopping my words.

"No. Let's just keep it to business, Skylark, okay?"

My smile died. I stared at her as a scalding wave of hurt corkscrewed through my body. She had no idea what I was about to say, and obviously didn't want to know. It could have been that I would drop looking into the murder, which I'm sure was what she was waiting for. It wasn't, but it could have been. I took a deep breath and turned my head away.

"Fine," I said, my voice almost a hiss. "If that's what you want, then that's what we'll do. Business."

I turned back to her as I spat out the last word and she blinked at me, as though surprised by my reaction. Well, hell, she wasn't the only one who could do angry. And if she wasn't careful, there'd be two of us who had a lot to get over before we could get back on an even footing. If we ever could.

Then Garrett's words echoed in my head—*give her time*—and I clenched my teeth before taking a slow breath in an effort to tamp down my anger. I'd give her time, all right, but I sure as hell wasn't going to be the one to break the uncomfortable silence that had fallen. After an eternity-long moment, Reenie took a sip of her foamy concoction—she was a total girly-girl when it came to her coffee—and nodded.

"So," she said, an amused glitter in her eyes. "Dunwitty? Lawsuit?"

I couldn't help my answering grin. This one was definitely full-on.

"You better believe it."

"I wondered if it would motivate you." I frowned at her, and she clarified. "I saw your picture on Facebook. And Instagram. And Twitter. And—"

"Yeah," I sent a glower her way, "you and about two million other people."

"I think you were even 'trending' for a couple of days." She grinned full out at me, her fingers busy air quoting. "Might even have hit a few porno sites as well."

"Social media should be banned. And damned to hell," I growled.

"I assume that's what brought about this change of mind?"

"Absolutely. Dunwitty had no right to drag me out of my house like that. He should have let me get dressed, at least."

"And because he didn't, we all got to see way too much of you."

Her grin widened even more; damn, she was loving my humiliation way too much. My hands tightened on my cardboard cup and it crushed between my fingers. Good thing I'd almost finished it, or I'd have been wearing its contents. I narrowed my eyes and unclenched my jaw enough to speak. I wondered if she could see the steam I could feel shooting out my ears. My voice came out in a harsh growl.

"I want to take him down, Reenie. Destroy him. Make him hurt. Take everything he's got, and all the stuff he doesn't, too."

"Well," Reenie gave me a nod, one regal dip of her head: down, up, "it's about time you came to your senses. What about the county? You're not still going to let them off easy, are you?"

I looked down and fiddled with my crumpled cup, trying to fit the plastic top back on. A losing battle.

"I don't really have anything against the county." I glanced up and saw Reenie's expression harden, so I let my voice do the same. "But then, they did hire the jerk, didn't they?"

"They did." Her expression froze; her eyes grew watchful.

"And they should have fired him, long before what he did to me. But they just keep letting him run loose."

"So...?" Reenie stared into my eyes. Her lips twitched.

"So, I'd say they're fair game, too. But I'm not sure what that means, money-wise, I'm too pissed to be rational about it. So, whatever you decide, I'll go along with. For all of it. Do whatever you think is right. Just... don't try to make this into a landmark case, Reenie. Be fair about it, as much as you can. Please." I smiled and kowtowed to her with head and hands. "Oh, great and wise legal guru."

"Well, it's about time you admitted that." Reenie laughed out loud. Mr. Non-descript looked up and frowned; I watched as he folded his newspaper, rose, and ambled out of the shop. "You can be so dense at times."

"Yeah, unlike some people around here."

"Bite your tongue."

This time I laughed with her. Then we rose and hugged, and it felt like the winter ice had melted, especially when she whispered in my ear that she loved me. And had missed me. I promised not to compromise her ethics again, and together we headed out to the parking lot and our cars. I was in the middle of telling her about my conversation with Duff when I saw it—my classic 1980 Jeep CJ7, sitting lopsided on the blacktop.

"What the hell?" I started to rush forward. Reenie pulled me back, out of the path of an oncoming car I hadn't noticed. "If someone smashed into my baby..."

My heart thudded and I could barely breathe as we circled around the vehicle. It took me a moment to realize what had happened, since there was no sign of any damage on the body itself. Nor had anyone invaded the interior. But three of the tires were flat as pancakes, the wheels sitting down on their rims. Three of them. At the same time. Three of the high-end set that had emptied my coffers not six months before, and that had carried me just fine the whole mile-and-a-half to Starbucks.

"Running over something in the street couldn't do all this, not unless it was a spike strip." I waved at the lopsided vehicle. "A nail or piece of glass might flatten one tire, maybe, but not three."

"You're right. This looks deliberate." Reenie nodded. "I'd say someone's pretty unhappy with you, Skylark."

"You don't mean..." I turned and stared at her. "*Him*?" Rage began building inside me. My whole body shook. I began to hyperventilate. "Damn that Dunwitty, I'll kill him, I swear I will!"

"Calm down."

"Calm down?" I screeched; I was practically spitting, I was so angry. I groped in my purse for my gun, praying Dunwitty would show his face. "After what he did to my car? He's a dead man, Reenie, he—"

"Listen to me. It wasn't Dunwitty, Skylark. It *wasn't*." Reenie put a hand on my arm and my breathing eased a bit, though I still felt like I might pass out. Still, I released the gun and let it slip back into the purse.

"It damn well was," I growled, scanning the parking lot for his huge, hulking form. No way would he not be around to see what his handiwork did to me.

"No, you're wrong. I wouldn't put it past him, but I really don't think he did this. He knows he's already on thin ice with you—and me—especially since I gave him an earful after seeing you online, barely dressed." I blinked at her; I hadn't realized she had intervened with Dunwitty on my behalf. "No, this smacks of someone other than Dunwitty. Someone even more twisted." She pulled out her cell and punched in 9-1-1. "Who else have you been screwing with lately?"

She gave me a saucy grin that I so wanted to wipe off her face. But I refrained. We'd just made up, and I didn't want to fracture our fragile peace. Not yet, at least. While she called it in, I steadied my breathing then crouched down to inspect the tires. They'd been slashed all right, all three of them; long, deliberate—and unrepairable—gashes that had opened up the sidewalls. We stood silent, Reenie's presence keeping me under control—I was still so angry I'd have happily wrung the neck of anyone who looked sideways at me—while we waited for the cops. Once I calmed down enough to talk without screaming, I called Smitty's, the only repair shop I'd let touch my ride—nothing but the best for my Jeep—and Mark said he'd send out a tow truck in about half an hour. Fifteen minutes later, two uniforms showed up. I breathed a sigh of relief. I'd feared it might be Dunwitty, and I wasn't sure I could restrain myself in the face of his delighted smirk.

The uniforms took a report, little as it was, and a few pictures of the tires, then walked around a bit to see if they could find any witnesses. I knew they were just going through the motions; in a busy shopping center lot, with everyone on a spending mission, nobody hung around looking at cars or even other people. All someone needed to do was, with knife at the ready, pretend to drop something, crouch down to pick it up, and slash away. Then stand up again, unnoticed and free to walk off uncollared.

The uniforms took off just as Smitty's truck arrived and loaded up my baby. Reenie offered to drive me home, sparing me the long, mile-and-a-half, sidewalk-less trudge. Which was a good thing, since I couldn't see very clearly with all those tears in my eyes from watching my Jeep hauled away like a pile of trash.

"So," she said as she pulled out onto Los Osos Valley Road, "what about those glasses?"

"Don't ask me." I shrugged, startled she'd brought up the subject. "I don't have them anymore. Garrett took them."

"Really? What did he do with them?"

"I don't know," I said, grateful I could answer truthfully, without any fudging. "I haven't a clue. And I haven't asked him, either. Haven't even wanted to."

Okay, maybe a little fudging.

"Good. You scared me, Skylark, taking them like that."

"I know. I'm sorry, Reenie."

And I was—sorry I had scared her, not that I took them. But I didn't bother making it clear for her, just let her interpret my apology as I knew she would. After all, why bother being imprecise if you're going to ruin it by offering clarification?

We turned left onto Palomino, as did the older pickup behind us, then pulled into my driveway. The Silverado—black, or maybe dark navy—continued down the street and disappeared around the curve, and I wondered who the driver was visiting. There were only three houses around the bend, and I didn't remember seeing that truck before. Not that I was privy to every car that belonged on the street, but still.

Not wanting to let Reenie go until I confirmed our reconciliation, I made arrangements to have dinner with her at the Galley Seafood Bar & Grill in Morro Bay on Sunday night. She agreed and I breathed a silent sigh of relief; she truly was back in my corner. She said she'd call and twist Garrett's arm to join us, then put the car in reverse. I stood in front of the house until she backed out, then waved to her as she drove away, turning right onto Los Osos Valley Road for her five-minute journey back to her aerie-like home in Cabrillo Estates.

I was heading for the mailbox beside the entrance to my driveway when the pickup came back around the curve. The driver's head kept twisting, as though he was searching for an address. Or maybe a cross street that didn't exist. Every day we got a few drivers who thought they could use our street as a shortcut—for some reason discounting the "No Outlet" sign on the corner—then had to turn around and retrace their route.

With the westering sun in my eyes, I couldn't tell much more than it was a man, not young and not old. He'd turned his head to the opposite side of the street when he passed me, so I couldn't see his face. He didn't seem beefy or look too short or too tall in the seat. Average, I'd have said if asked. Nondescript.

He didn't stop to ask questions or slow down or even look over at me, just accelerated on toward the main road. In my peripheral I saw his turn signal flash for a right turn as I headed back toward my side door, mail in hand. Mourning my Jeep, I went on into the house to check my bank balance to see if I could pay for a full round of new tires without having to sell everything I owned.

CHAPTER EIGHTEEN

"Well, aren't you cheerful this morning," Garrett said the next day when I bounced out of the house and into his car. "And you haven't even talked to me yet."

"I do have a life outside of you, you know." I gave him my best arch look and stuck my nose in the air. "Reenie and I made up and—"

"Yes, she called me. We're doing dinner on Sun—"

"—*And*—" he wasn't the only one who could step on people's words, "Araceli Aguayo called last night and said she changed her mind. Did an electronic transfer of the retainer and everything. So now I have three jobs, money coming in, and Dunwitty by the short hairs." I grinned and stretched my arms above my head. "And tomorrow afternoon I'll have my Jeep back. Life is *so good*."

"Yeah. Reenie told me about the lawsuit, too." Garrett stopped at the corner, looked both ways, then hung a right onto Los Osos Valley Road. "She's asking for mega-bucks, baby. You'll be set for life. I guess your on-line porno act was worth it."

"You are such a jerk."

I smacked him a good one, but not even his teasing sarcasm could dampen my mood. Thanks to Araceli Aguayo's change of heart—and her retainer—I could afford to bail out my Jeep and still have enough left over to buy a week's worth of groceries. And I'd already made good headway on her problem this morning; the internet was truly a Godsend for those of us who knew how to use it in all the wrong ways. My spidey sense had started tingling not half an hour into the research. I knew I was on to something big, though Miss Aguayo might not be happy to hear it. I wasn't any closer to discovering who was doing the damage, but I was pretty sure I knew how it was being done.

Garrett swung off Los Osos Valley Road toward Starbucks, but he passed the coffee shop building on the left and headed on toward the two-story L-shaped office complex that sat toward the back of the lot on the right.

"Hey, you missed Starbucks," I said, turning to look at my caffeine-distribution center.

My spidey sense started tingling again, and not in a good way. I knew what was housed in that office complex, and I don't mean the pizza place, the accountant or the insurance agent. Or the real estate office. My eyes narrowed.

"Just where are we going?"

"You'll see." Said with smug look and teasing tone. He pulled the car into a slot and shut off the engine, then took the infamous purloined reading glasses out of the center console. "Come on, let's go."

He was so not being serious, was he? I sat still, waiting until he stood outside my door with arms crossed and annoyance flickering across his face before I unfastened my seatbelt and got out to join him. I matched his crossed-arm stance and glared at him.

"Okay, what are we doing *here*?"

"We're seeing what's up with these things." He waved the glasses in my face. "I thought you wanted to know."

"I am *not* going in *there*."

I looked up at the second story of the office building, at the window we were parked beneath, with its black and red sign decorated with arcane symbols. *Psychic Lillia*, it read. *Palmistry and Psychometry*. The Open sign flashed sedately in a corner: amber - white - blue - amber.

"Why not? She can read these, tell us what they mean."

"She can't do *anything*, Garrett, she's a *fortune-teller*."

"So?"

He started for the building. I trailed behind, wanting nothing more than to whack some sense into his head.

"Are you kidding me? None of what she does is real, and you know it. These so-called psychics, they're all scam artists!"

He stopped and turned incredulous eyes on me.

"How can you say that? You, of all people, with your powers, what you can do."

"At least mine are *real*. And I don't use them to bilk unsuspecting people out of their hard-earned money. Not like," I glared up at the window, "her!"

"You don't know anything about her." Garrett grabbed my arm and hauled me with him into the building and up the stairs. "I've heard that she's legiti-mate."

"Yeah," I muttered, unable to pull my arm from his grasp. Damn, he'd leave bruises and Dunwitty's still hadn't fully faded. "A legitimate *fake*."

He pulled me to a stop in front of the door to Psychic Lillia's lair.

"Just keep your snarky mouth shut and let's see what she says, what she can tell us about the glasses."

"Fine. But I'm not paying her, *you* are."

"Fine."

"Fine!"

We glared at each other, then he opened the door and waited until I entered before stepping in behind me and shutting the door with a sharp crack. Okay, yeah, he was pissed, but so was I. With all I had to do on my three new cases, I was about to waste who-knew-how-many-hours-long-minutes suffering through some charlatan's psycho-babble. I knew how it would go: *I see someone dark and handsome in your future, keep an eye out for him, that'll be a hundred bucks.*

The waiting room wasn't what I expected, though. No weird artwork on the walls. No pentagrams or Celtic symbols. No dark, arcane colors. No warbling, mystic music. Instead, it resembled any legitimate business waiting area, with soft pastel blue walls, chairs and a couch upholstered in a blue and rose flower print, dark oak end tables, and a glass coffee table on which were scattered a selection of magazines. They, however, lived up to expectation—I noted issues of *The Psychic, Palmistry, Mind-Reading,* and others I didn't want to know the names of.

I was about to turn around and leave, even if I had to knock Garrett on his ass to do so, when the inner door opened.

"Mr. Gallivan? You're right on time," a smoky voice behind me said. I grimaced; she had the scam-artist personna down to a 'T'. "Please, come right in."

Garrett glared at me and I rolled my eyes. Then I turned to face the so-called psychic.

She, too, was not what I expected. No flowing robe, no turban, no jangling jewelry. She stood maybe five-feet-seven and was slightly plump. Dark blue eyes gleamed in a heart-shaped face. Her long, dishwater-blonde hair was parted in the middle and held back at the sides with glittering cat-shaped clips. She wore a yellow and green sundress, topped by a crocheted cardigan, and wedge-soled sandals on her feet. She looked more like an elementary school teacher than a cold, calculating scam artist.

Garrett gestured me to preceed him and I walked into the inner sanctum, again expecting the trappings of Lillia's pseudo profession. And again, I was mostly disappointed; the small room was almost barren, the walls off white, a circular brown rug on the tile floor. A small white round Formica table sat in the center of the rug, three straight chairs grouped together on one side, opposite a lone one. Centered on the table was a stand holding at least one of the things I'd expected, a crystal ball.

But nothing else. No drapes, no artwork, no arcane symbols, no other psychic paraphernalia, not even Tarot cards or a Ouija board. No discreetly hidden speakers peeking from the ceiling, no cabinets to hide other tricks. Just what kind of "psychic" was this woman?

"Please, have a seat," Lillia said, gesturing to the trio of chairs.

We sat and I watched her drift around the table to sit opposite us. Drift is the only way I can describe the way she walked, never quite seeming to touch the floor, her body swaying as though in an unfelt gentle breeze. *Interesting,* I thought, wondering how long it had taken her to perfect that portion of her performance.

Garrett set the glasses on the table. Lillia looked at them without touching them.

"What can you tell us about these?" he asked. I rolled my eyes and asked my own question.

"How much is this going to cost us?"

I stared at Lillia's eyes, looking for the tell-tale flickers that would betray her, but I found none. Hers remained steady and calm.

"It depends on the glasses," she said. I rolled my eyes again and Lillia smiled, her full lips curving up into a cupid's bow. Oh, wasn't she just so sweet? "What I mean is, if I can't get any useful information for you, there won't be any charge."

"And if you *do*? How much *then*?"

"Stop." Garrett's warning tone stepped on my words. Lillia just laughed.

"No, it's fine. Most people who come here are skeptics. Many have been cheated before by others like me, those who are just in it for the money, and who don't really have any actual powers. That's not me."

She took a deep breath and stared right into my eyes. I felt the room shift around me; I lost awareness of everything but that blue gaze staring into me, and that smoky velvet voice stroking down my spine.

"What I do is real. What I want more than any-thing is to help people. I hope to make enough to live on by what people pay me, but often I don't. My charge is fifty dollars an hour, or whatever you can afford to give me, whatever my information might be worth to you. If it's only a dollar, or five, or ten, that's okay. My job is to help you by using my gifts. That's all." She blinked, releasing me from her spell. "Does that answer your question?"

I nodded, not yet able to find voice. What the hell had she done to me? I was not the personality type that succumbed to hypnosis; God knew, enough head doctors had tried it when I was young, only to give up in total frustration. Garrett's eyes shifted back and forth between us. His mouth opened, but he closed it before saying what he was thinking, and I was pretty damn sure I knew what it was. Smart man.

"Now," Lillia reached for the glasses, "let's see what these can tell me."

She sat still, eyes closed, the glasses cradled in her cupped hands. Not a sound broke the silence, not even our breathing. She didn't moan, or groan, or writhe in the chair, as I'd expected. Nevertheless, chills ran down my spine the longer we sat there. This bitch was really milking the atmosphere for all it was worth. Just when I was at the point of walking out—walking the whole mile-and-a-half home if Garrett wouldn't leave with me —Lillia took in a deep breath.

"What I see is strange, and jumbled," she said, her eyes still closed.

Oh, I'll just bet, I thought. Her fingers spasmed on the glasses. I looked at Garrett and again rolled my eyes at the typical psychic double-speak. He shook his head, narrowed his eyes at me, and pressed a finger to his lips.

"It was a very disturbed mind that wore these glasses. It's difficult to see the images clearly. I'm getting glimpses of... oh, streaks... of, of different colors... and... bars of wood, one after the other, leading up toward the sky." She twisted her head to the side, frowning. "What is this? Trees and darkness... and a cave?... but no, it's built out in the open, away from everything else. It holds his secrets, that cave, things no one else should see."

She fell silent again, let both her head and shoulders drop. I stretched my spine and neck, wishing I were home, at my computer, working on my neglected cases and earning my retainers, when a soft glow caught my attention. The crystal ball on the table's center now emitted a soft, blue light that swirled slightly, deep within the orb. I gestured to it with my head; Garrett's eyes grew huge as he stared at it.

Oh, come on, I thought. *You don't think it's real, do you?* Obviously, she'd pressed a switch somewhere under the table, probably with her knee. Turned on the ghostly glow to open up our purse strings. A clever, if clichéd, trick. I'd thought Garrett too smart to believe in such hocus-pocus, but from the look on his face, he wasn't. I shifted in my seat, ready to crawl under the table to look when Lillia spoke again.

"I'm getting… what is it?" Lillia frowned, her eyes flicking back and forth beneath her lowered lids as though she was looking at, or for, something. Yet another cliché pulled from her repertoire. "Images… numbers, a one and a nine, repeating over and over... And a... yes, a butterfly…" Another long pause, then a sigh, "Uhhh," long and drawn out, "oh, the steps, so

Susan Tuttle

many steps, beware the steps," her voice deepened, seemed to reverberate slightly, "they are dangerous, deadly. Stay away from the steps. And I see a ship, a sailing ship, ancient, sails afurl in a heady breeze."

She gave a sharp gasp and her eyes popped open. She blinked, looked at Garrett then at me. Then down at the table.

"Oh."

It was only one word, one tiny little syllable, but a world of surprise and fear rode in her tone. I didn't think she was faking that. She set the glasses down and reached a hand toward the glowing globe, cupping her palm near it but never quite touching its surface. She sat motionless, staring at the globe as time seemed to stretch into infinity, then, as the glow slowly faded, she spoke without looking up. Her low voice held an echoing quality and her words hit me like bullets, shredding my insides.

"Be very careful, Skylark, there is danger all around you, danger you cannot yet see. You were left alone, abandoned, to keep you safe, but the safety is beginning to break down. It's breaking because of who you are, which is more than even you yet know. Seek answers about yourself in the past, Skylark, for the past holds the key. The past is your key."

Lillia closed her eyes, shuddered, and sank back in her chair. Huge breaths lifted her ample chest. Her hands shook when she pushed her hair back from her face. After a moment of composing herself, once her breathing evened out and her hands stopped shaking, she drew in a deep breath and gave Garrett a thin smile that didn't include me.

"That's all I have on the glasses, all I can see. I hope what I said will be of help to you." She paused and drew in another breath. "But I'll tell you, I've never before seen the globe light itself before I look into it. And it's very, very unusual that that something comes in the crystal when I'm doing a psychometry reading." Her gaze shifted to me. "I never remember much of what I say when I look into the globe, but please, Skylark, this is important. Pay attention to whatever I said, it's even more important than the images I saw from the glasses. Much more important." She closed her eyes and bowed her head. When she looked up again her face had cleared. She gave us another smile and then rose, prompting us to do likewise. "I know that what I saw about the glasses wasn't as clear as it might have been, but each of those images have their own meaning that could bring you to the answers you need if you can decipher them. If I can help further, please let me know."

I stood staring at Lillia, my teeth clenched, my blood boiling. What a money-grubbing, fawning, sadistic imposter she was. Garrett shook his head at me, warning me not to give voice to my opinion of Lillia's performance. He peeled off a few bills from the wad in his pocket and pressed them into her hand, then picked up the glasses and escorted me from the place, leaving thanks ringing on the air. His, not mine.

Hard as it was, I kept my peace until we were back on Los Osos Valley Road, heading toward my house. Then I lit into Garrett.

"I don't even *want* to know how much you gave her," I said, not even trying to keep the acid from my tone. "And for such oh, so *illuminating* information. Swaths of color, bars of wood, a cave that's out in the open under trees and darkness—which is not only ridiculous, it's *impossible*. And on top of that we get repeating numbers, butterflies, and oh, yes, let's not forget those dangerous, deadly steps. Where the hell will we find what she terms 'so many steps' here on the Central Coast? Only a handful of places have even a *second floor*, much less any *steps*." I shook my head, totally ignoring Lillia's crystal ball performance, which came much too eerily close to the truth for my comfort. I didn't even want to think about that. "What a waste of time—and money. We don't know any more now than we did before."

Garrett turned onto my street, then into my drive. He turned off the motor and we sat there in silence, listening to the pings as the engine cooled off while I tried to get my agitated breathing under control. In spite of my resolve, I thought about Lillia's last words, about me being abandoned, about seeking my past. And I realized with a shock it had all been a set-up. My heart rate finally slowed down. I shook my head and gave a half-laugh.

"Good job, Gar. You really got me. You two cooked this up between you, didn't you? It was a nice touch, giving her my name and history ahead of time. If I was more gullible, I'd have actually believed her."

"You're wrong, Skylark." Garrett shook his head. "When I called for an appointment, all I told her was my name, and that I needed a psychometry reading. Didn't even tell her about the glasses. That was it, I swear." I turned and stared at him. "I never said a word about you, your name, or your history. Never even told her you were coming."

 CHAPTER NINETEEN

The phone rang just as Detective Soto was about to bite into his meatball sub. He closed his eyes and sighed, then set the sandwich back in its wrappings, reconciled to eating yet another cold lunch. He wiped his fingers and caught the phone on the sixth ring.

"Sheriff's station, Detective Soto."

Silence met his ears. He was about to repeat his greeting—or maybe just hang up and catch whatever warmth was left in his food—when a soft, low male voice echoed in his ear.

"I… I think I know who that man is, the one who was killed two weeks ago."

Soto frowned and snapped his fingers at Dunwitty who was enthusiastically chewing away at his own lunch. Dunwitty frowned back at him as Soto pointed to the phone, then snatched up his receiver and pressed the button for the open line, his mayo-and-mustard-smeared fingers leaving multi-colored streaks on the keypad.

"May I ask who this is?" Soto kept his voice calm and soothing, though his heart was beating like a drum in a heavy metal band.

"I'd rather not say."

"Okay, can you tell me who you think it is?"

"I… I think it's Justin Yarrow. He hasn't been at work and no one has heard from him. I went by his house and there's no sign of him. He had an important presentation yesterday that he missed. And he'd never miss it, never. It was for a major client."

Soto shared a look with his partner. Was this guy a kook, or was there any reality to what he was saying?

"Can you tell me where he worked?"

"Um… Okay. Mason's Insurance, in SLO. We—I mean, they—do a lot of investment stuff for people. Justin, he lives in Los Osos." The man rattled off an address that Soto scrambled to write down. The caller's voice began to shake. "Oh, no, I-I hope it's not him, n-not Justin."

"Well, we'll check—"

The connection broke with a sharp click. The two detectives looked at each other for a long minute, Dunwitty again gnawing on the remains of his sandwich, dropping pieces of tomato onto the papers littering his desktop. Soto wrapped up his own aborted lunch and stood.

"I'm driving," he said as he shrugged into his suitcoat. "You've got too much crap on your hands, you'll grunge up the steering wheel. Come on, quit stuffing your face. Let's go see if we've finally got an ID on our dead guy."

Soto headed out of the office, leaving Dunwitty to follow behind. He had the car running and waiting at the entrance when the huge detective finally left the building. The car bobbled as Dunwitty heaved his solid frame into the passenger seat.

"You're a real pisser lately, you know that?" Dunwitty fumbled for his seat belt as Soto took off down 9th Street toward Los Osos Valley Road. "I'm the senior partner here, I get to give the orders."

"Yep. Whatever you say." Soto grinned at him and hung a right on the main road.

"You think it's maybe our guy? About time someone wondered about him. Missing at work for two weeks and no one cared enough until he missed a presentation that would have brought in money....Shit for brains, that's what they have. One track minds. Dollar signs."

"I wonder why the guy wouldn't leave his name." Soto squinted in the bright sunlight that glinted off the car ahead of them. "Sounds like maybe they worked together."

"Sounded a little light in the loafers, you ask me." Dunwitty squirmed in his seat to adjust his sport coat. "Reason enough not to want to be identified. Who'd want that kind of label, especially if the other one's already dead?"

Soto snorted.

"Trust you to think something like that. There's nothing wrong with same-sex relationships, not these days."

"There's everything wrong with them any days. Damn faggots." Dunwitty pointed to the left. "Follow the bend, here." One block further on, he pointed to the right. "That's the road."

They slowed down, eyeing house numbers that stood either on houses or mailboxes, when they were visible at all. At last, between Humboldt and Inyo, Soto braked, then pulled into a drive and cut the engine.

From the front the house appeared compact, a one-story rose-beige stucco with an attached one-car garage. A red tile roof snugged against the walls. A chimney broke the roofline on the left side of the structure about twenty feet back from the front wall.

Dunwitty sighed and released his seat belt.

"Let's go see what we can see. Then we'll head in to that insurance investment firm in SLO and talk to this Justin Yarrow's boss."

They walked up to the front door, mounting three steps onto an abbreviated porch on which stood a small white plastic garden table and two chairs, and a pile of yellowing newspapers still in their plastic sleeves. Dunwitty punched the doorbell; chimes rang, but no one answered. They waited a few minutes, then he rang it again. Still no answer. Dunwitty inched behind the table to peer in the front window, hands cupped around his eyes and pressed to the glass.

"Don't see much, no obvious blood on the floor, but it looks like a table in the entry might be tipped over."

"Let's check around back."

Soto led the way around the side of the house, past a row of overgrown magnolia bushes that half-blocked the walkway. The house was larger than Soto had first thought it to be, its impressive length not visible from the street. At the back they found a concrete patio facing a large back yard. A small shed perched in the back left corner. Between it and the house a neglected garden sprouted a multitude of weeds choking out the remains of last year's tomato and pepper plants.

On the patio, to one side of the back door, a small wood picnic table with detached benches crowded a large barbecue grill. Two lounge chairs with a small occasional table between them sat on the other side of the door. Which was ajar.

Dunwitty and Soto looked at each other, then drew their weapons.

"Backup?" Soto whispered.

"Hell, it's been two weeks. Whoever was in here has had plenty of time to get out. Come on."

He led the way, pushing the door open further with the barrel of his gun. Soto glanced down, then poked Dunwitty in the back.

"That doesn't look good," he said, his voice almost non-existent.

Dunwitty looked down and nodded, then stepped carefully over the dried remains of whatever it was— *Catsup? Barbecue sauce? Blood?* Soto wondered—and moved further into the house.

They stood in the kitchen, the room neat, almost sterile except for the rust-red stains that trailed across the floor. A small kitchen table and one chair stood cocked, as though they had been shoved a bit askew. The stench of rotting food emanated from both the trash can and the refrigerator. Mushy black bananas and slimy peaches covered with green mold sat in a bowl on the counter near the sink. Whether this Justin Yarrow was their body or not, he hadn't been home for a long time.

They followed the rust-red stains down the long hallway, checking the three bedrooms—the middle of which bore signs of a struggle—and two baths on the right and the dining room and den on the left to make sure no one hid in them, until they reached the living room and entryway at the front.

Dunwitty had been right, a side table in the entryway had been tipped over, but there was no sign of any blood trail this far into the house. No sign of anyone home, injured or dead. And no sign anyone had been in the house for quite a while, to judge by the amount of rot in the kitchen and the abandoned newspapers on the porch.

Wordless, they returned to the largest bedroom, the middle one. It appeared to have been ransacked. Dresser drawers gaped open; clothes had been torn from hangers in the closet. Dried splashes and spatters of blood littered the floor, the bed, and one wall.

"It went down here," Dunwitty said. "This is where she did it, that freak-o."

"Skylark?" Soto blinked at his stubborn ox of a partner. "You're not still on that kick, are you?"

"Damn it, José, the evidence is right in front of your eyes!" Dunwitty pulled out his cell and punched in the station number. "Yeah, we need officers and a Crime Scene Unit here, right away." He gave the address as he watched Soto roam the room, cataloging the destruction. He snapped the phone shut and shoved it into his pocket. "I'm gonna get her for this, you watch me. She left something of herself behind, and we're gonna find it."

"I don't think so." Soto shook his head. "First, we have to be sure this place belongs to our dead guy and not just someone who hurt himself and is in the hospital somewhere. Second," he raised his voice to drown out Dunwitty's snapped reply, "we can't prove a thing unless there was evidence left behind. Concrete evidence. And third," he pushed past Dunwitty and headed toward the front door as sirens sounded in the distance, "I don't think she has anything at all to do with this."

"She did it," Dunwitty called after him, staying in the room as though afraid if he left all the evidence he needed would vanish like smoke in a high wind. "You mark my words. That Skylark bitch is going down for murder."

On Saturday afternoon Carstairs stood grinning, hands on his hips. He gazed around the changes he'd made in the old barn. Serendipity had led him to it—or, rather, Intervention Number Four.

He hadn't understood at first how he could have left the latch on the damn bitch's cage open, or the cabin door ajar. Even though he'd drunk himself into almost a stupor—he'd needed it after the week he'd had—he was sure he'd checked everything with his usual precision.

Still, somehow, during the night, the damn dog had gotten out—out of the cage, then out of the house. His rage had known no bounds when he woke that morning; his little angel was still unconscious six hours later. But once he calmed down—and recovered the fucking dog—he finally understood.

Intervention Number Four had gifted him with the next phase of his evolution. Had the puppy not gotten loose and hidden out in the barn, Carstairs would never have so much as thought about it. It was just always there, on the edge of his property; old, dilapidated, abandoned, half-hidden in the bushes that grew everywhere in rampant profusion. A piece of the background, like the broken-down machinery in the overgrown field, that's all it had been, not inhabitable, not worth a second look. Invisible to him, most of the time.

But no more. As he knelt over the quivering body of the puppy he'd beaten half to death, he'd understood the perfection of it—the barn. It had taken him half of Saturday morning to dig a trench in which to bury the electrical lines he'd tapped from the box on the back wall of the cabin, and a few more hours to string up lights in just the right places. All the while the word "expansion" had echoed in his brain, keeping time to the whimpers of the stupid little dog that lay in the far corner, too spent—or perhaps injured—from the punishment to so much as move. That'd teach the little bitch to try to run off.

After the lights were finished, he'd driven twice into Atascadero and loaded up on lumber and sound-deadening wall board, then attended to partitioning the inside walls. Another trip to the pet store in Los Osos snagged him a half dozen large metal cages that now sat against the walls. In one lay his lovely angel, still unconscious, curled into a fetal position and leaking blood onto the rancid straw that covered the floor of her new home. On the far wall of the innermost room he'd built his stage, embedded eye-bolts in the platform and the floor around it, and set up the camera. It was ready, and it was perfect.

All he needed now were more chains. And another bitch or three. And a couple more dogs.

Grinning, he left the barn, padlocked the re-inforced doors, and headed back into town.

"Go on home, Mike. I'll finish up the closing."

Yvonne Avila grinned at the coffee shop manager who, she knew, was anxious to get back to his wife and six-day-old daughter. In her opinion, he should have stayed home for a couple of weeks—taken male paternity leave, not that the company offered it—and let his assistant manager do what she'd been hired to do: fill in for him when necessary. And what was more necessary than being home with your newborn?

"Listen, it's okay. Leave. Denise and little Marina need you, and there's not that much left to do."

"Are you sure, Yvonne?" Mike Miller wiped his hands and threw the towel on the counter. "I don't like the idea of leaving you here alone this late at night."

"Oh, come on." Yvonne laughed, a sweet tinkling that soared her amusement to the ceiling. "It's not that late, it's barely eleven-thirty. And this is Pismo Beach, not LA. I'll be fine. My car is just down there," she pointed out the window to the right, where a grouping of three cars huddled at the end of the lot where the McDonald's anchored the far end of the plaza, "and Andy should arrive in about fifteen minutes. I promise, I won't stick my nose outside the door until he gets here. Go home, and kiss that sweet little baby girl for me."

"Are you sure?"

"Mike." Yvonne gave him a gentle push in the direction of the door. "Go."

"Okay, okay. Thanks. Make sure you take a flashlight with you with you leave, Andy or no Andy."

"Yes, Daddy, I will."

"See you tomorrow, Yvonne."

Mike grinned at her, then pulled on his jacket and let himself out the front door, locking it behind him.

Yvonne shook her head as she watched him walk away. He was so protective of his staff—overprotective, really. Nothing would happen to her, not in Pismo Beach. Even though the outlet mall across the street was long closed there were still some cars in its lot, and Mickey-D's was open 24/7. Every ten minutes or so someone pulled around to their drive-through window. She couldn't think of a safer place to live, or work, at any hour than beautiful, laid-back, carefree Pismo Beach.

Humming to herself, Yvonne finished wiping down the tables and counters, then got out the broom to do a final sweep of the floors, hoping to finish up before Andy arrived. Her ring caught the lights as she swept and her tune morphed into "Here Comes the Bride." She held up her hand to admire once again the lovely two carat solitaire set in platinum that she'd received just a month ago. Andy had spent a fortune on it. She still couldn't believe he had asked her to marry him, and on her birthday, no less. On his knees in a crowded restaurant. He was such a romantic. *What a way to turn twenty-one... I'll be both legal and married*, she thought, breaking into a laugh.

She put the broom away and shut off the lights, then picked up her purse and went out to wait for Andy. From within the purse's depths she heard the notification tone for a text message. She rummaged around in it, pulled out her phone and entered her passcode, then frowned at the message.

'Got hung up, Babe. Can we meet at home in about an hour or so?'

Yvonne frowned. "Hung up", she knew, was Andy-speak for "I'm winning, don't want to leave the game just yet." She'd been looking forward to snuggling in bed with him and going over the wedding plans; she had six magazines with gowns she simply couldn't decide among and they still had to thrash out how many bridesmaids and attendants to have. And which place to choose for the reception. Then again, if he was winning, maybe he'd come home with enough to pay for that destination wedding in Tahiti they'd been teasing each other about.

For some dumb reason, she just couldn't stay mad at him for more than a minute or two.

Her thumbs moved over the screen. 'Okay, I'm leaving now. One hour and no more, and you'd better have lots of cash in hand, Tahiti is calling', she typed, a grin breaking out once more.

'You got it, Babe, making reservations now', he answered back, adding a smiley-face emoji.

Damn, but she loved that guy.

Laughing and trying to decide which wine would go best with bridal magazines, Yvonne locked up the coffee shop and strode down the parking lot to her car. After a dozen steps she hesitated. It seemed much darker than usual. The shadows looked like inky puddles that seemed to undulate toward her as she walked. When she looked around she realized that the security lights out near the street were dark. And for the moment no cars moved on the roadway. The lights from McDonald's windows only lit up the parking slots in front of the restaurant; they didn't reach the area across the way where her car was parked, along with an older pickup nearby, the only cars now on that side of the lot. The wind rattled the palm trees and bushes that formed a break between the street and the lot, affording a modicum of privacy but also collecting wavering stygian shadows. She shuddered, not really scared, but definitely feeling uneasy.

Maybe I should go back for that flashlight, she thought, turning to look at the shop door. But it was as far back as it was forward, and she had her keyfob in hand, she could click the car lights on, that would give her some illumination. And she could hit the panic button if need be, her horn was damned loud. *Don't be a ninny*, she told herself. *It's Pismo Beach, perfectly safe, right?*

She continued on toward her car, faster now, all thought of wine and bridal dresses vanishing from her mind. As she walked, she shuddered again. It wasn't like her to be a such a scaredy-cat, she'd closed up lots of times before, even later than this. But something about the deserted street and the non-working lights felt wrong to her. Weird. Eerie.

She breathed a sigh of relief when she reached her car. She clicked the fob twice and the car beeped; the doors unlocked. As she reached for the handle, she caught a glimpse of a nearby shadow detaching itself from the murk below the adjacent palm tree. Before she could react, the shadow moved behind her and grabbed her, pinned her arms down, and pressed a sweet-smelling cloth over her face. She tried to scream, tried to break free, but in seconds her head began to whirl. Her strength fled and her body collapsed. The keys dropped from her fingers onto the pavement.

"You're mine, now, bitch," a harsh voice grated in her ear. "I've got a place all set up for you."

Andy! Help me! she thought, then knew no more.

 *CHAPTER TWENTY*

I didn't make as much headway as I should have on any of my cases—the skip-trace, the background checks, or Araceli Aguayo's vanishing profits—because Lillia-the-fake-psychic's words kept ringing in my head and destroying my concentration.

How had she known my name? Or the fact that I'd been abandoned by my parents, though who really knew what her definition of "abandoned" meant? That was if Garrett was telling the truth, and he hadn't revealed all sorts of secrets about me to her. But he usually owned up to stuff like that, once the gag was over and done with and I'd been thoroughly humiliated. I couldn't dismiss the sober look on his face, the almost scared expression in his eyes, when we talked about what Lillia had claimed to have seen in that crystal ball.

I thought about the damned sphere that had glowed. Man, I so wished I'd crawled under the table to get a closer look at it, to find out just how she'd made it do that. Yeah, I know; since I have paranormal abilities, I should be the last one to pooh-pooh someone else's so-called "gifts". But I'd never yet met anyone else who had any real paranormal abilities—except for Bass Ehrler, and I'd never actually met the real man, only got to ogle his see-through image—and I'd been dealing with mine for sixteen-plus years now. You'd think in all that time there'd have been at least one or two real psychics in the mix.

But no. There was just me, the freaky weirdo who saw the past superimposed over the present and weird lines of light that connected people. And who also had an ectoplasmic mentor who showed up at the most inopportune times. The rest of them were just phony money-hungry scam artists hogging the limelight and bilking the gullible.

So, what was up with Lillia? Who the hell was she, really? Was she the one Ehrler had told me to watch out for, and listen to? The one who held the key to the next so-called phase of my life? I snorted at the notion. Like hell, not that little conniving fake. No way was one word of what she'd said even close to true. Or real. Though I knew it would cut into necessary money-earning work time, I'd definitely have to do some deep research into what made that pretend psychic tick. Then I could chop her into little pieces.

I was still stewing over that "psychic" reading, wondering what color swaths, steps, run-on numbers, and butterflies had to do with the price of beans. And I was pissed as hell that I'd lost so much productive work time on both Saturday and Sunday to what amounted to fruitless brain farts when I met Reenie and Garrett for dinner at Galley Seafood in Morro Bay on Sunday night. I barely tasted my shrimp scampi as I sat there in silence, listening to Garrett's half-hour-long, overly dramatic rendition of our visit to Lillia-la-la-land.

Funny how Reenie had no problem talking about the infamous stolen glasses, or the so-called psychometry session, when I was the butt of the joke. I suffered through about as much humiliation as I could stand without pulling my Glock on them, then threw my napkin atop my half-eaten dinner and stood up. I didn't even try to use my indoor voice.

"Since you two are having such a wonderful time talking *about* me instead of *to* me, I see no point in staying." Damn, but I loved the looks of dismay on both their faces. "And I don't see any point in paying for what you've made sure I can't eat, either. So, see you around. Maybe."

I shut my ears to their protests and stalked out of the restaurant, my progress marked by shocked whispers from other diners who'd overheard my scathing remarks. I wasn't any cooler by the time I reached the Jeep; angry breaths lifted my chest, and my hands—my whole body—shook like a leaf in a high wind. There was no way I could go home, I'd probably just smash something I cared about, given the state of my nerves. So I did the only thing I could think to do.

I pointed the car at Montaña de Oro State Park in Los Osos, barely six miles from my house, and drove from Morro Bay to Spooner's Cove where there was a natural rock jetty I could walk out on and commune with the ocean. If I was lucky, maybe the tide would be coming in, huge waves that would crash over me and hopefully drown my temper. It was my secret place, that jetty, the main reason I lived where I did. When life got to be too much for me, I'd go stand at the end of it, facing the endless, fathomless ocean, and let the enormity of the universe pull me back into sanity.

Granted, I rarely did it alone at night, in the dark, especially if the tide was roaring ashore. Too dangerous. But tonight I was just too pissed off to really care.

I turned off South Bay Boulevard onto Los Osos Valley Road and headed out toward the park, my hands clenched numblingly tight on the steering wheel. The fact that I had to pass Cabrillo Estates, where Reenie lived, to get to the park entrance, pissed me off even more. I sighed as the road curved to the left, the place where it changed name from Los Osos Valley Road to Pecho Valley Road, and braced myself. Just a half mile further on, Cabrillo Estates climbed the hills on the left. I hoped I'd be able to pass it by and not drive up to Reenie's house and egg it or something.

I caught a flash of the street sign from the corner of my eye just after the curve straightened out. I drove another fifty feet then pulled to the side of the road.

Had it said what I thought it did? Once again, Lillia's words poured through my brain. I tried to shake it off, but it was no use. Foolish as I felt, I would have to go back and check it out.

I hung a U-ey and drove back, then again pulled to the side of the road and stared at the sign across the street.

Monarch Lane.

Monarch.

Butterfly.

Taking a deep breath, I pulled out, then turned left onto Monarch Lane and continued slowly on.

I don't know what I was looking for. The houses were sparse along this street; most faced the cross streets, and it was darker than Hades along here since Los Osos didn't believe in street lights. I caught house numbers when my headlights illuminated the few mail boxes that stood streetside: 18732, 18964. And then I saw it. I mashed the brakes and sat in the middle of the road, staring at the mail box. Number 19191.

I see... a butterfly... numbers... a one and a nine, repeating over and over. Lillia's voice resounded in my head. A butterfly plus ones and nines. 19191 Monarch Lane?

A chill ran down my spine as I started forward again. I hung a left on Humboldt Street and drove a block to where it curved around and became Butterfly Lane—whose house numbers were only in the double digits, so it had nothing to do with Lillia's vision—then pulled over and parked. I sat a while trying to talk myself out of it, but in the end I dug out my cell and dialed Garrett.

"Hey," he answered. "Listen, I'm sorry, Sky—"

"Doesn't matter. I found it, Gar. The house, the one Lillia was talking about."

"House? She didn't mention a house, Skylark."

"She did, we just didn't know that's what she meant. It was the butterfly and the repeating numbers; 19191 Monarch Lane, it's off Pecho Valley Road, just past Pecho Street."

"Well, that's a possibility."

"No, it's more than that." As I spoke I could feel certainty cover me like a warm blanket. My shaking stopped, my breathing evened out. "The place is dark, no one is there. I'm going in to check it out—"

"What do you mean, you're going in?" His screech jabbed into my ear and I pulled the cell away for a moment. I almost missed his next words. "Don't do anything until I get there, promise me, Skylark. I'm leaving now, it'll only take me about ten minutes. Wait for me, you hear?"

"Yeah, I hear. Don't attract attention. Park around the corner on Humboldt, not on Monarch."

I ended the connection and switched the phone to vibrate. Didn't want any calls to interfere with my plans, or alert nosy neighbors to my presence. Leaving the car where it was, I walked in the cool darkness, beneath a night sky awash with stars, around the bend back to Monarch Lane and up to the house Lillia had spoken of when she'd held the glasses. No lights shone in any of the windows, no hint of a TV on in any room, no sound of a radio playing. Nothing but darkness and silence, at barely nine o'clock at night.

Who lives here? I wondered as I stood in the shadow of a live oak and waited for Garrett to show up. *Is it the guy who was killed or the guy who owns the glasses?* Considering what Lillia had picked up from the broken frames, it didn't seem like they'd belonged to the victim. More likely the killer. So this place could belong to either person. Providing, of course, that anything she'd said held even a modicum of truth.

But then again, here I was, standing on Monarch Lane, looking at number 19191... a butterfly and repeating numbers. If that much was true, what else had she said that might also be true?

I waited as long as I could. Only one car drove past me—a pickup, not Garrett's Lexus. It went on another block, then turned up Inyo, a block and a half from where I stood. I waited until the engine noise faded, checked to make sure no one was around, then slowly made my way up to the house, keeping to the dense, dark shadows—which wasn't hard, given that there were no streetlights in a five-mile radius.

Packets of plastic-wrapped newspapers littered the small front porch. Crime scene tape barricaded the door. *So*, I thought, *it's the victim's home, not the killer's*. I inched around the bushes that half-covered the south facade, but found no easy way to get close to the house. The back yard was even darker than the front, and also offered no way in. More crime scene tape criss-crossed the sliding glass doors.

I moved on and found a window on the north side of the house that was bushless and unlocked. I had just eased it open enough to crawl through when someone tapped on my shoulder.

Garrett caught my fist in his hand when I whirled to attack him. He grinned at me, then shook my arm.

"I thought I told you to wait for me," he whispered.

"You took too long," I whispered back. "Come on."

"Wait." He moved between me and the window, effectively blocking me from getting into the house. "How do you know no one's home? They could just be asleep."

"No." I smiled, taking in his all-black attire; he looked like a stealthy Ninja. "No one's here. There's police tape on all the doors. This is the place."

I turned, edged past him, and boosted myself up and into the room, a spare bedroom, it appeared to be. Garrett pulled himself in after me, then closed and locked the window.

"Just a precaution," he whispered.

I nodded and looked around as best I could. The room was almost midnight dark. I could just make out a single bed pushed up against a side wall and a multitude of boxes littering the mattress. When I took a step, my foot smacked into yet another box.

Garrett snapped on the small flashlight he kept on his key ring and shone it around the room, which was indeed filled with cardboard boxes. They lay scattered as though dropped haphazardly, a legacy from the cops' forensic search, no doubt. I eased up the open flaps on one of them to find books, thick, leather-bound tomes with titles like *Ulysses*, *The Aenead* and *The Divine Comedy* stamped in gold leaf on the spines. Another box held a welter of papers that appeared to have been shoved in willy-nilly: circulars, junk mail, magazines, old bills that hadn't even been opened. Yet another held items of various clothing.

"Looks like this is Chuck's room," I murmured to Garrett.

"What?"

"You know." I grinned at him. "If you don't know what to do with it but don't want to throw it away, or if company's coming and you need to get it out of sight, you 'chuck' it into the spare room. Chuck's room."

"Cute." He grinned back at me, then nodded at the doorway. "Come on, let's get this over with before we're arrested for B&E."

We didn't go far. Garrett lit the way into the hall, shielding the mini-flashlight as best he could. We checked out the kitchen and bathroom first and found nothing but lots of black powder, then stepped into the disaster of a master bedroom. The glint of the flash picked up spatters of dark blood on the bed, the floor, and one wall, as well as the dishevelment left by the forensics team. Black powder littered all horizontal surfaces.

"Wow, I'd say Lillia was right," Garrett breathed.

He looked at me, but I was barely aware of him. Time shifted around me; the bottom dropped out of my stomach and my breathing clenched in my throat. Lights flashed like the beginning of an old movie newsreel, then burned steadily—the ceiling light and the dresser lamps that in current time were still dark. Two figures barrelled through the doorway, straight through both Garrett and me. He didn't feel anything; I, however, felt the impact as though a dagger of ice had impaled my ribcage. I groaned from the pain.

The taller man, though trim and in shape, was no match for his assailant, whose muscles bulged as his arms rammed into the victim's face and body like pistons. The attacker snarled, looking like a rabid dog as he battered on at his victim, who obviously had no experience with fighting. They twice bounced off the far wall, fell onto the bed and rolled off again, then smashed into the dresser, whose drawers gaped open. The slimmer man—the dead man in the morgue, I was sure —fell to the floor and the attacker began kicking at him.

"Oh, my God!" I could barely breathe, my body shook so with cold and shock. "He's killing him!"

"Skylark? What are you seeing?"

In my peripheral I saw Garrett reach out to me, then pull back his hands. He knew well what would happen if he touched me while a vision unfolded. As much as he might want to share my pain, or wish he could take it away, there was nothing he could do until it was over.

"Please, please, stop," I moaned, not wanting to see more of the vicious, insane attack, but helpless to stop it.

The assailant beat his victim half conscious on the floor. Blood poured from the man's temple and his mouth; one arm looked to be broken. I could see the attacker screaming at him as he took one last good kick, his booted foot landing square on the man's spine—though I couldn't hear a thing—then the assailant straightened up and looked directly at me. I gasped in a horrified breath, a reflex only since I knew he didn't—couldn't—actually see me. After all, I hadn't been there when it had happened, all this was simply a remote-view replay of sorts. No matter how real it felt.

His face twisted as he looked around the room again, then stalked to the dresser. He bent to grope in a lower drawer, and when he straightened up he was holding a revolver. He finished ransacking the dresser, pocketing jewelry, money and papers. He then crossed to the closet—taking a few boot-swipes at the man on the floor on the way—and rummaged through it, hurling clothing onto the floor as he ransacked. Dimly I was aware of a rattling sound coming from the front of the house. Garrett moved out into the hallway, returning a moment later to stand close behind me.

"Someone must have seen us," he whispered, "or maybe the light, the cops are checking the doors and shining lights in the windows. Can you move?"

I couldn't answer him, couldn't do anything but stare at the murder taking place before my eyes. Though my ears heard the sound of the window being tested in the room next door, and my brain recognized the flare of light outside the window as the cops approached it with flashlights blazing, I was caught in the past. The horror of it dribbled out of my shuddering mouth in little bursts of wordless protest.

"They'll see you if we don't move," Garrett said again, but I was frozen, unable to move. "And hear you if you're not quiet."

The light from outside moved closer; seconds, only, until we would be discovered and arrested for breaking into a crime scene. And still I could not move, could not stop moaning.

"I'm sorry, Skylark," Garrett whispered.

He grabbed me from behind, clamping a hard hand over my mouth and dragging me across the room and up against the wall beside the window just as the killer aimed and shot the man on the floor in the heart, and the beam from a flashlight angled through the window and lit up the room.

White hot agony tore my body apart. Burning sparks seared through my eyes and into my brain. I felt as though my entire essence was being shredded into microscopic bits. Pain ricocheted through me and I screamed behind Garrett's hand. Then blessed darkness clamped down and pulled me far from the torment that his touch had bequeathed.

 *CHAPTER TWENTY-ONE*

"That fucking bitch!" Carstairs screamed, pounding the steering wheel with both fists. "Who the hell is she, how does she know about this?"

He'd spent hours that day camped out on the bitch's street when he should have been home, acclimating his newly acquired angel and testing their new quarters. Then he'd followed the woman with the weird name to a restaurant in Morro Bay. She looked to be busy for a good hour or more, so he took a chance and left to pick up some fast food, only to arrive back at the seafood place about thirty-five minutes later to discover her walking toward her car.

Anger consumed him. How dare she? He'd almost missed her! All that time spent searching for her, then watching her, would have been wasted. This bitch had a lot to answer for.

He followed behind her, hidden in the darkness, hoping she'd take him somewhere where he'd be able to snatch her. His hands itched with the need to feel her neck between them. She drove back to Los Osos, then headed out toward the park, but surprised him when she turned around about halfway there.

Then drove up Monarch Lane.

What the fuck was she doing there?

He'd hung back, watched her brake in front of The House, then pulled around the corner onto Humboldt. Should he follow her? No. Butterfly connected Humboldt and Glenn in an arc only one block up, and both Humboldt and Glenn decanted onto Monarch. He stayed where he was, parked near the corner of Glenn, almost a block away from The House, and watched out both the front and back windows. He'd see her if she just circled around and came out behind him.

But she didn't. About twenty minutes later, he saw her move down the darkened street like a cautious cat, keeping to the shadows. She stopped, almost invisible beside a tree, and studied the house. Carstairs put the truck in gear and drove past her, then turned up Inyo. He parked halfway up the street and walked back in time to see the woman, that bitch Skylark, moving stealthily around the side of The House.

A few minutes later, a tall, lean shadow detached from the surrounding bushes and inched over the lawn to where the woman stood trying to break into The House.

Think you're so smart, don't you? he thought. *Well, I'll show you smart, you stupid bitch!*

He pulled out his cell and dialled 9-1-1.

"Yes, I was just leaving my girlfriend's house on Monarch Lane in Los Osos and I saw two people go into that house the cops were at... the one that has crime scene tape on the doors? I saw them open a window on the side of the house and climb in... I can see a light in there, I think they have a flashlight. Wait, what? I can't hear you. What?"

He rubbed the phone on his clothing to simulate static, then snapped it off and stuck it in his pocket. Through the windows, he watched the thin thread of light waver through the house, then stop in the master bedroom, until he heard sirens approach. He turned and walked back to his car.

He felt so pissed, he could barely walk straight. His hands, his whole body vibrated with an all-consuming rage. All he wanted was to smash that bitch's face, teach her what her place was, and now she was out of reach. Sure, the cops would arrest her, make her life miserable for a while, but she was a woman. She'd use her eyes, her lips, her body, sleep her way out of trouble. That's what women did. He knew he hadn't inconvenienced her for very long.

The rage built in him until he thought it would break him apart. By the time he reached his car, he would have killed anyone out on the street. His hands shook so hard he could barely open his car door. It took him three tries to get the keys in the ignition, and all his strength not to lay rubber when he pulled out and thereby awaken the neighborhood. He shot down Inyo to Howard; the tires squealed when he threw the car too fast into a right hand turn, and he had to pump the brakes so as not to skid onto someone's front lawn.

"Shit, fuck and crap!" he screamed.

He couldn't go any further, he knew, not without first releasing a good portion of this tension. If he kept driving, he'd just end up crashing somewhere. Then what would happen to his angels, who were anxiously awaiting his return, who so needed his ministrations?

He'd barely had time to introduce himself to sweet little Yvonne.

No, he needed to stop. He needed to vent. He needed to find a substitute for that Skylark bitch.

He pulled over on Howard and turned off the car. Darkness settled around him; country quiet covered the area like a blanket. The cops, obviously, had turned off their sirens to better catch the intruders unaware. He left the car and scouted across the front lawns of the nearby houses, looking for one with no car—or perhaps only one car—in the garage. Around the corner on Fresno Street, three houses in from the corner, he found what he was looking for.

Amy Lipschitz sighed and snuggled beneath the covers, searching for sleep that would not come. Didn't matter that she had finished more than half the bottle of wine, the special wine she had bought for the trip that hadn't happened. Didn't matter that only a couple glasses of wine usually made her unbelieveably sleepy. Didn't matter that she had spent a few hours—oh, okay, days—in tears, and that alone should have made her pass out from sheer exhaustion.

There was just no getting around it. Her mind would not shut down, would not stop rewinding and running over and over the pictures of Harry—her Harry —naked and tongue kissing Lisa. Her naked best friend. In his bedroom. In his bed.

No, make that her one-time, never-again, not-in-this-lifetime, *former* best friend. And her boyfriend, a boyfriend she'd hoped would end up a fiance by the end of their eagerly-awaited, excitedly-planned trip to Hawaii. Instead, he ended up in the one-time, never-again, not-in-this-lifetime, former category, too. The dirty rat.

Amy sighed, threw off the comforter, turned over for about the fiftieth time and lay still, searching in vain for the oblivion of sleep. She found only cold air that in about ninety seconds made her start to shiver. She groaned and pulled the comforter back up over her shoulders, knowing she would be sweat-hot in another ninety seconds. She sighed again, thinking once more of the aborted Hawaiian trip.

The tickets sat on her dresser top, mocking her with their silent presence. Departure date: three days ago. Useless now, except perhaps to cut into confetti. If she cut it small enough, maybe sprinkled some poison on the pieces, then snuck over to Harry's house and sifted them into that stupid bark-and-gravel, health-food cereal he insisted on eating—or mixed them in Lisa's oatmeal—would she get caught?

Tempting, but she thought better of it. No way would she going to risk a lifetime in jail because of him. Or her. It was bad enough she was missing out on Hawaii; no way would she miss out on the rest of her life because of them. Maybe she should just skip the poison, make the pieces bigger, and just hope they choked to death on them. That would be their fault then, not hers, right?

She turned over and sighed again, knowing it was only a morbid fantasy. Wishful thinking. As were, it'd turned out, her future plans. What hurt so badly was that she hadn't just gone anyway, by herself, without the rat. She had wasted the ticket, and the money it had cost. She shouldn't be here, in good old everyday Los Osos, where she'd been born and raised. No, she should be in exotic Maui right now—even if she wasn't snuggled in Harry's arms—rocked by Hawaiian liquor and the sounds of rustling palms and island music. Instead, she lay alone in her lonely, unexotic bed, rocked only by her inability to put this gigantic fiasco behind her, the occasional coming-home-late-from-somewhere car that chugged past the house, and the creak of the loose floorboard in the dining room. Her life had really gone to the—

Wait. Creak? Floorboard? Dining room?

Amy sat up, her heart pounding, and listened to the silence that enveloped her dark bedroom. The comforter slid from her shoulders to puddle in her lap. Was someone in the house? Or was she simply going insane, hearing things that weren't there, thanks to Harry and Lisa?

Her nerves stretched ever more taut as the silence lengthened. Should she turn on the light, or would that simply advertise her whereabouts to whoever had broken in—if anyone actually had? Should she get up and get dressed before going out to confront whoever it was, so she didn't scandalize them with her dogs-with-halos-print PJs? Or maybe she should sneak out to the garage and grab the baseball bat her brother had given her for protection, and that she kept forgetting to stash under the bed.

So many decisions for so late at night. After so much wine. And still she heard nothing, no further noise, no second or even third creak from the dining room. Maybe it was just the house settling. *Do one-story houses actually settle?* she thought. *Do dining rooms?*

That did it. Thinking about the dining room—creaking floor or no creaking floor—made her hungry. She glanced at the clock: 11:53 p.m. Too late for dinner, too early for breakfast. *But,* she decided, *it's just the right time to drown my sorrows in chocolate-coconut mint fudge ice cream, since I won't be swirling down any Hawaiian Mai Tais or Coconut-Pineapple Mojitos.*

That made her smile. If she couldn't have Hawaii—or Harry—she could always have ice cream. It was the one constant in her life she knew she could depend on. She shoved off the comforter, swung her legs over the side of the bed, and slipped on her flip-flops. She didn't bother with a light; ice cream was all the illumination she wanted for now. Smoothing down her shoulder-length corkscrew curls, she padded to the door, then paused to lean her ear against the cool wood and listen for any sounds out in the hallway, just in case. Then she realized what she was doing.

"Oh, my God, you're an idiot," she muttered to herself, shaking her head. "There's nothing out there."

Opening the door, Amy shuffled out into the dark hallway, automatically checking the window in the front door down to her right. Yes, the outside light was still on. No nefarious characters had broken the bulb so they could invade her home in unseen safety. All was well.

She breathed a sigh of relief as she turned left and headed for the kitchen, clomping past the closed doors of the spare bedroom and powder room. She wished she had more than one lousy half gallon of yummy goodness in the freezer. This was definitely shaping up to be a two, or maybe even three, half-gallon night.

She stepped into the kitchen and reached for the wall switch. Just as her fingers touched it, a hard arm snaked around her neck from behind. Another wound around her waist, pinning her arms to her sides. A deep, evil voice breathed into her ear.

"Ready for some fun, bitch?"

Amy's scream strangled in her throat, caught behind the tighening arm. He licked the side of her neck, her cheek, then bit her ear lobe so hard, stars burst in her head.

"Mmmm, your blood tastes so good," he whispered.

She wanted to struggle, tried to struggle, but he held her too tight. She couldn't breathe, couldn't scream. Her vision darkened; the room swam around her. Her bones turned to water, and her body collapsed. The last thing she felt before she passed out was being dragged down the hallway away from the kitchen. When she woke to find herself naked, tied to her bed, and his hulking form looming over her, a screwdriver and a pipe in his hands, she wished to high heaven she hadn't ever regained consciousness.

 *CHAPTER TWENTY-TWO*

I woke in the dark with my head pounding, my body shuddering, and my nerves on fire. It was lucky I hadn't eaten much for dinner. The way my stomach rocked and rolled, nothing much would have stayed in it anyway. What little there was, was about to come roaring out. I needed a bathroom, fast.

Where the hell was I? I rolled to my side and tried to open my eyes. Wasn't going to happen until the pain in my head eased up, and it didn't feel like that would be any time soon. A groan wormed its way out from behind my clenched teeth, a deeply pained sound that seemed to echo in the air. And in my body. Which only made matters worse. Now it felt like my head was about to explode.

I lay still and pressed my hands hard on my skull, hoping to keep it in one piece—I figured brains worked much better when they weren't splattered all over someone's walls—and groaned again, finally managing to crack open my lids. The room's door opened, flooding in light from the hallway. It stabbed into my head like a heated, double-edged, serrated knife.

"Shit!" I yelped.

I screwed my eyes shut, and clamped my lips together even tighter, fighting the nausea for all I was worth, since I knew I hadn't the strength to even get out of bed, much less walk—or even crawl—to whatever bathroom might be around. Strong, gentle arms enfolded me. They slowly and carefully lifted me up to a semi-sitting positon.

"Here, take a sip of this."

I cracked open one eye to find Garrett holding up a steaming mug of something rancid smelling. My stomach gave yet another lurch. I closed the eye and shook my head.

"I'll only throw it up," I muttered.

"Come on, you know it's what you need. It'll settle you right down."

My stubborn streak chose that moment to interject its oh-so-intelligent two cents.

"I hate that stuff. It's gross and disgusting."

I moaned even louder and held up my hands to fend off the offending brew.

"And it'll cure what ails you. Unless you want to continue suffering."

I dropped my hands and raised both lids to find I was ensconced on the bed in Garrett's spare bedroom. Garrett sat on the edge of the mattress, grinning at me, totally enjoying my discomfiture. The jerk.

He knew that, for me, the taste of both chamomile and ginger were next to anathema; mixed together they destroyed all hope for the future and induced thoughts of suicide. But he—and I—also knew it was the only combination that could take away the long-lasting effects of being yanked out of a past-over-present trance, which is why he'd brewed up the evil concoction. And oh, he so enjoyed watching me make the ugly decision to either suffer the taste, or the days-long pain.

To me, both were equally horrendous.

I shuddered and moaned again, then grimaced as I gave in and took the mug of ginger-chamomile tea from him. I forced down the first sip, then sat struggling not to eject it right back up. I kept my teeth clenched tight until the first taste finally settled and my queasy stomach eased up just a bit, then lifted the mug for a second equally gross sip. Much as I detested the taste, I knew I had to drink the whole mugful, or for days I'd suffer the aborted-vision aftereffects of debilitating nausea and stabbing headache.

It took me almost a half hour to finish the liquid; each sip had to settle fully before I could take another without hurling. Garrett sat beside me the whole time, holding my hand, not talking, just letting his presence help to soothe me. When I finally finished the hideous drink, he took the empty mug, set it on the night stand, and sighed.

"I'm so sorry I had to grab you—"

"It's okay." I gave him an anemic smile, the best I could manage at that point. "You didn't have any choice. I knew what was happening, that the cops were there, I could hear you, hear them, I just couldn't break myself out of it." I shook my head and gave a half laugh. "I can just imagine what they would have thought if they'd caught us and I told them why we were there. If they waited until the vision ended, that is."

"They wouldn't have. They'd have grabbed you and then had your unresponsive, half-dead body on their hands. And the hurling aftereffects when you woke up, since they don't know about the tea." Garrett grinned back at me. "That would have been a laugh riot."

"Good thing you'd thought to lock that bedroom window."

"It's the Boy Scout in me; you know, always be prepared."

"You were never a Boy Scout, Garrett."

"That's beside the point." I rolled my eyes and Garrett laughed. "How are you feeling now? Semi-human, at least?"

"I think so. What time is it, anway?"

"Three-seventeen," Garrett said, checking his watch. "You were out almost four hours. Started to scare me for a minute, there, it doesn't usually last so long. I'm glad you finally woke up on your own."

"Me, too." I nodded, took a deep breath, and then remembered.

"My car. It's parked where Humboldt turns into Butterfly. I better go get it. I don't want the cops to find it," I added, thinking of Dunwitty. That's all I needed, Dunwitty back in my life.

Garrett set his hands on my shoulders to stop me from getting up, which was a good thing. I could tell my legs were still too shaky to hold me. I'd only have ended in a heap on the floor, and given him even more ammunition with which to tease me.

"Don't worry, it's not there anymore. I had Dane take care of it. It's here, in the driveway."

"What did you tell him?"

"Just," Garret said with a grin, "that I needed it picked up and brought here."

"Really? Well, thanks." I settled back in the bed and pulled the covers over my still-shuddering body, grateful that Garrett had trained his people to take unexplained orders any time of the day or night. "Thank Dane for me, too. I hope you're paying him what he's worth."

Garrett laughed, then leaned over and kissed the top of my head.

"He's well compensated, though tips are always appreciated." I rolled my eyes. "Do you remember much of what you saw?"

I shook my head; that was another side effect of being forcibly pulled out of a vision, losing the thread of what I had seen. I sighed, exhaustion now setting in with a vengeance. My sojourns into unconsciousness never seemed to alleviate any need for sleep. Inexplicably, they increased it.

"No, it's all a jumble. Flashes, bits and pieces, that's it. Maybe in a day or two, more will come back to me." I shrugged. "If you hadn't grabbed me..."

"Yeah, well, there was no help for it. Listen, it's late and we both need to get some sleep." He tried to stifle a yawn, but his working jaw and half-closed, tearing eyes gave him away. "We'll go over what you remember in the morning, maybe some shuteye will clarify things a bit."

"Maybe," I said, though I doubted it.

Garrett left and I closed my eyes, not sure how much sleep I'd actually get no matter how tired I felt. This was the first time figures from the past had touched me—or, rather, barrelled through me—and I could still feel the icy coldness that had impaled my body. Every few seconds shudders whipped through me. I wasn't sure my core would ever fully warm up again.

I lay worrying about how to piece together the bits and pieces of the vision that were all that was left to me, and gradually sank deeper and deeper until the sunlight streaming in the window woke me six hours later.

There were no daylight revelations. I remembered only the two forms penetrating my body and lots of blood splashed around, though I felt deep inside that I'd seen something important, something that stayed just out of reach. No amount of forcing made it any clearer, and after about a half hour I gave up trying, hoping that maybe in a day or two, if I gave it time and space, enlightenment would burst upon me. Not that it ever had, but hey, hope is supposed to spring eternal, right?

I drove home around eleven-thirty, showered, and set to work on Araceli Aguayo's little problem, finally figuring out the mind behind the mischief. I called her to give her an update, but she insisted we meet face-to-face; I could tell by her tone she didn't want to hear what I had to say. She said she needed some time to prepare, and I wondered who she feared was at fault. We agreed to meet the following day, again at Starbucks, around three-thirty. I finished up my report for her, then dove into the background checks for the insurance company until, sometime around four-thirty, a dire need for coffee urged me up onto my feet.

On the way into the kitchen, I found Bass Ehrler once again hovering in my living room.

She woke shivering, naked, in complete darkness. Her head ached, and pain radiated between her legs when she tried to move. Something hard and cold encircled her wrists and ankles; a metallic clanking echoed in the dark when she shifted position. Her mouth felt like it had been stuffed with cotton wool. Her breasts hurt with every breath.

Where was she? What had happened to her? Memory shifted; she'd closed the store, started for her car, and then...

What?

She reached out into the darkness only to be brought up short by whatever was around her wrist. The metallic clanking—*like chains*, she thought—resounded on the cold air.

Chains? She was chained? In a flash, she remembered someone grabbing her, the sweet-smelling cloth over her face, falling into oblivion. Panic burst in her chest.

"Oh, my God, what's happening to me?" she cried. "Where am I?"

"Be quiet," a shuddery voice whispered close by. "He gets angry if you make any noise. You don't want to make him angry."

"Him? Who?" She couldn't help it; her voice rose with every word until screamed out her terror. "Who are you? Where am I?"

"Don't yell, please. He'll only hurt both of us."

The terror in the whispered plea clogged the rest of the words in her throat. She froze and held her breath. In the sudden silence she could hear breathing nearby that seemed to shiver in and out, quaking a staccato, semi-silent tracing into the blackness. The person with her, she realized, was hurt, scared, probably chained, too. Terrified as she was, she felt a slight bit of comfort that she was not alone.

"Who are you?"

The whispered words were so soft she almost missed them. She had to blink back tears before she could find her voice.

"Yvonne. Yvonne Avila."

"I'm Heidi."

"Heidi?" Yvonne gasped in a breath. "Heidi Coffey? But... you disappeared two weeks ago."

"Only two weeks? Feels more like two years."

"I can't believe it. They've been looking for you everywhere. Most people think you're dead."

A pained sigh echoed on the air and Yvonne cringed at the anguish it contained.

"I wish I were," Heidi whispered, a world of longing and hopelessness in her tone.

Panic again dug into Yvonne's body. She had to fight not to scream out loud again.

"We have to get out of here, now, before he comes back!"

"How? We're chained in cages in a barn with no one anywhere around. There's nothing we can do but wait, until he comes back. And he always does."

Tears streamed down Yvonne's face; her breath hitched in her dry throat. She forced her aching body to move, dragged the heavy chains until she encountered the hard, cold bars that held her prisoner. She knew what the pain in her body meant, what the man must have done to her while she was unconscious, her terror increasing with every movement, every breath. No way would she let him do that to her again. She had to get out, now, before he came back. She battered at the cold, unyielding bars with all her strength, gaining only throbbing pain in her hands.

"Oh, God, who is he, what does he want? What is he going to do to me?" she cried, her voice echoing up to the high rafters.

"Whatever he wants," Heidi moaned.

A door screeched open. A glint of light wormed a few feet into the huge space, a bare step above the pure darkness that had enveloped her. From her cage on the far wall, Yvonne blinked her light-starved eyes at the figure that stood limned in the doorway, then she shrank back against the bars of the cage when he stepped into the room. A mewling wordless plea shuddered from her mouth.

The man didn't look at her. He shut the door, walked over to the far wall, and snapped on powerful lights that lit up a waist-high platform. Only then did he stalk over to Yvonne's cage and unlock the door's padlock.

"Time for your film debut, my new little angel," he crooned as he reached in, unfastened the chains from the eye-bolts sunk into the floor, and wound those attached to her wrists around his hands.

He dragged her out of the cage and across the straw-strewn floor, embedding splinters deep into her buttocks and back, then hauled her onto the platform and secured the chains on her wrists and ankles to the eye-bolts in the floor. Yvonne couldn't help herself; the pain in her back and her tight-stretched limbs was so bad that, despite Heidi's advice to remain quiet, she kept begging over and over, her voice choked with terrified tears. She begged for mercy. For him to let her go. For him to stop.

"Let's see," he murmured as he contemplated the shelves on the wall, ignoring her pleas. "What to start with. That other bitch tonight wasn't nearly enough for me. I need more. Lots more."

Yvonne watched him make his choice, don a black ski mast, then turn on a wall-mounted video camera. Her body thrummed with terror; pain and panic dribbled out the side of her mouth when he turned to where she lay naked, spread-eagled, open and helpless. He gave her the cruelest smile she had ever seen.

"First lesson, bitch, is not to beg for what you can never have. Took that one over there a long time to learn it. How smart are you?"

He turned on the mini-torch, climbed on top of her, and sat on her thighs. He ran his ragged nails over her breasts, down across her stomach, then touched the flame to her abdomen. Yvonne's agonized shriek drowned out his laughter.

CHAPTER TWENTY-THREE

Ehrler lifted his glass to me. I held up my hand.

"No, not a word, not until I've got my coffee."

"You drink too much of that stuff," he intoned when I returned to flop on the couch beside him. "Caffeine isn't good for you, you know."

"And that stuff is?" I gestured at the deep red wine in his hand, lit by a shaft of light streaming in a window that hadn't astral traveled along with him. "Especially as much as you imbibe."

"Skylark, please." A pained expression crossed his patrician face. "You know—"

"Yeah, yeah." I waved a dismissive hand and took a sip of my luscious brew. "Unchanging picture, I get it. So, what brings you into my humble abode this time?"

I cringed as I asked, because I so did not want to know. I had enough to deal with; my mind was still spinning possible scenarios in an attempt to bring my aborted vision into clearer focus. Not that all my cogitating had helped. Nothing was clearer; all it did was make my money-earning work that much harder to accomplish because it kept me from concentrating. I didn't need any Ehrler-inspired advice screwing me up even more.

"So, now you've met her. Did you pay attention to what she told you?"

"Met her?" I gasped and turned incredulous eyes on him as realization hit me like a bolt of lightning. "*Her*? Lillia, that fake psychic? Are you kidding me?"

"Skylark—"

"No. She's a shyster, a money-grubbing quack. All she gave us was a bunch of malarkey that didn't make any sense."

"Skylark—"

"You want a recap? How's this: lots of stairs, swaths of color, bars of wood, and a cave out in the open under trees. It was all nonsense, I can't believe you'd tell me she's the one." No way was I going to get into the butterfly and repeating numbers. That was just a fluke. Wasn't it?

"Skylark, you know there was more and—"

The doorbell, then a loud hammering, stopped his words. I sighed; couldn't I have just one day without a ton of crap burying me neck deep?

"Hold that thought," I said as I stood up. "Better yet, go back to where you came from. I don't have the energy for this."

I stomped over to the front door and yanked it open. And froze.

They stood grim faced, staring back at me. Dunwitty and Soto, both. What now? I took a deep breath, then closed my eyes and let it out in a long, disheartened sigh.

"Come on in," I said as I turned and walked back to the couch, knowing full well I couldn't really keep them out. Much as I wanted to, I didn't sit down, I just stood staring at the two detectives who slowly advanced toward me. I glanced at Ehrler. "You happy now?" I muttered.

"I'm getting there," Dunwitty answered, obviously not aware I wasn't talking to him. I looked back at him and froze again, my stare caught on the cuffs in his hands.

"Are you kidding me? Again? This has to be some kind of a joke."

"Do I look like I'm laughing?" He glared at me. "Where were you last night?"

"Last night? Why?"

Dunwitty merely smirked at me. I frowned the question at Soto, who just shook his head. He rounded the couch, passing through Ehrler's ectoplasmic form on the way, then stopped short and shuddered, a look of incredulity on his face. He turned to look behind him, at where Ehrler sat grinning up at him. After a moment, Soto shook his head, turned back and walked up to me. Interesting.

"What happened? Was someone else killed?" I asked him.

"We're asking the questions, not you," Dunwitty said. "Cuff her."

He tossed the cuffs to Soto. I shook my head and took a step back, my not-fully-healed wrists throbbing in time to the alarm that thrummed through me.

"Come on, guys, that's not necessary. Really. Just tell me what's going on."

"Uh-oh," Ehrler said, amusement crinkling up his eyes. "Looks like they got the goods on you, Skylark."

"You're not helping," I growled at him.

"I can't, not this time," Soto said, as though I'd addressed him. "We need you to come with us to answer some questions. Now."

I looked from him to Dunwitty, who stood there with a look of anticipation on his face, just waiting for me to refuse. I sighed and nodded.

"Okay, just let me put my mug away," I said as I turned toward the kitchen, but Soto put a hand on my arm to stop me. He took the mug from my grasp and set it on the floor, then looked back at me.

"Are you *arresting* me?"

"You better believe it, Miss One Name Wonder," Dunwitty crowed.

"No. Not yet," Soto said, glaring at Dunwitty. "But you do need to come to the station with us." He paused and looked into my eyes. "Do we need these?" He lifted the cuffs.

"No." I grasped a throbbing wrist with one hand. "Not at all. Can I call Reenie before we leave?"

"Call her from the station," Dunwitty snarled. "Enough of this fucking white glove treatment, José. Put the cuffs on her and let's go."

Soto shoved the cuffs in his pocket. But he didn't let go of my arm.

"Come on, Skylark. Nice and easy, okay?"

"You got it, Javier."

Soto led me toward the front door, making a wide detour around where Ehrler still sat, enjoying his front row seat at the unfolding drama. He paused, looked toward Ehrler once again, then shook his head and continued towing me out of the house and into the back of the unmarked car that sat in my driveway. Dunwitty stomped behind us, slamming the front door with unnecessary force, more than unhappy with my uncuffed status. If he'd broken anything, I'd have Reenie add it to the law suit.

The two detectives got in the front. Dunwitty took off like a bat out of hell, taking his rage and frustration out on the street and the poor car's engine. Neither looked at me or spoke to me. I sat silent, shaking, feeling both pissed off and concerned—especially considering Soto's serious look. What the hell was going on? Something really bad had to have happened for both of them to come for me like this. What was it, and why did they think I had anything to do with it? Had they found out I'd broken into that house on Monarch Lane? Surely that wouldn't have been enough to cause two detectives to come after me, would it?

Then again, we are talking about Dunwitty.

In less than five minutes we once more sat across from each other in the interrogation room. I'd been there so often lately, I thought maybe I should just put a bed in the corner and move in on a permanent basis. Dunwitty looked smug and triumphant; Soto looked down at the file he'd carried in, unable to meet my eyes. I didn't say a word. Much as I wanted answers, I'd be damned if I'd be the first to speak.

After the silence had stretched from here to the North Pole and back, Dunwitty glared at me then cleared his throat.

"All right, let's have it. First, Saturday night. Where were you?"

I stared back at him and shook my head.

"Not without my lawyer."

"Skylark, please." Soto's quiet plea made me look over at him, at his somber face that held a trace of... was that disappointment? Did he really believe I could have done whatever had happened last night? "Just answer the question."

I took a deep breath, looked down at the scarred table, and nodded. I hadn't done anything, so they couldn't prove anything. It couldn't hurt to tell them, right?

"Okay. I was at home. Yes," I added when Dunwitty snorted his derision, "alone. I have three current cases, so I spent the day and night working online. I'm sure my browser history will back me up."

"I'll just bet," Dunwitty growled. "A computer for an alibi. That's rich." He pointed a thick finger at me. "And what about last night? Home alone then, too?"

"No, I went to dinner at Galley Seafood in Morro Bay." I glanced at Soto then back at Dunwitty. "With my lawyer. And Garrett Gallivan."

"And afterward? When you left?"

I took another breath and let it out as I looked at the door. What could I say? That butterflies and repeating numbers had made me break into not just a house, but a house sealed with crime scene tape? That while in there I'd had a psychic vision that had knocked me out for hours? That would only gain me a sojourn in a cell—or perhaps a rubber room—so I fudged the truth just a little bit. As in, left out the most juicy parts.

"After dinner," I said, turning back to the detectives, "I spent the night at Garrett's house."

"Oh, how convenient. You *'spent the night'* with him?" Dunwitty's disbelief rang clear in the small room as he air quoted the words. "With the guy you claim is like a *'brother'* to you? What'd I tell you, José? The absolute dregs."

"Yes. I was at his house the whole night," I said, refusing to rise to Dunwitty's bait. "Ask him, he'll tell you. And while you're at it, call Maureen. I'm done talking to you."

"Oh, don't think we won't ask him, Miss One Name Wonder. And check your so-called '*work history*', too." More air quotes. "You just sit tight. We'll be back."

The detectives rose and walked to the door. Dunwitty opened it, then turned to look back at me.

"Do I need to cuff you to the chair?"

I could see how much he wanted to, it was etched on his face. I shook my head and looked over at the two-way mirror that hid the observation window, wondering if anyone was in there, watching. I almost didn't flinch when the door shut behind the detectives.

I sat there a good hour, unable to initiate a Zen state because my stomach had decided to punish me for skipping lunch, before the door opened to admit the two detectives again. And with them came Garrett, who sat in the chair beside me and folded my cold, trembling hands in his warm, comforting grip. How had he gotten here? Had they dragged him in like they had me? Why?

"I came the minute they called, asking about you. You feeling okay?"

"Yeah." I tried to give him a smile, but wasn't very successful. "Kinda shaky still, but I'll make it."

"They tell you what this is about?"

I shook my head, but Dunwitty slapped photos on the table before I could say anything.

"*This* is what it's about. *This* is what *you did* Sunday night to Amy Lipschitz, and don't try to deny it."

I looked down to see another mutilated body, a woman, naked, tied to a bed, her body covered with bloody wounds, her face obliterated. Just like the one they had thought was Garrett.

My stomach rebelled. I clapped my hands over my mouth to stifle my gasp, and to keep the bile that had risen into my throat from spewing across the tabletop.

"She was only twenty-six, Skylark. She didn't deserve what you did to her."

"I didn't—"

"Time of death?" Garrett cut off my hand-muffled words in the quiet, even tone that I knew presaged an eruption of the steely anger he was famous for.

Dunwitty shook his head, his narrowed gaze boring into me, but Soto opened the file he'd carried in. He flipped a couple of pages, then looked up at Garrett.

"It's just a rough estimate until the autopsy is finished, but somewhere between midnight and four a.m. Probably closer to four than midnight, the coroner said. Whoever did this took a lot of time killing her."

"And *her car* was spotted in the area, parked just a few blocks away from the house," Dunwitty added, once again pointing at me, his voice filled with triumphant gloating. "We got you dead to rights, Miss One Name Wonder. You ain't getting out of this one."

I turned to Garrett, alarm shooting through my body. Who had seen my car? And how had they known to call the police about it? Garrett shook his head at me, warning me to stay silent, then he narrowed his eyes at Dunwitty.

"I beg to differ, Detective." Dunwitty blinked; Garrett's voice had acquired the steel it had promised. "Skylark was with me from about ten-thirty on, at my house."

"Figures you'd lie for her. You care to try to prove that?"

"Of course." Garrett leaned back in his seat and crossed his arms, the picture of unconcerned indifference. "We had dinner together at—"

"Yeah, yeah, we know about that. And we know you had a fight. *She*," Dunwitty nodded his chin at me, "left before the meal was done. So you weren't together *all night* like you two claim."

"But we were, Detective. Yes, we had a slight disagreement at dinner. Skylark was upset, and was on her way out to Spooner's Cove when she got sick. A reaction to something she ate, I assume." I looked down at the table and held my breath as I listened to Garrett rearrange history in my—our—favor. "She pulled over on a side street, hoping to wait it out, but it just got worse and worse. She finally parked and called me for help. By the time I got to her, she was barely conscious. She refused to go to the emergency room—she can be pretty stubborn about that," he added, giving me a grin, "so I took her home where I could watch her and make sure she was all right. We got back to my place just before ten-thirty; I have surveillance cameras on my house, Detective. They'll prove I'm telling the truth, and show that we didn't leave until the next morning."

I turned and stared at Garrett. I hadn't known about the cameras, but then he did own a security firm. Stood to reason he'd avail himself of his own products.

"As for her car, I had one of my employees go pick it up and drive it back to my house. You can see on the security tapes that it arrived around quarter to eleven."

Soto looked from Garrett to me. The frown on his face smoothed out.

"Well, what about this one, Yvonne Avila?" Dunwitty snarled, slapping down another photo, a head shot of a lovely brunette. I'd never seen her before. "She vanished Saturday night, after she left work down in Pismo Beach, just like Heidi Coffey vanished from SLO. We found her car in the parking lot, the door open, the keys on the ground. What did you do with her?"

"Dunwitty," Soto said, looking both apologetic and pained. "Enough."

"No, she—" Dunwitty roared, but I held up a hand to stop him.

"I have no idea who this is. I was not in Pismo Beach, I was at home Saturday, working, all day and night, didn't go to bed until around three in the morning. And as I said, my browser history will prove that."

"Oh, we'll check that out, Miss One Name Wonder, you can bet on that. We've already sent someone to your house to confiscate that laptop."

I winced at the thought of my computer in Dunwitty's hands and hoped he wouldn't keep it too long. It had not only the history of my searches, it also held the reports that needed to be sent to my clients so I could get paid. One look at the smug expression on his face and my hopes died. I had the feeling I'd never see that computer—or the work I'd done—again. Not in one piece.

So much for getting paid. Being on Dunwitty's radar was getting old, really fast.

But before I could formulate a plea for leniency—or tell him what I wished I could do to him—the door opened to admit Reenie.

I blinked. Who had contacted her? I doubted it was Dunwitty, even though I'd requested it. Then Garrett squeezed my hand, once, twice, three times, and I realized he must have called her himself before he came to the station.

"No," she said, giving me a wink, "you will not confiscate Skylark's computer. You do not have probable cause to so much as touch it. I stopped by her house before coming here. I have a printout of everything she did on Saturday, which shows she was exactly where she said she was."

She handed Dunwitty a sheaf of stapled sheets; I'd never been happier about giving someone an "emergency" key to my house. Dunwitty ground his teeth together as he looked down at the printout. I was sure he had no idea what any of it meant.

"That's it, Dunwitty." Soto slapped the file closed and stood up. "Like I told you, we're wasting our time. Skylark didn't have anything to do with this. You can go," he said to me, that faint hint of apology still in his eyes. "Thank you for being so cooperative."

I nodded and both Garrett and I rose. Reenie came over and gave me a hug, then we followed the two detectives out of the interrogation room. Dunwitty stormed down the hall and veered into the Captain's office, slamming the door behind him. Soto opened the door to the main entry foyer for Reenie and Garrett, then touched my arm before I passed through the doorway.

"Your house," he said, looking somewhat uncomfortable. "I think I felt something... There was a cold spot near the end of the couch, and I could swear I

saw... I don't know, a faint image, part of an image, I..."
He shuddered.

"I thought you noted something." I gave him a small smile. "My mentor was visiting."

"No one else was there." He frowned. "You were alone."

"No, I wasn't. He was in ectoplasmic form. Most people can't detect that. I guess you must have a bit of psychic ability in your makeup. From your *abuela*, probably. Dunwitty will be so pleased."

I left him standing open-mouthed, staring after me as I walked out of the station with Reenie and Garrett.

 *CHAPTER TWENTY-FOUR*

On Tuesday, I finished and fired off the report on the background checks of the three prospective employees for the insurance investment firm, then polished and printed the report for Araceli Aguayo. I still hadn't located the skip-trace subject; I had a sneaking suspicion he wasn't in my area any longer, but I still had a few things to check before calling the client with the bad news. If nothing else, I hoped to be able to tell them where he'd moved on to.

The psychic vision I'd had in the house still hadn't come any clearer, but then I hadn't gotten a good night's sleep, either. I couldn't stop thinking about those two women, one mutilated almost beyond recognition, the other vanished into thin air as she left work. Were they related in any way, even though one took place in Los Osos and the other in Pismo Beach? Who was killing random people in such a brutal way? Who was abducting young women off the streets? Were there really two violent assholes running around our peaceful little valley at the same time? It seemed impossible to me, but there also didn't seem to be much that connected the crimes. And why was Dunwitty so all-fired sure I had something to do with any of it, despite all the evidence to the contrary?

These questions rattled round and round in my brain, keeping me awake half the night. I have to admit, I wasn't at my best when I left the house to meet Araceli Aguayo at Starbucks at three that afternoon. A headache had started pulsing behind my forehead, a faint but steady tap-tap-tap that I hoped wouldn't grow into anything I couldn't handle. At least not until my meeting was over.

She beat me to Starbucks. I found her sitting at "my" back table, her hands clasped around another frothy concoction, an untouched sesame bagel on a napkin in front of her. I bypassed the coffee counter and sat opposite her, noting the disapproving look she gave me. Animosity rolled off her in waves, but her eyes held a note of fear. I had the feeling the anger wasn't directed at me; she simply wasn't looking forward to hearing the results of my search.

Well, this should be fun, I thought as I pulled out the report. I tried to hand it to her, but she waved it away.

"No, just tell me." Her voice sounded as pinched as her face looked. "I can read all the details later, right now I just want to know the what and the who."

"All right." I nodded and set the report to the side. "You've got what I call a back-door worm attached to your website. It took someone with a lot of skill to create it and it's wreaking havoc with your profits."

I explained to her that a very clever and knowledgeable someone had installed a trojan-horse-type program that gained entrance to the protected areas of her website through the back end of her computer system. It monitored each purchase, then stole the payment for every sale over three hundred dollars by shunting the customer's payment to a bank somewhere in the Cayman Islands. Her company received the purchase order; payment was logged as it was made, as it should be, and the item or items were shipped, but the funds did not appear in her bank account. Instead, they were deposited into an account not connected with her company. Her own bank accounts were never touched. She featured one-of-a-kind, hand-made items, a good portion of them priced at three hundred dollars or more, and the loss of payment for those sales was very quickly depleting any profits she might be making from the lower payments she did receive.

"Who would do such a thing to me?" Her whispery voice shuddered. She looked ready to cry.

"It's not anyone on the list you gave me." She sighed her relief, then her face hardened and she nodded for me to continue. "It took a bit of doing to find it, but everything leaves a footprint in cyberspace. No matter how careful the hacker is, there's always a trail to follow. This one led to a Rogelio Sanchez, in Denver."

"No." It was more breath than word. She shook her head, denying what I'd said. "It can't be Rogelio. It can't."

"I assure you, it is. I've documented it very carefully." I set my hand on the report cover. "Do you know him?"

She nodded, her eyes clouded with tears that did not fall.

"*Sí.* Yes. He's my brother—my step-brother, but we grew up together, our parents married when I was seven and he was six. We've always been so close. I love him. How could he do this to me? Why?"

Her pain was hard to watch. I took in a deep breath and bit my lower lip, wishing I could take some of it away. Especially since I was the one who'd led her to it.

"In my experience, I've found that the need for money often trumps everything else—love, friendship, even family. It can make some people do very reprehensible things."

She looked down at her frothy drink, then up and out the side windows at the traffic flowing along Los Osos Valley Road. I watched her process the information, watched her shoulders stiffen, her face grow hard, her eyes condemning. She looked back at me, a searing glare that made me blink.

"No. You are wrong. This is impossible, you have no idea what you are talking about. Rogelio could not do this. You said it takes a lot of skill, and he does not have any. He does not know computers, he can barely use his laptop to do email. It cannot be him."

I nodded, understanding how difficult this was for her.

"Nevertheless, the trail does lead to Rogelio Sanchez. With enough motivation, computer skills can be learned," I added. "Or he could have simply paid someone to do it for him. Or he might have a partner."

Araceli Aguayo froze and stared at me. Her breath pulled in through her teeth. She looked as though she were a thousand miles away.

"Carlos," she spat. "Carlos Villa. I warned Rogelio about him. But Rogelio was in love..." She blinked and shook her head, coming back to the coffee shop where we sat. "Could someone do this without my brother's knowledge? Use his equipment, and keep it a secret?"

I thought it over and nodded.

"If Rogelio is as clueless about technology as you think he is, then yes, someone probably could. It'll be up to the police who deal with technology and internet crimes to figure that out. Of course, Rogelio will be considered the culprit. It'll be hard to prove otherwise, given that his computer was used to steal the money."

"*Dios mio,* I can't deal, I... I..." Her voice, her hands, her whole body began to shake. She blinked as tears escaped her eyes and tracked down her cheeks. "Excuse me, I... I have to..."

She grabbed her purse and headed into the women's room. I sat rubbing my aching forehead and wondering if she'd return to the table for the report, or if she'd just leave once she was done in the bathroom. At least I didn't have to worry about any family members betraying me like hers had, since I had no family. And didn't want one, either. My fractured upbringing didn't exactly prepare me to deal with motherhood. And there wasn't a man on the face of the earth who would want to share his life with a freak like me.

One huge, honking bullet dodged. Too bad it didn't make me feel any better.

To my surprise, Araceli Aguayo returned to the table. She didn't sit down, she merely picked up her copy of the report, the half-empty coffee cup and her uneaten bagel.

"I must thank you for this," she said, her face filled with deep sadness. "Even if it was not what I wanted to hear, you have saved my business. It is now up to me to make sure this back door worm thing does not continue." She handed me an envelope with my name handwritten on the front.

"I just wish it had been someone you *didn't* know." I frowned at the envelope. "What's this? I've already been paid, the retainer is more than enough to cover my services."

"It is my gratitude," she said as I opened the envelope and took out a check. Made out to Skylark Investigations. For ten thousand dollars.

I blinked up at her.

"I can't accept this. In fact, I owe you back some of the retainer."

"No." She held up her hand when I tried to give the check back to her. "You have saved my business, and made me look at some very painful, if necessary, realities of the world. I have simply been too trusting. Of everyone. It has not made me happy to have learned this, but it has made me wiser. What you have done for me... it is worth much more than this. You owe me nothing. It is I who owe you."

She turned and walked away without another word. And she didn't look back. I sat a moment longer staring at the zeros on that check, trying to decide if I could, in good conscience, keep it, then sighed, tucked it into my purse and left for home. I'd have to think on it some more when my head didn't hurt so much. It was strange, though, to think that my financial situation, in crisis just a week ago, was now looking rather healthy. *If* I kept Araceli Aguayo's check, that was. I wasn't sure what to do with it, cash it or send it back to her. Maybe Reenie and Garrett would have some advice on the subject. I'd call them after I managed to grab some sleep.

Weariness dogged my footsteps as I dragged myself into the house. With my thoughts on the few inches of Glenlivet that remained in the bottle, or a few of those Ibuprofen tablets from the bathroom cabinet—or maybe both—I slogged into the living room, heading for the bookshelf on the far wall where I would deposit my purse. Maybe it was the exhaustion that lapped at me after night of broken sleep, or the way my head was pulsing. Or it could have been my bemusement at having received a ten thousand dollar tip, that made me unaware. Or maybe all three. But I heard nothing, suspected nothing as I shuffled past the couch.

Hard arms grabbed me from behind. A fist smashed into the side of my face and my legs buckled. Before I could blink, I found myself on the floor, fighting to stay conscious.

CHAPTER TWENTY-FIVE

He was on me in a flash, straddling my pelvis, pinning my arms with his knees, screaming words I couldn't understand and smashing his fist into my face, over and over. I felt the bones in my nose crunch; blood flooded down my throat, then spewed out my mouth to coat the front of the sweatshirt he wore. I writhed and bucked, trying to throw him off, but nothing worked. I could feel myself fading; my eyesight dimmed to a pinpoint and the only way out I could see was to flee as far as I could from the pain searing into me, even if that meant plunging into death.

But no way would this son of a bitch force me down that path. I grabbed onto the last vestige of consciousness I could find and held on for all I was worth. By the time he administered the last blow and stood up, I could barely breathe, my eyes were swollen almost shut, and I couldn't move. I used what little strength I had left to hold onto a tiny spark of awareness as he dragged my arms up and bound my wrists together.

"I got plans for you, bitch," he growled. "You got a fuck-load of lessons to learn."

He dropped my bound hands onto my chest, rippling more pain through me, then stepped to my side and looked down at me. I squinted my swollen eyes to bring him into semi-focus and forced words out in panting breaths.

"Fuck... your... self..."

His face contorted with rage. He drew back his booted foot and started kicking, hitting my left shoulder, my ribs, and my hip, over and over, as again he screamed at me.

"Shut!"

Kick.

"The!"

Kick.

"Fuck!"

Kick.

"Up!"

Kick.

"Bitch!"

Kick, kick, kick.

I must have passed out around then, because when next I became aware of a life that didn't seem to have much going for it other than agony, he was nowhere to be seen. I lay half on my side, facing the back bedrooms and shuddering from pain that shot through my body like a lightning storm jacked up on crack. My wrists were still bound, my face felt like it had been through a meat grinder, and I could draw only sips of breath into lungs that refused to expand.

He was still in the house, though, I could hear him tearing apart my bedroom, heard things rip and shatter as he screamed his frustration to the high heavens. What was he looking for? What did he want with me? Just who the hell was this jerk-off?

It took maybe a minute for it to register on my fogged brain. My purse lay about three feet away from me. In that purse was my Glock. And in my hands, that Glock was my salvation. Problem was, to reach it I'd have to move at least one part of a body that was refusing to even consider listening to my brain's directives: move my upper body, move my arms, my hands. None of it seemed doable, not for a few hundred years or so.

Then the screaming stopped. Echoing footsteps headed in my direction and I closed my eyes, feigning unconsciousness that I so hoped wouldn't become real; I needed to be somewhat awake to hold and fire that gun. A boot toe nudged my shoulder. I forced myself not to react to the surge of pain that played a snuff game in my torso.

"Bitch!" he snarled. What an extensive vocabulary.

Then the footsteps receded. Something in my office crashed to the floor and again I forced open my eyes. I needed that gun, now, pain or no pain, snuff game or not. Gritting my teeth, I inched my arms out, gasping for air that for some reason my lungs refused to process. My fingers stretched out, but missed the purse straps by about six inches. Hissing in the anguish that moving caused, praying he wouldn't hear it, I wriggled my shoulders forward until I could snag the straps. I dragged the purse closer, then fumbled inside it until I wrapped my fingers around the pistol's grip.

The damn Glock felt like it suddenly weighed a hundred pounds. I almost despaired at being able to drag it out of the depths into the daylight. But I persevered, inch by inch, knowing it was my only chance. When it finally cleared the purse I spared myself a few seconds to lie with eyes closed, trying to marshal enough strength to lift the damn gun—that now weighed at least thousand pounds—and aim it in my attacker's direction. A deep, steadying breath would have helped, but at the moment that was far beyond my ability. I didn't need to see him; I had seventeen shots, all hollow-points that would drill right through the wallboard that separated us. If he was anywhere in those back rooms, with an ounce of luck I would hit him. Or come close enough that he'd run for the hills.

Faint sirens sounded in the distance as I lifted the Glock and clutched it in both hands—working like the devil to keep it from wobbling and praying the kickback wouldn't knock it from my grasp—and squeezed the trigger. Once, twice, three times; on and on as holes opened in my walls, plaster dust rained onto the floor, and agony shot into my head from the noise and through my body from the exertion. I heard the asshole yelp, heard him swear up a storm, then start to run. I followed the sound with bullets, my eyes too bleary to see anything but a faint blur of movement as he ran from office to bedroom. I kept pulling the trigger until I became aware that the boom of the shots had stopped. Only a faint clicking remained.

Out of ammo.

I was back to being helpless. Damn, I hoped the asshole had crawled out a back window and fled. Or, better yet, was bleeding out on my bedroom floor.

As the sirens drew closer I rolled halfway onto my back, my weapon still clenched in my bound hands. The heat from the barrel stung into my cheek. I searched for air, but the change in postition didn't help; there was none anywhere, not for me. I couldn't seem to get my lungs to expand. My fingers began to tingle, then my hands went numb. I didn't know if I still held onto the Glock. When I cracked open my eyes to look, the room whirled around as though it were caught in a funnel.

I heard shouts, the sharp snap of wood breaking, stomping feet, then someone touched me. He was back! I jerked and tried to lift the gun that somehow had gained even more weight. I could feel it wobble in my frozen fingers. I tried to move, to push away from the probing hands, but lack of air and pain defeated my efforts.

"Skylark, it's okay," a deep voice said. It sounded familiar but I couldn't quite place it. Warm hands covered mine. "It's Detective Soto-Osorio, Skylark. Javier. Let me have the gun. Let go of the gun, Skylark."

"No," I moaned, rolling my head on the hard floor. "Need... it...." No way would I give up my only protection. Numb hands or not, I did my best to tighten my grip.

"There's blood back here," someone shouted. "And a broken window."

"Come on, Skylark, I can't help you if you're waving a gun in my face," the voice above me said.

I squinted my eyes the tiny bit they'd open, fluttered the lids to clear my vision, and caught sight of a blurry Javier Soto kneeling beside me. I gasped again for breath that stayed just out of reach and loosened my hold on the pistol grip. Soto eased it from my hands.

"Can't... breathe..." I gasped.

"All right, let me look," Soto said, cupping my face in gentle hands.

"Guy's gone, but she hit him," Dunwitty barked over Soto's shoulder. "There's a trail of blood out the back window. How's she doing?"

"She'll be fine," Soto said, but I knew he was lying. I could hear it in his voice, see it in his face, feel it in my body.

"No," I said, or tried to say. It came out more like a pained moan than a word.

Soto's hands moved, turned me fully on my back, straightened out my legs, cut the bonds on my wrists and laid my arms at my sides. Then he pulled up my shirt. He winced and drew air in through clenched teeth.

"You got a pen on you?" Soto asked.

He looked up at Dunwitty who frowned, then pulled a ballpoint out of his shirt pocket and handed it to his partner. Soto unscrewed it and discarded the insides, then pulled a pocket knife from one of his pockets and bent back over me.

"I'm sorry, this is going to hurt, Skylark, but I've got to do it. Got to relieve the pressure."

"What the fuck?" Dunwitty yelped. "She'll sue the shit out of you, you cut her, José. Wait for the ambulance, I already called for it."

"There's no time." Soto glared up at the huge detective. "And it's Javier, not José. Just once will you remember that?"

With Dunwitty hovering overhead, Soto bent back over me, knife in hand, but by this time I wasn't really aware of his intentions. Everything had narrowed to a tiny pinpoint. Sounds echoed as from a far distance. I didn't seem to even have a body anymore. It was like I didn't really exist.

Until Soto cut into me. Pain screamed me back into existence. I felt it issue from my throat in an elongated howl, then a hissing sound shot into the air and suddenly I could breathe again. I gulped air, terrified it would vanish just as suddenly.

My head cleared—well, as much as it could given the beating I'd taken. Tingles started up in my hands as blood circulated with a vengeance, as though they wanted to punish me for denying them their life-giving oxygen. I forced my sore lips into a mini-smile and gusted out words with each breath.

"Thanks. That's... so much... better."

"We've got an ambulance on the way. Just lie still, you'll be fine."

"No. No... ambulance. I'm... fine. Just... help me..."

I shifted, tried to sit up despite the pain that dug into me with each tiny movement, but Soto's hands on my shoulders held me down. He frowned into my face.

"I said, don't move. You've got a mashed face, broken ribs and a punctured lung, and God only knows what else. You need an ambulance and a hospital. Don't argue," he said, forestalling my protest, "and don't give anyone any grief, or I'll have you put on the lockup ward and cuffed to the bed. Got it?"

I nodded, knowing I had no choice. Even as stubborn as I was, I knew I needed help. Professional, medical help. Still, I wasn't going to let Soto off scot free. I reached up, grabbed his tie, and pulled him down closer to me.

"You've... been hanging... around... Dunwitty... too long," I managed to gasp before I passed out, his chuckle echoing in my ears.

CHAPTER TWENTY-SIX

I woke hours later in a dimly lit room with even dimmer memories of the emergency room's controlled-panic scramble playing tag in my mind. Soft beeps echoed around me. My whole body felt like someone had soaked me good then wrung me dry with more than one vicious twist. My eyes only opened to half mast, and when I tried to move my head every cell in my body protested. But at least I could breathe—as long as I didn't expand my lungs more than an inch. If I went any deeper, the ribs on my left side punished me with a jab of white hot lightning.

My mouth and throat were drier than the Sahara, and my tongue felt swollen to twice its size. My vocal cords had glued themselves together. I'd have sold my soul for a sip of cool water, but just the thought of moving any part of my body depressed me—mainly because I knew I couldn't do it. I must have made some sound, though, because the rustle of clothing emanated from my right side and then Dunwitty's ugly mug loomed into view.

How long had he been sitting there, watching me sleep? The thought gave me the heebie-jeebies. Now he stood hulking over me, a secretive little smile on his thick lips that did nothing to erase the venom in his eyes. I sighed.

"I'm really not in the mood for you," I managed to whisper.

Then the dryness in my throat caught me up in a spasm of coughing. I thought my ribs would fly apart and my whole left side crumble into dust, to say nothing of the pain that seared through my bruised face. Tears leaked from my eyes, not really something I wanted Dunwitty privy to. He had enough ammunition against me as it was.

"Here," he said, holding a cup of water near my mouth. "Try some of this."

I glared at him, wondering why he was being nice to me, but he flexed the straw between my swollen lips before I could attempt any more words—not that I was capable of forming any. I managed to suck in the amazing elixir, one, two, three swallows of pure relief, if I'd ever tasted any. I guess I got greedy, though, or gulped too fast, because he pulled the straw out from between my lips when I tried for a fourth mouthful, then set the cup aside.

"That's enough. You need to go slow with that stuff or it'll come right back up. And that's not something I ever want to see."

I knew he was right—not that I'd let him know that —so I merely closed my eyes and sighed out the half-breath I could take without re-awakening the pain monster that crouched inside me. Then I opened my eyes and looked at Dunwitty again.

"What day is it?"

"Wednesday, late afternoon. You been sleeping a good twenty hours."

He glared at me as though it were my fault, the jerk.

"Why are you here? Looking for a way to prove I did this to myself?"

"Ah, if only I could. But I doubt even you could mess your face up this bad."

My heart clenched in my chest as a shot of panic pierced into me. It's not like I'm vain, or anything, but— my face? Damn it! I lifted my hand, the one that didn't have an IV stuck in it, and silently ordered it to go on a fact-finding mission since getting out of bed and finding a mirror was out of the question—for about twenty years. My searching fingers touched a bandage over my nose and white hot stars exploded in my vision.

"Ah!" I yelped.

"Yeah, that nosy little nose of yours is gonna have a nice creative bump in it." He crossed his arms and shook his head. "Don't let it upset you, though. It gives you character."

"I already have character enough, thank you very much," I muttered, wishing I could have another sip of water. Before I could ask, Dunwitty spoke on.

"Didn't say it'd be good character, did I?" He shook his head. "Somebody was pretty pissed at you, Miss One Name Wonder. I bet it was your partner in crime, the guy you search out those young women for. Guess you had a bit of a disagreement, huh? What happened? Didn't he like the last one, or something?"

"Crap, give it a rest, will you?" I gave him as searing a look as I could manage from half-closed eyes;

he twisted his lips in a sarcastic little moue. "Why don't you get lost and send in Soto? He's at least somewhat open minded."

"Your newest convert?" He snorted. "I wouldn't let him near you anymore with a ten-foot pole. He'd probably believe whatever lie spewed out of your mouth. I left him at your pig sty, going through the mess. Do you really live like that?" He raised an inquisitive brow; I sighed and closed my eyes, hearing echoes of the intruder trashing my bedroom and office. "Now, give me your version of the truth so I can get the hell out of here. I got more important cases waiting for me, ones that deserve my attention."

Insult or not, that was exactly what I wanted, Dunwitty gone. As Mr. Old School pulled his notebook and pen from a pocket, I pressed the button to raise the head of the bed. I didn't even get halfway up before rising pain made me stop it. Still, it felt better than lying flat. I shallow-panted, eyes closed, until the throbbing eased, then took a tiny bit deeper breath, opened my eyes, and told him what had happened, step-by-halting-step. I didn't bother looking at him, I could see his disbelieving sneer in my peripheral.

"I think he was going to take me with him," I said at the end, "when he finished looking for whatever it was he wanted."

"What makes you say that?"

"It makes sense. Why else tie my hands? I was barely conscious on the floor, he could have just left. I couldn't have stopped him. But tying me meant he had something else in mind. And he told me he had plans for me. How did he put it?" I tried to frown, but my facial muscles weren't having any of it. "Oh yeah, I had 'a

Susan Tuttle

fuck-load of lessons to learn.'" I blinked up at Dunwitty. "He didn't like it when I told him to fuck himself."

Again, Dunwitty snorted.

"Only you, Miss One Name Wonder. Only you." He shook his head. "So who was this guy? Gonna give me his name?"

"Don't know it, don't know who it was. I didn't see his face, just his fists. His sweatshirt has my blood on it, though. Lots of it."

"And one of your bullets somewhere in his body." *Good*, I thought. "He left a blood trail right out the busted back window, which is how he got in. Coulda saved you some damage had you just given your boyfriend a key."

I closed my eyes in an effort to close out Dunwitty, since I couldn't get up and leave him in my dust. The guy just wouldn't quit.

"What do you have that he wants so bad?"

"Don't know. He never said." I licked my lips, my voice hoarsening from dryness, and winced to try to keep the cough from getting loose again. "Just screamed like a banshee when he didn't find it."

Dunwitty held the cup for me again and I managed another sip before he played Evil Nurse Nellie and pulled it away—dribbling water down my chin, this time.

"For your own good," he told me. As if.

"How did you guys get there so fast?" I swiped a careful palm over my bruised chin—the last thing I needed was cold water drying on my face and making me shiver—leaned my head back and closed my eyes. I could feel exhaustion spreading its insulating blanket over me. "I'd barely finished shooting at him when you showed up."

"Neighbors called, heard all kinds of screaming, stuff breaking, figured something was major wrong. The, uh," he pulled out his notebook and flipped a few pages, "Mobleys. They style themselves the neighborhood watchdogs. You ask me, they shoulda saved themselves a call, pulled up chairs and watched the show til it was over. Be a lot more fun investigating your murder than just a stupid domestic situation."

"You're an ass, Dunwitty," I muttered as my eyes closed of their own volition.

"I'll be back." I heard his notebook slap shut. "Don't go anywhere, and don't leave town, Miss One Name Wonder."

I know I made a sound, I could hear it, but audible words were now far out of my reach. I drifted away, Dunwitty's laughter and receding footsteps echoing in my aching head, knowing I owed the Mobleys one hell of a thank you for saving my life. I wondered what I could possibly give them, since no one would ever eat anything I cooked—not even me—and this hospital stay would effectively drain my just-refilled coffers, even if I deposited Araceli Aguayo's bonus check. Assuming it hadn't been stolen, that is. I'd be on unpronounceable-ingredient, no-name, boxed mac 'n cheese rations for the next six months.

Seemed that no matter how fast I spun the rat-race wheel, I just couldn't get ahead.

"Who the hell does that bitch think she is?" Carstairs screamed as he poured iodine over the bullet wound in his leg. "How dare she fight back? How dare she shoot at me?"

He'd passed out when he'd gotten home, waking around ten a.m. to assess the damage, take care of the injury, and call in sick to a boss who'd threatened to fire him for not calling at the crack of dawn.

He'd been lucky; the wound wasn't that bad, a through-and-through in the meaty part of his thigh. Nothing major had been hit, it had almost stopped bleeding by the time he got back to his truck. But it would be enough to keep him from mounting ladders, so work was out of the question for at least the rest of the week, and maybe next week, too. Now, instead of having that uppity bitch to educate and tame after a hard day's work, he'd lose money and have to doctor the wound himself because he couldn't take a bullet wound to those asswipe doctors who thought following the rules was like a law or something. They'd not hesitate to report it the second he limped through the door. And wouldn't that fuck him?

Because of Skylark, he was out both money and decent medical care as well as his reading glasses—and maybe a job. He'd torn that place apart, but couldn't find them. He knew she had them, he'd seen her with them. Just the thought of her being able to hide them so well pissed the hell out of him.

She should be in his hands right now. In the barn, in the cage, naked, chained, beaten to a pulp. She should be begging for mercy he'd never give her, not being molly-coddled by goody-two-shoes doctors in the hospital. He'd had it all planned out. She had no right to fight back, no right! She should be his, damn it, *his*!

"Shit, fuck, and damn!" he screamed as he bandaged the wound.

Someone will have to pay for this, he thought, his anger like a flaming veil of fire half-obscuring his vision. And since he didn't have the one with the weird name— the one whose cage sat empty, waiting—he'd have to use what he had at hand.

Chucking the bloody cloths toward the garbage can, he limped out of the house and headed to the barn. Once there, he snapped on the lights over the stage, turned on the camera, and fit the ski mask over his head. He picked up a hammer and toured the cages, smashing at the bars just to hear the women cry and plead.

The Yvonne bitch jumped and yelped, then glared up at him with defiance despite not having been fed more than one bowl of oatmeal in the last three days. With what he'd done to her and the lack of food, she had to be hurting bad. He grinned at her, well pleased; she had staying power, that one.

The new little bitch, Casey, the one he'd picked up Monday night after the cops had hauled in the Skylark bitch, making him postpone his plans for her, wailed long and loud. He'd have to cure her of that. But his first one, Heidi—she didn't move, didn't even look up at him. He banged another time on the bars, but there was no response other than what looked to be an involuntary twitch.

Looked to him like she'd given up. Already, after only two frigging weeks. He'd really made a mistake with that one. What was the point of going through all this work if they croaked before they learned anything? If they had no staying power? His internet audience would get disgusted with his show if he had to keep breaking in new bitches. He had promises to keep—the show was called How To Train A Bitch, after all, so they had to get trained, not give up, right?—and this Skylark was ruining even that for him.

He unlocked the cage door, then unhooked the chains from the eye-bolts in the floor and dragged Heidi out. He dumped her on the floor a few feet from the stage set-up and nudged her with his boot.

"Get up."

Nothing. No hint of movement. He nudged harder, a little kick to her shoulder.

"Up, bitch! Do what you're told."

Again, nothing. The rage that had been simmering ever since Skylark had fired at him blew up into clouds of hellfire. He drew his foot back and gave her a good shot on her hip.

"Did you hear me? Do you know what I'll do to you for disobeying me? Get. The. Fuck. Up!"

Heidi nodded her head and moved, got halfway to her hands and knees, then collapsed with a low moan. Carstairs ground his teeth together. A nasty sounding growl issued from between his lips.

How dare she defy him? How dare she just lie there? How dare she give up? He'd teach her who was boss.

He kicked her, over and over, screaming at her to get up. She curled into a ball and wrapped her arms around her head, not even trying to obey his orders. The image of Skylark superimposed itself over Heidi's head, her body, and Carstairs' fury knew no bounds. He raised the hammer and brought it down, over and over, obliterating that face, that head, that body. Skylark's face. Skylark's body. When at last the red seeped out of his vision and the frenzy abated enough for him to be aware of where he was, who he was beating on, the Heidi bitch was nothing but a pile of broken bones and shredded flesh.

He stared down in disgust, the air throbbing with the horrified sobs of the two remaining caged women. This was all Skylark's fault. Now, on top of everything else, he had a body to get rid of, and a new bitch to find. Disgusted, he threw the hammer on the ground, found a plastic tarp, and rolled Heidi in it. No way was he going to let all that blood, tissue and brain matter soil his truck. As he hauled the body out of the barn after shutting off the lights, it hit him.

The Skylark bitch had actually done him a favor.

Heidi, as fond as he'd been of her because she was his first, had been a bad choice. She was too weak. She had disappointed him over and over, almost from the beginning, whining and begging day and night. What he needed was a girl like his second, Yvonne. She was more like the Skylark bitch. Defiant, strong, bold, and rebellious. A woman worth the work of taming. Casey was still too new to evaluate.

He started to lift the plastic roll into the bed of the truck, when inspiration struck. Or, to be accurate, Intervention Number Five, courtesy of his good friend, Fate. A way to send a message to Skylark, his pledge to her of what was to come.

Wouldn't that just make her day?

He grinned as he hauled the unwieldy bundle behind the barn and dumped it in the tall grass that had grown up around the abandoned machinery that littered the field.

A woman worth taming. Yes, that is what I need, he thought as he drove out of his isolated compound late Wednesday afternoon, headed for Los Osos. *Another woman or two like Skylark.* And he knew just how, one day soon, he'd thank Skylark for her help. Over and over and over.

 *CHAPTER TWENTY-SEVEN*

"I'm so sorry," Garrett said for about the hundredth time on the fifteen-minute drive home from French Hospital late Friday morning.

"Garrett, it's not your fault," I murmured from beside him in the car. Maybe if I said it enough times, he'd start to believe it.

"It is, Skylark. He got in because there was no security system in the house. Damn it, that's what I do for a living! How the hell could I let you move into a house that wasn't properly secured? It sure as hell *was* my fault."

"No, it wasn't, Gar. He'd have gotten in, one way or another, security system or no security system. You know that."

He braked for the red light at Foothill and Los Osos Valley Road, and looked over at me. The pain in his face was hard to take.

"And look at what he did to you. My God!"

"It's not a big deal. I'm fine. All this is just part of doing the kind of job I do. In a couple of weeks it'll be all healed up and you'll never know anything happened."

Untrue, and we both knew it. As Dunwitty had so magnanimously pointed out, my nose, even swollen as it was, now sported what he called a "creative" bump in the middle. And there were a total of 13 stitches in various places on my discolored cheeks, temples and chin, to say nothing of the deep tissue bruises and 31 stitches holding the left side of my body together. Or the three broken ribs and the collapsed lung. There'd be scarring, lots of it, both physically and emotionally. Good thing I'd gotten used to both early in life, or I might have been tempted to agree with Garrett. Or stop doing work I loved. But I knew, from years of experience, that scars faded, bruises vanished, and the emotional leftovers eventually withered and died. Mostly.

Except sometimes, in the small hours, in the darkest part of the night, when it all came back for a visit.

But I'd weathered that more than once, too, and I could do so—would do so—again. That was what insomnia, chocolate-chip cookie-dough ice cream, and my stash of Glenlivet was for.

"It's fixed now," Garrett said as we whipped past animal-dotted meadow and plowed-and-sown field; Garrett was well-known for his lead foot. "I'll give you the default code when we get back, and the instructions on how to change it. Doors and windows are all wired. Anyone breaks so much as a window pane, an alarm will sound in both our monitoring center and the sheriff's substation."

"Thanks for getting it done so fast. I hope you didn't put any paying jobs on hold. This could have waited, you know."

"No, it couldn't." I drew in a breath—every day a little deeper—at the grimness of his tone. It'd be a long while before he'd let himself off a hook he didn't deserve to be on. "But the exterior security lights out in the back yard, they can't get them done until this weekend. I hope that's all right."

He glanced at me, his puppy-dog eyes begging forgiveness, then looked back at the road as we sailed down the hill, passed the Los Osos welcoming bear on the left, and started up the other side.

"It's fine. Whenever they can do it without delaying any other jobs is okay with me. And don't worry, this will all heal up." I waved a hand to indicate my body.

Garrett merely shook his head as he turned right onto Palomino.

"My main problem now," I added, "is trying to figure out what I can give the Mobleys as a thank you. I can't very well poison them with any of my cooking or baking. Nosy little so-and-sos did save my life, after all."

That earned the chuckle I was going for, though it was way more anemic than I wanted. Garrett pulled into my drive and parked behind my Jeep, then came around to help me out of his high-riding SUV. Sliding out and down into his arms didn't ramp up the pain quite as much as climbing into the damn vehicle had, but I still wouldn't recommend it as the ideal home-from-hospital ride. Of course, beggars and all that. It took a minute of wincing, teeth-clenched, gasping little breaths before I felt strong enough to unlock my knees, shuffle alongside my Jeep while clutching Garrett's arm, and mount the three steps into the house.

Reenie was waiting in the living room. She bounced up off the couch and stood staring at me, wringing her hands. I held up the one of mine that wasn't clinging to Garrett's arm.

"Don't say it. It's not your fault, any more than it's Garrett's."

He led me to the couch and eased me down until I sat nestled in a plush corner. I let myself relax—as much as possible from within the cauldron of pain the bouncy ride home had stirred up—and sighed. Painful ride or not, it felt so good to be out of that hospital, and out of the reach of the medicos' probing fingers.

Reenie sat beside me and clasped my hands in hers. I smiled at her, as much of a smile as my still-sore facial muscles could manage.

"Don't look so worried. I'm fine, really. No permanent damage. Give me a couple of weeks, three at most, and I'll be back to normal."

"And we're going to pamper you for about half of that." She gave my hands a gentle squeeze and smiled back at me. "I need to go to 'Frisco tonight, I have meetings on Sunday morning and all day Monday, but I'll be back on Tuesday. Garrett will stay with you until then—"

"Whoa there, hold on a minute. What do you mean, stay with me?" I looked from one to the other; their sheepish expressions gave them away. "I'm not a child, I don't need a babysitter. Besides, I have a security system now. No one can get in. I'm perfectly safe by myself."

"Yes. We know that." Reenie looked at Garrett, who shrugged his permission for her to continue. "But you shouldn't be alone, not for a while at least. It'll help to have someone here, with you. For... you know."

I shook my head though I couldn't really argue with her. Flashbacks were par for the course after the kind of trauma I'd suffered—something I'd learned from experience—and being back at the scene of the crime, so to speak, would probably make them worse. She was right, a friendly face would make the aftermath less distressing. But damn it, I didn't want an audience. I wanted to lick my wounds in privacy.

"That won't work," I said, feeling my body beginning its slow slide into the state of drugged mummification that had become familiar these last few days. I knew I'd be asleep in about ten minutes. Damn pain meds. "I'll be camping out on the couch, it's way more comfortable than my pull-out, and there's nowhere else to sit. Except the kitchen chairs, and they don't lend themselves to longevity. Garrett won't fit on the pull-out, so don't even go there. And you," I eyed Reenie's designer-clad body—Balenciaga today —"wouldn't sleep in such a poor excuse for a bed if your life depended on it." I shook my head again. "Besides, the bedroom's trashed. It's uninhabitable. Let's face it, guys, I'm just not set up for overnight company. Or all-day company, for that matter."

"Never fear." Garrett winked at me. "It's all taken care of."

Reenie stood and tugged gently on my hands. With a lot of wincing but only a few pained grunts, I regained my feet. Reenie led me into my bedroom, which— miracle of miracles—had been cleaned up, a new window installed, even new drapes hung; sometimes friends did come in handy.

But what really held me motionless was the bed standing centered on the far wall: a gorgeous queen size sleigh bed carved from gleaming pecan wood, a lovely patchwork quilt in my favorite colors of blue, purple and green draped over the mattress.

"What?" I stared in shock, barely able to catch my breath. "Where did this come from? Reenie—"

"Yes, it's my doing. Your intruder ripped apart the mattress on the pull-out, and the couch, soft as it is to sit on, isn't good for sleeping. Not in the shape you're in."

"Reenie," I said, traitorous tears misting my eyes. I'd be damned if I let them fall, though. "I can't afford anything like this."

"Then it's good I can. And no, it's not a pity gift. Consider it an early birthday present."

"Yeah, for the next twenty years," I muttered as I tottered closer to the most beautiful piece of bedroom furniture I'd ever seen.

Reenie pulled back the quilt to reveal soft lavender sheets. Silk, to judge by the delicate sheen picked out by the light streaming past the half-open curtains. The Reenie I knew would settle for nothing less.

"I really can't let you do this." I turned to Reenie and shook my head. "It's too much."

"No, it's nowhere near enough," she replied, easing me down onto a mattress that felt soft on the surface but with a foundation of firm support. I had the feeling it would be like sleeping on a cloud. She knelt at my feet. "Now, let's take off your shoes, get rid of these clothes, and you can take a nice little nap." She began unbuttoning my sweater after pulling off my sandals.

"When you wake up, we'll have dinner waiting. Or, rather, Garrett will, I need to leave in about a half hour to pack for my trip."

"Reenie—"

"Not another word, Skylark. Just smile, lie down, and think 'thank you, Reenie' as you drift off to sleep."

Garrett left while Reenie helped me into my night clothes—she'd even purchased a nightgown for me, saying it'd be too hard on my broken ribs to pull on my usual camisole and boy shorts—then settled me into my newest piece of heaven with a smile. After a last pat on the quilt she left. I was three-quarters asleep before she reached the bedroom door, cradled in the arms of unbelieveable—and expensive—luxury.

"Sleep well," I heard her whisper, "see you Tuesday," and I was out.

I will admit, it was probably the best sleep I'd had in a long time—if ever—despite the lingering pain in my body. Two hours later the sound of voices out in the living room woke me. Male voices, one of which I'd hoped to never hear again.

I rose, moving a bit more easily, donned the silken robe that matched the nightgown, shuffled into the bathroom, and then out into the living room where Dunwitty and Soto awaited me, seated on two wooden kitchen chairs that had been placed facing the couch.

Garrett escorted me to the sofa and handed me a cup of the elixir of life in a mug I'd never seen before. Large and silver-gray, it sported a legend in sparkly purple: *Hide the Evidence, There's a PI in the House*. I frowned a question at him as he seated himself beside me.

"Came in the mail yesterday," he said. "No card, no return address, but the postmark was Minneapolis."

I smiled into the dark, luscious liquid swirling in the mug. Ehrler had sent a replacement, just as I'd demanded. I liked the other sentiment better, but the purple sparkles tickled my fancy. I wondered if he'd had it made special for me. After a moment I took a sip, then looked up at the detectives, my smile gone.

"What now?"

"We have a few questions—"

"Two more girls have gone missing." Dunwitty's harsh grate stepped on Soto's words. Soto glared at him, then subsided in his seat. "Know anything about that?"

"I've been a bit out of commission, Dunwitty. So no. Haven't got a clue."

Garrett stirred at my side, annoyance rolling off him in waves. I gave him a sidelong glance and shook my head.

"Come on, Miss One Name Wonder, these are innocent girls. Andrea's only fifteen, for God's sake." I caught the pleading tone in Dunwitty's voice, but I wasn't in the mood to play games with him. "They don't deserve what's happening to them. Give me something. Anything."

What was with this guy? After all that had happened he still thought I was involved? Well, that was it; I had had it with this moron.

"Okay, Dunwitty, you got me. All of this," I indicated my face, my body, "isn't real, it's just makeup. I've been faking it. Soto didn't really reinflate my lung, it was all an act. I doctored the x-rays, so everyone would think my ribs were broken, then snuck out late one night, dressed in my lovely backless hospital gown, called a cab—without any money or phone—kidnapped those two girls, stashed them somewhere far away, then had the cabbie drive me back to the hospital. He's my new partner. It only took one," I held up a wavering index finger, "little kiss to make him promise not to tell." I took another sip of coffee; beside me, Garrett sat trying not to laugh. "I'm really that good."

"You think this is funny, Skylark?" Dunwitty growled.

"No, I think it's tragic. Tragic that two more girls are missing, and even more tragic that you're the one assigned to find them. You won't do that hanging around here, trying to pin it on me."

Dunwitty's face turned a lovely shade of maroon, but before the lid blew off Soto took over the interview.

"Enough, Carrick. Let me." He glared at Dunwitty then turned to me. "Please, Skylark, can we go over again what happened to you? Maybe, now that you've had a chance to begin healing, you'll remember something that will be of help."

That was more like it, sane and rational, polite and somewhat sympathetic. All the animosity tucked out of sight. I nodded, keeping my gaze on Soto, but wasn't able to tell him any more than I already had. It all had happened too fast, and after the beating I'd taken, and the strong pain medication I was on, my memory wasn't at its best. I still had a lingering feeling that there was something important I'd seen during my vision at the crime scene on Monarch Lane, but it hadn't come clear and I wasn't about to muddy the waters by confessing to breaking and entering. The detectives left unenlightened —Dunwitty giving me one last glower before he slammed the door—and Garrett and I settled in to a quiet soup-and-sandwich dinner.

I had no plans to go anywhere or do anything except maybe finding where that skip-trace I'd been trying to locate had absconded to. But the intruder had smashed my laptop, along with the rest of my office. Garrett had taken it in for repair and it wasn't scheduled to be released until sometime tomorrow. And Garrett adamantly refused to allow me to go anywhere but the bedroom, the bathroom, and the living room. So I filled myself up on luscious coffee slurped from my new mug, cut creamy fudge wedges from the block Reenie had cooked up, and made inroads on the leisure reading I was always too busy to do, starting with the first volume in Lisa Lutz's *The Spellman Files* that had been languishing on my bookshelf for over a year.

I could only hope my surrogate-brother-enforced in-house recovery would keep me off the detectives' radar for the forseeable future, foreseeable meaning forever. Unfortunately, forever ended less than twenty-four hours later.

CHAPTER TWENTY-EIGHT

Despite one rip-snorting nightmare of a faceless monster flailing at me on a cliff above a roaring ocean—took a good half hour and Garrett sitting bedside, holding my hand, to bring my heartbeat into the vicinity of normal—I had my first really good night's sleep since I'd been attacked, thanks to the pain meds and the world's most comfortable bed. And the fact that no nurses came in every couple of hours to poke, prod, and wake me up just to ask me if I was sleeping okay. Sometimes the logic of hospitals totally escapes me.

I woke on Saturday ready to face the rest of my life —okay, at least the weekend. Garrett made wonderful bacon and avocado omelets for breakfast, then I took a leisurely shower—not that I was capable of moving any faster—and pulled on lounge-around clothes: yoga pants and an oversize sweatshirt, neither of which impinged on the bruises and stitches that dotted my left side. It was amazing what some good sleep, a shower and real clothes did for me; I felt somewhat energized and almost human for the first time since Tuesday afternoon. And if I didn't think about it, move too fast, or breathe, I could even believe what I'd been telling Reenie and Garrett, that in a week or two I'd be fine, back to normal.

Garrett took a run into the office just after lunch, taking my key ring with him to ensure I'd stay put, the rat. When the doorbell rang around two-thirty, I hoisted myself up off the couch—setting aside the second volume in The Spellman Files series—and shuffled my way to the front of the house. I opened the door to a short, husky, bearded, t-shirt-and-jeans-clad man in heavy work boots. He held a clipboard and blinked his shock when he took in the black, blue, and stitched-up state of my face.

"Oh, I'm sorry, I don't mean to bother you. Are you all right?"

"Yes, I'm fine. It's not as bad as it looks. What can I help you with?"

After a moment, his expression of uncertainty morphed into a friendly smile, and he handed me the clipboard.

"Mr. Gallivan sent us. I'm Henry Blodgett, crew foreman for Gallivan Security. We're here to light up your backyard, Miss Skylark."

"Yes, Garrett said you'd be coming." I scanned the work order, and the schematic beneath it, not bothering to correct Henry's assumption that my first—my only— name was a last name. Some things just weren't worth the effort. "Do I need to do anything?"

"Just put your signature here." He pointed to a line and handed me a pen. "And we need access to the back yard, so we'll have to move your car."

"Oh, I'm sorry, you can't." I signed where indicated and handed back the pen and clipboard. "I don't have the keys right now."

"No worries." He grinned at me. "Mr. Gallivan dropped them off to me around noon-thirty."

"Oh, he did, did he? My, how considerate of him."

Henry blinked at the sarcasm in my tone, but recovered quickly and gave me another of his jaunty smiles.

"Mr. Gallivan said not to bother you, he'd sign the work order later, but I wanted to let you know about the car, didn't want you to think we were stealing it or anything. We'll just park it out on the street, then pull it back in the drive when we're done."

"You do that, and I'll think of the perfect way to thank Garrett," I said, not bothering to rein in my snark; Henry's smile faltered a bit.

I didn't ask him to return the keys to me. I was sure he'd been ordered to give them to no one but Garrett. And who knew when I'd get them back? Not for the first time did I consider re-thinking this friend thing. Was some clean-up and a new bed really worth all this aggravation?

"It should only take about two-three hours, providing we don't run into any problems. The pole will go here," Henry pointed to a spot on the schematic about ten feet from my bedroom window, "with two halogen lights. One will cover the entire back yard, the other the side of the house opposite the driveway." He explained that they'd be attached to a timer mechanism, then added, "It might get a bit noisy while we're digging, sorry."

"No problem, it won't bother me. I'm just couch potatoing with a book. You go do what you have to do, and thanks."

I stood at the front window and watched them move my Jeep, making sure they had it pulled fully off the somewhat narrow roadway so it wouldn't get crunched, then went back to *The Curse of the Spellmans* as they drove a mini-digger up the drive. I had left Isabel in a sticky situation, and I was curious to see how she would extricate herself, hoping she could do so without making me laugh out loud, a hope I didn't have any trust in. These delightful books had me reading with a hand clasped on my already-aching side.

If only my own P.I. experiences could be as zany as Izzy Spellman's. Then again, she didn't have a Neanderthal called Dunwitty in her life.

A half hour later, my aching side needed a rest. I stopped to pour yet another cup of my flavor of the month, a bright, lemony Ethiopian Red Sea Reserve, just perfect for a lazy Saturday afternoon. Way too expensive for me, but hey, essential nectar of the gods, right? Well worth sacrificing a good portion of my meager food budget for a half pound of the aromatic beans.

A panicky-sounding shout from the back yard made me jump. Hot liquid splashed onto my hand.

"Shit!"

All I needed was a burn on top of all the cuts and bruises. As I ran my hand under cold water, more terrified-sounding shouts erupted from behind the house. What the hell was going on out there? An odiferous skunk? A rabid racoon? Had a coyote or a mountain lion descended from the hills and wandered into civilization? None of that seemed to warrant the amount of horror contained in those yells.

I left my coffee on the counter and headed out the side door to see what was going on. I'd have brought my Glock along if the cops didn't have it—again. *I really need to get a backup piece*, I thought as I rounded the rear corner of the house.

The crew had congregated near the back fence where the grass had been let go and stood about knee high. That was a good twenty feet from where Henry Blodgett said the security pole would be located. What were they doing back there? There were three of them: one staring motionless into the grass, hands pressed over his mouth; one bending over about five feet away— losing his lunch, I figured, from the way his back heaved —and one on his cell phone, waving a frantic hand in the air, his back turned to the site. Henry.

He snapped shut the phone, shoved it into his pocket, and looked up to see me shuffling my way across the bumpy ground toward him, though it was a lot less shuffle than the day before, and a lot more actual, though slow and careful, stepping. He came to meet me, his arms out as though to stop traffic on an LA freeway.

"Don't come any closer, Miss Skylark, you don't want to see this." He licked his lips, then swiped a hand over the sweat on his brow. "I've already called the police."

"Police? What for?" I shoved down his arm and stepped around him. I heard him take a deep breath, then he fell in step beside me. "What's going on out here?"

No one had to answer, I was close enough now to see for myself.

The naked body lay strewn in the high weeds on its back as though it were discarded rubbish thrown by a careless hand, limbs canting at odd angles. The face had been obliterated, the skull crushed, the torso nothing but a mish-mash of bloody flesh—shades of the man I'd seen in the morgue, and the pictures of poor Amy Lipschitz that Dunwitty had thrust at me. This, judging from the long, dark auburn hair and curvaceous torso, was another woman. But it wasn't the state of the body that weakened my knees and dropped me onto the ground. It was the handwritten note on the chest, pinned there by a large-headed nail driven into her breastbone.

This is your fault!

I don't remember getting back into the house, though I did have the sensation of moving: stand up; balance on unstable rubber legs; move one, then the other; repeat. By the time the fog semi-cleared from my head I found myself sitting on the couch with Garrett beside me, holding my hand. Who, I wondered, had called him? When?

A multitude of deep voices echoed through the open windows in the bedroom and office, letting me know I'd been fogged in a while; the cavalry and its entourage had had time to arrive. I blinked at Garrett and pressed a shaking hand to my lips.

"Dunwitty will have a field day with this," I whispered, trying in vain to erase the sight of that poor, tortured body—and the handwritten accusation—from my mind.

"Dunwitty's not getting near you, Skylark. He's not even here. We've got the weekend contingent out there."

"They'll call him. It's his case, he'll want in on the ground floor. And he'll want to ground me *into* the floor."

"Coffee?" Garrett asked, standing up.

I nodded, even though I wasn't sure I could keep anything down. But I felt so cold, despite the seventy-six-degree temperature. It shuddered from my core, that iciness, in waves that radiated out to torture every broken rib, stitched wound, and throbbing bruise that made up my body. I knew what that kind of cold meant, had experienced it more than once before, and the only way to stop it was to warm up from the inside out. All I needed was a visit from my ghostly failures when whoever—or Dunwitty—arrived to ask their probing questions.

My hands shook so badly when I tried to take the mug from Garrett that he insisted on holding it for the first few sips. And it seemed to work, as that amazing elixir always did. It soothed the gelid shades within me until they retreated back into their deeply buried cavern —at least for the moment—I could hold the mug myself, and the shudders finally stopped. I smiled my thanks at Garrett, who stood holding out one of my pain pills. I shook my head.

"Have you had any since this morning?"

"Haven't needed any."

"Yeah, right." He snorted his disbelief. "Well, you do now. Take it."

"No." I took another sip of coffee and let more warmth flood through my body. "I need to have my wits about me, and those things dull my mind. You know Dunwitty will show up, there's no way he won't."

"Maybe, but you need to be pain free even more or you won't think straight, you'll just spew. So, stop arguing and take this."

I knew he was right, even though it pissed me off. Pain shut off all my filters, which allowed me to say things I ordinarily wouldn't—not out loud, anyway. I snatched the pill off Garrett's palm and swallowed it down just as the back door opened and Dunwitty swaggered into the living room, Soto shadowing behind.

I hoped it was a really fast-acting pill.

The behemoth yanked a kitchen chair into the living room, set it facing away from me, then straddled it, his arms crossed atop its back. I'm sure he thought he looked cool and intimidating, but to me he looked more like a hippo trying to balance on a slippery rock. Soto remained standing at Dunwitty's right, looking almost embarrassed.

"Come on, Miss One Name Wonder," my nemesis said, his guttural voice a low purr, "make my day. Confess."

I rolled my eyes; Dirty Harry he was not. He wasn't even in the same universe as Dirty Harry.

"All right. Bless me, Dunwitty, for I have sinned. Except for one nightmare, I slept through the night thanks to some really strong pain meds. I had a good breakfast this morning for the first time in days. I've been sitting here all day reading because moving around still hurts too much. When I heard shouts I shuffled out into the back yard to find a mutilated body. And, worst sin of all, I went into shock over it."

Despite the hot coffee, I began to shudder; the shades had started to stir again. Garrett sat down beside me, his steely gaze locked on Dunwitty, one hand warm on my knee. I handed my coffee mug to Garrett and held out my hands, wrists a few inches apart.

"Slap on the cuffs, Detective, I'm guilty of it all."

"Skylark," Garrett murmured, his tone one of warning.

I looked at him and nodded. *Right. Watch my mouth until the pain med kicks in. Gotcha.*

"Who is that out there?" Dunwitty narrowed his eyes at me. "How did she get there? When, and how, did you do it? And what does *This is your fault* mean?"

It pierced through me. Hearing it in Dunwitty's accusatory voice destroyed my defenses. The ghosts moved out of the cavern and into the daylight. I gasped in a breath and closed my eyes, not wanting to see them. I could hear the men talking as though from a far distance as my own inadequacy took control.

Garrett: "Do you have a TOD yet?"

My fault. She's dead because of me.

Soto: "A rough estimate only, probably three or four days ago."

Beaten to a literal pulp. Mutilated. Shredded. My fault. I could feel wetness leak onto on my cheeks.

Garrett: "That's it, then. Three days ago, Skylark was in the hospital. She had nothing to do with this. Nothing."

Could I have stopped it? Done something different? Or hadn't I done something I should have done? Where had I failed?

Dunwitty: "Oh, she had something to do with it. How, I don't know, but I *will* figure it out. You hear that, Miss One Name Wonder?"

I opened my eyes. The room, the detectives, Garrett, all were gone. I saw only the ghosts. They lined up, fingers pointing, eyes glaring, condemning me.

Garrett: "You're way off base, Detective. I was here all night. Skylark never left the bedroom. I'd know; I'm a very light sleeper and I checked on her more than once. I heard nothing. Whoever did this was very careful, very quiet."

I'm sorry I failed you. I'm sorry. Forgive me, please. They stood in a line before me, all the ones I'd failed to save: Billy Cranston, Clara Modesto, Rene Miller, Jason Argus, Melissa Curry, Willa Porterman, Amy Lipschitz... and that faceless one, there, on the end. The one from my back yard.

"Who," I whispered to my line-up, my hands clasped so tight they hurt, "who... are you? Which one?"

Soto: "We won't know until we check dental records, but the Coroner thinks, from the age of the wounds, it might be the first one to go missing. Heidi Coffey."

Garrett: "You're truly insane, Dunwitty, if you still think Skylark's involved in this."

Heidi. The one he'd had for two weeks. The one he'd been hurting for two weeks. Why hadn't I tried harder to find her? Why had I just lived my stupid little life, when she was going through hell? It didn't matter that it wasn't my case. She'd needed me and I had failed. It was my fault.

Dunwitty: "I don't think it, I know it."

More joined the line of condemnation: ghostly images of the other missing young women: Yvonne, Casey, Andrea, Nicole. And there, lined up behind them, those I'd been forced to kill: Pietr Kaiser, Martin Lockhart, Abel Zuniga, Devon Christoff.

"No," I whispered, my breath hitching in my throat. "Go away."

Dunwitty: "Not until we get our answers, Skylark. So, start talking."

I clenched my teeth together and tried to stem a river of tears that had a mind of their own. They certainly weren't about to obey any orders from me. But tears didn't matter, they wouldn't block out the ghosts advancing on me, or banish the darkness swirling around them. I felt Garrett's hands on my arms, felt him bend over me.

"Skylark? What's wrong? Skylark?" He shook me, but still I could not respond, could see nothing but the ghosts. "Can you hear me? Talk to me, Skylark."

I can't, I thought, my vision, my whole being, filled with ghosts, my freezing body vibrating like a struck tuning fork, my breath gusting in and out of my mouth.

I felt his palm, warm on my icy cheek. Felt him turn my face to his. But I couldn't see him, couldn't see anything but the darkness, and the shades.

"Damn it. All right, that's enough. Skylark's not in any condition to continue, Detectives. You have to leave." Garrett enfolded me in his arms. "Now. And don't come back until her attorney is present."

"Oh, we'll be back, Gallivan. Don't either of you go anywhere near the yard, you hear me? It's a crime scene." Clomping footsteps, receding. Then: "That's quite an act, Miss One Name Wonder. But it doesn't change anything."

That was the last thing I heard before the emotional pain became too much to bear. I let the crowding darkness close in on me and take me far away from dead bodies, failure, and my sucky life.

 *CHAPTER TWENTY-NINE*

Garrett told me I was unconscious for close to six hours—long enough to scare him into considering hauling my carcass back to the emergency room—but I preferred to think of it not as a problem, but as a necessary break from reality. Considering the way my reality stunk these days, I was more than happy to forego six hours of it.

With my ghosts tucked back in bed where they belonged, I vegged around all day Sunday, alternately sleeping and reading The Spellman Series—the volume I had on hand, anyway. Then I sat at the repaired computer Garrett had picked up late Saturday afternoon and did some slightly dodgy digging on that skip-trace I thought had left town. At first, it appeared he had; he'd headed up to San Francisco about three weeks ago, going so far as filing an official change of address with the post office.

My spidey sense sat up and took notice. What kind of wanted fugitive leaves an easily-traced paper trail? A fugitive laying a false one, I'd bet. I traded dodgy digging for some a bit more illicit and found, wonder of wonders, he was still earning a paycheck at the local restaurant where he worked as a kitchen slug. Then I accessed the state's DMV records—and no, I'm not revealing how; moldering in a state-run facility isn't something I want to experience anytime soon—and discovered he hadn't bothered changing his address there. Plus, he'd been issued a parking ticket not two days ago, right here in little old Los Osos, in a location three blocks from the one listed as his current address on his work papers.

I know, I know; most criminals aren't the brightest bulbs in the pack, but this guy's filament didn't hold much light at all. Think about it; he was smart enough to pretend to move upstate—even if only on the surface —just to throw us off the trail, but then was dumb enough to keep his own license plates, and not park properly on his own street. Plus he worked a job with a legitimate paycheck. Did he really believe we'd all be fooled by a simple change of address at the post office, and not probe any deeper? Dumb doesn't begin to describe it; this turkey deserved to get caught.

I fired off an email with the idiot's current home and work addresses to my client, who would pass them on to the local authorities, took a moment to celebrate another job well done—and bonus earned—then went in to share a pizza and beer with Garrett. Well, he had the beer, I was limited to cola since I was still on the pain pills. Like I said, suck city.

By Monday, thanks to enforced vegging and three good nights' sleep under my belt—nightmares not-withstanding—my ability to walk without doubling over in pain was almost back in full. My bruises were turning a lovely shade of green, the stitches itched more than they hurt, breathing was fine as long as I didn't push it, and I only needed an occasional pain pill. I was ready to get back in the saddle: aka, go out hunting for the asshole who'd done this to me. But good old Garrett had other plans, and though he left for work at 8:30 in the morning, leaving me unsupervised, try as I might I could not locate any of my keys. Or my wallet. With no car and no money to pay a cab—a truly scarce, and expensive, commodity in Los Osos—I was stuck in the house. Without so much as an unread book to keep me occupied.

I spent a couple hours planning creative ways to eliminate Garrett from the gene pool, then my email dinged and brought me salvation in the form of another job, deep background checks for a local bank that was experiencing some odd shortages. They forwarded a list of nine employees, along with their social security numbers and other pertinent information, and I abandoned my list of ways to "off" my surrogate brother and set to work.

But I couldn't completely erase the image of that girl's body from my mind—or that handwritten "love" note—nor totally banish ghosts that hadn't been out to play in too long a time. It all played havoc with my concentration, and I missed things a rookie would catch. I had to retrace my steps more than a dozen times, and re-read reports over and over before the information sank in. I'd only managed to clear three of the nine employees by three-thirty when exhaustion set in. A dismal record for me.

I knew it wasn't over with the guy who'd taken those girls and attacked me, not by a long shot. There was a confrontation coming, sooner or later—Garrett's vigilance notwithstanding—and I'd need my strength back in full. Like, yesterday. So I gave in and took a siesta, not waking until Garrett showed up at six, laden with Chinese food and, to my everlasting relief and joy, my Glock.

"You know, if you treated men as well as you treat your weapon, maybe they'd stick around for more than fifteen minutes," he said, watching me put the gun through its paces.

"Seriously?" I cocked my head and frowned at him. "You insult me when I've got a gun in my hand?"

"It's not loaded." He gave me a saucy grin.

"I can remedy that in about three seconds." I shoved a couple hollow points into the empty magazine, rammed the magazine into the gun, chambered a round and grinned back at him. "You might want to re-think your opinion of me."

"Okay. How's this?" He stepped close, laid a hand on my cheek, and gazed into my eyes, his whisper soft, deep and intimate. "Babe, you're so hot. If I didn't consider you my sister, I'd drag you into the bedroom, caveman style."

My heart gave a thud, startling me, then I blinked and shoved him away as hard as I could. He only went back a few steps, since I wasn't yet at a hundred percent, but it gave me the space I needed.

"Oh, gross, now I have that ugly image in my head. Thanks a lot, Gar."

"My pleasure, Lil Sis."

"Blow it out your ear." I finished loading the Glock and set it on the bookshelf in the living room, then sat at the kitchen table as Garrett dished up the food. "Where are my keys? And my wallet."

"Safe." Garrett shoveled food in his mouth and grinned at me. "And no, you can't have them back."

"Oh, come on. Just a quick trip to the bookstore?" I tried on my most ingenuous expression and crossed the fingers on the hand not holding a fork. The one hidden by the table. "I won't go anywhere else. Honest. I'm out of reading material."

I gave him a pleading look. In answer, Garrett reached behind his chair and lifted up a weighty plastic bag that he set on the table in front of me. Paperbacks spilled from its interior.

"Not anymore."

I closed my eyes, shook my head and sighed.

"I hate you."

"I know."

He grinned at me and went back to shoveling food into his mouth. I picked at my meal in silence, knowing that, with no car and no money, there was no way I could even start on trying to find those missing girls. Or the asshole who had beat the shit out of me. Eventually, as Garrett dished up ice cream for dessert, I poked around the books in the bag, since I didn't have anything else to do. And in the mess I discovered the next two volumes in The Spellman Files series. I pulled them out and looked a question at Garrett. He shrugged.

"You seemed to be enjoying them, so I thought, why not?"

"Thanks," I said, touched that he had not only noticed what I had been reading, but also had cared enough to check out the shop for the next volumes.

"I know the downtime is hard, Skylark," Garrett said as I rose, books in hand. "But you have to take the time to let yourself heal. He's just playing with you, hoping you'll get careless. Don't let him force you into doing something you'll regret."

He might be just playing with me, I thought, *but he's also playing for keeps.* Still, I knew Garrett was right; if I went off half cocked, before I was physically ready to beard this lion in his den, I'd only fail. Again. I had no choice other than to be a good girl until I was truly ready. Not that I'd let Garrett know I agreed with him.

"Don't just rinse the dishes and leave them in the sink like usual, Gar. Use soap this time," I said as I headed into the living room to arrange my new books on the bookshelf, and start in on the next Spellman volume.

Tuesday was more of the same, though my rapidly healing body made the downtime even more torturous. Garrett made breakfast then left for work, still not relinquishing my keys or wallet. I sat alternately reading and working on the bank employee background checks until I walked out to grab my mail at one-thirty. By that time I was so bored and antsy, I'd have jogged to wherever had I been physically capable. But the thirty-yard walk to and from the mailbox just about did me in.

I sat at the kitchen table and ate the sandwich Garrett had left for me while I sorted the mail—one utility bill and a pile of junk ads—then toyed with my cell phone, wishing I could somehow dial up my attacker's location. What good was having GPS if it didn't do what you really needed it for? Every minute I had to wait to heal was another minute of his doing God-knows-what to those missing girls. Dunwitty's voice echoed in my head: *Andrea's only fifteen.* Too young to learn there was more to life than school, homework, and boyfriends. Too young to be in the hands of a monster. If only I—

The phone rang, cutting off my morbid thoughts. Reenie's number flashed on the screen.

"Hey, how were the meetings?"

"Loooong." Reenie's voice came through with its usual dramatic inflection. "Boring. Unnecessary. How are you doing?"

"As if Garrett hasn't kept you up to date. When are you getting in? Sorry I can't come get you, but Garrett's absconded with my car keys."

"Not to worry, it's all taken care of. I should be at your place by six-thirty at the latest. Thai?"

"Nah, I'm all Oriental'd out. And Mexican'd. What I really crave is a burger and fries—"

"From Valley Liquor, yeah, yeah." Silence, then an exaggerated sigh. "All right. But I'm only lowering my standards *this one time*, 'cause of what happened to you. Understand? See ya soon."

I sat a few more minutes before delving back into the bank's employees, savoring another cup of Ethiopian Red Sea Reserve—the beans were almost gone, a half pound didn't have any real lasting power in my house—and anticipating sharing dinner with Reenie. It felt like way more than four days since I'd last seen her. I needed to talk to her about the insight that was just out of reach. Maybe the two of us could—

The kitchen door burst open. I looked up with a gasp to find Dunwitty hulking in the opening, hands fisted on his hips. Damn, had he actually kicked it in? Or hadn't I locked the door after I went out for the mail? That was possible, I still wasn't used to having a security system.

"What the hell—"

"Who the *fuck* do you think you are, Skylark? How *dare* you do this to me?"

"What? What are you—"

"Don't act all innocent with me." He stomped over to me, the open kitchen door swinging on its hinges behind him, and leaned down until his nose was mere inches from mine. "You ain't got *no right* to do this, you hear me?" he screamed, spraying my face with spittle. *"No fucking right!"*

He slammed a fist on the table top, the blow less than an inch from my hand. His face turned a deep burgundy.

"Those girls need me to find them. You get that? They *need* me!"

His eyes glared at me like lasers, and I knew he wanted nothing more than to slice me into ribbons. I reached out, blindly, for the phone I'd set aside just a few minutes before. I wasn't about to look away from him for even one second.

"Dunwitty—"

"Shut the fuck up! I don't wanna hear one word out of you. You hear me? Not. One. Word."

He straightened up and turned away, stomping over to the stove where he stood, his back to me, his body thrumming with his rapid breaths. I thumbed on the phone, hit Soto's number and pressed send, still not letting Dunwitty out of my sight. Had I been able, I'd have been up, through the living room and out the front door before the Neanderthal could so much as turn around.

"Soto," I said when he answered his phone, "your partner is here, in my kitchen, acting like a crazy man.

Pounding on the table, screaming at me." Dunwitty turned around; his lip lifted in a nasty sneer. My heartbeat ratcheted up, as did my voice. "You better get here, fast, put a leash on him before—"

Dunwitty crossed the kitchen in three strides and snatched the phone from my grasp. He slammed it down on the table, cracking it into three pieces.

"Hey!" I yelped. "What the hell is your problem?"

He reached out a meaty hand, fingers grasping toward my neck as I pushed back in my chair, my ribs screaming at the movement. Was the detective about to strangle me? Then he froze, closed his eyes and gritted his teeth. His breaths whistled in and out of his mouth; his massive chest heaved. After a moment he opened his eyes and closed his fingers into a fist. Okay, was he now going to hit me?

We stared at each other a long moment in breath-held silence. Then he stood up, crossed his arms, and resumed glaring.

"It's always all about *you*, isn't it? What *you* want, what *you* need. No thought to anyone else, to those poor girls going through hell." He leaned again on the table, jutting his head toward me. "It's all about you and *your greed.*"

Greed? The light went on: the lawsuit. Is that what had brought this on? I knew Reenie had filed it early last week, but with all that had happened I hadn't given it another thought. Didn't even know how much she'd asked for.

I'd opened my mouth to say something—though I had no idea what—when suddenly Dunwitty deflated. All the rage seemed to bleed out of him. He blinked, looked around the room, then lowered his bulk into the chair across from me.

"Why?" He looked at me, his expression completely bewildered. "Why did you do it?"

"File the lawsuit?" He nodded and I stared at him, amazed that, after all that had happened between us, he still had no clue. "What choice did I have? The county wasn't reining you in, so *someone* had to. And no one else was stepping up." My own anger stirred, began to rise. "Did you really think you could just blithely go on flouting the law, *Detective*, year after year, doing whatever you wanted to anyone you decided you didn't like, and get away with it forever?"

Dunwitty's face darkened. His eyes narrowed. I looked out the open kitchen door, wondering how long it would take Soto to get here, if he'd arrive before Dunwitty squished me like a bug.

"You money grubbing little bitch," he growled.

"It isn't about money, I don't *care* about the money," Dunwitty snorted but I spoke over his derision, "I did it to *stop* you. I did it for everyone you've ever abused in the past, and for all the ones you'll mistreat in the future unless you get your head out of your ass and see what you're doing."

I paused for breath; the detective frowned and shook his head, then winced as though my words had made an inroad somewhere in his Neanderthal brain. Everything I'd gone through at his hands piled up on me. Tears congregated in my throat and I had to push the rest of my words out.

"You *hurt* me, Dunwitty. *Physically*. I have an emergency room bill and stitches and I'll have a scar because of you." My voice began to shudder; I blinked to keep tears at bay. "Then you dragged me out of the house half dressed, and made me the laughing stock of the internet. You didn't have any right to do that to me. You don't have the right to do that to *anyone*, no matter *who* they are or what *you* think of them."

I looked away, arms crossed, hands clenched on my sleeves as I struggled for control. Silence stretched as I counted—one, two, twelve, twenty—listened for Soto's rescue, and expected Dunwitty to lunge at me again.

But he surprised me. Instead of attacking, he merely sighed.

"You're right. I did hurt you. I shouldn't have done that, and I'm sorry. I really am. But you didn't have any right to throw me to the wolves." I looked a question at him; now what was he talking about? "Don't you get it? I'm out. Gone. They put me on paid administrative leave until this is all sorted out."

Paid leave? This is what had his panties all in a twist?

"Big deal," I said, finally hearing a car pull into my driveway. "You get to sit home for a while, drinking beer and watching sports on TV, and you get *paid* to do it. How's *that* such a *hardship*?"

"Damn it!" He hit the table again, a sharp slap of his open palm that made me jump. "Don't you get it? They took me off the case, Skylark! Those girls..." He shook his head. "My case. They're assigning it to someone else."

I lifted my chin and stared at him. Soto appeared in the open doorway and I hoped he could rein in his partner, because I couldn't hold back any longer.

"Good. Maybe now, instead of your prejudice leading you around by your dick so you can pin it on whoever you don't happen to like this month, they'll give it to someone who wants to do the job he's getting paid to do. Someone who'll find the person who's really behind these crimes—*before* anyone *else* dies."

"You frigging bitch!"

Dunwitty lunged up from his chair, pushing the table—and a bright burst of pain—into me, but Soto stepped forward and grabbed his arm before Dunwitty could do any more damage.

"Carrick, stop! You're not supposed to be here, you know that."

Dunwitty bared his teeth at Soto and tried to pull out of his grasp. Soto wrestled him across the room and up against the refrigerator, held him there with an arm across his chest. Have to admit, for a guy only five-six, he had formidable strength.

"No contact, Carrick, they said to stay away from her. It's up to the attorneys now. This isn't helping anything. It's only going to make it worse."

Dunwitty glared at him while the clock's second hands inched around the dial, once, twice, his jaw working, his angry breath gusting through his nose. Then he nodded at Soto.

"Let go of me," he said, his tone pure steel.

Soto studied him another ten seconds, then dropped his hands and stepped back. Dunwitty turned his head and pierced me with his glare.

"When the next one dies—and one of them *will*—it'll be your fault, Skylark. *Your fault.*"

Then he walked out the door, his words reverberating on the air: *your fault... your fault....* Soto looked at me, at the broken cell phone on the table, then back at me. I just shook my head and held up my hands; I didn't care about the phone, didn't care about the lawsuit, didn't care about any of it. I just wanted it over. I wanted the monster causing all this pain and death arrested and jailed, and I wanted Dunwitty out of my life. For good.

"I'll do my best to keep him away from you," Soto said.

He followed Dunwitty out. I got up and stood in the open doorway until I saw both cars drive off, then I shut and locked the door—it wasn't broken, I *had* left it unlocked earlier, my fault, my fault—and set the security alarm, wishing I could as easily lock out the world.

CHAPTER THIRTY

"We need to talk."

I paused with my mug partway to my lips and blinked at Reenie through the fragrant steam. This beginning, I knew from experience, was the opening salvo of a dump-on-Skylark battle.

What the hell had I done now?

It was three-thirty on Thursday afternoon. We sat in Starbucks, at my usual table in the back, on our way home from replacing my cell phone and what I hoped would be my last doctor visit until I turned at least ninety. The stitches were out, my wounds and ribs healing well, my face and left side a lovely shade of greenish-yellow, and I'd been cleared to drive— providing it was no further than San Luis Obispo for at least the next week. It seemed two concussions in less than three weeks made medical personnel slightly nervous, so they chose to err on the side of don't-give-Skylark-too-much-leeway. Egged on, I was sure, by Reenie and/or Garrett. Probably both.

I took a sip of my coffee, set the cup on the table with my hands clasped around it, soaking in the heat—I was still having trouble keeping my body warm, and the ghosts tucked away—and raised my brows at her.

"About?"

"Your keys."

"The ones you're giving back to me, right? I do have permission to drive. You were there," I added when she pursed her lips and looked away from me, "you heard what the doctor said. I'm fine, I don't need a babysitter anymore."

She looked back at me and nodded.

"You're cleared to drive *locally*. About a twelve mile radius. Do I think you're going to obey that directive?" She shook her head. "Not on your life."

"So you're what? Going to let your law practice go to the dogs while you stay glued to my side? Or abscond with my keys on a permanent basis, which will give *me* grounds to sue *you*?" I gave a sardonic laugh—a small one, no sense in overtaxing those healing ribs—and took another gulp of coffee. "I am an adult, you know. I'm capable of following orders—or not, as I choose. And even if *you* don't, *I do* have work that needs to be done. For some of which I will need transportation."

Yeah, I thought, *kinda hard to find abducted girls—and creeps who break in and beat the shit out of you—without a car.*

She didn't say anything, she just stared down at a spot on the tabletop halfway between us.

"Come on, Reenie—" I said, but she lifted her head and stared into my eyes. The pain in hers choked the words in my throat. When she spoke, her voice was so low I had to lean closer to hear her.

"You almost *died*, Skylark. If your neighbors hadn't heard the commotion and called the cops, if Detective

Soto hadn't known what to do..." She faltered to a stop and drew in a shaky breath. Tears sheened her eyes. "I'd be attending your *funeral* right now, instead of sharing coffee with my best friend. I don't know how to make you understand you're not invincible. You're not indestructible. I don't know how to make you be more careful."

"I wasn't doing anything other than going home, Reenie—"

"*No.* You were doing a whole lot more than that, Skylark. You wouldn't let this thing, whatever it is, go. You kept pushing, nosing around, and obviously you caught the attention of the wrong person."

She closed her eyes, shook her head, and gusted out a breath.

"I know that's all part of who you are," she added, "what makes you so good at what you do."

She opened her eyes and looked at me, her expression holding a hopelessness that seared right into my core, then spoke on.

"But it's *so hard* to watch. To see you almost *self-destruct* over and over. No, don't say anything."

She held up a hand to stop my protest; what was she talking about, self-destruct?

"I know it's not conscious on your part. You're not trying to get hurt. Or be killed. But you're so afraid to be wrong, to fail, to not measure up to some standard that only you can see, and that no one else cares about, that you don't know how, or when, to stop. It's going to be the end of you, unless you can somehow accept that you don't have to be better than everyone else. Or more perfect. Or worthy, or *whatever* it is that drives you."

Tears began to leak down her face. Her voice strangled in her throat. "And I don't know if you can."

I reached over and clasped her hands, my own heart breaking. I never wanted to cause her this kind of pain, so much anguish. But I also knew I could never stop being who I was. Saving someone else, helping life make sense of a sort for them, bringing them a semblance of peace and closure, brought a bit of all that to me, too. It brought me a sense of belonging—and yes, she was right, worthiness—and that was something I'd never had while growing up. And without that semblance, that little bit, my life wouldn't be worth living.

"I don't know if I can, either," I said. "I am who I am, and wishing won't make me any different. But I will promise you this, Reenie. I won't go off alone, anymore. I'll always make sure someone knows where I am, why, and what I'm doing. And that, along with Garrett's fabulous security system, should make up at least a little for all the rest of it, don't you think?"

I smiled at her and gave a tug on her hands. She blinked, then smiled back and gave me a watery laugh. We finished our coffee over a neutral conversation about her long, boring San Francisco meetings, the patent infringement trial that loomed on the horizon, and a cleaned-up—on my part, no point in further scaring her —recitation of Dunwitty's reaction to the infamous lawsuit, the requested payout of which Reenie still refused to reveal to me. All she'd say was that she always asked for the moon to ensure we'd at least get to the top of Mt. Everest. I was still wondering how those two places translated into numbers when she dropped me off at home—with both car keys and wallet.

Administrative leave.

Dunwitty heard the words over and over in his head, echoing his shame as the hands on his kitchen clock inched their way around the dial, and other detectives tried to do the work he should be doing: solving cases; getting the shitheads off the street; rescuing those poor girls.

All because of Skylark. Skylark and her damned greed.

How the hell could she put money ahead of the lives of those girls and live with herself? He didn't care what she'd said, that it wasn't about the money. It was always about the money. All she wanted was to pad her bank account so she didn't have to work anymore. So she could sit around and spout off that woo-woo shit of hers, and have everyone look up to her, the great, wonderful, wise private eye.

What a crock.

I should have just killed her. Strangled her. Stomped her into the ground. Mashed her until there was nothing left.

He opened the refrigerator door, looking for he knew not what, and glared at the three beer bottles, two bottles of salad dressing, and the container of something he'd cooked a few weeks ago—now green and fuzzy—in the almost-empty interior, then slammed the door shut. Something rattled; he heard a couple of thuds, then a sharp crack as though glass broke. The damned beer, most likely. Or the dressing. Or both.

Dunwitty glared at the door, wishing he could see through it, could laser his way inside the appliance, laser up the beer-or-dressing puddle that was probably dripping from shelf to shelf. No, he wished he could laser his way into Skylark, cut her in half. No, quarters. Mince her into pieces.

He'd never been so humiliated in his life—not even when his father had called him on the carpet when he was young officer—as he had when his Captain had lit into him.

"What the hell is the meaning of this?" he'd roared, not even trying to modulate his tone. He shook the report of the lawsuit in Dunwitty's face.

"Captain, I can explain—"

"It's too late for explanations, Dunwitty. The damage is done. IA's involved now, and the lawyers. She's named you and the county, it's out of my hands. I warned you about your behavior and you didn't listen. Well, now it's bit you on the ass. Bit all of us. The brass wanted to can you; you got any idea what I had to do to keep you on? To convince them you're our best detective? Despite this?"

In his peripheral, through the office window, Dunwitty could see the other officers standing motionless, listening to the dressing-down that reverberated through the closed door, though not one moved closer to the office, or even looked toward it. He felt his ears burn; acid chewed his gut. It got harder and harder to breathe.

"I've been ordered to put you on administrative leave until this is cleared up. You are not to go near this

Skylark woman. Don't call her, talk to her, email her, none of that other social media shit. You got that? Do you?"

Dunwitty forced himself to nod; there was no way he could say a word without taking off someone's head, and if he decapitated the Captain, even metaphorically, his career would be over. As the Captain continued to berate him, he clenched his teeth and fisted his hands—and tried to figure how to get even with Skylark.

"I need your badge, and your sidearm," the Captain said at last, his tone modulating from hot fury to cold carbon steel. "Go home, and don't come near this office—or your cases—until you're cleared. Take a break, get out of town, go on vacation, I don't care. Just get your head on straight so when you come back you can do the job you're paid to do without stepping over any more lines. You got that?"

Silent, Dunwitty'd pulled out his badge and his gun and slapped them down on the Captain's desk, his fury knowing no bounds. Then he glared into the man's eyes, unable to help himself.

"This is *bullshit*, Captain," he roared, "I was just doing my job, that's all. She's after the fucking *money*. A get-rich-quick scheme, that's all this is."

"That may be, Dunwitty, but as of now, you're on leave."

He'd slammed his way out of the office and strode through the station with everyone—his fellow officers, his own partner, for God's sake—watching his walk of shame, stripped of everything that made him who he was.

He paced the kitchen now, around and around the table that sat in the room's center, like a mouse on a wheel, his mind whirling. There were still girls missing, girls who needed to be found, girls only he could find. Girls who were counting on him to save them, girls who would turn up dead now because of this... this... knee-jerk reaction on the part of the so-called powers that be. So what if Skylark was suing him? She didn't have a leg to stand on, he'd only been doing his job. So what if he'd stepped on the line a bit? Sometimes, to get the job done, you needed to. It wasn't like he'd crossed it, or anything. This fucking suit would be dismissed, surely it would.

Wouldn't it?

He growled. Three days. Three *days* he'd been sitting idle at home, a useless lump on the ass of humanity. He couldn't understand why, how, he could be punished like this for simply doing his job. For keeping people safe. For ridding the streets of scum. *Maybe I should just quit. Not go back at all. Move away, start over somewhere else.* That'd sure teach those crap-shit mucky-mucks who only thought of money, of the bottom line, and not what the rank and file had to put up with on a daily basis.

But that wouldn't help those girls. It wouldn't save them. Nor would whoever the Captain assigned to the case. He was the best detective they had, even the Captain said so, no one else could do what he did because no one else cared as much. He couldn't just sit here anymore, he needed to get out there and find them. They needed him; he had to go *now*.

Dunwitty picked up his keys and strode to the back door. Then he stopped with his hand on the knob. Where the hell did he think he was going? He had no gun, no badge. He was off the case. On "administrative leave". He couldn't go look for them.

Fuck. He felt his shoulders droop as he stared through the translucent curtain on the door's window, seeing not his night-dark back yard but the pictures of the missing girls: newly-engaged Yvonne, college student Casey, fifteen-year-old Andrea. And Heidi Coffey, dead, mutilated. Who knew how many more before this was over? He had to do something, he had to—

Skylark.

The thought hit him like a freight train. She was involved, she knew who had taken those girls, she knew where they were. If he could surveil her, follow her...

Without authorization? His breath hitched in his throat at the thought. He'd lose his job if he worked the case now. He was considered a civilian, even if only temporarily. But he knew no one else would be watching that bitch. They'd be pussy-footing around her now because of the lawsuit. They wouldn't even try to bring her down. He was the only one who could do it, and yet he'd been forbidden to do it.

"Screw this!" he growled.

He dug his cell out of his pocket and punched in the number of his CI. In less than half an hour, after a meeting in the dark, deserted back parking lot behind the now-closed Grocery Outlet, and the exchange of an appreciable amount of cash, he had what he needed. Barry might be next-of-kin to the scum of the earth, but give him a judicious threat layered in between a few never-to-be-fulfilled promises and covered with a copious amount of cash, and he came through every time.

Dunwitty, parked in the darkest corner of the lot, locked his doors, reclined the driver's seat, and closed his eyes for a little cat nap. He figured he had about three, maybe four, hours before it would be safe to continue with his plan. He wanted to make sure the entire street would be fast asleep before he arrived. He couldn't risk anyone seeing him, or reporting his presence anywhere near Miss One Name Wonder.

At one-forty-five am he fired his engine and drove to Ito Lane, one street over from Skylark's house. He parked about a block in, then wound his way through dark backyards to Palomino, keeping to inky shadows, grateful the new moon that rode in a star-studded sky shed no illumination on the earth below. He kept both eyes and ears peeled for any sign of movement, any sound, but all was silent and still, all residents tucked in, fast asleep. He stood in the lee of a pine tree a yard away and watched Skylark's residence for about a half hour, but saw no sign of a light inside or anyone awake in the small frame house. He thought over his plan once more, then nodded and moved toward the Jeep nestled beneath the house's carport, keeping the car between himself and the house.

It took only thirty seconds to attach the gizmo deep inside the passenger side front fender. He reached into his pocket, took out the control unit, and pressed a button; a faint beep sounded as the two units synced.

Gotcha, he thought as, grinning, he made his silent way back to his car on the next block. *Now let's see you get away with it.*

 ## CHAPTER THIRTY-ONE

Work was almost impossible; my mind would not stay on any one thing for more than a few seconds. Everything I did consisted of one step forward, two steps back, leaving me with five bank employee backgrounds on which to keep starting over.

It was hopeless. If I was to get my concentration back to where it belonged—and earn my keep, to say nothing of paying the damn hospital bills that kept piling up—I needed to find those missing girls. And the jerk who'd broken into my house. I just didn't have any idea how to go about it. Not at first.

Something had niggled at me all day Wednesday and Thursday, a thin thread that I couldn't put into words. At least, not words that made sense. And I wasn't about to let either Garrett or Reenie help me figure it out, either, not when I'd finally gotten them to back off on the babysitting crap. But I had promised Reenie I wouldn't go off on my own, and I didn't want to go back on that promise, not unless I had no choice. Thankfully, I wouldn't have to—I hoped.

The idea that had been percolating for those two days burst fully formed in my head when I woke on Friday morning. I had to admit, it was dumb, totally stupid. And it had the potential to be truly humiliating in more ways than one. I almost dismissed it out of hand. But when I shifted it around and looked at it from all angles, I decided it was worth a try. Since neither Reenie nor Garrett would ever find out about it—I hoped—I wouldn't have to suffer their brand of derision. And if it ended up a bust, well, at least it had been worth a try.

No skin off my nose if Lillia couldn't deliver, right? Not that I thought for a second she could. But she had been right about the numbers and the butterfly. There was that. Maybe good old Lillia could, one more time, stumble on something we could actually use.

I called the Sheriff's substation on Friday morning and asked for Soto. My luck—such as it was—held. He was in.

"Thanks for hauling Dunwitty off the other day. You still speaking to me?" I asked once he picked up the line.

Silence met my question and I wondered if he'd just hang up. If he did, what would I do? A harsh sigh filtered down the line.

"I guess I am," he said in a cold, clipped tone. "But I'm busy, so make it quick. What can I do for you, Skylark?"

"You could lose the attitude, for one." I crossed my fingers he wouldn't simply cut me off. "And you could help me find those girls, for another. Or are you too proud to team up with a P.I.?"

"What do you mean, team up? This is an official police investigation. I can't bring a civilian on board."

"I think I'm already on board, at least as far as the culprit's concerned. Don't you?" Silence; I soldiered on. "Tell me... Can you get your hands on that note that was nailed to the body in my yard?"

More silence that stretched to the breaking point before I heard him groan.

"I can't give it to you, Skylark, so don't even ask."

"No, that's not what I'm saying. I have an idea how we might get some intel from it, and I definitely want you there. It's a bit... on the dicey side. Not illegal," I added when he snorted, "but very unorthodox, to say the least. *If* it works, it could tell us where those girls are being held. Or at least give us some viable clues."

"Yeah? What is it?"

"I think I'd rather you experience it firsthand, rather than tell you outright and have you hang up on me." I paused and took a deep breath. "So, you game?"

"I don't do cryptic," he said after another long pause. "But, given who you are, what's happened to you... Okay. Let me see if I can liberate it for a few hours from the forensics guys."

"Good. I'll call ahead, make an appointment for us, for tomorrow. Pick me up at eleven. That okay?"

"I'll make it work."

"Thanks. And... say hi to Betsy for me."

That earned me a deep growl. The phone slammed in my ear. I looked up the pertinent number with a grin on my face. Life was definitely a lot more fun—and interesting—without Dunwitty hanging around my neck.

The orgasm hit him like a jackhammer, revved even higher by the sound of her cries. He rammed himself harder, wishing he could split the bitch in two, then collapsed on top of her when it was over, crushing her, until his breath returned to somewhat normal.

He raised to his elbows and looked down. She had passed out, cute little thing that she was, and a virgin to boot. Imagine that, fifteen and still a virgin.

Not anymore, he thought with a grin. Then he looked up at the camera.

"And that, gentlemen, is how you deflower a virgin. Take her in the dead of night. Beat her into submission. Then a few restraints, a lot of pain, a little pleasure, and she's yours forever."

He climbed off the bleeding, unconscious girl and swiveled the camera to point at the cages. Leaving Andrea chained to the platform, he tucked himself back into his pants and went over to the hotplate where the day's rations were keeping warm, filling the air with a sour stench. *Time to feed the harem*, he thought, chuckling at the notion. He ladled the slop into a bowl, picked up a spoon and a hammer, then limped toward the cages that lined the far wall.

"Dinner, my lovelies!" he sang out, whacking the hammer on the bars of the first occupied cage to make its occupant look up at him.

Casey, the college bitch. Thought she was such hot shit, she did, majoring in Global Engineering, juggling those science books while she wiggled her hips across campus and spread her legs for her professors. Science was a man's work, she had no business learning that shit. He'd known the minute he'd seen her that she needed his taming hand.

After he'd shown her the only thing a woman was good for and then chained her in the cage, he'd had so much fun with her long hair, tying it in hanks to the bars that surrounded her. They held her in a sitting position even when exhaustion overcame her, and kept tears rivering down her face. The scalp was so very sensitive; it was a joy to see the effect the smallest movements had on her.

He opened the cage door and crawled inside with the girl, shoving the hot bowl in front of him.

"Please, please, untie me." He could barely understand the words, her voice was so choked. "It hurts so much."

"As it's supposed to."

He caressed her face, then filled the spoon with the stew and stuck it in her mouth. Her eyes widened and she shrieked as the the red-hot mixture of ground animal organs and shit burned the delicate tissue. He slapped his hand over her lips and held her steady as she gagged, unable to struggle with her hair tied around the bars. It took almost a minute before she swallowed, a convulsive spasm that left her shuddering in his hands.

He filled the spoon again.

"No, no, please, don't," she pleaded, then clamped her teeth together.

Carstairs squeezed her cheeks with iron fingers and her mouth popped open. He tipped the contents of the spoon into the gaping maw, then clamped her mouth shut with his hand, this time pinching her nostrils, too. She bucked and twisted, tearing hair from her head, before once again she convulsively swallowed. He patted her cheek, allowed her to breathe, then loaded the spoon once again.

This time she opened her mouth on her own. He fed her the entire bowl of slop, warned her not to throw it up or he'd have to punish her, then crawled out of the cage. He went over to Yvonne, who glared defiance at him even through the burns and cuts that covered her body. Shaking his head, he turned to the camera.

"Some of them you can feed, others you have to starve. Like these two. One whines and pleads, so she eats shit. The other is still defiant, so she eats nothing. Eventually, they'll both learn their lesson. Now." He pulled out an empty cage and centered it before the camera lens. "I have a special treat for you all. Someone very special for this cage. She'll be here soon, the beginning of my endgame. And won't we have fun with her?" He rubbed his hands together. "She's been lording it over men for years, and in a public forum. She deserves to be broken. And she will lure the one we've all been waiting for, the one woman who may never break, no matter what we do to her. And oh, the things we will do! Stay tuned, and have a wonderful, productive night, my friends, taming your own bitches."

He turned off the camera and removed his ski mask, then hauled the empty cage into a place along the wall where the lamps lit it like a spotlight. He sat a while to give his throbbing leg a rest, and devoured his own meal of steak and baked potato, washed down with a hefty micro brew from a local brewery.

All this work, this prep, hadn't been easy, still wasn't, not with his leg so bad. It wasn't healing well, despite the amount of antiseptic he'd used, no matter how often he changed the bandage. Driving was hard, shoving down that clutch, but he'd persevered. He'd gone back three times after dumping weak little Heidi's body in the cunt's yard, but hadn't been able to get near Skylark. That one-name bitch was never alone: cops roamed the grounds and friends stayed at the house, tending to her, loving her, making her life so damned easy. He still had trouble not blowing up and killing his whole harem just thinking about the way she'd shot at him.

Got the better of him.

Again.

But no more. He knew just what to do now, how to draw her into his arms. The plan had come to him just yesterday, when he'd followed her to and from her doctor, and it was brilliant. Yes, he needed to make some adjustments to the barn, put in a few more partitions, but it would be worth it. A few days to prepare, to set it all up, and he could put the plan into action. And this time, no one would stop him, especially not some uppity, untamed, one-name woman.

After checking his youngest little angel, who was starting to moan and roll her head on the rough platform—it'd be time to feed her soon, too—he went out into another of the barn's rooms to continue preparing the stage for his ultimate victim: Skylark.

 CHAPTER THIRTY-TWO

I spent a couple hours online, found what I needed, and came loaded for bear Saturday morning, not that I clued Soto in on the full game plan. Part of it was personal for me. Having Lillia "read" that note gave me a quasi-legitimate reason to confront her, and I wasn't about to lose this opportunity to de-feather this particular cuckoo bird in her den. Yeah, I know I'm mixing my metaphors, but you know what I mean.

The look Soto gave me when we pulled up outside Lillia's place was one part disbelief, one part disgust, and one part anger. It made me wonder if he'd drive off, leaving me in the dust, or maybe call in the men in the white coats. But after a tense moment of staring at the sign in her window, he put on his game face and followed me in silence up the stairs and through Lillia's front door. He had his stern cop face firmly in place by the time she emerged from the inner room.

She still looked like a kindergarten teacher, today in flats, a full blue-and-yellow flower print skirt and a pastel blue sweater set I was sure had gone out of style back in the seventies. I introduced Soto—placing emphasis on his title, *Detective*—and watched her smile stiffen just a bit, though she didn't voice any of the questions that crowded her eyes. She simply escorted us into the inner room and sat us in the same chairs Garrett and I had used. She drifted over to her place on the other side of the small round table, and I did my best not to so much as glance at the stupid crystal ball that sat quiescent in its center.

"I understand palmistry, Miss Lillia," Soto said, his voice creamy smooth. He ignored my evil eye. "But psychometry? I haven't a clue what that is."

"It's the ability to pick up images, sounds, and even words from inanimate objects, depending on the psychic."

"Really?" He crossed his arms and raised his brows. "And just how does *that* work?"

Lillia gave me a look that I interpreted to mean, *Are you trying to get me in trouble?* then turned her attention fully on the detective, complete with saccharine smile.

"We are all made of energy, Detective, everything in the universe, all vibrating at different frequencies. As we interact with people and objects we leave a trace of our own energy behind. I'm what's considered a conduit; I have the ability to pick up on that leftover energy and receive images from it." She looked down and gave a self-deprecating little smile, then looked back up at Soto. "To be honest, at times more successfully than at others. Mostly I pick up odd, disconnected images, and sometimes, though rarely, I'll see words. I've never heard any sounds, that's not part of my gift. And I have no idea what the images mean. They can be literal or figurative. Even metaphorical. I leave it to my clients to figure out their significance. I'm just thankful I have a gift that helps people."

Soto took it all in with a gleam in his eyes and an expression I couldn't quite decipher. He looked both fascinated and skeptical at the same time, and I wondered if he was remembering my reading his light lines, or the vision I'd had of Dunwitty and his father. Or maybe the half-glimpse he'd had of Ehrler in my living room. He sat silent a moment when Lillia finished speaking, looking deep in thought, then reached in his jacket's breast pocket and drew out the blood-saturated note, still sealed in its protective plastic covering. He held it out to Lillia who sat motionless, her stare glued to the clear envelope and its grisly contents, her hands clasped tight on her lap. I could tell, from the look on her face, that the last thing she wanted to do was touch the note. Even in the bag.

I didn't blame her, I wouldn't want to touch it, either. I wondered how thankful she was for her particular "gift," now.

"What can you tell us about this?"

"The whole thing," she said, blinking, her voice a bit shaky, "or just the paper inside?"

"Just the paper, please."

"I'll need to remove it—"

"No, I'm sorry, you can't. It's evidence in an ongoing investigation."

"I see." Lillia swallowed, then drew in a deep breath. "The fact that it's covered might cause problems. The plastic will block some of the note's energy, and I'll probably pick up images from whoever handled the covering. But," she let out her breath in a deep sigh, "I'll do my best."

You do that, I thought, not the least bit convinced about her act as she reached out and took the clear envelope into a trembling hand.

She went through the same routine as before, sitting quietly, eyes closed, her hands resting in her lap, the note resting on her fingers. I glanced at Soto wondering if he found all this as phony as I did, but he sat attentive in his chair, leaning a bit forward, inspecting every nuanced emotion that crossed Lillia's heart-shaped face. He looked totally smitten with the faker. It took all my will power not to sigh out my disgust. Men were all the same; give them a sweet-looking, curvaceous woman with a come-hither voice and they'd fall for anything.

I endured the motionless silence for about five minutes, until I thought I would explode. I was on the point of standing up and getting the hell out of there when Lillia flinched in her seat; I had to admit her timing was impeccable. She frowned and jerked her head. A sharp sound of protest grated in her throat.

"Oh, no, such rage," she murmured, her voice shuddering. "So much hatred." Her fingers tightened, crushing the plastic envelope. She grimaced and hunched her shoulders as though in pain, and bit her lip until she drew blood. All the while giving high-pitched little yelps from deep down in her throat. It sounded almost as though she were being tortured.

Then she drew in a sharp breath.

"No!"

The word burst out of her like a blast from a flame thrower. Her eyes snapped open. She leaned forward and dropped the note on the table beside the crystal ball, which started to glow, a swirling movement of violet-tinged gray deep inside the globe. I glanced at Soto, but his attention was glued to Lillia.

"I'm sorry, I can't do any more." She swiped her hands over her face, almost like she was wiping away tears though her skin was dry. "There's too much, I can't decipher it. The images..." She shuddered and shook her head, sharp, staccato movements side to side. "There's so much evil," she whispered. "So very much.'"

Soto leaned forward, wrapped his strong fingers around her clasped hands. I kept an eye on the movement in the globe, which at the moment seemed to be easing up. I could only hope it would die away completely before anyone else noticed it.

"Take your time, you're safe here." Soto again used his smooth, creamy voice. "Nothing can hurt you."

Lillia squeezed her lips together and nodded. She took in a few deep breaths, nodded, then fixed her gaze at a spot somewhere above and behind us—about as far away from the bloodstained note as she could get without turning her back to it.

"The... nicer images... a baby, candles on a table, a few red balloons... they're from the envelope, I think. But the others..." Again she shuddered and clenched her teeth. "It's pure evil. Torture, physical and sexual, done for the sake of pain, just to hurt, to shame and destroy. Both what he does and what had been done to him."

"Anything *practical* we can use to *find* him?"

I watched my sarcastic tone bite into her. She stiffened and blinked, then looked at me, deliberately not looking down at the note.

"I saw the ship again, and the steps, rising up and up. And colors, blotches of colors, splattered, as though they had been dropped from a height."

I drew in a breath and stiffened as the elusive vision from Monarch Lane suddenly came clear. Coveralls, the assailant had been wearing white coveralls splattered with blotches of different colors of paint.

"What? That mean something to you?" Soto asked. I shook my head.

"Later," I said, still trying to get my breathing back to normal.

"Detective, please." Lillia turned pleading eyes on Soto. "Find him, get those women away from him. Though after what I saw, I don't know how they will ever get over what he's done to them. He hates women, wants to destroy them, make them less than human. Look for a cave out under the trees, that's where he's holding them."

"What the hell does that mean, a cave under trees?" Soto frowned. "That doesn't make any sense."

"I don't know how else to describe what I saw. I don't think it's a literal cave, it's the way he thinks of it. His safe place. Far away from prying eyes. I saw cages, and chains. And tools... bloody tools." Her gaze dipped toward the table. She shut her eyes. "Please, put that away. I can't bear to look at it."

"Any idea where this so-called cave might be?" Soto growled as he snatched up the note.

"I'm sorry," Lillia murmured as she shook her head.

"Well, this was a colossal waste of time," Soto growled.

He rose and threw a few bills on the table, then turned and stalked out of the room.

"I'll be right back," I said to Lillia, then hurried after the detective.

I caught him at the main office door, hand on the knob. I grabbed his arm to keep him from leaving.

"I need to talk to Lillia for a minute. Will you wait for me?"

"Outside," he growled, his tone pure angry cop. I knew I'd be taking a chance, but he needed to know what I'd remembered.

"Listen, while you're waiting, do some research. See if anyone who reported a robbery also had the inside of their house painted. The theft was probably a few weeks or even months after the painting, this guy isn't stupid or he'd have been caught by now. I think this all started that way, and the guy who was killed came home unexpectedly and interrupted the robber."

"How do you know that?"

His eyes narrowed on me, and suspicion flooded his voice. I gave a half laugh and shook my head.

"If I told you, you'd probably arrest me again. Let's just say, something's been hiding in the back of my mind and what Lillia said triggered the memory. Those splatters of color, they're paint splatters. Go on, go see what you can find out, and I'll join you in a couple of minutes."

He stared at me, his eyes iron-hard, then he opened the door and stepped out of the office. I sighed out a relieved breath—had it been Dunwitty, I'd have been shoved in the back of a squad car by now—and returned to where Lillia waited for me.

She sat where I'd left her, staring at the flashing colors that still swirled in the crystal ball. I shut the door and leaned against it, arms crossed.

"Want to tell me how you make it do that?"

She looked up at me and smiled, but she didn't speak.

"You've got a nice little set-up here, don't you? Looks like a 'legitimate' psychic's lair." I air quoted legitimate. "You probably make a good living off the gullibility of the average person. I wonder what would happen if people knew who you really are." I walked over and sat in the chair I'd occupied earlier. "Clancy."

"I'm not trying to fool anyone. Lillia is my psychic persona's name. If anyone ever asked, I'd be happy to tell them my given name is Clancy D'Angelo."

"Psychic persona, I like that." I laughed. "Sounds so 'official'. Why the deception?"

"Expedience. Would you believe anything a psychic named Clancy said? Lillia is much more believable. All this," she gestured around the room, "is to help put people at ease. They've been conditioned to expect a certain atmosphere, and so I provide it. At least as much of one as I'm willing to create. It helps them hear and accept the messages I give them."

"The shit you shovel, you mean."

Her smile died. She folded her hands and rested them on the table, then looked into my eyes. Just as before, the room shifted around me and I felt drawn into her. I lost awareness of the room, the chair I sat in, the table before me—even myself—everything except those glowing blue orbs.

"What I do is real, Skylark. And what I see is truth, truth that those who come to me need to hear. Just as what you see is truth, truth that helps you solve the puzzles you take on. Why is it so hard to believe that others beside yourself have true gifts? There are more of us out here than you think. When you refuse to see, you become blind."

She released me with a blink and we stared at each other a long moment. How had she done that, and so easily? I'd never before been susceptible to hypnosis, yet for the second time she'd drawn me in with just a look.

"Your gifts were given to you to use, Skylark, not to be feared or ignored. If you will only trust them instead of denying them, they will open many more doors for you. Doors into both the future and the past."

I stood up so abruptly I knocked my chair over.

"I like my doors just where they are, thank you very much. Your cryptic crap doesn't interest me, Clancy D'Angelo. I'm putting you on notice. If I hear of you skinning anyone, stripping them of their money, for any reason, I'll shut you down. You get that? Don't fuck with me; you won't like what'll happen to you."

She just sat there and smiled at me. Then she looked down into the swirling teal in the crystal ball and her smile died.

"Be very careful, Skylark. Be sure you have a backup plan, or you won't succeed. You'll die, and so will those women."

I snorted my disdain and left her there, staring into that swirling orb, playing her part for all it was worth. But I couldn't shake the eerie feeling that her words held power, that they rang with a touch of prophecy. It kept me silent as Soto drove me home.

He'd been astonished at how easily he'd gained entrance to her house. People with her kind of money should be more careful.

She'd left a bathroom window on the downhill side of the house cracked open, probably to air the room after a hot shower, and even though the security system was on, that open window allowed him free access. Stupid of her not to have all the windows wired, even ones she considered inaccessible. Equally stupid not to have motion sensors inside.

That the window was on the side of the house with no other houses overlooking it, meant daylight posed him no problem. Despite the bright sunshine, no one could see him raise the sash and crawl in. Fate was still on his side. Intervention Number Six.

He roamed the huge structure while he waited, pocketing gold and platinum gem-encrusted jewelry that lay unsecured in her four-tier mahogany jewelry box. In the huge kitchen he raided the refrigerator and made himself a pastrami and prosciutto sandwich, washed down with a couple glasses of what tasted like a very expensive red wine. Then he took a piece of her monogrammed stationery and composed the note.

Not half an hour later, he heard the garage open and a car drive in. The garage access door opened. Beeps sounded, and he figured she was disarming the security system. It would make getting her out of the house much easier, as long as she didn't re-arm it. But if she did, there was still that open bathroom window he could drag her through.

Still, most people only used their system when they went out, never thinking they needed it while in residence. Well, she'd learn.

He slid into the walk-in pantry, leaving the door cracked. She walked in, a petite little thing, and set three bulging bags on the center food-prep counter. She began unloading her purchases: bread, cheese, cold cuts, meats, fresh vegetables, canned goods, spreading them out on the counter. He waited until she turned to open the fridge, then he stepped out and grabbed her from behind. Given her small stature, he figured she'd not be much of a challenge.

He was wrong. She fought like a demon and knew what she was doing, self-defense wise. They crashed into the wine rack, breaking several bottles, knocked over the stools that lined the eating counter, scattered the groceries she'd purchased onto the floor. She scratched, bit, kicked and kneed him between the legs; that sent pain ricocheting into him and he lost hold of her. He caught her halfway to the front door and dragged her by her hair back into the kitchen, punched her down to the ground, then grabbed a thin, sharp knife from the block that sat beside the stove.

She cut up as nicely as she screamed; blood bubbled and spurted and streamed down her arms and legs. Not enough to kill, just to incapacitate, to make her tractable. Then he used his fists again, rearranging her face with total glee, leaving her blood splattered all around the sunny yellow kitchen.

When she lay unconscious, and he stood over her, knife in hand. Fighting not to end it all here and now—which was what a bitch like her deserved—he closed his eyes and reminded himself of the plan.

She was not an end in herself, merely the means to the ultimate end. One he'd have fun playing with. He pulled the note from his pocket and set it on the counter, laid the bloody knife on it so it wouldn't blow away, hauled the unconscious woman out to his truck, then finished his work at the front of the house.

From a distance no one would notice; it was merely a little clue for the one he really wanted. Something to pique her interest and draw her in.

It won't be long now, he thought as he drove down the steep hill, heading for his secluded barn, and the cage that awaited this new bitch.

CHAPTER THIRTY-THREE

I should have known something was wrong when I didn't hear from Reenie all weekend. But I knew she had that patent-infringement trial coming up—preliminary motions in front of the judge on Monday and Tuesday, and opening arguments on Wednesday—so I just figured she was busy preparing over the weekend. Plus, I got selfish. After enduring almost two weeks of mollycoddling from both Garrett and Reenie, I was more than happy to have my solitude back again. It wasn't like I needed a babysitter anymore. I was back on my feet and doing just fine for the most part. My status was finally quo, and I reveled in it.

I didn't hear from Soto, either, though I called twice on Monday to see if he'd had any luck running down that painting lead. He supposedly wasn't in and he didn't call back, not even to say thanks. *Just like a cop*, I thought, *to shut a person out of the action once he got the help he needed*. I considered driving over to the station to ambush him, but I wasn't sure that would do any good. It wasn't like I was his partner; in his eyes, I was just a civilian, and cops don't share information in ongoing investigations with civilians, not even with ones who shared information with them. My PI license carried no status at all, at least not with anyone in law enforcement.

And as much as I was on my feet, I wasn't yet up to full strength. My breathing was almost back to normal, though I wouldn't be running marathons anytime soon —or even jogging around the block—and my ribs only hurt if I moved too fast, or too often. The bruises had faded to a faint pukey green I could have covered with makeup if I'd had any, and the stitches had healed enough that I no longer feared tearing open the wounds. A few more days of down time would only improve things, so I chose to let Reenie and Garrett go their own way while I hunkered down at home and finished working the background checks on the bank employees —two of whom came up a bit dodgy—and caught up on some much-needed sleep.

By early Wednesday afternoon I'd finished and sent off the final report for the bank, had two more job offers in my inbox—to which I'd sent gleeful acceptances— and had run out of the few cans and boxed goods that had sat in lonely isolation on my larder shelves. Figuring I should replace them in case of emergency, I wandered the grocery store aisles—finding nothing appealing, mainly because I'd have to cook it—wasting time until I could justify heading to Valley Liquor for an early dinner of their luscious hamburger plate. As I perused the offerings I wondered how Reenie's trial was going; she usually called to give me a daily blow-by-blow. It seemed strange not to have heard from her at all, but I dismissed the lingering feeling of unease and basked in my solitude.

In the produce aisle I picked up and squinted at a yucca root. *How the hell does one cook something that looks like it came out the ass end of a huge animal? I* wondered. *And why the hell would anyone want to eat it?*

My cell rang. I set the yucca back beside the jicama, dug the phone out of my purse and grinned at the number.

"Hey, Reenie, I was just thinking about you," I said. "How's the trial going? You hand them their asses in a teacup yet?"

"This is Danielle Munds, at Overton, Mills and Fortner." The dragon used her voice like a filleting knife; her icy tone dug into me. "I really need to speak with Miss Overton. Don't give me any of your tall tales, Skylark. This is urgent."

"What do you mean, Danielle? She isn't with me, she's in court."

"You know damn well she is not. What have you done with her?"

"What have I...?" Panic bloomed within me. I could hardly draw breath. My head whirled and everything around me turned white. I lurched up against the produce shelves. "She-she's not here, Danielle, I haven't seen or talked to her since she took me to the doctor on Thursday. She told me she'd be busy all weekend, she had a trial to prepare for."

"Well, she's not here, and Mr. Fortner is *quite* put out. She missed preliminary motions on Monday and Tuesday; we had to pull in a *junior* partner to deal with those. Without her notes, I might add."

Danielle spilling confidential information without having her fingernails pulled out—and to me, of all people? This was really bad.

"And Miss Overton did not show up for opening arguments this morning. It was a complete debacle until Mr. Fortner himself stepped in to request a continuance."

"She missed...? That's not like Reenie—"

"It most certainly *isn't*. I told Mr. Fortner that *you* must have done something to keep her *away* from her *obligations*."

"I what—"

"She's had to put so *many* things on hold for you in the past. The only thing that would make her miss a court date would be dealing with *you*."

I let her dislike and condemnation roll off my back as my heart pounded and my head reeled. Reenie wouldn't miss a court date, not for me or for anyone else. Something was very wrong, here.

"Have you called her—"

"No, of course not." Danielle's frigid tone cut across my words. "Why would I call any of her numbers to get ahold of her?"

"Home *and* cell?" I whispered, my eyes shut tight.

All I heard in response was Danielle's disdainful snort. I had to hand it to her, she had sarcasm, both verbal and non, down to an art form. Fear shuddered down my spine.

"Listen, I'll go out to her house right now, see if I can find her. I'll let you know."

I shut down the phone before the dragon could reply, left my close-to-empty cart where it was, and ran out to my Jeep. I was on the road out to Cabrillo Estates in less than two minutes. As I passed Monarch Lane, with its attendant memories, I punched in Garrett's number. The hell with DMV laws.

"I'm on my way to Reenie's house. The dragon called me," I told Garrett when he picked up. "She's desperate. No one's seen or heard from Reenie for more than three days. She missed two preliminary trial meetings, and today's opening arguments."

"Are you serious? That's not like her. Something's wrong, Skylark."

"Gee, you think, Gar?"

I punched off and threw the phone on the seat beside me as I turned into Cabrillo Estates. I wound up and around the interwoven streets until I pulled into Reenie's driveway. Nothing seemed amiss; the huge house sat on its raised lot three-quarters of the way up the steep hill, thumbing its multi-million-dollar nose at the poorer half-million-dollar houses in the lowlands below. Scattered neighboring houses turned blind eyes to Reenie's place from their distant lots. Palms swayed in the ubiquitous ocean breeze that swept the heights. Birds twittered; a rabbit scuttered through the low scrub of the vacant lot next door. A clear blue sky arched overhead, no clouds in sight. In the distance far below, Morro Rock rose from the depths of the Pacific like a gigantic paleolithic whale, slightly misted by the afternoon fog.

The garage sat to the left of the house, its door closed. I walked over and took a peek through the heart-shaped windows. Reenie's BMW sat tucked neatly within.

I had trouble catching my breath.

I walked back to my car and stood staring up at the two-story house. Its cream stucco siding glowed in the late afternoon sun. The red tile roof cupped the structure like a sheltering hand. The windows were shut tight, drapes pulled half across the wide clear panes on the lower floor, as usual. No lights showed anywhere.

Reenie should be home since her car was in the garage. So why hadn't she answered either of her phones? I grabbed mine off the seat and tried yet again. Her cell rang on and on until a drone advised of a full voice-mail box. No answer on her home number either, and the machine didn't come on. As an attorney, Reenie couldn't afford to be out of reach; she always answered her cell. Her home answering machine always picked up. Was she ill, injured, in desperate need of help? Had she had a heart attack, an aneurysm? A shudder ran down my spine as I started for the house, terrified I'd find her sprawled dead on the floor.

Not until I walked up the steep slope of the front walk did I see the signs. Some of the decorative cacti beside the steps had been trampled. The porch, always swept clean, was now littered with dirt and debris the highlands wind deposited there daily. Four plastic sleeves of daily newspapers hung out in one corner, something Reenie would never tolerate. And deep gouges marred the front door around the lock.

I mounted the steps, my breath hitching in my throat. It wasn't visible until I stood in front of the ocean-blue door: a partial handprint in rusty red up high, at my shoulder height. And a crack where the door should be nestled snug into the frame.

It wasn't completely closed.

The security system wasn't on.

I thumbed on my phone. Garrett answered on the first ring.

"Garrett, Reenie's car is here, but she's still not answering. The front door is slightly ajar, and I think there's... blood... on the edge."

"Don't go in there. Call the cops, Skylark. I'm on my way."

"No, wait, maybe I'm wrong. Maybe it's just dirt..."

"Skylark," Garrett said, but I'd stopped paying attention.

I reached out and pushed on the front door with my fingertips. It swung wide on well-oiled hinges to reveal the dark entry foyer.

"Reenie?" I called. "Are you here?"

Silence. Deep, dark, depressive.

"I don't hear anything, Gar. And I can't see anything out of place in the entry. I'm going in, she could be hurt, needing help—"

My voice choked off. I barely heard Garrett's shout.

"Skylark! Wait for backup, damn it! I'm on my way. Justin," Garrett's voice thinned as he turned away from his phone, "call the cops, get them out to Maureen Overton's place, fast!"

My footsteps echoed in the large, airy space, underscored by the slam of Garrett's office door and the roar of his Corvette engine revving up, filtered tinnily through our cell phones. I checked the living room, the dining room; all seemed fine, not a pillow or an ornament out of place. I glanced into the half bath, again finding nothing amiss. Then I stepped into the kitchen.

All I could do was stare in disbelief.

"Skylark! Are you there? Answer me, Skylark!"

Garrett's shout, issuing from the phone still clutched in my hand, penetrated into my head. I lifted the cell. I could barely form words, my despair was so complete.

"There's blood, Gar, lots of blood. In the kitchen. On the counter, on the floor, the walls. Spoiled food on the counter, broken wine bottles. Stools knocked over, one broken—"

My voice broke as I walked up to the center island. Words jammed in my throat. I set the phone on the counter and stared at the piece of paper, a sheet of Reenie's own monogrammed stationery, anchored down by a bloody knife. Five lines, short and stark, addressed to me in the same erratic handwriting as the note left on Heidi's body.

> Skylark—
> Bring my glasses
> 19765 Two-Tunnel Road
> Come <u>alone</u>
> No cops
> Tell <u>anyone</u> and the bitch is <u>dead</u>

My whole body felt numb. This wasn't happening, couldn't be happening. *No, please, not Reenie*, I thought, over and over. *Please, not her.*

I stood frozen, staring, until sirens sounded in the distance, drawing closer. Cops would be here soon, as would Garrett who was still shouting into his phone as he drove, both arriving too soon for me to figure out what to do. And I had to figure it out. Reenie's life was on the line.

My ghosts sent up their quiet, mournful chant from deep inside their cavern, *your fault, your fault,* and

I knew I was the only one who could make it right. The only one who could save Reenie.

Or die trying.

I knew I shouldn't have done it. I knew better, knew it was illegal to tamper with evidence, knew I'd be arrested if anyone found out. But I couldn't have stopped myself to save the world. I reached out and eased the note from beneath the bloody blade. Tremors ran up my arm into my body; my heart squeezed down until I thought it would stop beating. As I heard a car pull into the driveway and a screaming siren die into silence, I folded the paper and slipped it into my hip pocket.

Then I picked up the phone, from which Garrett's shouts still spilled, and found my voice again.

"He's got her, Garrett. The bastard's got Reenie."

"Just wait... til I get you... in a courtroom. You're gonna... pay so bad." She glared at him from where she hung by her wrists from the rafters, and tried to lift her legs to kick at him, but blood loss and abuse had drained her strength. "You won't... get away with this."

Dried blood coated her arms and legs; purple swellings twisted her face. Bruises dotted her naked torso. He could tell she was having trouble breathing from the way her words stuttered. Carstairs grinned at her as he pulled down the ski mask.

"I already have." He reached over and turned on the camera. "She'll be mine soon, you wait and see.

She'll be mine and I'll tame her, just like my father taught me."

"You're wrong. No one can... beat... Skylark."

"I've already beaten her." He winked into the camera and looked over the assembled tools.

"You'll never beat her. Skylark's... the strongest person I've... ever known. She'll take you... down."

Carstairs laughed and picked up the knife.

"Maybe I'll cut off your hooters. You won't be much of a woman without them, will you?"

"Doesn't matter what... you do to me. Skylark... will get you. She'll kill you, you... worthless moron."

Rage burst in him as he heard, in her derision, his father's voice: *You worthless mama's boy, letting girls get the better of you. Grow a spine, little Maggie. Be a man for once.*

"Shut up, you fucking bitch!" he screamed. "No woman talks to me like that!"

"You poor... pathetic... little man... thinking your... miniature dick is—"

"Shut up, shut up, shut up! I'll show you who's worthless! I'll show you what a real man is!"

He yanked her head up by her hair, set the knife near the outer corner of her eye and pressed down. She screamed as he dug it deep over her cheekbone and through her flesh, down past the corner of her mouth, the blade piercing through her cheek and nicking her tongue. Then he dug the point into her throat and cut through her vocal cords.

"Now you'll never speak to anyone again, you stupid bitch. No more doing a man's work in the courts. You'll be what a woman should be, silent and obedient." He gave her a shove. "Stupid lawyer bitch."

He turned and stalked away, out of the barn, leaving the camera running for his internet audience, recording the woman's moans, her swaying, shuddering, naked body, and the blood that ran from her ruined face onto the filthy straw-covered floor.

CHAPTER THIRTY-FOUR

Within ten minutes of the first car's arrival bearing two uniformed officers, a couple of detectives I'd not met before—Guzman and Stone—pulled up and stashed me in their back seat. I wondered where Soto was, if he'd put in an appearance. And thanked my lucky stars that Dunwitty was down for the count. Half an hour later, the whole contingent had assembled. A CSI unit began toiling away in Reenie's kitchen, while uniforms canvassed the neighbors. And there I sat, idle, wasting time while the note burned a hole in my pocket and acid ate away at my stomach lining.

I should have been home, figuring out where the hell Two-Tunnel Road was, not moldering away in the back of an overheated cop car. It was an odd name, Two-Tunnel; could there be more than one road called that? Or had the asswipe made it up? If it was real, in which of the dozens of towns scattered within driving distance would it be located? How long would it take to find it and then get there to save Reenie? If she was even still alive. What was he doing to her? My head felt like it would explode from the never ending questions; why didn't the damned cops just release me, so I could go find the answers?

I told my story over and over, first to the uniforms, then to the two detectives who seemed to think the details would change every few minutes. Or that I was lying, and multiple tellings would trip me up. If Garrett hadn't arrived just as they began questioning me for the fifth time, I might have lost hold of my temper and done something that would have landed me behind bars. As it was, he defused the situation and I only landed in the back seat of the detective's car—again.

"Take it easy, Skylark," Garrett said after he climbed in beside me. "Getting on their bad side won't help anything."

"I know," I muttered, staring out the open door at the uniform the detectives had left to watch over me. Did they really think I had something to do with this? "But I can't stand sitting here, doing nothing. I should be out there, trying to find Reenie."

"And just where would you start? She could be anywhere."

I drew in a deep breath and held it a moment. I wanted to show Garrett the note I'd found, have him help me in the search for Two-Tunnel Road. But I could still see the orders on the paper: *come alone,* and, *tell anyone and the bitch is dead.* I simply couldn't take the chance. Not with Reenie's life.

"I know that," I said. "But anything is better than just sitting here!"

I clenched my fists, ground my teeth, and screamed deep in my throat. Garrett put his hand on my arm.

"Calm down. Let's see if they find anything that can at least point us in a direction, okay? We'll find her, Skylark. We will."

Yeah, but in time? I asked myself as I fought the tears of anger and frustration that wanted to fall. The blood in the kitchen was dust-dry, the fresh food rotting beneath a film of mold; the asshole had already had her for days. Days! I turned to Garrett only to find Detective Guzman leaning down to stare in at us.

"Okay, Skylark, tell me again. Did you touch anything in there?"

I gasped in a breath and shut my eyes; Garrett's hand tightened on my arm. I shook my head then raised my lids and glared at the detective.

"How many times do I have to tell you? I got a call from Reenie's assistant, Danielle, and drove straight here. I looked in the garage window and saw her car, then went up on the porch and found the door not quite closed. I pushed it open with two fingertips," I held the fingers up, "went in and found the kitchen... with all that blood... And no, I didn't touch anything," *except the note*, I thought, "I'm a trained PI, I know not to mess with a crime scene."

"She called me right after she got here, Detective," Garrett added. "I was on the phone with her the whole time. I heard the first car arrive, heard the officers approach Skylark."

"And just how do you know Miss Overton?"

He was asking me. His stare hadn't wandered to Garrett for even a fraction. Of course, he already knew Garrett had arrived after the first cop car, unlike me, who was Johnny-on-the-spot when the festivities began. And who had called a friend instead of 9-1-1. Okay, that might make the detective a bit suspicious, but it didn't account for the animosity that rolled off him. I wondered if Guzman had Dunwitty on speed-dial, or if the whole damned Sheriff's department hated me because of him. Or maybe the lawsuit.

"I've known Reenie for more than five years. She's my best friend. As I've told you and told you and *told you!*"

Garrett leaned over me, blocking Guzman's view of my livid face.

"Let me, Skylark. Just stay calm for a few more minutes, can you do that?"

I didn't look at him as I nodded, mainly because I hated lying to him and I didn't know how much longer I could hold off exploding like a volcano. Garrett climbed out of the car and moved a few feet away with the detective. I couldn't hear their words, but Garrett's conciliatory tone and the detective's self-important bombast filtered clearly through the late afternoon sunshine. Then they smiled at each other, Guzman nodded, and they shook hands; the good-old-boy club was alive and well in San Luis Obispo County. Too bad I didn't have the right equipment to qualify for membership.

"It's okay, Skylark," Garrett said, holding out a hand to help me from the back seat, "we can leave now."

"But I want you at the station on 10th in two hours, so we can take a formal statement." Guzman glared at me. "You got that?"

I nodded, knowing full well I had no intention of keeping that appointment. If they wanted a statement from me, they'd have to wait until after I'd found and rescued Reenie. Or hell froze over. Whichever came first.

It took another ten minutes for the cops to shift cars so that I could pull mine out of the driveway, then Garrett followed me down the hill into Los Osos proper, all the way to my house. It took two cups of coffee and a lot of hand holding before he finally decided I could be left alone. The clock was edging up to 7:00 pm as I watched him drive away, then I pulled the note from my pocket and fired up my computer.

I typed "Two-Tunnel Road" into the search engine, deliberately not adding a location, or even a state, and to my surprise it popped right up. There was only one, right here in SLO County, out in the wilderness of hills and forest that connected the coast with Atascadero. It canted off Route 41, which I could access via Route 1 in Morro Bay. Practically around the corner.

"I'm coming, Reenie. Hold on," I muttered as I checked my pistol, grabbed an extra cartridge, and tucked a mini-switchblade into my back pocket.

Ten minutes after Garrett left, I was on my way to Two-Tunnel Road.

Soto sat staring at the printouts spread on his desk. *Damn if Skylark wasn't right*, he thought.

There'd been seventeen reported thefts in the last three years from homeowners who had been out of town and returned home to discover their houses ransacked and their valuables gone. Of the seventeen, eleven had had their homes painted within four to six months of the robbery. If the robber-turned-killer had been on a painting crew, he definitely was smart to have waited so long to hit the places. No one would have thought to link the painting with the thefts.

Two companies had handled the painting of the eleven houses in question: Diablo Canyon Painters and BrushStrokes. Because he didn't have a warrant, it had taken hours to convince the company owners to fax him a list of their employees for those three years, at least those who were on the payrolls. If the robber/killer had worked under the table—though both owners claimed all their employees earned paychecks—there would be no way to find him.

It seemed that painters moved around without much notice, especially apprentices and those doing peripheral work. And since he had no way of knowing what kind of work the killer did for these companies, Soto had to carefully comb each long list. He had spent all of yesterday afternoon comparing them, matching names and work dates with the houses that had been robbed. Then he'd spent this morning and half the afternoon comparing the employees' work histories.

He ended up with three names, three men who had worked on and off for both companies, and who had painted, or worked at—in some capacity—the eleven houses.

He jotted down the names, then spent another hour on the phone to find out where each man was working. Frank Burger, currently a prep man for Diablo Canyon Painters—he seemed to switch companies every few months—was at a house up in Atascadero. Soto's scalp began to tingle; Andrea, the fifteen-year-old, lived in Atascadero.

Mateo López, a senior painter for BrushStrokes, was foreman of a crew working a cluster of homes in Pismo Beach. Yvonne Avila had disappeared from her workplace in Pismo Beach. Either man could be the one he was looking for.

The third man, Magellan Carstairs, had worked a few days with the Diablo Canyon Painters crew currently at the SLO City Morgue, but he'd been out now with the flu for over a week.

The flu? For more than a week? Seemed like a long time to be down with something like the flu. *Or is it a bullet wound, perhaps?* he wondered, thinking of the intruder Skylark had shot.

He called the number the office manager had given him, but no one answered. Had the man gotten so sick that he was hospitalized? Or was he out scouting another victim? Or was one of the other men the one he was looking for?

It took three hours and a slew of phone calls to get each company to agree to hand over home addresses without a warrant; he played the "lives at stake" card for all it was worth. Soto jotted them down, and studied the short list. One man lived in Paso Robles, one in San Luis Obispo, the third in Morro Bay. Soto decided to start with the closest suspect, the one who was supposedly home sick, and work out from there. By the time he finished with Carstairs, the other two should be home from work. He grabbed his gun from the desk and headed out into the evening to hopefully track down one very elusive killer.

Dunwitty tipped the last of the beer into his mouth, then stared at the GPS tracker that sat on his kitchen table. She was on the move again, after being homebound for days, days that ate away at his patience and churned the acid in his stomach. She'd stuck around town for a while, probably running errands, then headed out toward Montaña de Oro and drove up into the hills. The car sat there for about four hours—most likely at The Overton's place, which surprised Dunwitty; he thought the lawyer would be in court, or at least her office, on a weekday—before the blip showed it headed back to Skylark's house. Almost two hours later, she headed out again.

He watched the blip crawl along her route: Los Osos Valley Road, then right on South Bay Boulevard, all the way down to merge onto Route 1, heading north. Where was she going? Cambria? Cayucos? Further north? Was she on her way to her bastard boyfriend, or was she on the lookout for a new victim for him? Or perhaps to a plane up in San Francisco that would take her far, far away from his reach?

What is she up to? he wondered. He stood up, grabbed another beer from the fridge, opened it, then walked back to watch the tracker. To his surprise, she'd turned off Route 1 onto 41, heading toward Atascadero. And the highway? She looked to be already a mile or so up the road; wherever she was headed, she was in a hurry. Had she spent her time at home packing? Was she on the lam?

Dunwitty fingered his cell phone as he watched the blip move further and further up the winding road. He should probably call Soto, let him know their—well, his —main suspect was fleeing jurisdiction. But then he remembered he was off the case; there was no way he should know anything about Miss One Name Wonder or her movements. The fact that he did, that he'd illegally tagged her ride, would get him in even more trouble than he already was in. Besides, the last time he'd spoken with his so-called partner, Soto told him the investigation had gone in another direction. The Skylark bitch was in the clear, as far as the department was concerned. So calling Soto would do no good.

He stood, beer in hand, staring at the tracker, trying to figure out what the woman was doing, where she was going. The blip moved along Route 41, up into the hills, then slowed, turned left, and headed out into total wilderness.

What the hell?

He pushed a button on the tracker and a name came up: Two-Tunnel Road. He watched her car navigate what looked like a sharp U-curve, then a group of S-curves as the road wound in toward a low mountain. Where the map said the road ended, the blip paused, turned right and continued on another couple of miles. Then it stopped.

He waited five minutes, ten minutes, twenty minutes, forty-five minutes, but there was no further movement. She was either sitting in the car, waiting for someone—her bastard boyfriend, perhaps—or she'd abandoned the Jeep and gone to meet him on foot.

Or maybe she's getting rid of the kidnapped girls for him. The thought took his breath away.

"Not this time, you don't," he growled.

Dunwitty thought again about contacting Soto, but couldn't figure out how to tell him how he knew what Skylark was up to, or where she was. So, it was up to him. He'd probably lose his job over this, but if he could stop her, if he could find and rescue those girls, keep them alive, it would be worth it. He grabbed his backup piece and some extra ammunition and shoved them in his jacket pockets along with his cell phone. Tracker in hand, he went out to his car, determined this time to run Miss One Name Wonder into the ground.

CHAPTER THIRTY-FIVE

Civilization fell away as Route 41 rose higher and higher. Four lanes became two. Trees crowded close to the edges and met in a dense dark canopy overhead. To the right, the land sloped down sixty steep feet to Morro Creek, the shoulder in places not much wider than two feet, making the winding road a bit harrowing to drive. Seven miles up from where 41 intersected with Route 1, Two-Tunnel Road led off to the left, a cut in the dense underbrush that streaked a lighter slash in the dark foliage. I'd have missed it if I hadn't been looking for it.

Not far from the turnoff, the road curved back on itself in a tight U shape. I found the edges of the road difficult to see in the dim, green-tinged half light beneath the thick canopy of trees, and had to slow to under 20 miles per hour. The light brightened as the road straightened into a series of gentle S-curves and the landscape slowly morphed from wild forest to treeless cultivation. I picked up a little speed, but not much, since the holes that pocked the deteriorating road jarred the Jeep's springs and rattled my teeth.

I wound through shorn fields, the few farmhouses I could see mere dots in the distance. Edging the pavement, horses, cows and sheep grazed on yellowed grass; alternating fields sown with vegetables spun orderly rows on a diagonal away from the road that gradually narrowed down to a lane-and-a-half. In the distance, growing closer with every mile I covered, hulked the shadow of a low mountain. The numbers on the few mailboxes I saw, all in the four-digit-range, didn't come close to the address in the note.

I drove slowly, the only moving dot on the landscape, hands slick on the wheel, heart pounding, wondering how long the road was, and what—or who—would be waiting for me when it ended. I left the last of the farm fields behind, this one a fallow meadow rampant with tall grasses not yet plowed under, and came to the end of the road where it abutted the steep slope of the mountain.

I looked around in the fading early evening light and managed to spot what looked like a track off to one side. With no choice other than to turn around—which I wasn't about to do before finding Reenie—I yanked the wheel to the right, bounced onto the track, and proceeded along a wild stretch with the mountain to my left. Its shadow made the light feel even more oppressive, gray and foreboding. The Jeep's wheels ground over rutty gravel that crunched with an ominous echo on the still, hot air. A molting wooden fence roped off entrance to the sloping side of the mountain; it rose and fell with the land, like a wave on a turgid ocean. Overgrown trees and bushes on the right masked any hint of other life from view.

Two miles further on, the disintegrating gravel pathway ended with abrupt suddenness at a decaying wooden fence. Gray clouds hid the lowering sun, dimming the light even further. Nothing stirred, neither bird in the sky nor animal on the ground. For all I could tell, I was the only living being left on the face of the earth.

I stopped the car before a dilapidated gate that hung from half-detached hinges. It gaped an opening barely wide enough for a vehicle to pass through. Painted on one upright post, weathered almost into extinction, I could just make out numbers: 19765.

I had arrived.

I turned off the Jeep and sat watching, listening. Nothing, not a rustle or a peep, no crunch of gravel or snap of twig, no sign of movement anywhere. Ahead of me, on the other side of the gate, stretched a barren expanse of field dotted with half-dead oak trees and low scrub bushes. Faint gravel tracks led through the opening and across the field to vanish in the distance, but I didn't want to commit my Jeep to the unknown. I executed a twelve-point turn on the narrow track to maneuver the car around so I faced the way I'd come—to facilitate a quick getaway, should I need it—then got out, eased the door shut, and went the rest of the way on foot.

I stayed to the side of the track so my footsteps wouldn't crunch gravel and announce my approach, and hugged close to the mountain. A few hundred yards in, the tracks curved to the left, around the side of the hill. I followed the curve with cautious stealth to find a dilapidated old farmstead spread out before me.

To my left, snugged up against the mountain, stood a rickety-looking machine shed, or perhaps garage, large enough to hold maybe three vehicles. All but one of the windows in the tight-shut doors had been broken and boarded over. Across a dusty, barren expanse of a front yard where chickens and dogs maybe once roamed, I could see a small, almost-shack-like farm house. Dried shrubs poked out of the arid soil in a haphazard line along broken pavers that formed the front walkway, leading to the rotten-looking boards of a minuscule front porch. Beyond the house, I could just make out a large barn standing on the far side of a neglected, overgrown field, ringed on three sides by a thicket of trees. The tall grasses half-hid what appeared to be abandoned farm machinery.

There was no sign of life around the entire area, no movement anywhere, and no sounds other than my own heartbeat and an occasional bird call from high above. Where was Reenie? In the garage? Or maybe the house, or the barn? Were the other missing girls here, too? What about the turd who'd left that note? Where the hell was he? Since he'd lured me out here, shouldn't he be here to greet me?

I slid my Glock out of its holster and held it at my side as I edged over to the garage and peered through the remaining window. My heart gave a lurch; inside sat a dark, rusted pickup truck, coated with dirt. In the open bed I could see a crumpled plastic sheet covered with dark stains. Blood? Had he wrapped the remains of poor Heidi Coffey in it to transport her to my back yard?

"Son of a bitch!" I whispered.

I gripped the Glock tighter and turned toward the farm house. Still no sign of anyone, no smoke from the chimney, no sounds of music or television from the interior. The asswipe had lured me out here, so where was he? And where was Reenie?

I crossed the open, pock-marked yard as quickly as I could with all senses on alert, noting footprints and drag marks on the dusty ground. Someone had been here not long ago. I pressed my back against the splintery siding and risked a peek through a side window, but dark curtains foiled my attempt to see inside. Clenching my teeth in a futile attempt to keep my breathing under control, I edged along the house to the front corner and peered around, down the length of the narrow porch.

I'd been right, half the boards were rotting away, though in places it looked as though some had been replaced. Still, it didn't look safe. Or squeak-proof. I figured I'd either fall through the deck or make one hell of a racket if I tried to cross it. Not conducive to a stealth entrance. I decided to look for a back door.

As I turned to head toward the rear of the place, the world tilted. My psychic curse surged into the fading daylight as the past once again arose to ghost over the present: a yard filled with sunlight, blooming bushes and flowers, chickens pecking at the dirt, a dog cowering near now gleamingly-new porch steps. And there, between the front walk and the garage/machine shed, not ten feet in front of me, a man and a boy maybe eleven or so, standing over the prone form of a woman.

"No," I whispered. "Please, no. Not now."

I stood immobilized, unable to turn away no matter how hard I tried, as the past held me captive and unrolled its secrets before my eyes. The man shoved a narrow iron pipe at the boy as he screamed at him. The boy didn't want to take it. The man grabbed him by his too-long hair and shook him. I could read most of the words on the man's lips, though I couldn't hear a sound: *Do it, Maggie... you stupid... Mama's boy... time... grow a pair... be a man.*

Then he hit the kid, smacked him down to the ground, and nudged him hard with a booted foot. *It's just a woman, Maggie,* he said. *It's what she's made for.* In the silence I could almost hear the taunting ring in his voice. *Make... fucking decision: her little baby, or my son.* The boy, blood dripping from his nose, finally nodded, rose, and grasped the pipe. He lifted the unconscious woman's skirt and—

My head exploded and I dropped into a deep, dark well.

I woke sitting in a wooden chair, my head throbbing and my stomach threatening to spew up its contents. I couldn't move; my hands were bound behind me, my ankles tied to the chair legs. A strip of tape had been plastered across my face. Every movement of my head brought the threat of up-chucking that much closer. I sat still, eyes closed, waiting until the pain died down a bit; the last thing I needed was to choke to death on my own vomit.

Three concussions in less than two months. Won't the doctors be thrilled? I thought.

Flickering light seeped through my closed lids, lighter, darker, then lighter again. I could hear talking and screaming from nearby, but it had an odd, tinny sound to it, as though it weren't live, but piped in somehow. It took me long minutes—minutes I couldn't afford to waste while Reenie needed me—to raise my head, open my eyes, wait for the world to stop spinning, then look around.

It was a small room, a tiny bedroom, perhaps, or a large closet, though walls made from rough planks made me question my guesses. There didn't seem to be anything other than the chair I sat bound to and one tight-shut door. I'd been situated facing an old plasma TV affixed to the wall beside the door. Some kind of torture and bondage show spread its vileness across the screen. A man, face concealed by a ski mask, dragged a naked woman—Heidi Coffey, I recognized her even through the cuts and bruises—over the floor and threw her onto a bed, then fixed the chains on her arms and legs to the bedposts. He climbed atop her and placed an iron pipe, much like the one I'd seen in my vision, between her legs. He looked up at the camera; I could see his thick lips stretch in a ghoulish smile.

"This, bitches, is what happens when you don't obey your man," he said, and thrust the pipe.

Heidi screamed as though her insides were being shredded. They probably were. Bile again rose in my throat and I shut my eyes, wishing I could as easily shut my ears. I tried to slip the rope on my wrists, but he'd tied me good and tight. I looked down at myself. My blouse—spotted with blood that still dribbled from my head—had been torn open and my bra cut apart, exposing my breasts. Stinging pain and a thin stream of blood let me know he'd used his knife on the left one, the turd. But I still wore my jeans. *Mistake number one, asshole*, I thought as I squirmed on the seat.

Silence fell, then a weird, ululating music rose. I squinted at the TV. *How To Train A Bitch, Episode 8* splayed across the screen. The music ended. The masked shithead appeared, dragging a young beagle pup by a rope around its neck.

"You can't be squeamish about it, no matter how cute these bitches are," the man said. "We're men, it's our duty to do what needs to be done. They will thank you for it, in the end."

He picked up a mini-blow torch and lit it. I turned my head away, refused to see what my ears heard, the poor little dog yelping and shrieking as though its soul was being torn free. Instead, sickened and pissed to hell and back, I concentrated on wriggling my fingers into my back pocket, thankful for once that the height I'd hated all my life also gave me long arms that afforded enough wiggle room to retrieve the little knife I'd tucked in there.

Teach that asswipe not to do a thorough pat-down, I thought.

I inched it out, and by feel, shifted it around until I could press the button that released the blade. It sliced into my thumb and I grunted at the pain, but kept working on shifting the blade until it sat against the ropes holding me prisoner. I went to work to the accompaniment of more female screams and pleadings: *Episode 9*, and not Heidi this time. One of the others, but I wasn't about to look long enough to find out who. Or what was being done to her. It took a while to saw through the strands—I almost lost the knife twice; the blood from my cut made things slippery, and the screams from the TV shredded my concentration—but eventually the rope fell from my wrists, freeing my arms.

I should have gone for the ropes on my ankles next, but I feared trying to bend down with my mouth still taped. So I first pulled the tape from my mouth, hissing as a few layers of skin came away with it, then bent and sawed through the ropes holding my ankles prisoner.

It took a few more long minutes before I could stand without either passing out, falling down, or throwing up, then I searched the small room to see if I could locate something to use as a weapon. Nothing; there was only me, the chair, and the TV. I cut off a thin slice of my shirt hem and wound it around the deep gash in my thumb to soak up the blood, then wriggled out of the ruined bra. There weren't enough buttons left to close the shirt, so I made do by tying the bottom together. Then I turned to the TV.

We were back to the poor, abused dog again. I picked up the chair and, despite my pounding head, swung it as hard as I could, grinning as the glass exploded into thousands of lethal shards. And the light I'd had, little as it was, vanished. Inky darkness surrounded me.

"Damn," I muttered. "Great plan, Skylark."

But it wasn't all bad. No one had come running in response to the noise. And the chair had broken apart; now I had both a knife and a sturdy oak chair-leg club for weapons, since my captor hadn't been considerate enough to leave behind my Glock.

I wanted to run to wherever Reenie was being held, but my body wasn't about to cooperate. I inched through the glass shards to the wall, and from there felt my way to the door, praying it wasn't locked. It was hard going. My head reeled, making the room see-saw around me. Spots swam before my eyes. My knees felt like wiggly jelly. But I wasn't about to let this piece of shit have any more time with his captives. Heart thudding, teeth gritted in an effort to find enough strength to stay aware and on my feet, I found the doorknob and turned it.

To my surprise, it wasn't locked. I stood a moment, listening, but heard nothing, no sign anyone was anywhere near me. Then I eased open the door and slipped out into even more darkness to begin the next leg of this increasingly dangerous rescue mission.

CHAPTER THIRTY-SIX

Soto eased his car to a stop, facing Skylark's Jeep. It sat just outside the open gate, as though set for a fast getaway. *What the hell is she doing here?* he wondered as he again checked the address for Magellan Carstairs, then peered at the faded numbers on the gatepost. Yes, this was it. He looked around: a place far out in the country, hidden from prying eyes, where noise— screams?—would go unheard.

A chill swam down his spine.

He got out, walked up to the Jeep, and laid his hand on the hood. Cold. She'd been there a while, then, a couple of hours at least. Doing what? He glanced up at the darkening sky, at a couple of pinpoint stars beginning to gleam in the firmament, then around at the land, which appeared devoid of any human habitation. After checking the address one last time, he opened the trunk of his car. He felt stupid, especially since he was no longer in uniform, hadn't been for over six years, but he could still hear his training officer's insistent voice: *Always wear your vest. Better safe than sorry.* His thoughts went to Betsy and their date set for

Friday night, the ring burning a hole in his pocket. *Yes,* he thought, removing his shirt and strapping on his vest, *much better safe than sorry.* He dressed again, straining the halves of his shirt front over the bulk of the vest, then donned his suit coat, checked his weapon, and walked with cautious steps through the yawning gate and along the faint tracks that led across the wide field.

He rounded the curve of the mountain and stopped to survey the farmyard that appeared before him. Nothing moved; no animals, no birds, no sign of habitation. Not even a light in the farmhouse window. Was this Carstairs character even home? The garage held a single small pickup; the flashlight on his keychain picked up the license plate—yes, it was his—and a crumpled sheet of plastic in the bed. Dirty plastic, dark with stains he could barely make out... He squinted. Was that mud? Or blood?

Blood... Another cold shiver raised gooseflesh on his arms. This could be the plastic sheet that had wrapped Heidi Coffey's body on its final journey to Skylark's back yard. His mouth went dry and he licked his lips, then blew out a shaky breath.

He tried the lift door; locked. Then he tried the side-access door; also locked. He turned and scanned the deserted yard once more, then headed for the small farm house.

He took the front steps with cautious feet, testing each one before trusting his full weight to them. They didn't look strong enough to hold a child, much less a full-grown man, but he navigated them without much difficulty. He edged up to the door and peered through the misty curtain that covered its dirty window. Without any lamps burning inside, and light fading fast outside, there was little he could see. He waited long minutes, searching for any sign of movement, and saw nothing, then carefully checked the knob. Locked.

If no one was in there, where was Carstairs? His truck was in the garage, he should be around, but this place felt deserted. And where was Skylark?

He finally left the door and moved to the one window on the front side of the house. His shoulders dropped when he realized it was covered by a thick opaque curtain. *Back door*, he thought. If he had to, he'd kick it in so he could make sure Skylark wasn't lying injured, or dead, somewhere in the small house.

Shielding the flashlight with his fingers, he made his way back to the front steps. Shots rang out just as he set his foot down on the first one: sharp staccato bursts that echoed eerily from the mountain at his back. Where had they come from? They didn't sound like they were outside, and were definitely a distance away, not in the house. There had to be another structure he hadn't seen in the gathering twilight.

He hurried down the steps and stood on the uneven front walk, searching for a direction. Screams split the air—Skylark? Or the other missing girls? Where? There, off to his left!

He took off at a run, squinting into a darkness unrelieved by his mini-flash as he made out a hulking shape outlined against the darkening sky on the other side of a large field—the farm's barn, probably. Then his foot dropped into a gopher hole. Pain shot up his leg as he fell. His keys flew from his hand and the flashlight flickered out. He landed hard, whacking his head on the unyielding ground. His teeth crunched into his bottom lip; the iron taste of blood flooded into his mouth. *Crap,*

crap, crap, he thought as darkness deeper than the night closed down on him.

I stood shaking, pressed against a rough wood wall in what appeared to be a narrow corridor, listening with every fiber of my being, wishing like hell I had at least a flashlight if not a lamp. Or a candle. I couldn't hear anything at first, then faintly, off to my right, the clink of metal. A chain of some kind? I turned toward the sound and inched down the narrow passageway. Mini-switchblade in hand, I slid the side of my fist along the wall for balance, wincing as splinters pierced my flesh—not the kind of walls one would expect in a house of any kind. After about ten feet, I stopped and blinked, not sure if what I was seeing was real or just wishful thinking.

Light. Faint, almost non-existent, but definitely lighter than the inky blackness that had surrounded me ever since I'd smashed the TV screen. I closed my eyes, shook my head, then blinked my eyes open again, hoping it was real.

It was. I could make out the very faint outline of a narrow archway about twenty feet further on. Some-where beyond that arch, wherever it led, were, fingers crossed, the captured women, Reenie, and the turd who had taken them. A turd who'd be very surprised—and unprepared—when I popped out and attacked him. I hoped. I took a deep breath and kept going.

When I reached the opening I stood against the side wall and peered through the arch into a massive room filled with menacing shadows. Definitely not the small farmhouse, this was most likely the farm's massive barn. Two small night-lights, low down on opposite walls, sent faint luminescence into the darkness. I could make out a series of cages lining the closer wall, the one to my left, though I couldn't tell how many there were, or if they were occupied. Shadows shrouded the far reaches of the room, and though something big and bulky hulked against the wall opposite me, it was too dim and too far away to tell what it was. A faint whimpering yelp echoed in the room, a dog in agonizing pain. I remembered the session with the puppy and the blow torch, and shuddered.

Is this what he'd done with them, stuffed them in cages, dragging them out one-by-one to play his games with them? The dogs and the women? Anger brewed deep and dark within me. *Just let me get my hands on him*, I prayed as I crept across the floor to the cage-lined wall. *Just give me the chance to rip his head from his body.*

The first two cages held young-looking dogs that blinked up at me with rheumy, fear filled eyes. Both looked so badly beaten and abused that I doubted they could be saved, or would be anywhere near normal if they were. The next two cages stood empty, doors gaping, chains secured to the floorboards of the second, manacles open and waiting to close on wrists and ankles. Mine? A small figure huddled frozen in a fetal position in the next cage; only the fact that she flinched when I yanked on the locked door, trying to free her, let me know she was alive.

"I'm going to get you out of here," I whispered, though I didn't think she was in any shape to hear or understand me. I couldn't see her face, so I didn't know which one it was, though it wasn't Reenie. The blonde hair told me that much. "Just hold on, okay? I need to find something to open this door. I'll be back, I promise."

I waited a moment, but she gave me no response, not even the flicker of an eyelid, or an intake of breath.

I moved on and crouched before the next cage; another woman, this one glaring up at me from defiant eyes. Yvonne Avila, barely recognizable beneath the bruises and wounds. We stared at each other for a startled moment before her expression morphed into shock, then into a desperate pleading. She reached out a hand; the chain secured to her wrist clanked loud in the stillness. Then she laid a trembling finger on her swollen lips, looked toward the far side of the room, and shook her head.

I nodded, tried her door and found it locked, also, and moved on without a word.

A third woman, again not Reenie—too old to be Andrea, so it was either Casey or Nicole; I hadn't seen their pictures long enough to be sure—sat propped in the next-to-last cage, her eyes closed, her face twisted with pain, her body shuddering, her lips moving as though in soundless prayer. When I got close, I could see her hair was tied in clumps to the iron bars, holding her semi-upright. Rage thrummed through me. Wasn't beating and torturing her enough? He had to do this, too? I set down the club and tried to open the door. No luck. I'd need keys to get to the prisoners, and keys to open the manacles on their arms and legs. An impossible task, I feared.

Well, if I couldn't unlock her cage, at least I could give her some relief from the pain. I flicked open the switchblade and moved to cut her hair away from the bars when a deep, menacing voice echoed in the room.

"How nice of you to come to me, bitch. You disobeyed my orders, but it saves me the trouble of dragging you into the training room."

I gasped and spun around, almost losing my balance. He stood some thirty feet away, silhouetted in another doorway, one that led to a more brightly lit room. I could feel—though I couldn't see—the cocky grin on his face. I rose slowly, my teeth clenched.

"You stinking son of a—"

He raised both arms; a volley of shots rang out. All around me bullets slammed into the floor, the wall, the rafters overhead, even zinged off the bars of the cages. The shithead wasn't trying to kill me, just scare or maybe wound me; if he wanted me dead, he'd have aimed directly at me, not around me. I was tempted to just stand there, motionless and defiant, and not let him see how badly he'd rattled me. But self-preservation engulfed me before the thought fully formed. I took off toward the end wall and the concealing shadows, ran as though the hounds of hell were on my heels, arms over my head, dodging bullets and shrapnel like a scared rabbit. Bullets flew everywhere, even toward the cages that held the captives. My heart stuttered in my chest; I could barely catch my breath. I had to draw his fire away before one of those poor girls was hit, I simply had to. I'd be damned if I'd be responsible for yet another death.

When I reached the shadows I dove behind what I discovered was a dense wall of hay bales. I crouched, trembling, trying to get my breathing under control as more bullets slammed into the front sides of the bales. Somewhere along the way I'd lost the knife, and when I attempted to worm my way further into the stack I discovered why. Pain shot down my right arm, through my shoulder and across my chest. My hand had gone completely numb; I had no control over my fingers. The bullet had hit my body near the shoulder joint; I hissed in as I clamped my hand over the wound. Blood bubbled through my fingers and spread like a river down my side.

In my panicked flight I hadn't even felt the bullet hit me. But I sure as hell felt it now. I crouched in the darkness listening as silence abruptly fell, my head swimming from both the exertion and the concussion. To say nothing of the blood loss. Moving at top speed was so not a brilliant idea. I squinted my eyes and looked around, trying to figure a way out from behind my wall of protection—not that I saw anything other than murky shadows. Were there any exits other than the way I'd come in? And where was the shooter? I couldn't hear a sound, not even a faint footstep. If I did get out without running into him, could I possibly get to the knife I'd dropped and use it on him before I either passed out or he finished the job of killing me? And what had he done with Reenie?

So damn many questions, the answers to which I wasn't sure I'd like. Sometimes I just loved my life.

CHAPTER THIRTY-SEVEN

Before I could gather my thoughts, or figure a way out of my predicament, the asswipe stalked behind the hay bales and grabbed me by my hair. Then he dragged me out and across the big room toward the lighted doorway. The women in the cages screamed at him until he shouted at them to shut up and fired off a few more rounds. I struggled and fought and, though it didn't slow him down any, it definitely made him work for it—until he hit my wounded shoulder with the butt of his gun and agony burst within me. All my struggles then went toward staying conscious.

He dragged me through the inner doorway into a smaller, better-lit room, then swung me around and threw me on the floor. Before I could so much as blink his booted toe smashed into my side.

"Get up, bitch!"

I gritted my teeth against the nausea that churned up into my throat, shifted around to take pressure off my wounded arm and shoulder, and looked up—straight in Reenie's horrified eyes.

She sat on a filthy, stained wooden platform that looked more like a narrow altar than a table. I could just make out the outline of a closed door a dozen feet behind her. She was stark naked, shuddering like an earthquake, and hunched over as though it hurt to sit upright. Bruises, cuts and blood covered her head to toe, and her face... My breath caught in my throat at the sight of what he'd done to her.

"Reenie!"

Her name burst from me as I lunged to my feet and stumbled a few steps closer to her. Our captor grabbed me, spun me around and slammed me up against the splintery wall. He held me there, fingers clenched tight on my face, his nails digging into my cheeks. White hot pain-starbursts flooded my vision like Fourth of July fireworks.

"Did I give you permission to speak?" he growled at me, his voice slightly muffled by the knit ski mask he wore. "Did I say you could move?" He pulled my head out then smacked it hard into the wall. I groaned and my legs lost cohesion. He held me upright by my face until I was steady again, then he let go, stepped back a few feet and grinned at me.

I glanced at Reenie; slow tears dripped down her ruined face. She gave me a look of exquisite anguish; it was obvious she didn't expect either of us to leave this place alive. But not me. No way was I giving up, not while there was one spark of life left in my body. What I planned was for this asshole to leave in pieces. Preferably a lot of them.

I straightened my spine, stood clear of the wall, and glared at our captor. I couldn't get my shaky voice to show full contempt, I was still reeling from his abuse, but I figured he'd get the message.

"All right, you've got what you wanted. I'm here. Let Reenie go."

"I don't think so," he said, his voice a low purr. His lips moved into a smile so evil it took my breath away. "I said she'd die if you didn't come, I never said I'd let her go. She still needs a lot of taming." He sent his slimy gaze down my body, lingering on my abused breasts. My blouse had come untied during the struggle, but I'd be damned if I'd give him the pleasure of seeing me cower away from his lust. "And so do you. The true star of my show."

He gestured behind himself. I looked and saw a camera mounted on a rafter and directed at the platform on which Reenie sat. So, this is where he filmed his torture and rape sessions. Which meant the stains on the platform weren't dirt, they were blood. Human and canine.

The man was beyond disgusting.

"Taming? That's what you call it? Is that what you did to Heidi? *Tamed* her?"

He shook his head and grimaced, his lips twisting the mask on his face. The room seesawed around me; the asswipe faded in and out of my vision. I leaned against the wall and clenched my teeth and my good hand, fighting not to pass out.

"She wasn't tamable. Not all women are."

"So you killed her instead? Why didn't you just let her go?"

"What good would that have done, Skylark? She'd still not be what she was meant to be. No." He shook his head again. "She's better off dead."

"Meant to be... Better off..." My knees failed me and I stumbled a couple of steps to my right, scraping my back on the wall. The creep turned to keep me in view, putting Reenie almost out of his sight-line. A light bulb went off in my head. If I could get him to turn a bit more, maybe she could get down off the platform and sneak out that door—if it wasn't locked—or hide somewhere before he realized she was gone. It wasn't much, and it was beyond risky, but it was all I had.

I faked another weak movement to my right, as though I were losing balance—which wasn't too far off the mark—then glanced at Reenie and gestured to her to get down and hide, trying to make it look like I was getting even more light headed. Again, not too far off the mark; I was still losing blood at an alarming rate. I kept talking to distract him further.

"So you think torturing and raping women will tame them somehow? Are you a complete moron?"

"You'll learn soon enough to keep that smart mouth shut. And to service a man the way you should."

"I wouldn't mind so much if there actually was a man around here." Another step to my right, and now he couldn't see Reenie at all. I shot her another look, then focused on the asswipe I wanted to kill more and more with every word that came out of his mouth. "A real man, not a pretend one."

He took a step toward me, his fist raised, and I slid along the wall another few steps to the right. A splinter jabbed into my back; I winced, but ignored the pain.

"Why are you hiding behind that mask? Afraid I'll laugh at you once I see your pathetic face?"

He froze, then snarled, snatched off the ski mask and threw it aside. I almost did laugh, he was so nondescript looking. I could have sat in a room with him for hours and not been able to remember anything about his face.

"I'm gonna love taming you," he growled, his eyes boring into me like the glowing ends of two cigarettes. "I'll make it last *years*."

"Really, *Maggie*?"

The epithet his father had screamed at him rolled off my tongue before I realized it. The man's—Maggie's—face reddened. But I was nowhere near done.

"Is that what you did to your mother, *Maggie*? You *tamed* her? Or did you just kill her and put her out of your misery?"

His eyes narrowed, grew even harder. Deep crimson suffused his face.

"How did you know—"

"I saw her on the ground outside the farmhouse. I saw you lift her skirt, and you just a little boy. I know lots of things about you, *Maggie*. It's what I do. I see things. Like how you had a choice, to be the human being your mother wanted you to be or turn into a deranged asshole like your father wanted." I glanced over at the platform; Reenie was gone. Good; I didn't know how much longer I could hold on. "Good choice, *Maggs*. Your prick of a father must be so proud of you."

"Shut up!" he screamed. Spittle flew from his lips. "Shut the fuck up, you bitch!"

"What's the problem, little man?" I had to force volume into my voice; a white fog crept along the edges of my vision and I knew I'd pass out soon. *Please, let Reenie have gotten away*, I prayed. "The truth too much for you to take? I'll bet you can't even get it up unless you're hurting women."

"I'll show you, bitch! I'll show you how I get it up! You'll *beg* for mercy, you'll beg to *die* before I'm through with you!"

He didn't come after me as I'd expected, though I'm sure he could tell I wasn't in any shape to go much further. Instead, he spun around to the far shelves and began pawing through the items, chucking a large-buckled belt, a box of matches, a pair of pliers onto the floor, cursing at me in full volume. I leaned against the wall, closed my eyes, and held onto awareness with what little strength I had. Then someone grabbed my arm. I let out a startled squawk and my eyes flew open.

Soto! With a swollen, bloody lip and a welt on his temple.

"Quiet, Skylark," he muttered, then he pulled me around and shoved me ahead of him toward the now-open door behind the platform.

"Police, Carstairs!" he shouted behind me. I stumbled to a stop and half-turned back toward Soto. "Put your hands up!"

The man I knew as Maggie spun around, holding a pipe in one hand and a gun in the other. His shriek would have raised the dead; it left me half-deaf.

"I said *no cops*, you fucking bitch! How dare you disobey me! *No fucking cops!*"

Maggie started shooting. Soto returned fire as he shoved me forward with his free hand. Maggie kept screaming and firing. Bullets gouged pieces out of the floor, the wall, even the platform; deadly shrapnel flew everywhere. Soto stumbled and fell into me. We both crashed to the floor, me buried half beneath Soto. His gun bounced out of his hand; I reached out and snagged it, wormed out from under him, then turned to see where Maggie was. He stood not ten feet away, drawing down on both of us, his face twisted into ugliness, hatred streaming from every pore in his body.

"You're not worth taming," he growled. "You're dead, bitch."

"No, you are," I said, my voice quavering as I blinked to see through the white mist that menaced closer and closer.

I raised Soto's service pistol; it shook in my weak, one-handed grasp. Maggie laughed.

"You can't shoot, not with your left hand. You'd never hit me."

"Wanna bet, asshole?" I said as I squeezed off a half dozen rounds.

Other shots echoed mine. Maggie's body jerked forward, then back, as bullets hit him from two opposite directions. The gun he held—my Glock, the fucker—dropped to the floor with a solid clunk; Maggie's body followed, his open dead eyes staring unseeing at me. Blood leaked from a dozen holes in his torso.

I gasped in a breath, then froze when heavy footsteps reverberated in the room, and Dunwitty materialized. He walked over to Maggie, kicked the Glock away, then knelt at his side to check his vitals. What the hell was Dunwitty doing here? With my luck, he'd charge me with murdering that murdering bastard.

I heard a pained groan beside me. Dismissing Dunwitty, I struggled to my knees and leaned over to Soto. He lay on his back, eyes closed, his breath hitching in his throat. His shirt was a charred mess of bullet holes; I could see the vest beneath the tattered remains, and glimpsed a few bullets lodged in the staunch fabric. Then the breath froze in my throat as I caught sight of the widening blood puddle beneath his shoulder, the jagged wound on the side of his neck.

"Soto." I dropped the gun and clasped my hand over the wound; blood bubbled from beneath my palm. "We got him, Soto. It's gonna be all right."

He shook his head. His eyes opened to slits and his fingers fumbled with the button on his shirt pocket.

"Take it," he whispered. "Please..."

I took my hand from his neck and opened the button, slid blood-slimed fingers into the pocket until I felt something hard. I pulled it out: a diamond solitaire in a heart-shaped platinum setting. The damned thing must have been two carats, at least.

"Betsy..." I had to lean close to his lips to hear his voice. "Tell Betsy... I love her. Give... her the ring... so she knows..."

"No, damn it, you tell her, Soto." I slid the ring into my jeans pocket and clapped my hand back on his neck. "You hold on, you hear me? She needs to hear it from you, so you hold on. Don't you dare die on me."

"Promise me," he whispered. "Promise..."

"Yes, okay, I promise. Just hold on, you hear?"

He gave me a faint smile, then the light in his eyes faded away. Tears burbled up from deep within me and poured down my face.

"No, don't do this to me! You can't die, you can't!"

I don't know how long I screamed at him to come back from wherever he'd gone, but Soto was far beyond my, or anyone else's, reach. The last thing I remember before my own blood loss made me pass out was Dunwitty, silent and stoic, kneeling in front of his dead partner, his strong, warm arms rocking me as I sobbed my heart out.

CHAPTER THIRTY-EIGHT

A week later, I stood on the sidewalk outside the open window of a church in San Luis Obispo, my right arm in a sling, listening to a succession of family members and cops eulogize Detective Javier Soto-Osorio. *Kind... considerate... a caring son... a fun uncle... a loyal friend... a great cop... a true hero...*

Every word felt like a sword in my heart. I knew I shouldn't have been there, not after what had happened a few days earlier, but I couldn't stay away. I needed to honor him as much as the rest of them did. But my strength still had a habit of deserting me when I most needed it, and I knew I'd need it more than ever to run the gauntlet of animosity and blame inside that structure. So I compromised by staying out on the sidewalk, hidden from view, while I said good-bye to Soto, aka Leopard, the man who had saved not just my and Reenie's lives, but those of the kidnapped women as well.

I'd woken in the hospital to find Dunwitty sitting at my bedside, engrossed in some kind of paperwork. I felt unreal, as though detached from my body, the effect of both anesthesia and really strong pain medication. My right side was totally numb, my shoulder and upper arm wrapped in thick, stabilizing, cast-like bandages. The rest of me felt as though a street sweeper had caught me up and whirled me around a few thousand times before spitting me out again. The sky outside the window glowed with pre-dawn paleness and I wondered how long I'd been out. I licked my lips and reached for my voice.

"What day is this?"

I winced at how weak I sounded. Dunwitty didn't look up, just kept jotting notes on the papers.

"Friday. Morning. You been out about thirty-six hours."

"I thought they put you on leave."

"We're short handed, so they called me in."

Well, no one would ever pass a test with the information they gleaned from a voice that indifferent. They were short handed because his partner had been killed. Didn't Soto's death affect him at all?

"So, you waiting here to arrest me for killing that asswipe?"

He looked up, blinked something I couldn't decipher from his eyes, then stretched his lips in more of a gloat than a smile.

"I seem to remember I helped just a bit with that."

"Not really."

"I'll say. You were dead on, unbelievable considering your dominant hand was out of commission."

"For your information, I happen to be ambidextrous. Sure surprised the hell out of Maggie."

"And me. But I'd say you did the world a favor with this one, so I'll give you a pass. Of course, he was trying to kill you, so it's probably a moot point."

I blinked at Dunwitty; he knew the word moot? And used it correctly? Had I just died and gone to hell? Then Dunwitty frowned.

"Wait—Maggie?"

"That's what his father called him. To belittle him, I'm sure, and make him turn against women, starting with his mother. I don't know his real name."

"How do you know...? No, don't tell me." He shook his head and held up a hand. "It's more of that woo-woo shit, right?" I nodded; he pursed his lips in derision and rolled his eyes. "He called himself Jerry, but his name was Magellan. Magellan Altamont Carstairs."

What kind of parent names their kid Magellan? Or Altamont, for that matter? Then it hit me.

"So that's what it meant," I murmured, remembering Lillia's vision of steps and an Old World sailing ship. How much misery might have been avoided had we only known how to interpret those symbols?

"What what meant?" Dunwitty scowled at me, but I just shook my head, a careful back and forth motion that seemed to last forever, an unpleasant side-effect of the pain meds.

"Nothing, it's not important. Who was he?"

"A house painter, if you can believe that. Worked for a local company, cased the places while he painted the insides, then robbed them a few months later when the homeowners were away. One of them came back early and Carstairs killed him, the one we thought was Gallivan. We found it all documented in Soto's notes." He paused and studied me as I shifted in the bed, searching for a comfortable spot that seemed to have left town a few centuries ago. "What were you doing there? How did you know where he lived?"

"How did you?"

Another lip twitch, this one with more amusement in it. Funny, I didn't think Dunwitty knew how to smile.

"You first."

"Okay, but you'll have to let me get a lot more sleep if you're gonna arrest me."

I told him everything, starting with the phone call from Danielle, driving to Reenie's house, the note left for me—that I hadn't turned over to the authorities, and didn't Dunwitty love that admission?—then driving out Two-Tunnel Road and finding the Carstairs abattoir. Dunwitty told me about kicking around rootless at home, finally putting a tracker on my car, then getting suspicious when I drove out into the hinterlands. He'd followed the blip to find both my car and Soto's, and the debacle in the barn.

"Wait, you put a tracker on my car? Without a warrant? Isn't that illegal?" He had the grace to blush as he shrugged. "Maybe *I* should arrest *you*."

"Wouldn't the brass love that? Mutual arrests." He folded the papers and rose. "I just wanted you to know that we believe Carstairs worked alone. So, it's over. We'll need a full interview later, but for now just work on getting better." His eyes hardened. "And keep your nose out of police business from now on."

By the time lunch on Saturday was over, I'd endured a number of police interviews—four of them, mainly because I hinted that Maggie's mother, and maybe others, might be buried somewhere on the property without saying how I knew it. The medicos had added some hefty mind-bending drugs and a lot of annoying medical probing to the lineup before I finally had had enough. Garrett arrived to find me sitting on the edge of the bed, systematically removing needles from my arms and sensors from my body as lights flashed and alarm bells rang. He placed a hand over mine, stopping me; a gaggle of nurses rushed in on his heels.

"What the hell are you doing?" he asked.

I blinked up at him, my upright balance still a bit precarious.

"I don't do hospitals. You know that."

"You do now. No, stop, Skylark," he insisted as I tried to finish my mission.

He forced me down onto the mattress—which didn't take much, given my weakened state—and pulled the covers over my bruised, battered, hospital-gowned body. He sat beside me as the nurses rushed around to repair the damage I'd done, though I refused to allow them to reinsert the needles into my flesh. Garrett spoke on as one of them reattached the probes that tracked my heartbeats and slipped a pulse-ox monitor on my finger.

"You have to obey the rules for at least a little while longer. Let the docs make sure you really are okay. You came this close, Skylark." He held his fingers a scant half inch apart. His eyes grew suspiciously moist. "Did you know you flatlined in the ambulance? Yeah, that's right," he said as I blinked in shock; I'd actually died? "Thirty seconds with no heartbeat, no pulse, before they managed to bring you back. So please, for me if for no one else, just follow orders for a couple more days?"

The doctor arrived then with his why-are-you-bothering-me-on-the-weekend attitude, and I let him reinsert the IV that was replacing my blood serum. Not because I thought I needed it but because of the pain in Garrett's face. Then the damned medico shot me up with something that swept me off to la-la land on a wave of warm undulation, and everything faded from my consciousness.

The next day I had to admit—at least to myself— that the enforced rest had done me a world of good. By mid afternoon I felt lucid and stronger, ready to at least leave this place of torture, if not for anything else. I'd been divested of all invasive accoutrements and allowed semi-solid food for lunch. I forced down the tasteless mashed potatoes, pudding, and jello, mentally adding a stop at Valley Liquor for a Skylark burger and fries on the way home.

Garrett arrived with a wheelchair around 2:00 pm, though I wasn't strong enough yet to get into it under my own steam. When I asked about home, all he said was, "Tomorrow," and wheeled me out of the room.

We took an elevator up one floor, and proceeded to a room halfway down a dimly lit corridor. Inside I found two occupied beds and two equally-occupied wheelchairs, all with patients even more abused and bruised than I. My heart almost stopped when I recognized one of the women.

"Come here, let me thank you properly." Yvonne Avila, propped up on pillows, held out a battered hand to me. "You're our hero."

Garrett wheeled me to the bed closest to the door, and I formally met the others who had shared Yvonne's nightmare: Casey Thurman, a twenty-year-old college student, whose haunted eyes didn't reflect the smile she gave me; and Nicole Baker, a thirty-one-year-old mother of two whose fear felt like another presence in the room. It would be a long time before any of them would ever again feel safe, or in complete control of their lives.

The other bed held the fourth victim, fifteen-year-old Andrea Armstrong. Yvonne noticed me glancing at the girl after we'd chatted for about ten minutes, me trying to hide my embarrassment at their effusive praise for my bravery in trying to free them.

"She just lies there, unmoving." Yvonne shook her head and sighed, her eyes tearing. "She won't speak, doesn't react to anything, she's just locked inside her mind. Nothing gets through to her."

Andrea lay on her side, facing the wall, her body drawn into a half-fetal position. I had a nurse wheel me around to where I could see her face—Garrett had left us to our "hen party", as he'd called it—and leaned close to her.

"You're not alone, Andrea. I do know what you're going through," I whispered. "I was younger than you the first time it happened to me." I watched her face; not a flicker to show she even heard me. "But I'll tell you what I've learned. Women have an inner strength that can rise above anything, a strength that men, with all their muscles, can only dream about. Think about it; you won, Andrea. You survived, and he's dead. But he'll still win if you give in to this. Don't let him. Draw on that inner strength, and don't let him win." I stroked her hair back from her forehead. "You don't have to force it. Take all the time you need to heal. Just know that when you're ready, I'll always be here if you need, or want, to talk."

Andrea's body remained motionless though her pale green eyes moved. Her gaze slid to my face for a moment before it slid back, and her eyes closed. She had dismissed me. Then her lips slowly lifted in a faint, almost-not-there smile, and I knew in my heart that someday, after a lot of work and counseling, she'd find her way back from this nightmare.

I had Garrett drive me to Betsy's house on Monday, on the way home from the hospital—which I'd left against medical advice, per my usual routine—even though Atascadero was more than out of the way, it was in the opposite direction. I held the ring in my hand, feeling the weight of the stone, the vain promise it represented, and couldn't wrap my mind around what to say. I could only hope the right words would come.

It surprised me to see the number of cars lining her street, the clusters of uniformed and plainclothes cops dotting her front yard—since Betsy and Soto weren't married or anything—until I remembered she, too, was a part of the law enforcement family. Garrett pulled into the drive and stopped a few inches from the squad car parked there, his back end jutting out into the street. He shut down the motor and came around to help me out, since my right arm was still immobilized.

"You want me to go in with you?" he asked, his worried gaze on the men who stared their hostility at us.

I shook my head. This was something I had to do alone, a promise I had to keep. I made my way up the front walk on still-shaky legs, stopped three times by uniforms who stood in my way, arms crossed, faces hating. But they moved aside before I said a word, and before I was ready I found myself inside the small, one-story stucco house.

Betsy, shoulders hunched, face swollen and blotchy, red hair disheveled, sat on the couch in the living room, bracketed by an older couple who gave off a protective vibe, her parents I assumed. The room was crowded with even more Sheriff's deputies and detectives, civilian employees, family and friends. Voices murmured an indistinguishable background drone, as though actual words might shatter the illusion of quiet composure that appeared to reign.

I walked up to the couch and stood looking down at Betsy, who twisted a sodden handkerchief with her fingers.

"Betsy? I'm so sorry. You don't know me, we've never met, but—"

"I know who you are," she snarled, looking up at me with an expression of pure venom.

All sound, all movement stopped. Everyone stared at me. An aura of menace closed off the air in the room. I gasped in a silent breath, and swallowed down a stab of fear and anguish. *Soto asked you to do this*, I told myself. *You promised him.*

"I... I was with him, at the end," I said, my voice trembling with unshed tears.

"I know you were. They told me," she spat. Her hands curled into fists; her eyes sparked fire. "They told me *everything!*"

"He w-wanted me to give you this." I stretched out my hand; on my palm lay the beautiful, heart-shaped diamond, Soto's promise of love and togetherness. "He made me promise to give it to you, from him. So you'd always know." Tears I couldn't stop dripped down my face; my body trembled like a leaf on an aspen tree. "He talked about you at the end. He wanted you to know that he... loved you. He'll always... love you." It was hard, now, to force the words out, I kept losing my breath, but I persevered. "He... died... with your name... on his lips."

Betsy stood up, one slow, languid-seeming motion at odds with the fury that twisted her face.

"How dare you?" Her voice was so low I wasn't sure I was hearing her correctly. It slowly rose in volume as she spoke on. "How dare you say these things? How dare you be the one to have been there? How dare you *give me this*?" she screamed as she snatched the ring from my palm.

I shook my head and opened my mouth, but had no idea what to say.

"It's *your fault*, you bitch! He's dead because of *you!*" She threw the ring at me with the last word; it hit my cheek just below my eye with a sharp wasp-like sting, then spun off into the room. "I have *nothing* now, and it's *your* fault! Yours!"

She hit out at me, a woman wild with grief, and smashed a fist into my injured shoulder. Pain shot through me and I stumbled back a couple of steps. Her parents rose and put their arms around her as she screamed on, restraining her from attacking me again.

"He'd still be alive if if weren't for you! It's your fault. Your fault."

Her voice devolved down into unintelligible sobs and I turned blindly to flee the room. I got as far as the door when a plain clothes cop stepped in front of me and leaned close.

"You better be careful, Skylark," he muttered. "We'll be watching you."

I stood on the sidewalk outside the church now, Betsy's words blending with the ongoing eulogies, and felt my heart break as I reassessed my life. I couldn't do this any longer, the good just didn't outweigh the pain. What was the point, if all I did was get people—good people—killed? If all I did was destroy my friends' lives?

Reenie wouldn't talk to me, wouldn't even let me see her; Garrett said to be patient, to give her time, she needed space to process it all. But time and space wouldn't help, because we both knew: What had happened to her was my fault, because I couldn't let it go. I brought her to Carstairs' attention, her and Soto both. Now he was dead, and Reenie's body was scarred, her face ruined, her life destroyed. Because of me.

I'll leave, go far away from here, I thought as I turned away from the church toward where I'd parked the Jeep. *I'll get a job as a waitress, a store clerk, a barmaid—whatever. No more PI work. And no friends. Never again, no more friends.*

A huge form blocked my path. I looked up into Dunwitty's hard face. A stab of fear shot through me. I held up my good hand and took a step back.

"I don't want any trouble, I just wanted to pay my respects."

"You're not going in?"

I looked at the church door, standing open to the glorious midday sunshine, and shook my head.

"I'm *persona non grata* around here. I don't dare show my face in there. It'd probably start a riot."

I tried to step around him, but he blocked my way.

"You did good, you know."

"What?"

"Figuring this out. Finding Carstairs. You're good at what you do."

"Yeah." I shook my head and let an ironic laugh escape. "I'm good at getting people killed. Or maimed."

"You didn't do that, Carstairs did. He's the one who chose his path in life, not you. Who knows how many other women he'd have 'tamed' and eventually killed if you hadn't kept digging? I watched the tapes of his so-called show. The things he did? He was one sick puppy." He crossed his arms and looked down at me. "Let the blame fall where it belongs, Skylark. Don't try to hog it all, or it'll break you."

"It's weird." I shook my head. "I'm glad he's dead, and I'm glad I shot him. But at the same time, I wish I hadn't killed him, you know?"

"Who says you did? We both shot him, numerous times; who knows which bullet did the dirty deed?" He gave me another of his ironic smiles. "Like I said, don't hog the blame. Spread it around. Life's easier that way."

We stood silent a moment, me knowing my life would never get any easier.

"They found graves, you know, up there. On Carstairs' farm, like you said they might. Six of them..." Dunwitty sighed. "We've identified two so far, one Carstairs' mother, the other a hooker who vanished a few years ago. I'd bet the rest are more hookers; no one really looks for them if they go missing. Seems killing wasn't anything new to him, after all."

Music swelled from inside the church. Dunwitty looked at the open door.

"Sounds like things might be winding up in there. I better get back inside. You take care, Skylark."

I watched him stride up the steps to the church, wondering who had unzipped him and put a decent human being inside that Neanderthal body. I wasn't sure I could handle that. Halfway up, he turned and pointed at me, his bad-tempered scowl back in place.

"And don't interfere with any more of our cases. Leave police work to the cops or I'll arrest you, you got that?"

I smiled for the first time in over a week as I watched him vanish into the interior of the church. That was more like it. I'd been so unsettled since Leopard had been killed; nothing in my life felt the same to me. Now I could feel my nerves settle down a bit. At least one thing hadn't changed; Dunwitty was still Dunwitty. My spirit a few ounces lighter than when I'd arrived, I went home to a Valley Liquor hamburger and my bottle of single-malt Scotch.

CHAPTER THIRTY-NINE

A week later I walked through the gates of Los Osos Cemetery. I'd planned the visit well; at ten o'clock on a weekday morning, there was little chance I'd run into any of his colleagues. Or his poor fiancée. It was the last place I wanted to be, but I owed it to Leopard to come here alone. Or, maybe, I owed it to myself. Soto's death was, after all, despite what Dunwitty had said, my fault.

I parked close to the entrance, needing the long walk to soothe my nerves. The smell hit me first, clean, sweet and sharp, lavender from a nearby bed of flowers and chlorophyll recently released by the blade of a mower. Not a power one, there was no under-riding stench of gasoline, only the scent of the sun and of life in a place where there was no life. At least, not any life most people would notice.

Blades of grass near the stones tickled my ankles as I trod deeper into the enclave, eschewing the roadway and leaving behind the sound of the town outside the gates. Car engines, thrumming tires, horns, a dog barking, distant laughter—people living their lives—it all faded away the farther I went. I wanted to take off my shoes, let my feet indulge in the coolness of the land juxtaposed with the warmth of the brilliant sun overhead, but let that desire drift away.

This was neither the time nor the place for pleasure. Not for me.

I kept my head down as I walked. The sun caressed my hair, my shoulders, as though in an attempt to console, or bring solace. *A vain hope*, little birds twittered from the trees that dotted the gently rolling landscape. There was, I knew, no solace for me. Not here; not ever.

I couldn't help but read as I walked, wending my way past the plaques embedded in the earth in neat, soldierly rows. Harry Bencroft, aged 93; Sarah Langley, aged 41; Rogelio Gallardo, aged 22. Death, it seemed, was no respecter of age, or of possibility, future, or plans. As well I knew.

Was it the heat beating down on me or my own guilt that made it so difficult to see? By the time I reached the so-called Garden of Gladness—a misnomer if ever I heard one—my cheeks were damp and my vision blurred. What kind of gladness could there be in a place like this? A place Leopard would inhabit for the rest of eternity, a place I had put him in. He would never marry, or have children, never see them grow to adulthood, never again kiss Betsy goodnight, never hold her close, never again breathe in air scented with dust, lavender and chlorophyll, never solve another crime or help someone in need. All because he'd met me. Cared about what happened to me. Did his job too well.

I had never felt more inadequate, more useless, more like a failure.

I stopped before his grave and stared at the mounded earth, half covered by flowers decaying in the heat. I wrinkled my nose from the stench of their rotting, and wondered what his headstone would reveal to the world, once it was put into place. His name, of course. Dates of birth and death. Would it also say he'd been a detective? That he died in the line of duty? That a woman had sealed his fate by being who she was? That she—I—hadn't had enough skill to see the future, to warn him, to save him?

Not your fault. It showered down on me from above, from the feathered throat of a tree swallow perched on the limb that stretched its protection over Leopard's grave. *Not your fault.* The sweet, high, melodic song pierced my heart.

I clenched my hands, wincing at the pain that still rode in my injured shoulder. I would not cry, would not allow myself to cry. Because it *was* my fault. Somehow it was, just like all the others. Logic and sane reasoning would never change that fact.

It was time. Nodding, I took the flask from my pocket, unscrewed the cap, and anointed Leopard's final home with single malt. *Welcome*, I said to him, to the ghost I was sure hovered nearby. *Welcome.*

A cool breeze blew past my body and ruffled my hair—Leopard, letting me know he was there, with me. Letting me know he was ready to take his place among the others. I nodded.

My task done, I turned away and trudged toward the main gate, knowing the detective's ghost now dwelled in the hidden psychic cave deep within me, with all the other people I had failed to save. Waiting to pinpoint my every inadequacy, my every failure. I lifted my chin, took a deep breath, and squared my shoulders. It was time to begin packing. Time to choose a new hole in which to hide, and find another career that included less death. Less responsibility. Less guilt.

Halfway back to my car, my cell rang. I dug it from my pocket. I didn't recognize the number, so I let it go to voice mail. Two minutes later, it rang again, and two minutes after that, again. Same number each time. *Damn, people can be so persistent*, I thought. Well, I'd just answer it and let whoever it was know that Skylark Investigations didn't exist anymore. Would never exist anymore.

I thumbed it on and kept walking toward my car.

"Skylark Investigations, I'm sorry, we're—"

"Please, please," a tear-choked voice cried, "you have to help me. I don't know what to do."

I pulled the phone from my ear and shook my head at it, even as my heartbeat sped up. Then I put it to my ear again.

"Listen, I'm really sorry—"

"It's my husband, he was supposed to be on a trip, but they said he never got there, and now I got this letter, and the cops say they can't help, he left on his own, but I know he'd never do that, he just wouldn't... I don't know what to do. Please, I don't know who else to call."

I leaned against the Jeep, the phone held at my side as words still spewed from its depths. I looked up at the sky, seeking guidance, and again the birds shared their wisdom from a nearby live oak: *it's who you are... it's who you are...*

Well, I thought, *one more case can't hurt, can it?* I'd need the money to relocate, anyway, and I couldn't deny that my mind was already chipping away at the puzzle, my hands trembling with anticipation...

With a resigned sigh, I lifted the phone. Whoever this was, she was still on the line. I could hear her muffled sobs.

"All right," I said, wondering if I was making yet another mistake even as some of the ice that encased me melted away. "I'll meet with you. Are you familiar with Los Osos?"

"Yes, I'm right here in Baywood Park."

"Good. Meet me at Starbucks at," I glanced at my watch, "one thirty, can you do that? I'm tall, I have long black hair, and I'm wearing jeans and a dark blue T-shirt."

"Thank you, thank you. Oh, my name's Nancy Roessler. I'll see you there at one thirty."

"Bring the letter," I said just as the connection broke.

Had she even heard me? I shook my head again and thumbed off the phone, then stood there a moment, wondering at life's vagaries, at the way fate plays with our destinies. Then, smiling, my heart a thousand pounds lighter, my ghosts all packed away, I piled back into the Jeep. I had just enough time for a Valley Liquor burger and fries before heading out to meet my new client.

The End... of the Beginning...

Tough Blood

ABOUT THE AUTHOR

Susan Tuttle grew up in Buffalo, New York, and has lived in New England; Lexington, KY; and Ossining, NY. In 2004 she picked up and drove across the country, landing on the Central Coast of California where she lives in a small town whose motto is (yes, she coined it): *Wherever you want to go, you can't get there from here.* She has found her passion and her place there, where the weather is always perfect—even when it isn't.

After arriving in California, she discovered and got involved with other writers in SLO NightWriters, the premier writing organization on the Central Coast (www.slonightwriters.org). She has served as board president and treasurer, is the newsletter editor, and offers professional critiques at the monthly meetings.

Susan is also a member of Sisters in Crime (SinC) National, the Central Coast Chapter of SinC (she currently serves as treasurer and newsletter editor), and the Public Service Writers Association (PSWA). She is also the owner of the newly formed WriterWithin Publications, an independent publishing company. (www.WriterWithinPubs.com).

A professional editor and writing teacher, Susan is an award-winning author who writes in various genres: suspense, mystery, fantasy, sci-fi and young adult, and poetry. She also has a 6-volume work-book series for writers of fiction and creative nonfiction titled *Write It Right.*

Under the pen name Susan Grace O'Neill, she has published the first of six volumes of spiritual meditations on the Parables, and a book on journeying with Jesus through Lent. Her work has garnered numerous awards and has appeared in Mind Prints Literary Journal, Tolosa Press, Simply Clear Media & Marketing, If & When Literary Journal, The Feathered Flounder Literary Journal, and Central Coast Kind Magazine.

Susan is currently working on the second and third volumes of the Skylark series, as well as two young adult fantasy series, and several stand-alone books. In case you haven't guessed, writing is her life. She lives on the Central Coast of California with her imaginary cat in a house filled with her (mostly unfinished) handmade quilts and (mostly finished) knitted scarves. Find her on Facebook (susanwriter), Twitter (stuttlewriter), and her website, www.SusanTuttleWrites.com.

PUBLICATIONS

Fiction (writing as Susan Tuttle):

    Suspense: *Tangled Webs*
                     Piece By Piece
                     Sins of the Past

    Paranormal Suspense:
                     Proof of Identity

    Historical Suspense:
                     A Matter of Identity

    Short Mystery Stories:
                     Death in the Valley

    Flash Fiction Stories:
                     Tiny Tales, Flash Fiction
                     Tiny Tales, Mystery/Suspense
                     Tiny Tales, Sci-fi/Fantasy
                     Tiny Tales, Skylark PI
                     Tiny Tales, Romancing the Muse

(All available in print from Amazon and as Kindle e-books.)

Audio Books (available from Audible and Amazon):
    Proof of Identity
    Sins of the Past

Susan's short works appear in the following Anthologies:
Somewhere in Crime
The Best of SLO NightWriters in
Tolosa Press
Deadlines: Murder and Mayhem on
the California Coast, Vol. 1
Deadlines: Murder and Mayhem on
the California Coast, Vol. 2
Tales from a Rocky Coast, Vol. 1

Non-Fiction (available in print from Amazon):
    Write It Right Workbook Series:
        Workbook #1: Character, Setting,
            Story
        Workbook #2: Point of View (POV)
        Workbook #3: Plot, Dialogue
        Workbook #4: Scenes, Style/Voice
        Workbook #5: Conflict/Tension,
            Subplot
        Workbook #6: Brilliant Beginnings,
            Extraordinary Endings

Poetry (available in print from Amazon):
    Mirror Eyes

Writing as Susan Grace O'Neill:
    Spiritual Meditations: The Journey Series
        Lord, Let Me Grow: A Journey with Jesus
            through the Parables, Vol. 1
        (Coming soon, Vol. 2-6)
        Lord, Let Me Walk: A 3-Year Journey with
            Jesus through Lent

(Available in print from Amazon)

Books in Process:
  Obsession
Paranormal Mystery/Suspense Series:
  The Skylark Series (Vol. 1 coming soon)
    Vol. 1: *Tough Blood*
    Vol. 2: *Words Left Unsaid*
    Vol. 3: *Death Duties*
    Vol. 4 : *The SomeWhen Murder*
    Vol. 5 (novella): *Dead Ringer*
    Vol. 6: *Taking a Chance*
    Vol. 7: *The Dead of Winter*
  Stand-alones (connected to Skylark):
    The Eyes of Death (Mackenzie Straite)
    Not Even Death (Linnea Keszeli)
    The Unhonored Past (Clancy D'Angelo/Lillia)

Sci-fi/Fantasy/Paranormal Books in process (writing as T'Kon):
  YA/Adult:
    Destany's Daughter Series
      Vol. 1: The One
      Vol. 2: The Restoral
    Demon's Run Series
      Vol. 1: A Deadly Shade of Gray
    Stand-alone: *Impossible Girl*

  Adult Fantasy/Paranormal Books (writing as T'Kon):
      Stealing Shyon
    The CPW Series:
      Vol. 1: Cursed in California

Tough Blood